PRAISE FOR *NEW YORK TIMES* AND *USA TODAY* BESTSELLING AUTHOR GENA SHOWALTER AND THE ALIEN HUNTRESS SERIES

Dark Taste of Rapture

"A literal taste of rapture."

—Fresh Fiction

Ecstasy in Darkness

"A glued-to-your-seat kind of book. Pick it up and you won't want to put it down. The action is hot and fast-paced. . . . Showalter is a master of creating unique, fun, and super-sexy characters. The banter between Victor and Ava will stick with you days after you're done reading."

—RT Book Reviews

Seduce the Darkness

"Imaginative and sexy, this story teems with nonstop action!"

—BookPage

"[A] compelling and entertaining story of lust, deception, intrigue. . . ."

—RT Book Reviews

Savor Me Slowly

"Hot, hard-hitting science fiction romance. . . . I'm so glad she took the characters to their sensual and emotional limits—and beyond!"

—Susan Sizemore, *New York Times* bestselling author

Enslave Me Sweetly

"A roller-coaster-like adventure. . . . Sizzling romance and nail-biting suspense."

—Booklist

Awaken Me Darkly

"A heady mixture of speculative fiction, romance, and chick lit."

—*RT Book Reviews*

"Brilliantly written. . . . Sizzles with intrigue. . . . Similar to Laurell K. Hamilton's Anita Blake series."

—*Fresh Fiction*

"A fantastic read. . . . Fascinating characters."

—*A Romance Review*

"The final spin will shock. . . . Mia Snow is a fabulous 'bad girl.'"

—*The Best Reviews*

MORE PRAISE FOR THE NOVELS OF GENA SHOWALTER

"Gena Showalter delivers an utterly spellbinding story!"

—Kresley Cole, #1 *New York Times* bestselling author of *Shadow's Claim*

"Combining passion, humor, pulse-pounding action and just plain fun, Gena Showalter's books are always a refreshing escape!"

—Lara Adrian, *New York Times* bestselling author of *Deeper Than Midnight*

"Showalter at her finest."

—Karen Marie Moning, *New York Times* bestselling author of *Shadowfever*

"Sizzles with sexual tension!!!"

—Sharon Sala, *New York Times* bestselling author of *Next of Kin*

Also by Gena Showalter

Awaken Me Darkly
Enslave Me Sweetly
Savor Me Slowly
Seduce the Darkness
Ecstasy in Darkness
Dark Taste of Rapture
Deep Kiss of Winter

And coming soon:
Book Two in the Otherworld Assassin series

Gena Showalter

Last Kiss Goodnight

Pocket Books
New York   London   Toronto   Sydney   New Delhi

Pocket Books
A Division of Simon & Schuster, Inc.
1230 Avenue of the Americas
New York, NY 10020

This book is a work of fiction. Names, characters, places, and incidents either are products of the author's imagination or are used fictitiously. Any resemblance to actual events or locales or persons, living or dead, is entirely coincidental.

First Pocket Books paperback edition January 2013

POCKET and colophon are registered trademarks of Simon & Schuster, Inc.

For information about special discounts for bulk purchases, please contact Simon & Schuster Special Sales at 1-866-506-1949 or business@simonandschuster.com.

The Simon & Schuster Speakers Bureau can bring authors to your live event. For more information or to book an event contact the Simon & Schuster Speakers Bureau at 1-866-248-3049 or visit our website at www.simonspeakers.com.

Manufactured in the United States of America

10 9 8 7 6 5 4 3 2 1

ISBN: 978-1-4516-7159-9
ISBN: 978-1-4516-7161-2 (ebook)

First, to God, who picked me up out of a very dark place, ushered in the light, and inspired me on every level.

To my darling Jill Monroe, for reading the first draft and offering invaluable advice.

To my bold, beautiful editor, Lauren McKenna, who isn't afraid to tell it like it is. You are gold!

To my sister, Christy James, for pointing me in the right direction.

To Roxanne St. Claire, for the encouragement, the phone calls, and the e-mails.

Acknowledgments

To my Wednesday night girls (and sometimes Saturday night girls). You know who you are, and I hope you also know you are so, so dear to me. Thank you for the prayers, the support, and the sharing of the truth.

Prologue

⤟⤞

FOURTEEN-YEAR-OLD VIKTORIJA LUKAS RACED between the circus tents, her throat and lungs burning as she gasped for breath. Though it was well past two in the morning, many of the performers were outside talking, drinking, and laughing raucously around blazing fire pits, celebrating their last night in a prosperous town.

The closer Vika drew to her destination, the more the scent of animal permeated her every inhalation. It was a scent she'd come to adore. A scent her father wanted to forever take away from her.

He planned to sell her babies—in pieces.

Righty, the gorilla with a penchant for stealing necklaces and bracelets. Angie, the horse too shy to look anyone but Vika in the eye. Gabbie, the prancing camel. Gus, the zebra who often hid behind objects too small to cover him. Dobi, the overly excited tiger she had caught peeing in all kinds of inappropriate places. Barney, the food-poaching llama, who was, needless to say, obese. Sammie, the obsessive-compulsive ostrich now missing several patches of feathers. Mini, the sweetly sensitive elephant who cried at the slightest raise in Vika's voice. Zoey, the sugar-addicted bear.

And then there was One Day, the brave lion Vika loved above all others.

"Those mangy creatures cost too much money to keep," her father had grumbled only this morning. To him, that was a good enough reason to kill them, but she'd cried and begged, willing to say anything to save them, and so the litany had continued. "They take up too much space. They're too old, too feeble, and they no longer cause people to gape with awe and wonder. They fill people with pity and disgust."

Her father hadn't cared that each animal was beautiful to Vika, faults and all. He hadn't cared that One Day and the others were her only friends, the only solace she'd found since her mother's death and the loss of her childhood playmates two years ago. Jecis Lukas owned Cirque de Monstres, and he cared only about profit.

And profit now demanded he make room for a new menagerie—one that would showcase *people*. Otherworlders, to be exact, males and females from different planets, whose families had come to earth almost a hundred years ago to enjoy protected, peaceful lives.

Sadly, there had been nothing protected or peaceful about their earthly "welcome." Worldwide war had broken out, nearly destroying *this* planet. And even though a truce had been reached eventually, allowing otherworlders to live alongside humans, the innumerable races were still an oddity. Some were strange colors, some abnormally shaped. Some had powers beyond imagining. Humans *would* pay to view and scoff at them, especially in the dark, seedy recesses of a place like this.

"Anything goes if the price is right," Jecis liked to say.

What had happened to the man he used to be? The one who had carried her on his shoulders and tickled her feet? Wait. She already knew the answer. Greed had killed him.

Killed—like her babies would be if she failed to free them.

By the time Vika reached the cages, her blood flowed white-hot in her veins. A fine sheen of perspiration glossed over her skin, and tremors rocked down her spine, vibrating into her arms and legs.

So happy to see her, each of the animals erupted into beautiful song.

"Shhh. Be quiet, my darlings." She reached out to unlock One Day's door but dropped the ring of keys. Frantically she patted at the dirt. As dark as the metal was, and as little light as there was in the area, she couldn't see—there!

Thank the Lord! She straightened and carefully inserted the key. *Click.*

"Vika!" Her father's shout cut through the distance.

No! No, no, no. He'd noticed her absence.

One Day roared in protest, firing up the rest of the animals. In seconds, the tone of their cries changed from joyous to frenzied.

"*Pleeease,* be quiet," she whispered fiercely.

Of course, the soundtrack continued to play.

Not a single creature liked Jecis. They feared and despised him, and with good reason. He treated them poorly, was always spitting on them, yelling at them, and poking at them with electric rods.

Vika had protested the abuse—once. It was a mistake she'd never made again.

Hinges squeaked as she opened the cage door, and her gaze fused with the dark, feverish eyes of her best friend. His mane of golden hair was tangled, twigs and dirt clumped in several of the strands. Despite the fact that she always gave him portions of her own meals, he was so thin she could see every indention of his ribs. There was an oozing sore on his left paw, still festering despite the salve she'd applied every morning, afternoon and evening for the past few weeks.

"Finally, the day I told you about has arrived," she said in pristine English. As an emigrant from New Lithuania, she'd had to steadily whittle away at her accent to fit the new identity her father had bought for her, to save her from being deported. Jecis had been her tutor, and his reward-and-punishment system had ensured quick success.

One Day mewled, peeked out, and tried to nudge her hand.

"Go, baby. Go."

Another nudge from him.

"Go on, now. Jecis wants to hurt you, but I will not let him."

One Day lumbered to the ground, but rather than sprinting to freedom, he rubbed against her leg, causing her to stumble forward and drop the keys a second time. He wanted to be brushed, she knew. He loved when she cleaned and groomed him, his purrs of approval so rich and deep they always settled over her like warm honey.

Tears burned the backs of her eyes, clouding her vision. "You will run now. Please."

How many times had she promised her precious lion freedom? *One day we will escape together. One day I will grow tall and you will grow strong, and we will protect each other. Yes, one day.* She'd said the words so many times they'd finally become a name.

He deserved a chance to run and play and do whatever else he desired.

"Go."

"Vika!" Her father's voice boomed closer . . . so close his booted footsteps echoed in the background.

She shoved One Day toward the line of trees in the distance. She wouldn't be able to save the others, she realized with a flood of sorrow, but she could save her precious lion. She had to save him. "I said go!"

He resisted, again rubbing at her leg.

A shocked gasp sounded a few feet away. "You did it," her father said. "You actually did it. You betrayed me. Me! After everything I've done for you."

He had arrived.

Her heart thundered in her chest as her gaze found him in the darkness. He was tall, with wide shoulders and a barrel chest. Not necessarily bad things—until a temper as hot as the inner core of the earth got the better of him. Fear she'd managed to ignore now consumed her. Suddenly her feet felt as heavy as thousand-pound boulders, and she couldn't force herself to move.

She rarely disobeyed this man. His punishments were too severe. "I . . . I . . ."

Jecis stomped to her, grabbed her arms in a painful vise grip, and shook her. "I buy you the best clothes, the best food, and gift you with the greatest treasures, and yet you dare defy me?"

One Day roared with long-suppressed rage, and slowly stalked around them. But he didn't attack. He couldn't. Jecis used Vika as a shield, always ensuring she blocked the way. The rest of the animals banged against the bars of their cages.

"Atsiprašau," Vika managed to choke out.

Jecis glared down at her through eyes the color of violetiniai, the same as hers. She only prayed her own were not laced with such cold, hard cruelty. "I have told you only to speak English. Or do you speak the mother tongue hoping someone will realize you are foreign and try to take you away from me?"

"I—I am sorry," she translated with a tremor.

"Not yet, but you will be." He released her—only to backhand her.

She tumbled to the ground. Blood filled her mouth, a copper tang coating her tongue, and pain exploded through her head.

One Day jumped toward her father, but, sick as the lion was, he was sluggish, and Jecis easily dodged the creature, grabbing Vika and jerking her upright.

The lion crouched, ready to initiate another attack, clearly desperate to rip his enemy in half.

"I love you more than life itself, Vika, but that love will not save you from my wrath."

When has it ever? she wanted to scream. Wisely, she remained quiet.

Another roar tore through the air.

"You think to threaten me, eh, lion? To hurt me?" Jecis withdrew a gun from the waist of his pants and stretched out his arm. "The man who paid for your care, all these many years?"

"No!" Vika shrieked, trying to tug that arm down but making no progress. "Please, no. Do not do this. Please," she repeated, nearing hysteria.

"Before, I would have been merciful, would have done this without causing any pain. Now . . ."

"No!"

One Day couldn't contain his aggression any longer and leapt. Jecis squeezed the trigger.

Boom!

Despite the sudden ringing in Vika's ears and the bright white stars winking through her vision, she heard One Day's agonized mewl and watched as he collapsed on the ground. Big dark eyes, now filled with anguish and regret, found her. His body twitched, and he yelped with agony.

A cry of denial burst from her.

"I will deal with you in a moment," her father snapped, shoving her away now that the threat was gone. "First . . ."

She scrambled to One Day to stroke his trembling body. *Oh, my darling. Oh, no.* Her shock and horror ate up her strength as she looked up and watched Jecis turn, aim. *Boom.*

Turn. *Boom.*

Turn. *Boom.*

One after another, her beautiful animals were gunned down, their cries ending abruptly. Her chin quivered, finally dislodging the tears welled in her eyes. Droplets spilled onto her cheeks, raining down, burning and stinging the cut her father's ring had left behind.

She wanted to look away from her friends. She couldn't bear to witness their suffering, but she refused to allow herself the luxury of retreating mentally. These precious beings had lived terrible lives here at the circus, and she could not let them die alone.

When the last of them stilled and quieted, only One Day hanging on—*oh, One Day, I'm so sorry*—her father yanked her to her feet and slapped the gun in her hand.

"One bullet left," he said, grabbing her wrist to ensure she never pointed the weapon at him. "You will finish him."

Bile burned a path up her throat. "No. Please, no."

"Do it," Jecis growled, getting in her face, putting them nose to nose. "Do it, or things will be much worse for you."

"I—I don't care. I won't. I can't."

His eyes narrowed. "Do it, or I'll skin him while he's still alive." Spittle rained upon her face.

Your lion is in pain. This is for the best. Was that true, she wondered, or was she simply trying to comfort herself? Either way . . .

Shaking, she stretched out her arm, the gun heavy in her palm. Though Jecis still held her, he offered no support.

Crimson leaked from One Day's mouth.

Her finger wound around the trigger, and her vision hazed.

Her beloved released a long breath, as if he knew what he planned. As if he waited for the inevitable end.

"I'm so sorry," she croaked. "Forgive me."

Boom.

The lion stilled and quieted like all the others. Sobs racked her body, and her arm fell to her side.

"Good girl." Jecis claimed the gun and stuffed it back in his pants. He rolled up his shirtsleeves, cracked his knuckles. "Now, my heart, it's your turn. Clearly, you have not learned the proper respect for me. But you will, I promise you, and we'll never again have a problem like this."

One

∽∾

The Song of Songs, which is Solomon's.
—SONG OF SOLOMON 1:1

SIX YEARS LATER

MICHAEL BLACK LEANED BACK in his chair, his hands forming a steeple over his mouth. He studied the three agents he'd recruited for Operation Dumpster Dive. Each was an otherworlder who had been raised here on earth. Each had lost his biological family soon after birth, and because of Michael, each had been quickly adopted by a human family under the condition Michael have complete access any time he so desired.

He'd begun their training at the age of five, though he'd only taught them little things at first. Target practice had eventually morphed into hunting living, breathing game. Camping had morphed into surviving a week in the jungle, alone, without any kind of weapon. Creating strategies for winning video games had developed into creating strategies to save one another from whatever disastrous situation Michael had staged.

Now the boys were adults, the best of the best—and about to face the biggest threat of their careers.

"Are we just gonna sit here in silence?" said John No Last Name. He'd refused to accept the surname of his adoptive parents, and by the time Michael had realized why and gotten him out, the boy had wanted nothing to do with the Black name either.

"Obviously not," Michael replied easily. "We're talking now, aren't we?"

John gave him the finger. He was a Rakan and from his curling locks to his glittering skin, he looked as though he'd been chiseled from a brick of solid gold. Michael was pretty sure there was no man more beautiful.

Corbin Blue snickered, and John gave him the finger too.

Blue was an Arcadian, a race known for its people's pale skin, white hair, and lavender eyes, and he was one of the fiercest warriors Michael had ever encountered, over six and a half feet tall, with the muscle mass of an artificially engineered specimen on a steady diet of steroids and growth hormone.

Of the three males, Blue was the only one who kept a public persona. He played professional football as a cover to get into the right parties, attended by the right people, where alcohol flowed and secrets spilled. Well, that, and because he enjoyed knocking other men around for money.

Beside him sat Solomon Judah. Michael wasn't sure of the male's origins. All he knew was that he'd never encountered anyone like him, and everyone who met him feared him. Including Michael! Solo either burned hot or iced cold, and there was nothing in between.

Solo kept to himself, only emerging from his "hick, backwater bat cave," as Blue called it, for a mission. But then, Solo had to be solitary. He was taller than both Corbin and John, monstrously so, with an even bigger muscle mass, but while the others were fantasies of urban beauty, Solo was a nightmare of hellish ugliness.

And okay, yeah, that was way harsh. He only resembled a creature from the underworld when his temper overtook him. Right now, he was actually what Michael's female assistant referred to as barbarian chic. And she always used a hushed, deferential tone.

Solo had unevenly chopped black hair, thanks to his affinity for cutting the strands with his own blade, and deeply bronzed skin. His eyes were blue and heavily lashed, his nose strong and aristocratic, with a slight bump in the center from one too many breaks.

Whenever he experienced a surge of anger, Solo's skin would darken to a frightening shade of crimson— the last color his enemies saw before dying horribly. His teeth would elongate into something far worse than fangs. His cheekbones would double in size and his ears would grow and develop sharp points at the end. Metallic claws would sprout from his nails.

By the time the last of the physical changes occurred, no one would be able to calm him. He would rage until becoming too weakened to move, everything in his path already totally and completely obliterated.

That hadn't always been the case. Once, his adoptive parents had had great success in the soothe-the-savage-beast arena. In fact, the pair had taken countless years off Michael's life, terrifying him as they'd approached the crazed boy, not to try and subdue him but to wrap their arms around him and hug him close. And Solo had let them!

When Mary Elizabeth and Jacob died, Solo had been inconsolable—and once again unstoppable.

He must have felt Michael's gaze, because he looked up and locked on him. They shared a silent moment of communication.

Michael: *How are you doing, son?*

Solo: *If you don't get started, I'll rip out your heart and have it for breakfast.*

That was just a guess on Michael's part, of course, but he was suddenly certain Solo iced cold today.

"I received a great piece of intel," Michael said, getting down to business. He sat upright and pressed a few buttons on his computer.

"Uh, I hate to break it to you, boss, but that's not exactly a news flash," Blue replied. "The only time you call us together is when you've received intel. Get to the real stuff, will you?"

"Why do you care whether or not he delays?" John said. "It's the off-season for you, so you've got nowhere else to be."

"Speak for yourself." Blue hitched his thumb in the Rakan's direction, all *Can you believe this guy?* "I have a wedding to pretend to help plan."

Unvarnished truth, right there. And Michael was still shocked about the impending nuptials. He kept track of his boys, and knew Blue hadn't known the girl long. A few weeks, nothing more. But that wasn't the shocking part. After a failed relationship a few years ago, Blue had become a serial one-hit batter. Yet now he expected a lifetime of wedded bliss? Please. And the girl? Blue's philandering was well known. Did she truly believe she would be the one to change him?

Well, she wouldn't. The fiancée had no idea Blue worked in the shadows of the government as a hired killer, and she never would. Eventually, she would realize he was lying to her about his whereabouts, and she would demand answers he couldn't give. She would assume he was having an affair—and he might be doing that, too—and leave him.

Michael had seen it happen to his operatives time and time again, but they kept trying, hoping to build ties with someone, anyone, and create an illusion of normalcy. When would they learn? When your life was a big fat lie, happily-ever-after was impossible. And yes, Michael knew that firsthand.

He would have released the boys from his employ, but they would have told him to go screw himself. They were brothers by circumstance rather than blood, and deep down they truly loved each other. Michael, too. Besides that, they knew of no other way to live. He hadn't let them learn. A mistake on his part, yes, but one it was too late to rectify.

At least John and Solo would not make the same mistake as their friend. The pair had waded through too much filth to try the marriage thing, and Michael knew they both felt as if they were tainted all the way to the bone. And Solo . . . well, he wasn't wrong about that.

Other agents made messes, and Solo was the one to clean everything up, destroying evidence that was never meant to make the light—whether living or not, whether guilty or innocent.

Michael would call him, give him a location, and tell him what had gone wrong. A few days later, Solo would have everything in order. And oh, the things he'd had to do to succeed . . .

"What's got your panties in such a morose little twist, boss?" Blue asked. He'd always been the most observant of the three. "You thinking about my wedding? Wanting to cry because you didn't get an invite?"

"Cry, when I'd rather kill myself than attend?" he asked, already knowing he would be there, hidden in the shadows. "Hardly."

His gaze returned to Solo. Would *he* go? The guy was slouched in his chair, his shoulders slumped in a wasted effort to make himself appear smaller. His eyes were narrowed and still locked on Michael, now piercing as sharply as a sword.

"All right, moving on," Michael muttered, taking the hint. He punched a few buttons and a screen appeared on the wall behind him. Images formed. "Meet Gregory Star. Human. Thirty-three. Married with two children, a boy, twenty-one, and a girl, nineteen. Both are heavily into drugs. We've traced the disappearance of several Alien Investigation and Removal agents to Mr. Star's door."

"Location of the agents?" Blue asked.

"Scattered. We haven't yet acted because we aren't yet sure if they're dead or alive."

A few more buttons were punched, and a picture of each agent flashed over the screen.

"So you have no idea what Star wants—or does—with those agents," John stated bluntly.

"Correct."

"But you're sure it's him?"

"We are. We had him under surveillance for something else and overheard a few phone conversations. While we can pin him to the crimes, we can't figure anything else."

"Well, I've spoken with him at several parties, and I gotta say, I'm baffled," Blue said. "He's a wealthy businessman with an eye for the pretties. Gambling is a weakness and drugs are a hobby, which is probably why the kids are addicts. Bodyguards are a staple, and mistresses as disposable as underwear, but he seems harmless enough."

Solo snapped, "Yes, and everyone is always exactly what they seem, aren't they? Why don't you think before you speak? *Idiot.*"

Blue, who sat in the middle of the boys, twisted to face him. "Why don't you say hello to the cherry slushie I'm about to make from your brain?"

He could do it, too. He possessed extraordinary abilities no human, and very few Arcadians, could even dream about.

"Go for it," Solo said, unconcerned. "Unlike you, I've got a few cells to spare."

"Children," Michael said, clapping his hands. "Enough." If they decided to reenact the gimpy-gazelle-versus-hungry-lion scene from *Animals of Old Earth*, Michael would be down two agents and probably missing a few limbs after trying to pull them apart.

Hired guns were *such* babies.

"Just let them play," John said, his tone now edged with an emotion Michael couldn't name. Something spiked with poison . . . deadly. "They need to get it out of their systems. They're due."

"Uh, that's not happening." Blue knew how to play; Solo did not. Blue would unintentionally insult Solo (more than he already had), and Solo would leave—with carnage in his wake. Nothing and no one would be able to bring him back until he was ready. But he would never be ready. "If it does, I'll have to pull all three of you from this case and assign you to work with my daughter, Evie."

"Enough!" John shouted, and the other two immediately zipped their lips.

They might be able to dismiss Michael, but they'd dance through fire for John.

"We good now?" Michael asked.

Blue nodded.

Solo ran his tongue over his teeth . . . teeth slightly longer than they'd been a few moments ago.

Michael knew Solo had been insulted by people all of his life. Because of his height and muscle mass, the kids at his elementary school had called him Ogre Boy—until his temper had gotten the better of him and he'd partially morphed into his other form. Then they'd called him Monster Mash and Ugly-O and had even thrown rocks at him.

Once, to protect himself, he'd nearly beaten a kid to death.

His mother had been phoned, and she'd arrived in

time to calm him before he'd harmed another child, but the damage had already been done. He was pulled from the school system, and would have been locked away for life if Michael hadn't intervened.

"We're good," John said, his face pale. "Evie is now off the table."

A well-known secret: John would protect Evie with his life as long as he didn't have to talk to her. It was Michael's fault. He had spoiled his youngest daughter, and she now felt as if it was every man's duty to do the same.

"I mean this in the nicest way possible, Michael," Blue said with a shudder, "but Evie needs to be put down."

"I'll take that under advisement." Michael cleared his throat. "Now, as I was saying, the agents were snatched while on the job."

"Human? Otherworlder?" John asked. His color hadn't yet returned to normal.

"Both," he replied. "Male and female, too. The only common thread is the fact that they work for AIR."

"Are they young? Good-looking?" Blue asked.

"Some of them, yes."

"Maybe they're being sold into the slave trade. That's the best way to hide multiple living bodies, as well as the best way to make fast cash when you're trying to support a drug habit." Blue worked two fingers over the smoothness of his jaw. "Have any civilians been taken?"

"Yes," Michael said, impressed by the jump his quick mind had made. It had taken Michael two days to connect that particular dot. "We don't think this has anything to do with trafficking, though. We have men on the inside of every major auction and whorehouse, but none have seen any hint of the agents or the civilians."

"What *do* you have?" Solo asked. "How do you know the victims were snatched by the same guy?"

Another excellent question. "Mr. Star has a calling card. He uses the victim's blood to draw the Chinese symbol for revenge somewhere in their home."

Blue rolled his eyes. "Are you sure the symbol is for revenge? A guy I know got a tattoo of what he thought was the symbol for strength, but it was really the symbol for indigestion."

"A guy you know? Dude, I've seen your back," John quipped. "The tattoo is yours."

Unapologetic, Blue said, "I thought the story had more spice the other way."

Anyway. "Yes, we're sure," Michael interjected. "We think he uses it to throw us off and confuse his motives. There's no reason for him to seek revenge against the seventeen people who were abducted. None of them have any connections to him or each other. Outside those from the agency, of course."

John pursed his lips. "Let me guess. You want us to find out what Star has done with all seventeen people before we kill him. Well, forget that. If we end him now, no one else will be abducted, and the problem will be solved," he said, spreading his arms. "You're welcome."

"When one of those people is a senator, we don't take out the only man who might know where she is."

But there was no question Star would die when all was said and done. "So here's how this will go down. John, you'll join the New Chicago AIR team as a transfer from Manhattan. They've lost two agents to this catastrophe."

"Got it."

"And no one can know who you really are or why you're really there. Not your new boss and not your partner, Dallas Gutierrez." Michael tossed him a mobile folder with all the information he would need.

John caught the device and immediately dug in. "And why am I really there?"

"To listen to office gossip, and to study the agents. If someone's got a connection to Mr. Star, I want to know about it and I want you to make friends. Sleep around. Whatever."

He nodded.

"Blue, the world is about to find out about your new drug habit."

The pro-baller's eyes slitted dangerously. Good. He understood. He'd have to pretend with the fiancée, too.

"Now that you're spinning out of control, you'll throw a party. You will invite Mr. Star's kids, and you will make nice. If you can, become the son's new supplier. And if the daughter's interested, sleep with her. Just be careful. I'd hate for you to disappear, too."

Like John, he nodded.

At least he hadn't protested the affair.

Michael focused on Solo. He was still slumped in his chair, his gaze still narrowed. "You will become

Blue's new, most trusted bodyguard. The man who gets things done. The one Blue relies on for the darkest of deeds."

A flash of panic before Solo's features smoothed out, revealing nothing else. "Very well."

He hated going out in public, and Blue led a very public life. His photo would be taken, would be plastered across every newspaper, and he would have to relive every moment and tolerate every insult. But he would do it. He always did what Michael told him.

"Good," Michael said. "You each have four days to prepare. On the fifth, I expect you to be entrenched in your roles. Dismissed."

In unison the boys popped to their feet. As they stomped to the door, Blue grumbled. John rubbed the back of his neck. Solo was quiet, his arms at his sides, his footfalls purposely soft.

The sensors above the door caught their movement and caused the soundproof metal to unlatch and slide open. Blue crossed the threshold first, John right on his heels, and Solo right on his.

Whoosh.

A sudden, violent gust of heat slammed through the entire office, lifting Michael out of his chair and propelling him into the far wall. Fire licked at his skin, and lances of pain battered at him as he slid to the floor. He tried to breathe but couldn't. Something heavy pressed against his chest, and he blinked rapidly in an effort to focus. A desk was now on top of him, he realized. What the . . . How . . . ?

The answer clicked into place. Someone had bombed his home office.

He laughed at the unlikeliness of such a situation, and blood bubbled from his mouth. As he coughed and fought to suck air past the liquid obstruction, his pain intensified and his eyesight dimmed.

Where were his boys? he wondered dazedly. *Were they . . . ?* Darkness closed in on him . . . *hurt . . . hurting . . . was hurting so badly now . . .* The boys had been closer to the blast, and he wasn't sure they could have survived . . . but they were so strong, so vital . . . surely they had . . .

The darkness finally reached him and he knew nothing more. . . .

For Solo, consciousness arrived in slow degrees. There was smoke in his nose and down his throat and his body throbbed as if every bone had been broken. He wasn't sure where he was or what had happened to him.

"—with this one?" a voice he didn't recognize was saying.

Despite the fog hazing his vision, he was able to distinguish two males leaning over him. One was tall, thin, and around thirty years old, with dark hair and dark eyes. The other was a living version of the man Solo had seen in the picture projected on Michael's wall. Gregory Star.

Star was a short human with silver hair, brown eyes, and skin tanned and lined by the sun. "Look at him," he said, his lip curling in disgust as his gaze roved over Solo's body. "Sell him to the same circus we sold the AIR agent to. He'll fetch a decent price."

"And this one?"

Both men vanished from Solo's line of sight, yet still he heard Star sigh. "Finish ashing him. As fried as he is, there's no way he'll survive transport anywhere else, and that way, there will be nothing left of him for anyone to find. A shame, though. I kind of liked him."

"And this last one?"

A pause. A purr of relish. "Do nothing. I'm keeping him."

Two

∽

Oh, that I had wings like a dove!
I would fly away and be at rest.
—PSALM 55:6

ONCE AGAIN, CONSCIOUSNESS ARRIVED in slow degrees for Solo. Darkness gradually faded from his mind, little thoughts forming. *I need to wake up. Something's happened. Something's wrong.*

He was enveloped by heat, sweating, his skin stinging. With every inhalation, the inside of his nose burned. With every exhalation, his chest throbbed as though it had been scraped with broken glass. He flexed and straightened his fingers. The joints were stiff, swollen. He arched his back, stretching. Every vertebra cracked, some even popping back into place with painful force.

He was Allorian—a race the humans knew nothing about—and because of the power of the guardian given to him by his biological parents, he healed quickly.

He forced his eyelids to part, grimacing as tender flesh pulled. He blinked once, twice, then again and again. Someone had flipped on a too-bright lamp and was shining it directly into his eyes, blistering his corneas. He could make out nothing but blinding white and gold.

He closed his eyes again. Sounds penetrated his ultra-sensitive ears. The rattle of metal against metal. A moan of pain. Multiple sets of footsteps. The slosh of something being dumped into a bucket.

His still-burning nose twitched as smells assaulted him. Dirt, grass, old oats, body odor, stale perfume, even the tang of corroded copper. Blood.

No longer caring about the damage from the light, he opened his eyes and kept them open. Gradually the stinging ceased, for which he was thankful. He looked around, only to realize no one had turned on a lamp. He was outside, the sun responsible for the high beams now spotlighting him.

And . . . he was inside a cage.

The knowledge hit him with the electrical power of a lightning bolt, and he jerked upright. Dizziness set up camp in his mind, but he didn't allow himself to react. He'd experienced worse a thousand times before, and with the life he led, he would experience worse a thousand times more.

All around him, men and women were locked in cages similar to his own: big, with thick bars, a red roof on top and four wheels on the bottom. The men wore loincloths and nothing else, and the females wore some type of transparent fabric over their breasts and around their hips.

"It wakes," someone said.

Snickers of "it" reverberated.

He knew they were talking about him. He'd been

referred to as "it" for most of his life. Usually, a person only made that mistake once.

He scanned the cages a second time, his mind processing several details at once. There were ten cages in total, forming a wide circle with an opening at the east and an opening at the west, allowing freemen to enter the clearing without hindrance. Not a single cage was empty. There were five males, including himself, and five females.

Each person was an otherworlder of some sort, and none were of the same species. There was a Teran, he thought, but he could only see the back of the woman's tawny hair and couldn't be sure. There was a female Delensean, with blue skin and six arms. A male Mec, with an oddly shaped baldhead and skin that would change color according to his mood. Right now he was clear, almost transparent, as though he had no emotions at all.

Next was a male Ell Rollie, with a big physique and, as with the rest of his race, probably less going on upstairs than a one-story house. A female Morevv, one of the most beautiful species ever to walk the earth, with silver skin and silver eyes. A female Rakan, with a more radiant golden sheen than even John No Last Name. A male Targon. A male Bree Lian. A female Cortaz.

Each wore thick metal cuffs around their wrists. Solo lifted his too-heavy arms. The same cuffs squeezed *his* wrists. He frowned. The skin around the metal was a darker bronze than usual, with an underlay of red, as if he verged on the edge of morphing into his other form. When he wiggled his fingers, sharp pains shot through his arms all the way to his shoulders. He'd had pins drilled into his bones before, and recognized the sensation. But why pin him if not to heal bone? To limit his range of motion, perhaps?

But why limit his range of motion as well as cage him?

Calm.

"Do not be afraid."

Recognizing the voice, he glanced to his right.

About the size of Solo's index finger, X had silver hair that had once been an inky black, and dull eyes that had once been a vibrant blue-green. A torn and dirty robe draped his emaciated frame. Skin that had once been luminous, glowing with all the colors of the rainbow, had become pallid and paper-thin over the years.

X. His guardian.

The being always looked undernourished, but when he fed Solo what little strength he still possessed, like he must have done after the explosion, he looked like death walking.

Solo was the only one who could see X, the only one who could hear him. He just hoped Dr. Evil, his other companion, maintained radio silence today.

Dr. Evil. His tormentor.

Dr. E hadn't been given to him, he had just shown up and refused to leave.

"I'm not afraid," he finally replied. He wasn't sure what was going on.

He remembered X telling him to stay away from the meeting with Michael. Remembered ignoring him and stomping inside Michael's office. Remembered . . . the explosion. Yes, that's right. Blue had opened the door, and a bomb had gone off. Solo had been thrown across the room and had instantly blacked out. After that, he remembered . . . what?

"You should be very afraid," another voice spoke out.

Dr. Evil. His hopes were slashed and burned.

Solo looked to his left. Where X had become aged and worn down over the years, Dr. E had thrived. He had thick blond hair, and eyes of the palest jade. His skin was tanned, unlined, and blazed with health. He, too, wore a robe, but his gleamed a brilliant white.

E—short for Laevus.

X—short for Adiutrix.

Solo had been too young to pronounce such complicated names. He had also been somewhat freaked out. But the pair had kept popping in and out, arguing, offering advice, and he'd eventually gotten used to them.

"You will find a way out," X said now, always the optimist. Not once had he ever believed Solo would fail in any regard, which always wrought crushing disappointment when Solo did, in fact, fail.

"Will he? Really?" Dr. E retorted. "Because I seriously doubt he can chew through the bars. No matter how big his teeth are!"

Solo looked beyond the cages, taking stock of his options. More humans walked about now than before, hurrying in one direction or another, while some were practicing on different apparatus. There was a barbed trapeze, with spikes protruding from a thin bar. A man climbed on top of a life-size cannonball seemingly made of glass, with snapping fish swimming through its walls. A woman performed flips on a trampoline, careful to avoid randomly placed rings of fire.

. . . sell him to the same circus we sold the AIR agent to . . .

The words reverberated in Solo's head.

. . . sell him . . . circus . . .

Star, a man who had abducted and maybe even killed sixteen people, had loomed over him and said those words.

Sell him to the same circus we sold the AIR agent to. He'll fetch a decent price.

The truth hit him with the force of a sledgehammer. Star had directed those words to an employee, about Solo. And then the two had done it, he realized. They had sold him to a circus. *This* circus.

Dread flooded him, a corrosive acid that scorched and ruined. This was—should have been—*impossible*. Star could not have known where the black ops agents tasked with his capture would be meeting, when the agents themselves hadn't known until an hour before-hand. More than that, there was no one on this planet who possessed the skill to bypass Michael's security. A system *Solo* had set up.

But okay. Star had known, and Star had somehow bypassed. As many years as Solo had worked for Michael, he'd learned to search for a solution the moment he realized there was a problem. Star could be dealt with later. Right now, only escape mattered.

And it should be easy. He was in a cage, yes, but

there were no armed guards posted at the door. The bars were metal, yes, but they lacked—he reached out—an electric charge. Good.

One of the captives scoffed and muttered, "Dummy. You'll never get free."

He would have to remember that there would be witnesses to his every deed. If only John and Blue were here. They would be—

Finish ashing him. As fried as he is, there's no way he'll survive transport anywhere else, and that way, there will be nothing left of him for anyone to find. A shame, though. I kind of liked him.

And this last one?

Do nothing. I'm keeping him.

The conversation played through Solo's mind, and he ground his molars. Whatever Star and his employee had said, John and Blue were alive. Michael, too. Solo would believe nothing less. His friends were strong, wily, and resourceful. Death didn't stand a chance.

As soon as he blew this circus, Solo would hunt the males down. Then they would complete their mission and destroy Star.

Wait. Their mission.

Sell him to the same circus we sold the AIR agent to.

"The AIR agent," Star had said. One of the missing.

Solo studied the captives one more time. His gaze snared on the Teran, who had finally twisted to face him. Her. She was the agent. He'd seen her photo on the wall of Michael's office.

Her name was Kitten, and she was with New Chicago's Alien Investigation and Removal team, trained to kill with her bare hands, to withstand the worst of torture, and, if necessary, to "catnip the hell out of someone," whatever that meant.

Her tangled hair belonged to a tabby cat, shades of gold, brown, black, and even streaks of flax intermingling. Her ears were tipped into sharp little points, and far cuter than his when he was angry. She had uptilted eyes of amber, high cheekbones, and lips curved into a deep frown. She was pretty in a very feminine, mischievous way—or would have been, with a little weight added to her body. Had she been starved?

Probably. But even still, a flicker of relief sparked inside his chest. To find and save this agent's life, he would have been willing to endure another explosion. He wouldn't leave without her.

As he adjusted his plan of escape to include two, she hissed at him. "What are you staring at, newbie? I will gut you!"

Dr. E puffed up with anger. "She won't be able to gut you if you remove her hands!"

"Search for understanding as for hidden treasure," X said. "She has been hurt, and so in turn she hurts others to try and protect herself from further abuse."

Solo forced himself to look away from the ungrateful Teran before he allowed his temper to overtake him. If he did, Kitten would kill herself just to save herself from being killed by him. And she'd be smart to do so!

He would still escape with her, but now he doubted he'd be nice about it. He didn't care whether she'd been hurt or not.

Fine. He did. Whatever.

A man who had to be on stilts crossed his path. And yet, the male's legs were covered by pants, and he looked to be balanced on bare feet rather than wooden posts. But . . . that couldn't be right. He was too tall, those legs too thin.

A female no more than three feet high waddled behind him. At least, Solo assumed she was female. She had large breasts and wore a pink tank and glittery micro-miniskirt, but she also had a long, thick beard, with beads interwoven throughout the dark locks of hair—

No, not hair. Couldn't be. The strands moved and hissed and bared tiny white fangs. Snakes, he realized. Her beard was comprised of hundreds of tiny snakes, their eyes red and glowing.

Another female trailed behind her, spraying fire from her mouth without any help from a torch. She laughed as the otherworlders in the cages scrambled backward to avoid being burned, but that laughter died the moment her gaze landed on Solo. She stopped midstep, her gaze sweeping over him.

"Well, well. What do we have here?"

He studied her in turn. Young, with a definite muscle tone someone of Solo's size and strength needed in a female. Otherwise he could accidentally snap her spine in two.

She was attractive, with bold features, green eyes that would have been pretty if they had not been glazed with inflated pride, and a slick fall of dark, shoulder-length hair streaked with pink. There were three spiders tattooed on each of her arms, each of a different size.

"Rebuke her," X commanded, surprising him. X was the lover, not the fighter. "Send her away."

"Don't rebuke her. Look at her. She likes it naughty, guaranteed," Dr. E replied.

X growled low in his throat. "Evil spreads, and we must not catch hers."

Dr. E rubbed his hands together with glee. "Hello! I'm willing for Solo to catch whatever she's got."

Yeah. Dr. E wouldn't mind if *Solo* caught something nasty, just as long as the little hell-raiser could watch him catch it.

X snapped, "Beauty often hides a beast."

Dr. E hummed his approval. "Good point. Let's get her clothes off and make sure."

They could go on all day.

Solo lifted his chin, gripped the bars in front of him, and shook the entire enclosure. He hoped to scare the woman and assert his dominance, but also to stealthily check the lock on the door. With only a glance, he could tell it was new, meant to open only when the proper fingerprint was scanned. Unfortunately, it was also titanium and held steady.

Unfazed by his outburst, she sauntered closer to him. "Did you see my new talent? Spraying fire? I just acquired it, and already I'm quite good."

She spoke as though it would have been just as easy to acquire a new shirt.

"But enough about me and my magnificence," she continued. "Jecis finally took my advice and brought in an attraction the masses will fear. You're as big as a bear and as fierce as a lion, aren't you? I am pleased."

Solo reached through the bars, determined to grab her. Grinning, she jumped out of reach.

"Uh, uh, uh. None of that, or I'll be forced to punish my tasty new toy."

He had been called many things in his life, but never that.

"I want her more with every second that passes," Dr. E said with a dreamy sigh.

X shook his head, saying, "She's not the woman for you, Solo."

"Ohhhh, what a shocker. X doesn't want to throw a party in your pants. Well, guess what? I do! It's been too long."

"Silence," Solo growled, and the female began to sputter with indignation. Dr. E wanted every woman Solo encountered, and X wanted none. But Solo wasn't a slave to his desires. The handful of times he had taken a lover, he'd walked away feeling dirty and disgusting. Because—shame fought to overtake him—if the females did not leave broken and bloody, they did not leave happy.

He only attracted women with a dark side: those who wanted the monster in their beds rather than the man—those who wanted a slap rather than a kiss, a slice of his claws rather than a caress.

On the job, that was fine. Whatever. He would do anything to anyone, without any remorse. He simply blanked his mind, buried his emotions. That was the only way he could do the terrible things that supposedly needed doing. But to harm the very females he was supposed to protect? The very females he wanted only to please? His parents had taught him better.

The female quieted and glared at him. "You did *not* just order me to be silent. I am your mistress, and you are my slave."

"Actually, you are nothing."

Rather than issuing another insult, she grinned. "I think I'll take great pleasure in teaching you the proper way of things."

Enough. "If you hope to survive the carnage I'll bring to this circus, you'll free me."

"Free you?" she asked with a seductive purr. "And what will you give me in return, hmm?"

"Do not bargain with her," X rushed out.

Solo pressed his tongue to the roof of his mouth. As if he would do something so foolish. Other people could bargain, but not Solo. Never Solo. To go back on his word was to suffer painfully. A curse of his race, perhaps.

"I told you," he said. "I'll allow you to live."

"How sweet. But no, I don't think I'll let you go. I like you right where you are. And maybe one day you'll even thank me for my refusal. I promise I'm not a biter and that you'll find heaven on earth in my arms. But guess what?" she added in a whisper as she leaned toward him. "I *am* a liar—and I do bite. Hard."

A mouthful of feminine curses echoed behind her. He moved his gaze over the otherworlders. All but the Teran still hid in the shadows of their cages, their expressions frightened. The Teran—Kitten—sat in the same position as before, but she was shaking the bars, her gaze locked on the human.

"Why don't you come over here and play with me?" Kitten snarled.

The girl paled.

Most likely the pair had tussled, and the girl had lost.

"Free me," he repeated, snagging her attention. "I promise you. It's the only way to save yourself."

A tinkling laugh bubbled from her, her encounter with the Teran already forgotten. "Aren't you just the most adorable thing? I know I hinted, but now I'm sure: I'm really going to enjoy your taming."

Very well. By sunset, she would not be able to enjoy anything ever again.

"My name is Audra, by the way. I'm the star of the trapeze, as well as the circus owner's lover. I'm someone of worth."

Someone needed to teach her the definition of "worth."

Gasps of horror erupted behind her.

"He's coming," one of the otherworlders said.

"Jecis is coming," another cried.

Once again, the human paled. Backing away from Solo, she said stiltedly, "Until next time, slave." Then she turned and raced from the clearing.

Three

∽∾

Deliver me from the mire and do not let me sink.
May I be delivered from my foes and from the deep waters.
—PSALM 69:14

X AND DR. E REMAINED silent as a big human male stomped into view. The newcomer stopped in the center of the clearing, bracing meaty fists on his hips and bringing Solo's attention to the gun sheathed there on one side and the large blade sheathed on the other.

He was armed for war.

Solo studied the rest of him. He had dark hair and sun-weathered flesh, wide shoulders and a large chest, and legs as thick as tree trunks. All of that was normal, if oversize for a human, but there was a paper-thin quality to the skin on his face, and despite his tan, Solo thought he could see his facial bones, as though looking at him through X-ray goggles. Only, the bones were bigger than they should have been, considering the shape of his face, and his teeth sharper than daggers.

"We do not fight the man," X said soberly, "but the wickedness inside him."

Solo had no idea what that meant, and at the moment, he didn't care. He just wanted out of the cage.

The male surveyed the captives with smug pride, before meeting Solo's gaze. His lips curved into the semblance of a smile, revealing teeth that didn't match the daggers Solo had seen.

"Good, you're awake."

"Free me," Solo demanded.

A booming laugh scraped against his ears. "A fighter. I'm glad."

Another refusal. Anger returned, a flash fire in his chest.

The silhouette the man cast on the ground suddenly moved. Frowning, Solo focused in on it. There was no way such a tiny silhouette belonged to such a brute of a man. It had to be—

A female, he realized.

A young woman stepped out from behind the male, and every nerve ending in Solo's body perked up and took notice. She was absolutely, utterly exquisite. On the small side, with long, curling blond hair and eyes that hovered somewhere between jet-black and deep, rich purple—plum eyes.

She was a fairy-tale princess come to dazzling life.

He could not force himself to look away, could only drink in every detail. A smooth forehead, delicately sloped nose, high cheekbones, and heart-shaped lips created the most luminous face, a canvas of perfection. She was rosily flushed, a flower dusted with morning dew and someone please stab him and put him out of his misery because he sounded like a deranged poet, but he couldn't help himself. The girl was a taste of heaven, sweetness and light, and he was suddenly starved.

The only flaw to her was the fresh bruise on the right side of her jaw.

He didn't like that she had been hurt.

As if she sensed his gaze, she glanced his way. Their eyes locked. Her mouth formed a small O. He knew what such a reaction from her meant. She considered his size monstrous, just like everyone else did. But she never severed the connection, as though disgusted or frightened and desperate to hide. She continued to stare, those plum eyes growing wide, softening.

The air between them crackled with . . . something, and every muscle in his body clenched agonizingly on bone.

"Her," X said, sounding dazed. "She's the one. She's yours."

"No way," Dr. E replied, incensed. "Just no way. She'll never want anything to do with him, and even if she does—which isn't likely, if I haven't made that clear—he'll kill her with his gigantor hands."

"She's the one," X repeated.

Yes, she's mine, all mine, Solo thought, then shook his head. Surely that thought had not budded inside his mind. She was too little, too delicate. And yet he heard, *She's mine,* a second time, a booming roar now, and he knew beyond any doubt. Yes, he *had* had that thought.

Jecis pivoted to say something to another captive, and Solo stretched his arm through the bar, reckless in his bid to touch the girl. Just touch her. He had to learn the texture of her skin. Would it be as soft as it appeared . . . or softer?

With a gulp, she darted behind the male named Jecis.

Finally Solo had frightened her. He bit back his bellow of frustration.

The crackle faded from the air at least, but Solo's body failed to relax. He wanted to carry the girl away caveman-style. He wanted to bang his fists into his chest, proclaiming to every man breathing that she belonged to Solo. He wanted to throw her enemies at her feet and bask in her adoration.

He would never do any of those things, and she would never adore him.

She wasn't the type to crave a monster in her bed. She wasn't strong, like the fire-breathing female, or rough, with an addiction to danger. As fragile as she appeared, as timid as she acted, she would scream for help the moment he approached her.

"Told you," Dr. E said in a singsong voice. "There was just no way."

His angry retort received the same treatment as the bellow.

Like him, X remained silent.

The little man had never before picked out a female for Solo, had even complained every day Solo had spent with his only long-term girlfriend, Abigail. The fact that X had chosen a girl who most likely belonged to the slab of beef about to announce he was the owner of the circus—and there was no doubt in Solo's mind the human was the owner—was almost too much to take in.

Jecis was moving his mouth, obviously speaking to Solo. As entranced as Solo had been by the girl, he'd lost focus. "—accept this welcome to Cirque de Monstres. As I said, and as I'm sure you have already heard, I am Jecis Lukas, owner, operator . . . your new master. Might equals right, and considering our different positions, I've proven mine. If you do what I say, when I say, you will have an easy life ahead of you. If you don't . . ."

Cirque de Monstres. French for "Circus of Fiends," yet Jecis certainly wasn't French. Solo had traveled the world many times over; names, languages, and dialects were a specialty of his. The name Jecis Lukas was Lithuanian, as was his very slight accent.

Solo hadn't heard of this particular circus, run by this particular male, but he had heard of similar traveling performing groups. They were illegally operated, with unsafe rides, unfair games, prizes that were nothing more than stolen goods, tents where drugs and women were sold, and unparalleled violence waiting in every corner.

Jecis continued his speech, saying, "You do not speak to, spit on, or harm anyone who approaches you. You just sit in your new home and look pretty." He snickered at his own joke. "You might have trouble with that last one, giant, but that's part of your appeal. Never forget that you are my pet. My animal. And if you behave, you are rewarded. If not, you are punished."

One word echoed in Solo's mind: *animal.*

He considered the cages more intently. There were

letters scripted atop each one, though someone had tried to scrape those letters off. He read *Lion. Tiger. Ape.* And on and on the titles went. *Bear. Alligator.*

Forget anger. Rage shimmered just below the surface of his skin. The trapped otherworlders were to be the animals. They were to be viewed by circus attendees, studied and degraded. They were to be . . . petted? Fed? Ridden?

He would *die* before he allowed a human to pet him. He would die before he allowed a human to feed him by hand. He would burn the entire world to the ground before he allowed a human to saddle him up and ride.

"I told you," X said. "Fear not. A man will eat the fruit of his own way."

"If that's true, our boy should have a panic attack," Dr. E replied with a smirk. "He hasn't exactly planted the best of trees, now has he?"

X ignored him, saying, "Jecis will destroy himself. And you, Solo, you will find a way out."

"Doubtful." Dr. E checked his cuticles. "Sure, you've broken out of a prison before, S, my man, but the first time was a training exercise and the second was with help. Now, you're alone. These people have weapons, and they won't be afraid to use them. You're unarmed."

"You will succeed—and you will aid all the others."

"You will fail—and you will heap more suffering on everyone's head. Just behave and wait for rescue, and you'll be better off."

Jecis said something else, drowning out his companions, but Solo didn't hear him either. For the first time since waking up, he studied his own body. Like the other males, he was dressed only in a loincloth. His chest, arms, and legs were cut and scabbed, with black-and-blue bruises branching off in every direction. He was a mess.

His skin was redder than it had been five minutes ago, the first sign of his still-growing rage. He twisted his arms to look at his tattoos. His mother's name was etched into his right forearm, and his father's name etched into his left. There was an irritated gouge bisecting the M and the first A of MARY ELIZABETH, but JACOB was untouched.

His entire cage shook, and his gaze snapped up. A scowling Jecis stood right in front of him.

"You listen when I speak, giant. Tomorrow the circus opens, and I expect you to be on your best behavior." His voice boomed through the daylight, the skull beneath his skin seeming to move without the prompting of his body, coming forward, closer to Solo. "I mean that."

Evil left a cloying film in the air.

I'll be long gone, he told himself. "And if I'm bad?"

Behind the human, men lumbered into the clearing and placed buckets of—he sniffed—enzyme soap on the ground. The buckets were followed by piles of rags, and bottles of—another sniff—perfume.

"If one customer complains, just one . . ." A dramatic pause as Jecis lifted his arms and rubbed his fists together, "I'll put a bullet in your brain, no questions asked."

When Solo gave no reaction to the threat—been there, done that—Jecis punched the bars of the cage, the film thickening. "If you doubt me, just ask your fellow animals. Many of their friends already have died by my hand."

Four

∾

I am the rose of Sharon, the lily of the valleys.
—SONG OF SOLOMON 2:1

A S ALWAYS, VIKA WAS revolted by the induction of a new "animal." Whether male or female, young or old, the newcomer always begged her to show mercy and grant freedom the moment her father marched away. Mercy she would not show. Freedom she would not bestow. Could not.

Not yet.

Years ago she'd assumed the beating Jecis had given her for attempting to release One Day was the most savage he had to offer, that her father would never be able to inflict more pain than that, and that, to save someone else, she could bear such pain again. But then, the day she'd freed his human animals, he'd taught her otherwise.

He could *always* do much, much worse.

And what could be worse than losing her hearing? Easy. Losing her eyesight, too. Oh, yes. Her father was *that* vile. He'd destroyed her hearing with no hope of repair, simply to make her reliant on him, and he had threatened to take her eyesight if ever she betrayed him that way again.

If she wanted out, and she did, she had to adhere to a very strict escape plan. A plan that demanded she remain at the circus for another year. Just a year, and then she could free the otherworlders and run. She could hide forever and never have to fear being found.

Jecis finished his speech about rules and expectations, and motioned Vika forward. She stepped beside him like any other obedient robot. He placed a big hand firmly on her shoulder, and she looked up to watch his lips.

"This is your caregiver," he said to the otherworlders. "You will treat her better than you treat the customers. You will keep your hands to yourself and your mouths closed, or my men and I will have fun with you before you get that bullet."

He didn't wait for their replies—to him, they were irrelevant—but pivoted to face Vika. She met his gaze, no longer surprised to find eyes no longer the color of flowers, but black, like endless cesspools.

He cupped her cheeks and kissed her on the tip of the nose. "If you have any trouble, my heart, do not hesitate to shout for me."

I will never seek your help. "Thank you."

"Anything for you." Instead of moving away, as she'd hoped, he remained in place, his lips pursing. "My new animal is big and fierce and unlike any you have dealt with before. Perhaps I should summon your guard—"

"The circus opens tomorrow," she interjected quickly,

hoping to stop him before he talked himself into it. "There's so much to do, and there's no reason to waste anyone's time watching over me. Besides, no matter how fierce he is, the newcomer would never dare to hurt me. He now knows the consequences of defying you."

Her father's grip tightened, nearly crushing her jawbone and defiantly worsening what remained of last week's "lesson." "I will waste whoever's time I wish. You are more important to me than a successful show, and if I think there's a threat, there's a threat. I'm far wiser about these things."

Won't cry out. "Of course," she managed to say. If, however, the show *did* prove unsuccessful and he *had* forced her bodyguard to remain at her side, preventing Matas from properly preparing for his magic act, Jecis would blame her. He would reprimand her. She would hurt.

With a sigh, he released her. "As if I can deny you anything. Very well, I will allow you to work alone since there are no townies nearby and the otherworlders are contained. But if you come home with a single bruise, my precious one, I will be very upset."

Well, then. She wouldn't point out the myriad of bruises already decorating her body. Besides, there was no need. He knew they were there; *he* had put them there. But while he was allowed to abuse her, anytime, anyplace, no one else was ever extended the same privilege.

He delivered another kiss to the tip of her nose before stalking away, fully assured she would do everything in her power to safeguard herself. He wasn't wrong. She would. She might dream of leaving her father, might even be planning to do so, but she would never disobey him while she was here.

Did the newcomer have any idea what was in store for him?

If he hadn't been convinced of Jecis's malevolence, he would be soon. Jecis punished his animals for the mildest of offenses, though the punishments themselves were never mild. His temper would get the better of him and he would erupt into a fit of rage. He would maim . . . he would ruin . . . and he would kill indiscriminately. . . .

Sadly, those who died were the lucky ones.

Vika walked to the supplies her father's worker had left behind, never allowing herself to shift her gaze to study the lips of the otherworlders to discover what they were saying about her—and they were saying something, she knew they were, because she could feel the vibrations of their words against her skin. At times like this, she was almost grateful for her deafness.

I'll escape this hellhole and take you with me, Vika, Wicked Witch of the Worlds. I'll put you in a cage and oh, the things I'll do to you . . . This had once come from the Mec she called Rainbow.

You're nothing more than a circus whore, and you deserve to be in this cage, not me! This had once come from the Cortaz named Crissabelle.

They needed a target for their frustration and rage, and she was the safest bet. She knew that, and had stopped letting it hurt her feelings a long time ago. She would never harm them and certainly never tattle, but it was almost impossible to keep a secret from Jecis. One day, he would find out about the two offenders and bloody their toast.

One day.

The words left a sick taste in her mouth.

The rest of the otherworlders refused to look at, talk to, or talk about her, too afraid of what Jecis would do. Actually, no, that wasn't true. The Targon actually seemed to enjoy her.

Is it time for my sponge bath yet, Vika I Wanta Licka? he was fond of saying. He often referred to himself as Daddy Spanky, and once a day asked her to do the same.

"Eat up, everyone. I'm feeling generous today." She threw vanilla cookies into each cage, even the Mec's and the Cortaz's. Rewarding the Terrible Duo for bad behavior was beyond foolish, but some part of her wanted to make their lives better, even in so small a way.

As the otherworlders dove for the desserts and devoured every crumb, she grabbed a bottle of enzyme spray, a brush and one of the rags, and approached the cage belonging to the Bree Lian she'd named Dots.

His race was known for the multicolored fur that covered their bodies from head to toe, and Dots was no different. He resembled a long-haired cheetah, with an underlay of gold and spots of black, yet his mannerisms were as uncatlike as possible. As muscled as he was, he didn't walk so much as thunder from one end of the cage to the other.

Still, he kind of reminded her of Dobi, the beautiful

tiger who had peed on everything, including Vika, and every time she looked at him, a pang sliced through her heart.

Don't go there. Right. The past was off-limits, and for good reason. Looking back brought only regret. Regret brought sorrow. Sorrow brought depression, and depression brought torment. She'd had enough of that, thanks.

So. Moving on. Each of the different species bore different physical characteristics, as well as different innate abilities. Some Bree Lians could poison an enemy with their teeth or nails. Some Cortazes could teleport. Some Mecs could hypnotize with the changing colors of their skin. Some Terans could leap a mile in a single bound. But it was utterly impossible to know each and every one of the abilities these particular otherworlders possessed, which was why her father had gone black market and purchased slave bands.

The shackles were thick and bronze with long, sharp needles honed from some kind of alien metal that drilled into each wearer's bones, dripping a steady and constant supply of a potent inhibitor straight into marrow.

When Vika needed to get inside a cage, either to wash it or its prisoner, she had only to press the remote activator to send a different drug—a sedative—through the otherworlder's system, knocking him out for at least an hour.

The closer she came to Dots, the more fervently he prowled the length of his cage. Usually, he was the incarnation of composed. He ate when he was supposed to eat. He never spoke without first being spoken to, and he remained seated in the back corner whenever Vika approached.

But he'd been here long enough to learn exactly how her father operated.

The otherworlders were kept in the menagerie as long as they were healthy and humans remained fascinated with them. Eight days ago, the most senior of the slaves had been relocated to games because he'd appeared "feverish."

He was a Rslado-el, a delicate race, easily breakable. Many times she'd come close to freeing him. Close— but not close enough. Now he was the star of Mole Smack Attack, forced to bob his head in and out of holes, while humans tried to hit him in the face with padded bats.

The past few weeks, Dots had lost a lot of weight. Despite his muscle, he was beginning to appear gaunt. Vika had given him extra portions at every meal, but so far, the food hadn't helped.

He would be the next one to go to the chopping block.

She wanted to free him before that happened. She did. And if he could just hang on for a while longer, she would. He just had to hang on. But she couldn't tell him that, could she?

Stomach twisting with a stinging blend of guilt and remorse, Vika jumped up to press the button that would render him unconscious. How she disliked her lack of height! In a blink, the Bree Lian was lunging at her, roaring, "I'll kill you before I let you move me!"

and spraying cookie crumbs all over her face. He managed to reach through the bars and scratch her before he collapsed, already snoring.

There was a throb in her shoulder, and she felt the warm trickle of blood, but such a minor injury was barely a blip on her radar.

She performed a quick spin, making sure the Bree Lian's roar had not roused the attention of a nearby performer. A minute passed, then two. No one came running. Good, that was good.

But what about your father? she thought, the first spark of panic blooming. *You aren't to come home with a single bruise.*

An open wound was worse, wasn't it. Motions frantic, she tied her shirtsleeve around her shoulder, applying pressure to the claw marks. As soon as the blood stopped flowing, she would properly bandage the thing and change shirts. Something long sleeved, maybe. And if she finally wore one of the necklaces her father had given her, he would be too pleased with her to notice anything else. Surely. Hopefully.

"Anyone else tries that," she forced herself to say, never meeting anyone's gaze, "and I'll forget to feed you tonight." And oh, how she loathed making threats like that. Threats she wasn't sure she had the ability to see through. But she couldn't risk another injury. Her father would kill each and every otherworlder, just to make a point.

Well, that, and a profit. He had paid top dollar for them, and while he made a lot of it back with the menagerie and the games, he received the biggest return to his investment when he sold the bodies—in parts.

Hands trembling, she unlatched Dots's door and climbed inside. She spent half an hour cleaning his skin and brushing his hair, as gently and noninvasively as possible. All the while, pity welled inside her. His modesty was a thing of the past; common courtesy had been forgotten; and torment was a daily occurrence.

One day, I'll be able to help him.

Ugh. There were those words again.

She finished with the Bree Lian and locked up. The Targon was next. And though she had no nickname for him, she refused to refer to him as Daddy Spanky.

As always, he stretched across the floor of his cage and smiled at her. He was a beautiful man, with pale skin that glittered as though dusted with diamond powder and hair as black as the night with pinpricks of sapphire. Only one thing had ever bothered him, and that was the appearance of Matas.

The Targon *erupted* any time he caught sight of her bodyguard.

"I'm *very* dirty," he purred. "Make sure you scrub really, really hard."

She placed her hand on her throat to feel the reverberation of her voice box and better judge her volume. "If only I could scrub your mind."

"Honey, no matter where you scrub you're gonna need an industrial-size—"

Rolling her eyes, she jumped up and pressed the button to render him unconscious.

As she sprayed the enzyme mixture that would clean him inside and out, then rubbed away the excess oil, she could feel someone's gaze boring into her, burning deep and sure. There was no reason to look up. She knew the newcomer was the culprit. *Everyone* watched her in the beginning, hoping to learn her habits and discover the best way to overpower her and, as Criss had often said, "blow this hellhole."

But Vika recalled how, at first, this one had looked at her with curiosity, crackling awareness and stunned awe, rather than suspicion. A heady mix that had shocked her. Men simply didn't regard her that way.

How quickly his countenance had changed, however, when her father announced she was in charge of his care. Awareness and awe had given way to barely suppressed ferocity. And that, she was used to.

If freed, he could crush her in seconds.

Could. She rolled the word through her mind. But would he? Had the awe returned, or was the ferocity tugging at its reins?

Dare she glance up and find out?

Just the thought caused her palms to sweat. As big as this Targon was, the . . . whatever he was would stand many inches taller and be many inches wider. He was the epitome of power, and she was quite certain she'd never seen so brawny a male.

If he threatened her, she'd . . . what? Scream? Hardly. There were only two things that scared her. An angry Jecis—and a happy Jecis. The newcomer wasn't either of those things. But okay, yes, as hot as his temper had appeared to be, he might just be able to slide into third place without any real effort.

But . . . his eyes. He had such lovely eyes. They were

large, and the most glorious shade of baby blue, like the sky on the brightest of mornings, fringed by a thick black fan of lashes. For a moment, she had lost herself in those eyes, and oh, that had been the most amazing feat.

Lost, she had forgotten about her miserable life.

Lost, she had found strength.

Would she lose herself again?

Fine. She had to know. Vika glanced up.

Five

∽⌇∾

Do not withhold good from those to whom it is due,
when it is in your power to act.
—PROVERBS 2:27

VIKA MET THE NEWCOMER'S gaze—and her entire body reacted, every cell she possessed coming alive, buzzing, heating. But she didn't lose herself. Not even close. He was far more than angry. He radiated white-hot fury, his skin actually darkening to a deep, rich red. His eyelids were narrowed into dangerous slits, his cheekbones protruded, and his nostrils flared with his every inhalation.

His teeth had even grown, she realized with intensifying horror. They were so long they stretched over his bottom lip. And his ears had changed, now pointing at the ends. And his nails . . . oh, sweet mercy . . . they were *claws*.

Surely he was capable of slashing the bars of his cage. And when he did, he would stomp over to her. He would raise those heavy fists and destroy her. The pain would be too much. He would hit her face, and he would finally blind her. No!

Panic threatened to overwhelm her as she dropped her rag. Breath caught in her throat and crystallized, leaving a hard, jagged lump that choked her. Black winked through her line of sight as she scrambled to the back corner of the Targon's cage.

Gonna hurt, gonna hurt, gonna hurt so bad.

Except . . .

Pain was never forthcoming.

She blinked, unsure how much time had passed. The newcomer . . . had not moved an inch, she realized. He hadn't tried to get to her. And even if he had, she thought, courage at last making an appearance, he was cuffed and drugged, as helpless as a newborn babe. There was nothing he could do to harm her.

Bit by bit, the rest of her panic receded. Gulping, she looked him over. His skin had returned to its original bronze color. His teeth had shrunk and his claws had vanished. His eyes still blazed with a furious fire, but they were also wounded.

The same wound her reflection often showcased.

What had she done to offend him? She hadn't locked him up; she had fed him delicious cookies. Cookies he had ignored, she realized. The little round treats rested on the floor of his cage. But she already knew the answer, didn't she? She had flinched when she'd looked at him, scrambling away to create distance between them, as if he were disgusting, tainted.

Such a reaction would have offended anyone. But even still, a warrior such as he should have pounded his chest with pride. Her father loved the terrified reactions his power elicited, for they stroked his ego. But, okay, not all men were like her father. Or Matas. Or the other men at the circus. Or a good portion of the men who visited the circus. She knew that. She'd seen fathers with their children, smiling and protective. She'd seen husbands with their wives, adoring and loving. Real love, not the kind Jecis was selling.

I can't leave the poor guy like that. His entire world had just collapsed, and a new one—a darker one—had taken shape around him. On this first day of his new, terrible life, she could grant him a kindness. Couldn't she?

Determined, Vika scooted out of the Targon's cage, engaged the lock with her thumbprint, and padded across the clearing toward the newcomer.

A pebble thudded against her arm. Frowning, she looked to the left and caught a glimpse of the female in the cage next to the newcomer's. The Cortaz grinned smugly—and launched another pebble. This one hit Vika in the chest.

Vika didn't bother asking Crissabelle if she wanted to die. Vika could guess the answer. Yes. *Sorry, darling, but I'm not going to oblige you.* "The fact that you remember I collect rocks is probably the sweetest thing ever," she forced herself to say with a breeziness she didn't feel. "Is it our anniversary?"

The otherworlder's grin took on a darker edge. Despite the dirt smudging her cheeks, she was breathtaking. She was tall and slender, all long limbs and willowy elegance. Her skin was as flawless as the most expensive pearl and her hair a fall of black velvet.

"When my brothers come and get me, and they will, you'll be burned alive while I watch and laugh."

A pebble hit Vika from behind. She spun around

to glare at the culprit, only to take a *bigger* rock to the chest. The Mec—Rainbow—was cackling and pointing at her, as if there was something wrong with her. He loved doing that.

The first few times he'd done it, Vika had run away to check herself in a mirror. A stain on her face? Ripped clothing? Something in her teeth? But not one time had she found anything out of place, and she'd realized he only wished to torture her.

"You found a few for my collection, too? That's so thoughtful. But guys, I didn't get you anything."

The cackling stopped, and he hissed at her. His skin began to glow bright red, a sign of his growing fury.

At first, he and Crissabelle had tried to build a rapport with her. Criss had told her how nice she was, and Rainbow had told her that he hated the way her father talked to her, that he could help, if only she'd free him. After a while, Vika's continued refusal had ruined all hint of goodwill.

Their transgressions had started out small, and they had hurtled insults, nothing more. When they realized Vika would not tell Jecis, they had graduated to straw, then food, and now rocks. They assumed that, in this, Vika would take, take, take, and never give back.

They were so—right, she thought with a sigh.

Head held high, she closed the rest of the distance with the newcomer. He was in the same spot, in the same position, but his gaze had narrowed on the Mec and the Cortaz. Like the Mec's, his skin had once again taken on a cast of red.

"Hello," Vika said.

Those baby blues swung to her, and she shivered.

She drew in a deep breath, hoping to suck in a little more courage and stop the sudden tingling in her veins. She failed at both. The tingling even increased. Hints of peat smoke, pine, and mint filled her nose, making her think of midnight bonfires in an enchanted forest. It was such a rare fragrance that she closed her eyes and inhaled again, and again, until she was light-headed.

There weren't many forests left in the world. Most belonged to the government and trespassers were never allowed. In fact, she'd only ever seen them from a great distance because, while the circus traveled from city to city, state to state, and sometimes other countries, all year round, they were only ever allowed to stay in clearings where forests *used* to be.

Ultimately the glare of the sun and the man's sizzling gaze reminded her that she was outside in view of anyone walking by, it was midday, and she had a lot to do. Failure to complete a single task would invite punishment, and punishment would put her out of commission for several days.

Heart hammering, she focused. The captive now radiated enough heat to melt the Arctic in a matter of seconds.

"Why don't you come a little closer, female?" he asked.

Thankfully, panic did not assail her and she was able to draw on the audacity that only surfaced in her father's absence. "I think I'll stay right here, but I appreciate the suggestion."

Vika squared her shoulders and looked over the male. Up close, she could see that his skin appeared to be as smooth as glass, the red fading into the beautiful bronze. His facial bones were slightly overgrown, but they were perfectly put together, creating a picture of rough, undiluted masculinity. In fact, he was as fierce in looks as One Day had been during the prime of his too-short life.

A sudden longing for what could have been swelled the chambers of her heart.

The otherworlder's mouth was moving, she realized, but she'd missed his words. Rather than admit the truth, she remained silent. People often repeated themselves, saving her from having to ask.

Finally, he said, "What are you staring at, human?"

"I'm staring at you. Obviously."

He grabbed the bars, his knuckles bleaching of color. The words NPRY ELIZABETH and JACOB were etched into his arms. Elizabeth and Jacob she understood. They were names, and she wondered what the people meant to him. But Npry?

"Woman!"

Pulse points dancing to a wild beat she couldn't control, she said, "Here," and withdrew the piece of chocolate she'd stuffed in her jeans pocket to enjoy later. "Take it. It's yours."

She tossed, but he didn't catch. He didn't watch where the candy skittered to a stop, either.

"If you fail to eat it now, it will melt and you'll have to lick it up. That can be embarrassing, believe me. But chocolate is good in any state, so it's up to you whether or not—"

His mouth was moving again. Such a lush, pink mouth. "—asked you a question, female."

Feigning nonchalance, she flicked her hair over her shoulder. "Ask again," she said. None of the captives had guessed her infirmity, and she would never admit to it. As desperate as they were, as much as they blamed her for their confinement, they would use the handicap against her. "I was distracted."

"Very well. Do you want to die?"

"How wonderful," she replied in the driest tone she could manage. "My eighth death threat today. I'll be sure to make a notation in my diary."

"Yes, you want to die," he said with a slow nod. "Otherwise you would free me."

"Let me tell you how the rest of this conversation will go and save you time, yes? If I fail to set you free right this moment, you will escape. You will be the one to kill me. You will make me hurt. I will regret the day I was ever born. The end. So . . . you eat that?" Frowning, she shook her head. "I mean, you will eat the chocolate now, won't you?"

Without ever looking away from her, he snatched up the treat, unwrapped the foil—and smashed the nugget into one of the cage bars, rubbing . . . rubbing . . . little crumbs falling into the dirt below.

A mewl of mourning slipped from her. Yes, she had a million more pieces in her trailer, all given to her by her father, just because he "loved" her. But that didn't alter the fact that the otherworlder had just destroyed something she had earned with blood, sweat, and a whole lot of tears.

"Your loss," she forced herself to say blithely.

"You have no idea the terror you have brought to this circus, little girl."

Little girl. That's what her father often called her. His beautiful little girl. His dearest little girl. His beloved little girl. Vika raised her chin and gritted out, "Don't call me that. And I didn't bring you here."

One brow arched, turning his entire expression into a dare. "Doesn't matter. You are guilty by association."

"Am not."

"Are too."

"Am not!" she said with a stomp of her foot.

His eyelids slitted dangerously. "We are not children. Let me go."

"No," she replied without a single beat of hesitation.

"Very well. As I said, you will die with the rest."

"Blah, blah, blah. I know." Vibrations at her left caused her gaze to dart in that direction.

"—kill her, kill her, kill her," Rainbow chanted as he jumped up and down in his cage.

Another vibration at her right. Her gaze returned to the newcomer . . . whatever his name was. He had decided to use her distraction to his advantage, was reaching through the bars, trying to contort his body to gain enough length to grab her.

She stumbled backward, out of reach. Frustrated, he snapped those saber teeth at her—sweet mercy, they grew before her eyes and were even longer than before!—his features radiating a dark rage she'd seen one too many times today.

Trembling, she barked, "I was trying to make your day better, and you decided to murder me for it? Perhaps you deserve to be in that cage, eh?" and stomped away to finish her chores.

Six

∞

But examine everything carefully,
and hold fast to that which is good.
—1 THESSALONIANS 5:21

SOLO WATCHED AS THE female the captives called Vika—a young girl the owner of the circus had called "my heart"—sedated and bathed the rest of the otherworlders. She still labored over the last, the Cortaz, leaving only Solo.

Her touch was always tentative, shaky, and gentle, and he was highly curious to know if she would treat him with the same deference, considering all the threats he'd made. A curiosity he despised. He shouldn't care one way or the other. To bathe him, she would have to tranquilize him, and the thought of dropping like a bear in the wild was utterly humiliating. Besides, if he slept through the entire episode, the sickening curiosity would never be assuaged.

And yet, he still liked the idea of having her hands on him.

Stupid. He needed to be smarter where she was concerned.

Already he'd made two grievous mistakes. The first? Attraction. Men forgot their purpose when they lusted after a woman. The second? He'd experienced a measure of pity for her. Because, here she was, a beautiful human girl surely clothed in the skin of God's most treasured angel, yet she had a bruise the size of a fist on her face. The size of Jecis's fist, to be exact.

Solo had come to the conclusion that Jecis was forcing her to work for him and that, if Solo could only convince her to trust him, he could flee with her. Her—his very own female, according to X. He'd truly thought he would have a chance to convince her, too. If she were being beaten, she would crave some sort of protection. *Any* protection, even from a monster. Protection he would have vowed to give. But when he'd offered to help her, she hadn't bothered to reply.

After that, frustration had become a living force inside him, and out had come the death threats. Rather than cowering, as an abused female would have done, she had taunted him with her disregard.

That's when the truth had settled deep. She was cold and cruel, without a heart, and he would have to take her down with everyone else. And he was totally okay with that, he told himself. He had always lived by three little words, the strongest words in creation: *whatever proved necessary.*

In fact, if ripping the door from his cage was a problem, he would remove her thumb—perhaps the only key to the locks—and he would do it with a slash of his claws or a swipe of his teeth. She would scream and she would cry, but nothing she said or did would stop him. She did not deserve Solo's compassion and, to his mother's shame, she would not receive it.

X had screwed up royally. Vika was to be Solo's woman? Hardly. Either she liked to crawl into bed with Jecis Lukas or she had sprung from his loins. Either way, she deserved what she got.

So what if she had exhibited moments of kindness?

So what if her expressive face had revealed hurt, courage, and grim resolve when peering over at Solo, and all three emotions had caused his chest to ache. And okay, yes, the ache had actually sprung to life when the Bree Lian had scratched her shoulder. Solo had been forced to fight the compulsion to bust free of the cage simply to tear the otherworlder into innumerable pieces. A compulsion he'd once again battled as the Mec and the Cortaz had thrown rocks at her.

Silly of him, considering *Solo* would be harming her tonight. But he remembered all the times the kids at school had thrown rocks at him. Remembered the day his emotions had gotten the better of him, and he'd turned another kid's face to pulp. Remembered that was the day X, who had been with him since birth only to disappear after the death of his biological parents, had returned. That was also the day Dr. E arrived. He remembered wishing he had a different life—but Vika hadn't seemed to care.

He didn't like that he had to wait to act, but patience was his best friend right now. He hadn't quite recovered from the bombing, weakness still swimming through his veins, affecting his limbs. His grip wasn't as strong as usual, and he doubted his footsteps would be steady.

"I can feel your anger, Solo," X said, sitting down on

Solo's shoulder, balancing his elbows on his upraised knees. "Why? The girl has done nothing wrong."

"Nothing wrong?" Dr. E snorted, pacing. "Maybe we're thinking of different girls, because this one tried to poison him!"

"Do not be ridiculous. She didn't try to poison him."

"Prove it."

X remained silent, knowing there was no need to speak. Solo was well able to smell the essence of poison, and he had smelled nothing in the chocolate. So . . . why had she given it to him? Had he hoped to soften him or perhaps even to seduce him? Had she slept with any of the other imprisoned males, enjoying her power over them? Just the thought caused his nails to elongate and cut into his palms.

He homed in on her, watched intently, and realized she was showing the female the same detached gentleness as she had shown the males. He relaxed, his nails shrinking to their normal size. No, she hadn't slept with any of the males.

She'd hoped to soften Solo, then. But why?

Dr. E stomped a foot and growled, "If you aren't on Solo's team, you're against it. She's against it and needs to be eliminated. That's all I'm saying."

"Oh, that's all? And yet, by lying in wait to destroy another, you will merely ambush your own life."

As Solo listened to the pair, he fought another wave of fury. Apparently he could think about harming Vika, but if anyone else so much as suggested it, he had major problems—even with a tiny male no one else could see or hear.

X said, "Look deeper than the surface, Solo, the way you've always wanted people to do for you. Vika is not what she seems."

Dr. E wasn't one to be ignored. "Wait. You're trying to tell us that you don't think she's like every other female Solo has known? Please. They either bolt from him in fear, or throw him down and demand he unleash his big, bad beast. She bolted. Give her a few days, and she'll do the other."

Yes, she had bolted, but she had also approached him afterward and offered him a gift.

"Listen to her, whistling so loudly and off-key," Dr. E continued, his tone dripping with disgust. "It's obvious she enjoys her work."

"Perhaps she needs a distraction from so horrific a task," X replied.

"Yeah. Right."

Both possibilities had merit. Each time she had finished with an otherworlder, she had left a treat inside the cage. A pile of cookies for the Bree Lian, a rose for the Delensean, an extra blanket for the Morevv. A book for the Teran, and a tube of sunscreen for the Rakan. Kind gestures, sure. Something to assuage her guilt, maybe. Something to prevent the captives from rising up in revolt, definitely.

She finished with the Cortaz and locked up. Gaze downcast, she approached Solo's cage, stopped, raised her foot as if she meant to take another step, placed it back on the ground. A second later, she shook her head and closed the rest of the distance with strong, determined strides.

"Don't do it," he said.

Her arm trembled as she leapt up to press the button to sedate him.

He was bigger than the others and didn't expect to drop as quickly as they had—but he did. Between one heartbeat and the next, his arms and legs felt as heavy as boulders. His knees gave out, and his face hit the cage floor with a thud.

The high-pitched squeak of the cage door nearly sent Vika running. Somehow, she found the strength to climb inside the small enclosure. The newcomer's chest was rising and falling steadily with his breaths, but his limbs were utterly still.

Okay, then. She left him to gather her cleaning supplies, her attention snagged on the special sandalwood oil she'd brought. Always she carried it here, but never had she actually used it. Now . . . she thought it would blend nicely with the otherworlder's natural peat smoke scent, and she couldn't help herself. She added the liquid to the spray bottle and reentered the cage.

I can do this. Really.

She started at his feet, shocked by how adorable his toes were. Never before had she seen toenails that resembled the purest of diamonds, sparkling in the light—and if she didn't hide them, she would never again see them. Jecis would remove them.

Nibbling on her bottom lip, she left the cage only long enough to gather a handful of dirt and a little cup of water. She created a thick, dark paste and smeared it over each of his nails, hiding their beauty. When the mixture dried, she was happy to note it remained intact, none of it flaking away.

Back to work. She toiled her way to his knees, spraying the enzyme wash and wiping with the rag, spraying and wiping, shocked all over again by the lack of hair on his legs. That shouldn't have caused her heart to pick up speed, but it did. It was just . . . he was put together so well, all muscle and sinew.

She'd bathed other males, of course she had, but there was something spectacular about this one. Something spectacular even despite the multiple patches of soot, each one hiding a wound of some sort. Bruises and scabs she was very carful not to injure further. Poor thing. What had been done to him?

Her cheeks heated the moment she reached his thighs, and she decided *not* to clean under the loincloth. She was curious, she wouldn't lie about that, but even the thought of looking at that part of him, even to do her job, was wrong. So she moved her attention to his very muscular, utterly drool-worthy stomach, and sweet mercy, he had to be smuggling iron bars under his skin—iron bars that were twitching, she noticed with a frown, as though they were coming to life. She—

Watched as a bruise on his ribs faded, there one moment, gone the next, and the twitching mystery was momentarily set aside. How could an injury vanish that quickly? She traced the rag over the area, but the skin remained bronzed, healthy.

Amazing. Her gaze swept over him, and she realized

several other bruises had faded, too. He was healing right before her eyes. What a wonderful, miraculous gift—one she would have paid a fortune to have.

Vika cleaned his arms and hands and then his chest, and the twitching increased. An allergic reaction to the drugs, perhaps? Concerned, she flattened her hand over his heart. The beat was strong, if fast. No, no allergic reaction. Had to be a characteristic of his race, then.

As she leaned over him to scrub his neck, her chest brushed against his and she lost her breath.

She straightened with a jolt, thoughts tumbling through her mind.

You should have seen him before the circus got hold of him, her mother had once said about her father. *He used to take my breath away.*

The loss of breath was a sign of attraction. One Vika had never experienced before. Why here? Why now? Why this male . . . who was as soft as velvet yet as hard as rock, and as warm as a winter blanket.

Well, that answered that, she supposed.

Her attention slid to his face. His surprisingly lovely face. Long, thick lashes cast shadows over cheekbones sharp enough to cut glass. He had a proud nose she wanted to touch . . . shouldn't touch . . . couldn't help but touch. Her fingers tingled.

His lips were surely a work of art. They were lush and the same color as the roses her mother used to pick every morning and keep in their trailer. A tradition Vika had missed every day since her passing.

What would it be like to belong to a man like this

one? Did he protect the things he loved, or did he hurt them? What was he like in his other life, the one before enslavement?

Her fingers migrated to his lips. Lips as soft as they appeared. No, softer. Like little pillows.

For the first time in her life, she wondered what it would be like to kiss a man.

You can find out. . . .

The question sprang from a hidden place inside her, drifted through her mind, the most insidious of temptations. What would a single kiss hurt? He would never know, and she would never again have to wonder what it would be like.

A quick look around proved that all of the other-worlders were sleeping and none of the performers or workers were hanging around. There would never be a more perfect time.

Inch by inch, she leaned down. Finally, she was there, hovering just over his mouth.

You shouldn't do this.

A moment of reasoning, springing from a place she knew very well. Self-preservation.

One she ignored.

She pressed her lips against his.

He offered no reaction, yet still the sweetness of the act astonished her. An intoxicating blend of emotions racing through her, she lifted her head, looked around. They were still alone. His eyes were still closed, his breathing still even. Again she lowered her mouth. This time, she applied more pressure, and oh, she liked this feeling so much better. He was there, she could feel him, and could savor the intensified scent of him.

I wonder if he tastes as wonderful as he smells.

Another irresistible temptation. Her tongue swept out of its own accord and traced the center of his mouth. At the moment of contact, a moan escaped her. He tasted even better, and that should have been impossible, but here, now, *nothing* was impossible.

No wonder people enjoyed doing this. There was a communion of bodies, a complete loss of worry. The world and its troubles simply ceased to matter.

More, she thought, and her belly quivered.

Yes. More. She sucked his lower lip between her teeth, careful, so careful not to hurt him. Another moan slipped from her—just as his eyelids flipped open and his gaze locked on her.

Seven

Let his left hand be under my head,
and his right hand embrace me.
—SONG OF SOLOMON 2:6

WELL, HIS CURIOSITY WAS certainly assuaged, wasn't it? Solo thought.

She'd kissed him, confused him, overwhelmed him. Stunned him. Because she'd done it of her own free will. He hadn't asked for it, hadn't demanded it. She'd simply given. A gentle meeting of lips, followed by the sweetest little nibble.

His body had been immobile—was still immobile—but his mind had been working just fine both then and now. The entire time, in fact. He'd been highly attuned to her every action, her every breath. Her every caress.

He'd known the moment she spread mud over his toenails. It had taken him a few minutes to figure out what she was doing, and why, and when the answers had slid into place, he had reeled. She'd hoped to protect him.

Then she had begun cleaning him. While she'd been gentle but businesslike with the other males, she had been sweet and affectionate with Solo, lingering, doctoring—arousing. From the first, his blood had heated to a fever pitch.

His muscles had knotted as he'd tried everything within his power to move, to grab her—not to toss her away and escape, but to pull her closer. To strip her and take her, here and now.

And when she'd kissed him . . . a growl of need had razed the inside of his throat.

His desperation for her had finally given him the strength to open his eyes.

"I'm so sorry. I don't know what came over me," she mumbled, and scrambled from his cage. After shutting and locking the door, she ran from the area and never looked back.

Solo wanted to shout and demand she return, but he couldn't work his mouth. His absolute, utter helplessness enraged him.

He *needed* to hold Vika in his arms and return her kiss properly. It was the sweetest he'd ever had. And he had enjoyed it immensely. She had treated his mouth as if it were a treasure, and she an explorer. She had been gentle, and oh, so tender. She had lifted her head, then once again fit her lips over his, and the second time, she had tasted him. Had moaned, as though she'd adored everything she'd discovered.

"Solo," Dr. E said, drawing him from his thoughts. "We're basically alone. Shouldn't you be planning your escape and the murder of everyone here?"

Escape. Yes, that was all that mattered. No warrior worth the kind of paycheck Solo received would have gotten lost during a time like this. And over so innocent a kiss, of all things.

But . . .

Why had she done it?

"You will save Vika and take her with you," X announced.

"Wrong! You will kill Vika, as you threatened," Dr. E replied. "But feel free to bring her better parts with you."

A pulse of anger sprang from deep in his chest. He ran his tongue along his teeth. Good. Movement. "Both of you do me a solid and zip your lips." Words. His jaw now worked.

He tried to roll his neck from one side to the other—success. He rotated his shoulders. That took a bit more effort, but still he managed it. The drugs were wearing off, then.

A deep breath in . . . out . . . and he was able to force himself into a sitting position. He surveyed the cages. All of the captives were sleeping soundly.

Beyond them and the equipment he'd already noticed, he could see a big red tent with multiple smaller white tents lined up along the sides. There were no trees to use as cover on the off chance he was spotted and chased, which meant there would be no limbs to use as daggers on the off chance he failed to find a weapon before leaving this clearing. That wasn't a big deal. His hands were weapon enough.

His ears twitched, and he picked up a bickering conversation about . . . sixty yards away, was his guess.

"I'm telling you, he's big and red and as ugly as sin,"

a male voice he didn't recognize said. "He's got to be the devil himself."

"And I'm telling you, we work for the devil himself."

The two cackled with humor.

"You gotta get a peek at him."

"Vika's probably there."

"So?"

"So, she'll make us fetch and carry sooner rather than later, and we won't be able to say no to Jecis's precious daughter," was the sneered reply, "or we'll end up disappearing in Matas's magic act."

Relief cascaded through Solo, a warm waterfall he didn't understand but wasn't going to question. Vika was Jecis's daughter, not his lover.

"If you can stare into the creature's eyes, you can withstand Matas."

A pause. The sound of spitting. "Fine. But only 'cause I don't believe anything can be as ugly as you described."

Two sets of pounding footsteps.

Solo knew the men were coming to check him out. Annnd . . . sure enough. About thirty seconds later, two stocky men with rotund bellies and swarthy skin stormed into the circle of cages and spun to search for the new guy. The one on the left spotted Solo, and his eyes grew wide. He stumbled backward, only to catch himself and shake his head.

"I'll be. You was right, Leonard."

"Yeah, but you gotta get a closer look to really appreciate the ugly."

The pair stalked to just in front of him, allowing

Solo to study the fourth and fifth people who would fall under his coming attack. Both had yellow teeth, and the man on the right was even missing a few. Tobacco filled their mouths.

"It's hideous, ain't it?" one said, and Solo realized his skin had once again taken on a crimson cast.

At any other time, in any other situation, he would have erupted. Here, right now, he had to control his temper.

The other spit a stream of black. "We should take pictures, you know. Prove we tangoed with a beast. Women'll be so excited by our bravery, they'll drop their panties and beg us to show *our* beasts."

"You ain't never gonna tango with a creature like that."

"Oh, yeah? Watch me." The speaker grabbed a few of the rocks that had been tossed at Vika and launched them at Solo.

Some slapped against his chest, some against his legs, but each one provided a slight sting, reminding him of all the times he'd walked outside for recess, the humiliation, the anger. Humiliation and anger even now rising to the surface. And if *he* experienced all of this, what had the much smaller Vika experienced?

His narrowed gaze strayed to the sleeping Mec and Cortaz. They had hurt her. They would pay.

"I think you're ticking it off," the other said with a laugh.

The word *it* echoed in Solo's mind, and his nails elongated into sharp-tipped claws.

"Calm down," X commanded.

"Get madder," Dr. E retorted.

The two men clomped off, murmuring about finding a camera. Every word was quieter than the last, until Solo could no longer discern their voices. He wanted to shake the cage until the bars popped loose. He wanted to try *something*, anything, but he still wasn't at full strength, and until he was, he was too vulnerable and couldn't afford to put his plan on the fast track.

Shouldn't have to wait too much longer, though. He would be stronger and ready to go by sunset, at the very least, but he would wait until everyone else was in bed. Then . . .

Yeah. Then.

A few hours later, the captives awoke. Most sat up with a jolt. Some eased up and stretched. All muttered and complained about Vika.

As though summoned by the complaints, she reappeared, wearing a new T-shirt and jeans. The top was pink, lacy, and the pants sparkly. She looked as though she'd just come from a nightclub after dancing for hours with the man of her dreams.

Solo's hands fisted, a hot surge of irritation blasting through him.

She'd touched him, kissed him. He didn't want her dancing with another man.

Stupid of him, yes. Did he care? No.

The tobacco-spitting men—who had never returned with a camera—trailed behind her, both carrying buckets and leering at her. When she stopped and faced them, their expressions cleared. She pointed to the ground, a queen with her subjects, expecting absolute and immediate obedience.

She got it. They placed the new buckets where she wanted and picked up the old ones. She busied herself with what was inside, but the pair remained where they were for several long moments, watching her, leering all over again now that her back was to them, elbowing each other with masculine intent.

"I think I'll sneak into her trailer tonight and have me some fun with her."

"You do, and you won't have to worry about Matas's magic act. He'll straight-up murder you."

A shrug. "Might be worth it."

"'Course, he'll only murder you if Jecis don't get to you first."

"I could take 'em both at the same time," the guy grumbled under his breath.

"Fine. Go ahead, and do it. Shank the meanest thugs ever to walk the face of the earth, and I'll sneak into her trailer while all three of you are too dead to stop me."

They snickered.

Matas had been mentioned on several occasions. Who was he? And why was Vika showing no reaction to the conversation? A conversation about her possible rape? Instead, she concentrated on her task, lifting bowls from one bucket and filling them with bread and grain from the other. Only when one of the men did what Solo had wanted to do the first time he'd seen her and reached out to pinch a lock of her hair did she give a reaction. Her spine went rigid as she whipped around to face the culprit.

Solo gripped the cage bars.

"Touch me again," she said, "and I'll be wearing your body parts as jewelry within the hour. Got it?"

One man's lip curled in fear. He nodded and strode away as fast as his feet would carry him. The other, the bigger one, kept his attention on her for longer than was decent, his gaze roving over her, lingering where it shouldn't.

"You really think you're strong enough to take me, Miz Vika?" he asked silkily.

She grinned with relish. "Let's ask Jecis what he thinks about that, shall we?"

Before the man could respond, Solo jerked at the bars, the entire enclosure shaking and rattling, creating a ruckus. The man yanked his attention Solo's way, and their gazes locked. His was brown. Solo's was bloodred—and growing brighter by the second.

Paling, the man at last backed away. He crashed into one of the cages, turned, and darted from the clearing.

Vika's shoulders sagged with relief.

Without the guards to dissuade them, the Mec and the Cortaz erupted into cruel taunts. Although Vika's motions were stiff, she gave no other indication that she noticed as she leapt back into work.

Solo had never encountered anyone capable of tuning out the rest of the world with such success.

He watched as she slid a bowl of food into each of

the cages, never getting close enough for anyone to grab, instead balancing the bowls on the end of a shovel and forcing the captives to accept from a distance.

"I want to talk to you," he said when she reached him.

She ignored him, even refused to look up.

Most of the otherworlders thanked her, but the Mec threw his bowl at her, the grain flying free and slapping at her. Solo expected her to shout, to threaten, but she simply bent down, picked everything up, and gave the whole thing back to him with a muttered, "I'll pretend that was an accident. *This* time."

That . . . made no sense.

Why so generous? Why so kind? Why not let the offender starve? That's what a cold, calculating witch lurking underneath an angel's skin would have done. That's what *Solo* would have done.

"I know what you're thinking, and the answer is simple," X said. "She sympathizes with those under her care."

"Wrong! No one's that good. She's just plain pathetic," Dr. E said, "hoping the creatures will behave if she's nice."

Solo didn't know what to believe anymore.

"Stupid little cow," the Cortaz shouted. "I want you dead!"

The otherworlder threw a handful of her own grain at Vika and several pieces stuck in her hair. Every muscle in Solo's body tensed. Vika faced the culprit, and the Cortaz threw another handful, the grains slapping at her face this time.

Dr. E laughed. "I love watching people get what they deserve."

X moaned, as though in pain.

Solo held his silence, though his jaw was clenched so painfully he could hardly stand it. He wasn't sure Vika actually deserved what was happening, but he wasn't going to get involved. He wasn't going to be her protector or her defender; it wasn't like she needed one, anyway. She was a freewoman. He wasn't going to care what happened to her.

Yes, she had been gentle with the captives. But she'd still done her father's bidding. She could have freed everyone and run away, but she hadn't.

"Fine," Vika said with a twinge of sadness. "Your loss. You'll starve, and make it easier for Jecis to over-power you."

They were basically the same words she'd given him over the chocolate. For some reason, that caused an ache in his chest. But judging from the Cortaz's dark expression, starving was exactly what she wanted. Huh. She must have lied about the brothers. A woman with hope wouldn't act that way.

Although Solo could understand wanting to die rather than remaining a slave.

"Help her," X said.

Which "her"? "No," he whispered, because the answer was the same either way. The Cortaz had hurt Vika, and even though Solo had decided not to protect or defend the girl, he wasn't going to aid those who harmed her. Just the thought of doing so caused his anger to return.

Maybe . . . maybe he wouldn't kill Vika when he escaped. He would burn the entire circus to the ground, spring Kitten, lock up Vika at his farm, and go to Michael. Together, they would gather an army, come back here and make Dr. E laugh.

What he would do with Vika after that, Solo wasn't sure.

Eight

Wisdom will save you from the ways of wicked men.
—PROVERBS 2:12

THE MORNING SUN CRESTED in the sky, flames of gold, orange, pink, and purple streaking in every direction. Fluffy white clouds dotted the never-ending expanse, and a single black bird flew past them while crying a song of loneliness and despair.

Solo understood.

He was still trapped inside his cage.

He, an expert lock picker, a man stronger than ten extraordinary humans combined, who had once sprung John No Name from a prison in Shanghai with only a toothpick and a stick of chewing gum, and, okay, Blue at his side, had failed to free himself from an old rusty pen for animals.

He . . . had no words.

Actually, he did have words, he realized a second later; they were as black as night and full of barbs. He wanted to unleash them, but he also wanted a target and the otherworlders were sleeping, Jecis nowhere to be seen. How was this situation possible? *It should not have been possible.* He should be long gone. The circus should be nothing more than a memory. He should be free!

Why wasn't he free?

After trying to disable the lock and failing . . . after trying to cut through the bars with his claws and failing . . . after trying to punch his way through the floorboards, then the roof, and failing, he had allowed his temper to get the better of him. He had shaken the entire cage—but he hadn't even managed to turn the thing on its side.

He'd been too weak. And the madder he'd gotten, the weaker he'd become. Dr. E had snickered the entire time, only to vanish a few hours ago. X had stayed with him far longer than he'd liked, sighing every so often, radiating only sadness, before finally vanishing as well.

I'm actually stuck here.

No. No way. He would not accept that.

"Kitten," he said, using her name when she had not offered it, trying to reveal the fact that he knew she was an AIR agent with skills. She had experience with the circus; she might not have had the strength to free herself, but she would have observed the comings and goings and would know what to do. And two were always better than one—or so X had already tried to tell him.

She stretched awake, sitting up a few minutes later, her long hair knotted at the base of her neck. "Do yourself a favor, big guy, and preserve your energy."

"I know your coworkers," he said.

"Wait. What?" Eyes wide, she wrapped her fingers

around the bars of her cage. "Who are you? Who do you know?"

Good. He had her attention. "We're going to have a conversation, you and I, about what I wish to discuss, until I'm satisfied with your answers. All right?"

An eager nod.

"Vow it," he said.

Kitten gave another nod and said, "I do. I vow it. Now tell me what I want to know!"

He watched her, waiting, and knew the exact moment the vow took root and grew branches through her spirit, soul, and body—branches that would force her to do what she'd promised, or suffer terribly. Her eyes widened and a gasp parted her lips. Her hand fluttered over her heart, baby-bird delicate.

"What just . . . how did . . . you did something to me! I know you did something. I felt a jolt of electricity go all the way through me."

For Solo, vows were binding whether he spoke them or received them. They attached themselves inside him and the other person, a compulsion that refused to be ignored. Did he try, he hurt. Did the other person try, they hurt.

The ability, he'd learned, could be a blessing or a curse, depending on how it was used. He'd noticed it as a child, had experimented with it, tested it, and it had only grown stronger over the years. In the end, he'd learned he was either saved or snared by the things he promised—and others were saved or snared, too.

"I know your coworkers," he repeated.

She snapped her teeth in frustration. "You said that before and I'm ready for something new. This conversation is . . . is . . ." Deep grooves formed at the corners of her mouth, her frown intense. "This conversation is . . ." Her eyes closed, and a groan of pain left her. "Why can't I say the words I want to say?"

Because the words would have broken her vow, leaving him unsatisfied. Even the thought of such a thing pained her spirit, the source of her life, which in turn pained her soul, or her mind, will and emotions, and lastly her body.

She cast him an accusing glare as she gritted out, "Fine. You think you know my coworkers. I think you're wrong."

"I'm right. These people, they miss sitting around the fire with you and can't wait to have you back."

It took her a moment, but she finally caught his meaning. AIR agents carried pyre-guns, weapons capable of shooting streams of fire. Her coworkers missed her. They were on the case.

She pressed her forehead against the bar, beside her hands, trying to get closer to him. "Really?"

"Yes."

"Tell them I said hello."

Translation: Was he in contact? "I would, but they stopped taking my calls."

Her upper lip lifted, baring her teeth, and she gritted out, "That's probably for the best. As much as I travel, they're pretty much dead to me."

He knew what she meant. The circus moved around so much, AIR would never be able to track them fast enough. And she was right. AIR wouldn't. But John and Blue? Yeah. They could do anything—if they had survived the bomb.

Don't think that way. They survived.

"Tell me about your abduction," he said. "Every detail."

"No way. That's private." She turned away from him, trying to end the conversation. A moment later, she groaned and swung back to face him. Scowling, she said, "I will never vow to do anything for you ever again—so I was at home, relaxing." The words rushed from her. "Someone must have snuck in and drugged the beers in my fridge, because I had one, only one, and passed out. That had never happened before, not even when I was fourteen and had my—argh! So then, when I woke up, I was . . . I was . . ." She drew her arms around her middle. "I was soon sold to Jecis."

There was a lot she wasn't telling him.

"What happened between waking up and being sold? I need to know."

Red suffused her cheeks, and her gaze darted to the other captives to see if they had awakened. They had, and they were listening unabashedly. "Why? It's not like you can help me," she said through clenched teeth.

"Were you beaten? Raped?" Solo asked softly. They'd needed code to discuss a potential rescue, not to discuss events that had happened in the past. Events that could help Solo profile Star, figure out his motives, his means, and his agenda.

"No, but I was . . ." Again she stumbled over her

words. "It doesn't matter." A groan. She closed her eyes. "Please. It *doesn't* matter."

"All right," he said, taking pity on her. Immediately she relaxed, unaware that the conversation would resume when everyone fell asleep tonight. "Do you know a man by the name of Gregory Star?" He described the looks of the human he'd seen in the photo. "Do any of you?"

All but the Targon jolted into action, pretending to be too engrossed in counting specks of dirt to listen. The Targon blew him a kiss.

Kitten's brow furrowed as she ran the image through her mind. "No. I don't, and no one else has ever mentioned him. Why? Was he the one that . . . that arranged for me to be taken?"

"Yes."

"You're sure?"

He nodded. To the Targon, he said, "What's your name?"

"Kaamil-Alize. Why?"

"I was tired of referring to you as the Targon, but I think I'll stick with that."

"Aw, how cute. You have a crush on me and can't get me out of your mind. I'd love to say I'm surprised, but I'll just say I'm not interested and leave it at that, 'k?"

Solo rolled his eyes. Were all Targons as irreverent as this one? "How were you captured?"

Amber eyes lit with amusement. "As if anyone could capture me. I handed myself over."

Hardly. "Why?"

"I thought it'd be fun. Turns out, I was right." But a

hard gleam had entered his eyes, draining the amusement.

No, he hadn't thought it would be fun. That gleam said he was here for a reason. But what? "I don't believe you."

"He's telling the truth," Kitten said. "I was here when he arrived. Most of the others Jecis brought in himself after someone else brought them in and sold them. From what I've been able to gather, that someone has been different each time."

He wasn't sure what to make of that.

"So why would this Star person abduct *me*?" she demanded. A moment later, she added, "Unless . . ."

Solo pounced, insisting, "Unless?"

"I woke up and . . . someone was in my house. Someone I'd hurt a long time ago. After she . . . finished with me, I was drugged and later woke up while some strange guy negotiated my sell to Jecis."

Details, and he hadn't had to wait. Details that actually helped him. Michael had mentioned the symbol of revenge, but had assumed it was a means to throw them off. What if Michael had been wrong? What if people . . . what? Took their revenge, then hired Star to do clean up? Or maybe Star actually arranged everything. "Thank you."

Again, shame colored her cheeks but she nodded. "Which of my coworkers do you know?"

"Dallas." During their meeting, Michael had only mentioned one name in association with this girl's unit, and that was it. He only hoped the two knew each other.

She grinned with relish, saying, "Dallas. Things are gonna get ugly. Now, if you'll excuse me, I'm going to close my eyes and dream of all the pain he'll cause."

As she lay down, he picked up a few of the rocks on his cage floor and tossed them in the air and caught them, tossed and caught. Time to think. To plan.

"Be careful with those." As beautiful as a spring morning, the Cortaz leaned against the side of her cage. "You might need them later."

Or not.

"To hurt Vika?" he found himself snipping.

She flinched at the harshness of his tone. Afraid of him?

She should be.

Steady. Calm. He still blamed her for her too-harsh treatment of Vika, yes, but he also needed her on his side. In a situation like this, allies were important.

"Well, why not?" she said, lifting her chin. "That girl deserves it. And are you really so stupid that you don't realize we've tried every trick possible to bust free of this hellhole? Yet here we stay, and here you'll stay, too."

"You're wrong," he said. He just needed more time. Soon he would be completely healed from the explosion. Nothing would stop him, then.

"I've been here two months. I promise you, I'm not wrong." She moved her arm through the bars and twisted her hand in the light. "It's the cuffs. Whatever drugs they're pumping through our bodies keep us weak, and our superhuman abilities useless."

He studied the metal circling his own wrists—metal he'd forgotten about in his quest for freedom. He could still feel the thin rods embedded in his bones, screwing with his range of motion, *annnd* yes, he could feel a slight warmth drip, drip, dripping into his system.

The otherworlders weren't just drugged for their baths, he realized. They were drugged every minute of every day.

Anger returned, a hot fire in his chest.

Doesn't matter. You'll overcome. You always overcome.

A sad, *you'll see* smile curved the corners of her lips. "I'm Crissabelle, by the way, but you can call me Criss. Call me Crissy or Belle, and I'll cut out your tongue."

He didn't offer his own name. He wouldn't. The less these people knew about him, the better. Besides, he'd been named after one of the wisest males ever to live, and yet he'd often acted like the dumbest. Well, not here. Not now. Not anymore.

"Who has the key to the cuffs?" he asked.

"I don't know," she replied with an easy shrug. "I've never seen it. You'd think Jecis or his spawn would taunt us with it, but no. They never have, and I'm not sure whether that's been a mercy or a cruelty."

He dropped the rocks rattling in his palm. *Thump, thump, thump.* "How were you brought in?"

Fury mixed with regret, flaring in her eyes. "I was out late at night, partying with my friends, and had a little too much to drink. Matas showed up, and somehow talked me into going home with him. I say somehow, because he's sick and disgusting and I'm not into sick and disgusting. Only, he didn't take me home. He brought me here."

Matas again. The name was beginning to bug him.

"So . . . what should I call you?" she asked.

"Bob."

A slow smile bloomed. "No way you're a Bob."

"Fred, then."

The smile grew. "That's even worse. But go ahead. Keep lying to me, and I'll start calling you Jolly Red Giant."

He wouldn't give her a reaction, he told himself. He wouldn't rip her head from her body when he escaped, either.

"Has anyone successfully removed their cuffs?" He tucked the fingers of his left hand into the right, and the fingers of his right hand into the left—

"I wouldn't do that," Criss rushed out.

—and jerked. Immediately pain exploded through him, sharp, cutting from the top of his head to the soles of his feet. He fell to his side, spiderwebs of black weaving through his vision, colliding with pinpricks of white and forming a dizzying kaleidoscope.

"Told you," he heard Criss sing. "When you pull on the metal, a different type of chemical is shot through your body. One that causes pain rather than lethargy. And don't think you can leave and remove the things with bolt cutters or something. I was here when a guy got hold of a pair, and when he snipped, the needles in the cuffs motorized, chopping off his hands."

Eventually the black and white faded and Solo could see clearly again. He slowly eased to a sitting position. He looked at his wrists and discovered he'd done more harm to himself. The cuffs were still there, still firmly in place, but blood now trickled from underneath the metal.

"Next time, listen to Auntie Criss. She's very smart. And beautiful. And talented."

And modest.

"There are tubes running through the metal," she said, "and if you look closely, you'll find a little hole in each cuff. That's where the drugs are administered. We're put to sleep every few days so that the tubes can be refilled."

His frustration and anger intensified, bubbling up, another white-hot fire wanting to spill from him; somehow he managed to hold himself in check. Now wasn't the time for another temper tantrum. Especially when that temper tantrum would do no good.

In the distance, he could hear clomping feet, chattering voices, and the roar of car engines.

"And so it begins," Criss said with a sigh.

A deep breath in, and he caught the scent of coffee in the air.

He found coffee too bitter to enjoy, yet still his mouth watered for a taste of it, and still his stomach twisted hungrily. Yesterday evening's grain had tasted like dirt, and yet, if he were given another bowl of the stuff—or another piece of chocolate—he would have eaten every morsel. He had to keep his strength up. Obviously.

"How does this work?" he found himself growling.

Criss slid into a pool of light and stretched out her legs. Green eyes glittered with resolve, pearlescent skin shone, and finger-combed black hair tumbled over both of her shoulders, shielding what lurked beneath that transparent fabric. "In a few hours, the circus will open and there will be a steady stream of people walking through this area for the rest of the day. Some will simply look at you." Her voice hardened as she added, "Some will command you to lift your clothing or to turn around and bend over. Jecis will station two armed guards here, and no one will be allowed to touch you, but if you fail to do as you're told . . ."

Yeah, he remembered: a bullet to the brain. His skin darkened, and his teeth and claws elongated. The fire burned ever hotter, singeing everything in its path.

"Don't give him pointers," the Bree Lian called. "Let him learn firsthand like the rest of us."

Solo already had a beef with him. That just sealed the deal.

"Let him take the burden for a while," the Mec added.

Yeah, Solo had a beef with him, too.

Several others murmured their agreement. Meaning, they all wanted Solo to occupy Jecis's mind, so that they could act out without fear. *Nice.* But fine, whatever. He understood survival.

He also never forgot a slight.

Criss waved away their commands, saying, "Little Miss Mouse won't feed us until after the circus, and then only if we've behaved." She air-quoted the last word, the motion stiff with barely leashed rage.

That rage would soon tear free, he was sure, and it would make her reckless, willing to do anything to die. Not just throw rocks, but more. A whole lot more. And

Little Miss Mouse—Vika, beautiful Vika, with the wounded eyes and the bruised face and the siren's body and the angel's kiss—would bear the brunt of it.

He'd been so careful not to think about her last night. Now . . . there was no stopping the mental tug-of-war that followed.

She's mine. I want her.

Are you stupid? She's not yours. She belongs to Jecis—you don't want her.

I deserve her. After everything I've suffered here, she will be my reward.

She's not a prize.

He was as bad as X and Dr. E.

"Uh-oh. I recognize that look," Criss said with a moan.

He forced the muscles in his face to relax, revealing nothing more. "What look?"

A derisive snort. "Please. Vika's the big guy's daughter, you know, and nothing but trouble."

See? Vika is a bad apple from a poisoned tree.

"Besides, I thought you were interested in our sweet little Pussycat," Criss said with a tilt of her chin.

His gaze darted to Kitten, who still sprawled on the floor of her cage.

"Vika does what Daddy says, when he says, and even if you were handsome . . . uh . . . well, anyway, she wouldn't help you," Criss said. "I don't mean to be cruel, just honest."

"Enough with the honesty," the Targon called. "Let's go for amusement! I'd love to see you try to charm our little Vika, Mr. Fugly."

All but Kitten and Criss snickered.

As if on cue, Dr. E arrived on the scene, settling atop Solo's shoulder like a bird on a perch. He was paler than usual, a little wobbly on his feet. Why? "They dare tease you? Well, it's time to teach them better, don't you think? If you tell Jecis you're willing to do a little cage fighting free of charge, you can rip these creatures into a thousand pieces without earning a punishment. It's win/win."

"They are as frustrated and angry as he is," X said, appearing on his right shoulder. He was tanner than usual, for once steady on his feet. "They are lashing out at their circumstances, not Solo."

"Enough!" he growled, suddenly sick of the captives, of X, of Dr. E, and all of his many recent failures. He wanted out. He *needed* out. Drugged or not, there had to be a way.

Each of the otherworlders peered over at him with differing shades of emotion. Some with terror, some with glee. But no one castigated him, and Dr. E— laughing and suddenly alive with color—and X— sighing with regret and suddenly pallid—once again vanished.

Solo wrapped his fingers around the bars and shook, shook, *shook*. Of course, they held steady, causing frustration to rise and eat at what little remained of his control.

"Uh, I wouldn't do that, either," Criss said. "You'll regret it."

He didn't stop. Couldn't. *I'm strong enough for anything, even this.* Another shake. But again, the bars held steady. Anger blazed into rage, and the frustration formed jagged edges that sliced through him, making him bleed.

Now, now, now. Another shake, a harder shake. Shake, shake, shake.

Rage . . . melding with a sudden burst of weakness . . .

Frustration . . . blending with a sudden spring of icy water . . .

The drugs, he realized as his mind hazed. The drugs must activate with stronger emotions, because with every moment that passed, the weakness grew and the icy water flooded another part of him, until he no longer had the strength to grip the bars.

His arms fell heavily to his sides, and his head lolled forward, his chin hitting his sternum. He lost track of his surroundings and just sort of tipped over. Right before landing, he thought he heard Criss say, "I told you so."

Nine

∾

Break up your fallow ground, and do not sow among thorns.
—JEREMIAH 4:3

VIKA PACED INSIDE HER trailer, the second biggest vehicle in the lot. (Her father's was number one, of course.) The walls were covered with pink lace and draped with several jewel-toned tapestries. Every piece of furniture was plush, white, and expensive. The coffee table was Victorian and the legs carved to resemble dragons. The side tables were topped with crystal vases and ornate bowls.

A fairy-tale home fit for a fairy-tale princess, her father often said.

Fine fabrics were strewn about. Velvets, satins, silks, and even the highly expensive cotton. She knew how to sew, and was supposed to design herself "a wardrobe fit for the daughter of a king." She hadn't. And she wouldn't.

To go along with her clothing, she had jade necklaces, ruby bracelets, and sapphire pendants, plus a set of diamond fingernails with rings of gold that wound all the way to her knuckles, and a brooch in the shape of a lion head, its fur made of amber, its eyes of ebony.

Each piece sparkled as the overhead light cast out soft, golden rays. So pretty. So useless. They were items she was currently unable to sell, because her father would miss them.

"Why don't you wear the things I give you?" Jecis demanded at least once a week.

"They're not my style," she would say. And so he would try again, giving her something else, something bigger, not understanding she had no desire to wear his guilt offerings—which was exactly what they were.

But last night at dinner, all that had changed. She had worn one of the necklaces, as planned, and he'd ruffled her hair, quite pleased with her, never noticing the slight bulge of the bandage under her shirt.

Oh, what a life I lead.

Her mother would have loved the trailer and the clothes and the jewels. She would have sewn as many gowns as possible, and danced across the entire home, laughing and twirling, and making Vika giggle.

A sudden lance of sadness pierced her. Her beautiful mother, who had claimed to love her more than anything, but had left her only child to run away with her lover.

Within a few days, Jecis had found her and dragged her back. Then, the next morning, he had summoned all the performers in one place and announced that his wife had died of a black, rotting heart. And that was true. Jecis had a black, rotting heart, and he'd killed her.

Vika had no idea what had happened to the lover.

Anyway, she wasn't going to ponder the past, she

reminded herself. She would think about today: opening day for the circus in New Atlanta.

She was to stay inside her trailer until her father finished with all of his duties and performances. She was to relax, eat her many chocolates, and enjoy herself, as if hours and hours with nothing to do but count her savings (for the three thousandth time) was fun, while everyone else within their circus "family" worked for their food and lodging, not just by helping with clothing, tents, games and vehicles, but through performing.

Vika was only to care for the otherworlders after the patrons left. That way, the townies never saw her, never tried to harm her, and heads never had to roll. More importantly, the circus never had to move to a new location sooner than planned, simply to avoid the law.

Jecis wanted Vika safe—from everyone but him.

When will you learn, Vika? There cannot be two masters in one house. You do what I say, when I say, or you suffer. I love you, but I cannot make allowances for you, just because you're my only child.

A father who loved his daughter would not beat her. A father who loved his daughter would not maim and exile one of her only two friends, forcing her to give up the other for fear of watching the girl receive the same treatment. A father who loved his daughter would not murder her precious pets.

I just want to live in peace.

And yet, still she hadn't stayed inside today. She had spent five minutes out in the open, running through the zoo to check on the newcomer. Five minutes, that was all, but in her father's opinion that was five minutes too long.

A shudder nearly rocked her off her feet, and she tumbled onto the couch. How she wished Jecis was the man he used to be, the man who had listened to her stories about butterflies and tucked her in at night, but everything had changed when her grandfather died and he took over the circus.

The place had been in horrible shape, facing financial ruin. Money had quickly become Jecis's only concern and he'd begun selling drugs and women in between acts. He'd had to do terrible things to keep his employees in line and his secrets in the dark, and those things had destroyed the man she'd known. But his pockets had filled, and that had been all that mattered to him. Within a year, he'd turned the place around—and his own terrible transformation had been complete.

If he found out what she'd done today, he would punish her for placing herself in danger.

If. Ha. He would. Too many people had seen her, just like she'd known they would.

Why had she done it, then?

There was no need to ponder; she already knew the answer. She'd done it because she couldn't get the prisoner out of her mind. A thousand times she had remembered how she'd had her hands on him. Her bare hands. Male to female, heat to heat. A thousand more, she had remembered how she'd had her mouth on him—and just how much she'd liked it.

Suddenly she felt the vibration of someone's . . .

scream against her skin? Oh, yes. A scream. The fine hairs on the back of her neck stood on end. She nearly threw open her door to peek outside.

The newest addition to the zoo had finally reached the end of his tolerance.

Sympathy welled inside her. All night he'd desperately fought to free himself, yet he'd made no progress. Fearing her father would hear his curses and decide to act, she had waited nearby, ready to doctor his injuries. But Jecis had never appeared, and the newcomer had continued to struggle, until the realization that he was stuck in the cage had at last settled in. Anger had contorted his features and his skin had taken on that crimson cast. His teeth and claws had grown, and though she should have run away in fear, the alteration had fascinated Vika.

Because . . . no matter how much his body had changed, his eyes had remained the same: big and blue, with those long dark lashes better suited to a woman. Innocent eyes. Haunting eyes.

Otherworldly eyes.

Like everyone else, Vika knew about the inhabited planets out there. But unlike everyone else, she also knew there was an unseen world operating here, on earth, all around them. And it amazed her how close the two worlds actually were. As many times as she had fought death, she had caught glimpses of that world and knew that there was absolute good and absolute evil—and both were as real as she was.

One step, that was all it took, and the spirit could leave the body and enter that other realm.

The newest prisoner should have reminded her of the evil side, but he hadn't. Quite the opposite, in fact.

She'd returned to her trailer, and waited for someone to deliver her breakfast. A few minutes after that, she'd snuck out and returned to the zoo, where she'd thrown the food in his cage. Had he sampled the syn-bacon, biscuits, or cubes of honey? He'd been awake. He'd seen her, but he hadn't tried to catch the bur-lap sack, and if he'd said anything, she wasn't aware of it. She'd kept her attention away from him. Had they locked gazes, he might have tried to speak to her and she would have been tempted to stay.

She owed him another apology, after all. He'd been at his weakest, and she'd taken terrible advantage of him. It was just . . . wait. Was she going to do this? Was she going to think about the kiss now? When she'd avoided the topic all night?

Yes. She was.

Why had she pressed her lips against his? *Why?* That wasn't like her. Desire wasn't something she experi-enced, and yet she had been drawn to him on a primi-tive level. An undeniable level. Now, a part of her she'd thought destroyed long ago, a needy little girl who'd dreamed of a handsome Prince Charming coming to rescue her, kept stretching . . . stretching . . . finally awakening completely. Only, this prince was alone, just like her. He needed a friend, just like her.

Dangerous thoughts. Thoughts that had once got-ten her in trouble. First, she could only count on her-self, and she knew it. Second, she had befriended one of the first otherworlders to be captured, had actually grown to love and adore the girl. Had snuck out every night to spend with her, with her sweet Mara, and they had talked, shared stories about their lives.

Eventually, Vika had freed Mara and all the others.

And she had suffered terribly for her actions.

She knew better than to travel down that road again. And yet, all she'd seemed to care about was that the newcomer wasn't used to hunger, and more than that, he was in for a horrible surprise when the circus opened in a few hours. She'd wanted him to experience *something* nice today.

If he tossed away the food, fine. His loss. She would have done a good deed, and she could—

The overhead lights flickered, and she groaned. She didn't have a bell; instead, the lighting system was rigged to alert her to a waiting guest.

Her stomach cramped as she stood and shakily turned the knob. Thankfully, it wasn't her father come to chastise her for her disobedience. Unfortunately, it was Matas, her "bodyguard," and he radiated menace.

Meeting his gaze, she snapped, "What do you want?"

"Let me in," he demanded with his patented scowl. He had tousled dark hair and eyes the color of black ice. He possessed a dusty complexion, and he was big of chest and arm—and pride and ferocity.

Today he'd opted to wear pants but no shirt, revealing the thick silver barbell hanging from his left nipple. He was certain it made him look chilled. Was that the right word? Cold? Cool? To Vika, it made him look like a hammer. Wrench? Whatever! He looked like some kind of tool.

"Move aside, Vika."

Act casual. "No. This is my home. You aren't welcome." *Act brave.* "So go on. Leave."

"I will . . . after I've had my say." He shoved past her, and at the moment of contact, bugs seemed to jump from him and onto her, burrowing past her skin and into her veins.

A far different sensation from her contact with the otherworlder.

She tried not to cringe as she turned and faced him. "Make it fast."

"Why? Do you have somewhere to be?" he asked just to be cruel.

She wasn't surprised; he was a cruel man. Oh, he would never hurt her physically or anything like that. He was too afraid of her father. But he liked to poke at her in other ways.

He plopped onto her couch and fingered one of the necklaces hanging from a bowl on the side table. "We're going to talk. Understand?"

"I do." And she could just imagine how the conversation would go.

When are you going to stop being so stubborn and marry me? he would ask.

Never, she would reply.

Don't be ridiculous. When? I'm the best thing that could ever happen to a girl like you.

A girl like her. Deaf. Defective. *After I'm dead, I'll consider it. Maybe.*

He would curse. She would tremble.

So, yes, she *was* scared of more than just Jecis.

"I'll kick things off," she said, refusing to back down. "Have you forgotten rule number one?"

A muscle ticked below his eye, a clear indication of his growing anger. "No."

"And it is?"

"No touching precious Vika. Ever."

"And do you recall touching me on your way in?"

"Yes," he gritted.

"Here's another question. Do you recall rule number two?"

His fingers curled around the diamonds, and she was surprised the stones weren't ground into a fine powder. "If I break rule number one, I have to punch myself in the face or you'll tattle to your father."

She waited, blinking innocently. Jecis was the only power she held over this man or any other, and she wielded it often and severely.

Matas gave his jaw a pop.

"Well?"

Scowling, he slapped himself.

"Good boy," she said with all the sugar sweetness she could muster. She had seen him with other women, and knew he had attended the Jecis Lukas school of discipline. He wasn't afraid to punch to assert authority and prove a (stupid) point when angry . . . or even mildly disturbed.

"Now it's my turn," he said. "When are you going to marry me?"

See? "I'm thinking . . . never. Is that good for you?"

A flash of annoyance. "I'm the reason your father's people hate you, the reason even the otherworlders are turning against you. A word here, a word there, and the poison spreads. Marry me, and I'll make them love you."

How dare he! "What have you said?" she demanded.

He waved the question away. "I want you, Vika, and I will have you."

Actually, he was second-in-command of the circus and he wanted to be first. He didn't yet understand that would never happen. Jecis would never abdicate power, and Matas would never be strong enough to take it from him.

Before becoming ringmaster, Jecis had performed the magic act. After becoming ringmaster, he taught Matas the secrets of the dark arts, the two spending countless hours poring through books, practicing what they read, and even testing their powers on some of the patrons of the circus.

In comparison, the two men weren't even in the same league.

"You'll never have me," she said with a shake of her head. "You repulse me."

"Is that so?" Suddenly his shadow moved—while his body remained still—expanding over his shoulders . . . splitting apart, slithering in different directions, each gloomy limb inching closer to her.

Heart pounding, Vika squared her shoulders. She knew what those shadows were, recognized them from that other realm. They were evil. Evil so real, so vile it had taken some kind of living form.

Her father carried the same essence. In fact, that was where Matas had picked it up. She'd noticed it a few days after they had begun training together.

"That's so. Now leave," she snapped.

He grinned, all pearly whites and menace. "Make me."

The cramping started up again. "You didn't used to be this way, you know." Like her father, he had changed over the years—from a somewhat affable young man who enjoyed sharing cotton candy with her after every show to *this*, demanding and depraved, capable of any despicable deed.

"I know," he said, and he didn't sound as if he cared. "Now I'm better."

"Not to me."

"That's because you haven't yet evolved. But I could make you powerful, Vika. Think of it. I could make you powerful enough to kill your father and rule this circus by my side. I—"

"Turned Rasa into a freak." He'd used his magic to transform her beard hair into hundreds of little snakes.

He shrugged, unconcerned. "She was heard laughing about my act, and needed to be taught a lesson."

"And Audra?" He'd shared his "power" with her, too.

"I never cursed her. She came to your father and asked for the same gift I'm now offering you. He told me to work with her, and I did. Every day she begs for more of what I have."

His sneering tone made her think he gave Audra more than lessons about black magic.

"I want nothing to do with you *or* your magic."

She would *never* allow herself to slide into the cesspool Jecis and Matas shared. A hunger and thirst for money and the power he'd mentioned had ruined them both, rotted their souls. And yes, she'd always heard that the greedy bred the greedier and the beaters bred even crueler beaters—but she was breaking the cycle.

Long ago, Vika had decided not to be like the men in her life. She always told the truth. She refused to bemoan her situation (very often). She refused to hate the people around her. She forced herself to be kind. That didn't mean she had to like, accept, or support what people did to her. She knew it was possible to love someone and not support their actions. She knew she could fight against what was done to her, and always did, to the best of her ability, without being cruel.

And, like anything else of worth, such a decision required work. It was hard to be truthful when she knew a lie would temporarily save her. It was hard to walk in love when anger demanded she run in hate. It was hard work to be nice when she was hurting, and even harder to hang on to hope when she was feeling abandoned by, well, everyone. But really, at the end of the day, when she rested her head on her pillow, she knew she'd chosen the better road. They had to wade through the mud. She remained clean.

"Now," she said, "if you'll excuse me, I'd like a little alone time to replay this conversation through my mind and laugh at you. Actually, even if you won't, I'd like a little alone time. Enjoy your day. Or not. Mostly not." Okay, so she wasn't ever nice to Matas. But then, even nice girls weren't to play with evil.

She opened the door and waited.

He slowly unfolded from the couch and stuffed the diamond necklace he'd been fondling into his pocket.

She almost protested. Almost.

She might despise what the jewelry represented, but every piece was going to a great cause. In a year, she would have enough money in trinkets and charms to buy a new identity and a home hidden high in the mountains of New Colorado. A place she'd dreamed of owning for the last four years. A place no one would be able to take away from her.

Without the identity, Jecis would be able to find her. Without the home, she would have to get a job to pay rent, which would put her under someone else's control, as well as on the grid.

Plus, the time gave her a chance to look for the key to the cuffs the otherworlders wore. Cuffs that had to be removed, or the captives could be tracked to the ends of the earth—and maybe even other planets.

"If Jecis catches you with that," she said as if she was happy at the prospect, "you'll be in trouble."

"He won't catch me. It'll be gone within the hour." Matas swept out of the trailer, making sure to brush against her.

Shuddering as the bugs once again seemed to jump on her, she slammed the door.

Ten

No weapon formed against you will prevail.
—ISAIAH 54:17

VIKA HAD TOSSED HIM a bag of food. The knowledge held Solo immobile. She'd tossed him a bag of food, and she'd done it even with fear in her eyes.

Why fear?

What—or who—was she afraid of?

Just as before, when the two otherworlders had harmed her, Solo experienced an almost overwhelming urge to chew through the bars of his cage. Not that such an action would work, he now knew. But just then, the urge had nothing to do with earning his freedom and everything to do with slaying whatever dragons plagued her.

Desperate to avenge your keeper?

Maybe. He'd done the vengeance thing countless times before and had never felt better afterward, only worse. He wondered if he would feel different on behalf of a female. *His* female.

No, not his.

"Jecis is gonna beat her but good for running through the zoo," the tobacco-spitting male from yesterday said gleefully from the distance. "He's on his way right now. Do you know how badly I want to watch?"

Solo's ears twitched.

The other male from yesterday chortled. "As badly as me, I'm betting."

"It'll be a shame, though, seeing that pretty face all busted up."

"It's always busted up."

"True."

A pause. "Okay, here's a question for you. There's a gun to your head and you have to do Vika or the bearded lady. But if you pick Vika, Jecis gets to do your wife. Who do you pick?"

"Jecis can have my wife, the little witch. I'll take Vika for sure."

Vika. They were discussing Vika. Jecis was going to beat his own daughter? His "heart?" Surely not. Surely the man would spank her, and nothing more. But the males had mentioned a busted face, hadn't they.

Little black dots flickered through Solo's vision.

He didn't know the girl, and he didn't trust her. Why should he? He shouldn't want to help her. And yet . . .

She had thrown him the bag of food. He didn't have to look to know that was what was inside the burlap. He could smell the milk and flour in the bread, as well as the sweetness of the honey and the tang of the meat.

Why would she do such a thing, especially since, according to the brute, she wasn't supposed to enter this area today? She had risked—and would receive— punishment.

He *had* to help her.

"Vika!" Before Solo even realized he'd moved, his fingers were wrapped around the bars. He was shaking his cage . . . shaking . . . so angry his bones were vibrating. "Vika, come here!"

Just as before, warmth shot into his wrists and quickly spread through the rest of him. Within minutes, his arms felt weighted down with boulders. Frustrated, helpless, infuriated all over again, he ground his teeth and forced himself to still.

His mother was probably turning over in her grave. A woman was about to be beaten within his vicinity— he was right here, relatively strong, somewhat capable— yet he could do nothing about it, was just going to let it happen.

"We must do something, Solo," X said, materializing, looking stronger and steadier than yesterday.

No matter where the pair went when they vanished, they always sensed a change in his emotions and returned to him.

"I say good riddance to the girl. He doesn't want a female like that," Dr. E said as he, too, materialized, looking weaker and paler than yesterday.

A female like that. For some reason, the phrase irritated Solo. She was a female who had tended him gently. A female who had kissed him as if he were precious to her. A female who had nibbled on his lip as if she liked the taste of him and craved more.

But was she as concerned and kind as she seemed, risking castigation to feed him—why him?—or as deceitful as the serpent in the Garden of Eden, tempting him, luring him into a sense of safety before ultimately striking him down?

There had been true fear in her eyes, and he couldn't imagine she would endure punishment simply to trick Solo into . . . what? Not softening, as he'd first assumed, for softening was far too mild to elicit any true results in a situation such as theirs. Perhaps she'd hoped to trick him into trusting her. But why would she want him to trust her? He was already locked up and weakened besides. She had no need for his cooperation. To make her job easier?

He barely stopped himself from punching the floor of the cage. He was confused, and he did not like being confused. He preferred things in black and white. Or, in the case of X and Dr. E, right and wrong.

"What can I do for her?" he whispered fiercely. He so rarely asked the pair for advice, they sputtered in bafflement. "I'm trapped." But he had to do something. Had to repay her generosity.

In all his life, in all the precarious situations he'd been in, he'd only ever been trapped without any sense of hope once. He'd been a child, and as young as he'd been he probably shouldn't have retained the memory of what had happened, but he easily recalled sitting in his playpen, his biological mother kissing his cheek and telling X to take care of him while she showered . . . and Solo having to watch as three masked men burst into the house and gunned her down. Her body had fallen, a pool of crimson flooding her.

He'd smelled the tang of gunpowder, felt the warm stickiness of the blood.

His father had run in from the other room, his skin already changing from bronze to crimson, his eyes glowing with concern. He opened his mouth to speak, but the *boom, boom, boom* of bullets drowned out his voice as he, too, was gunned down. He toppled mere inches from Solo's mother, his own blood deepening the pool. Both of their eyes had been wide with fear and pain, the light inside dulling. . . .

One of the men asked the others what to do with him. All three had peered down at him, discussing the matter and deciding to shoot him, too. An argument ensued as the shooter was chosen. A gun was raised. Another *boom* thundered. The pain . . . the utter darkness that had descended over Solo . . . X cooing, "Sleep now." The return of consciousness, with Michael cradling him close, shouting for paramedics.

"Bid me to help Vika," X said now, his voice terse with the force of his determination. "Just bid me, and trust me to do it. You'll see. You can sit back and watch as miracles happen."

Dr. E snorted. "If you help the girl, you'll be in a weakened state and unable to help Solo if something happens to him. He's not stupid enough to allow that."

"Solo?" X said, ignoring the other being. "Come on. Bid me."

Solo didn't mind losing X's strength, not for something like this, but they had gone down this road before and X had only disappointed him. A best friend had never appeared. A good girl had never chosen him above all things. His adoptive parents had not risen from the dead. He had no more trust to offer.

"Solo?" X prompted.

But . . . maybe a good girl *had* finally chosen him. Vika had helped him despite the danger to herself. Such generosity was better than heat in a winter storm, light in a darkened cavern. Hope bloomed. "What will you do for her?" he demanded.

"Why are you even asking? You can't escape if you're weak. Therefore, you can't risk anything that has the potential to make you weak." Dr. E paced from one side of his left shoulder to the other. "Plus, when X fails, and he will, you'll be upset and unable to function properly. If you can't function properly, you can't, what? Escape."

And he wanted to escape more than anything. Right?

X remained focused on Solo. "I won't know how to handle things until I reach her, but I will do something. All I need is your permission."

"Don't do this, Solo. Please."

"X," he whispered. "Do it."

"No! Don't be an idiot," Dr. E said with a sharp shake of his head.

"What, exactly, do you want me to do?" X insisted, still ignoring Dr. E. "Be specific."

How well he knew the importance of words. "I want you to—"

"No," Dr. E interjected harshly. "Are you kidding me with this?"

"Save her," Solo finished. "However necessary, whatever the cost to me, save her."

"Consider it done." A grinning X vanished.

"Idiot!" Dr. E shouted, stomping his foot. "Do you have any idea what you've done?"

Yes. He did. He'd turned to the only avenue available to him, trusting in a power greater than himself. And he couldn't allow himself to worry about the outcome. Something he'd noticed over the years: worry always weakened X further, and strengthened Dr. E.

Solo glanced at the tiny man who so often fueled his rages, no longer surprised to find his skin devoid of color. "Go away."

"You cannot . . . how dare you . . . Oh!" Dr. E vanished too.

"Hey, no fair, I smell food," Criss said, drawing his attention to the cages.

Good. He couldn't allow himself to think about Vika, and a distraction had just presented itself. "Your nose is working correctly. I have food." Delivered by Vika.

When would that fact cease to shock him?

Criss stretched her arm through the bars and waved her fingers at him. "Share with me. I haven't eaten in days."

"That's your own fault. You wasted what you were given."

"For a good cause!"

Was that so?

He opened the bag. The corners of several of the biscuits had crumbled off, and the crisp bacon had broken into multiple pieces. His mouth watered and his stomach rumbled. "You want half?" he asked, taking a section of a biscuit and a quarter of a bacon slice and tossing them at her.

First rule of fishing: Use the proper bait.

She caught the pieces with surprising grace and, with a speed his gaze struggled to track, stuffed both portions into her mouth as if she feared someone would try and take them away from her. Her eyes closed as she savored the food, her skin brightening . . . radiating a pearls-in-sunlight sheen . . . making his eyes tear with its radiance.

When her eyelids popped open, her eyes were the same bright shade. "More," she said in a deep, throaty voice.

"Why will you take food from me and not from Vika?"

"I don't want to give her the satisfaction of watching me beg for every scrap."

"She offers freely."

A growl from Criss.

"Are you a fan of honey?" he asked.

"Honey? Give me!"

Caught you. "I will . . . after you vow never to harm Vika again."

"Sure, sure. Now give me."

"You will vow not to hurt her with words, food, rocks, or anything else, and I will give you half of the bag's contents."

Dr. E made another appearance. There was a fresh cut on his cheek, and his robe was torn. His shoulders were stooped, as though his head was too heavy to hold up. "Now you're going too far. That food is yours. You need to keep your strength up."

His? Or Dr. E's?

"The otherworlder has gone without nourishment far longer than Solo has," X suddenly said, causing Solo's attention to whip to him. "It's only right that he share."

His robe had a single singe mark, just over his heart, and his skin was pale, lines of strain branching from his eyes, but he was grinning just as happily as before.

"And haven't you heard?" X added. "It's far better to give than to receive."

"The girl?" he whispered.

Satisfaction radiated from the being. "She is safe."

"How?" He'd heard nothing, and so little time had passed.

"Darkness cannot remain in the light."

He wasn't sure what that meant in terms of Vika's safety, but allowed the subject to drop. Vika was safe. That was all that mattered.

"So you got a crush on our keeper, do you? I thought so," Criss said. "Well, the romantic in me approves. It's a real beauty-and-the-beast-type story, and I'm in! When my brothers come to get me, and they will, I'll make sure I only kill Vika a little bit so that there's something left for you to have as a souvenir. I vow it. You're welcome. Now, please. Give me the honey!"

Somehow, he managed to maintain a blank expression. He wouldn't discuss his feelings for Vika—whatever they were—and he wouldn't allow himself to react to being called a beast while there was nothing he could do about it. However, he knew how to keep score. That was strike two for Criss. At three . . . poor dead girl.

That's what everyone would call her.

"Not good enough," he said. "Vow what I demanded." He pretended to bite into half of a biscuit. "Otherwise, you get nothing."

"Okay, okay," she rushed out. "I vow it. I won't harm her again. Ever. With anything."

A moment passed, and her entire body shook as though hooked to an electric generator. Her spine jerked into total alignment, going ramrod straight. "What was *that*?"

"A reminder that you will not like the consequences of breaking your word," he warned.

She popped her jaw. "You're a tricky Jolly Red Giant, aren't you? Well, that's okay as long as you give me the rest of what you promised." Those long, elegant fingers waved with more vigor.

He tossed her the portion. Just as before, she caught the food and devoured every morsel.

"Can't you do anything right today? If you wanted to share with her, fine, but you should have made her work for it," Dr. E griped. "And by 'it' I mean half of the smallest biscuit, not half of the entire bag."

Sighing with contentment, Criss lay back in her cage, a rare gem in a sea of dull stones.

His life would have been easier if he'd speculated about Criss all night. Instead, it was Vika he was drawn to, Vika he wanted to talk to, Vika he wanted to learn about and . . . Vika he wanted to save, even from himself. His hands curled into fists. She was his ticket out of here. He had to do whatever was necessary, even to her.

"Hey!" one of the other captives called. "New guy. Hamburglar."

"What'd you give Criss?" someone else demanded.

"I want me some!"

Solo snapped his teeth at the speakers, and they went quiet. Two even bowed their heads, recognizing a predator far more dangerous than themselves—one they did not want to rile, even caged as he was.

The Targon blew him a kiss.

Kitten watched him with expectant impatience.

Without a word, he claimed a piece of bacon and tossed half of what remained in the bag to her, and the other half to the Targon. She caught her portion and dug in. The Targon shook his head and volleyed his portion to her, as well.

"Sweet gesture, but I can't eat this," the Targon said. "My woman—" He slammed his lips together, going silent. And he must have decided that wasn't good enough, because he spun, giving Solo his back.

Interesting.

"I'm too happy to be upset that you shared with Kitten without making her give the dumbest vow ever," Criss purred. "She's feral, by the way. I'm surprised you got her to talk to you rather than spit curses, but news flash, you'll never be able to tap that."

He ate the bacon, relished the flavors.

"I'm not a beer keg," Kitten snapped.

Voices from beyond the clearing caught his attention.

"They'll be here in less than an hour. Move your lazy carcasses, now, now, *now!*"

"Have you glued the spikes to the paddle?"

"Feed the snakes, Rasa! If they take one more nibble out of my hand, I'm gonna start biting back."

A bead of sweat rolled down Solo's back. Already the air was warm and humid, and it would only grow hotter and wetter as the day passed.

"What'd you do to make Vika like you, anyway?" Criss asked, rolling to her side.

He had no answer and, taking a page from the Targon's playbook, turned away.

"Whatever. Hint taken," she mumbled. "This isn't a beauty-and-the-beast story, though, is it? It's a sister-wife thing, right? You want Vika, Kitten—and probably me. Definitely me. I'm pretty sexy. Well, consider me no longer intrigued . . . unless Vika brings you something more to eat. If you get a meat loaf, I'll be your slave for life. Well, half a life. My brothers will kill you."

Again, he offered no response.

"Have you prepared your mind for what's about to happen?" she asked.

The reminder flooded him with apprehension. The circus, due to start.

"Just do what you're told," she said. "You'll hate yourself for it, but you'll be better off. Trust me."

He could not have prepared himself for *this*, Solo thought.

For fifteen dollars a head, one human after another was allowed to parade through the clearing. The humans would stop in front of each cage and study the starving otherworlders inside while eating cotton candy, melting ice cream, hot dogs, and pretzels laced with addictive chemicals.

Did they know they were being drugged?

Some would stare with awe and wonder. Some would offer a critique of flaws. Some would throw pieces of grain at the captives. Solo allowed those pieces to bounce off him, letting them fall at his feet, but he watched as the others picked them up and ate, desperate enough to take what they could get, when they could get it, despite what Vika had fed them.

He should have shared his bounty with all of them, he realized with a flicker of guilt.

Children ran through every so often, laughing, tossing pebbles rather than food, before being chased off by the armed guards. That certainly explained where the rocks hurtled at Vika had come from.

"Dance for me, Pearls," one man begged Criss while the two males with him nodded eagerly.

Never once uttering a derogatory comment or insult, Criss danced, lifting her arms over her head and swaying her hips. The men moaned and groaned their approval, even though her every motion was made while she gritted her teeth and hate shone in her eyes.

Just do what you're told. You'll hate yourself for it, but you'll be better off, she'd said. *Trust me.*

Even now, he believed the opposite. If you hated yourself for your actions, you were never better off.

Only Kitten challenged the humans. She spat curses, as Criss had said she would, and tried to scratch and bite anyone who stepped too close.

Some of the female viewers asked the male otherworlders to lift their loincloths, and they, too, obeyed. Even the Targon, who wore his customary grin—though it was now cut by shards of broken glass.

No one asked Solo to do anything. He'd partially morphed, his skin a light shade of red, his eyes probably glowing, and his fangs and claws at half-mast. However, those with stronger stomachs stared at him with morbid curiosity until realizing he would not be the one to first lower his gaze, and that the fury blazing through him might give him the strength he needed to burst through the bars and do some damage before the guards could shoot him.

He heard murmurs of "ugly" and "hideous," just as he'd heard all his life, only now there was nothing he could do about it. He just had to take it. To react was to pass out, and to pass out was to be far more vulnerable, as he'd already realized, and this was not a place or time to welcome any type of vulnerability.

"I bet you want to kill these people," Dr. E said. He was paler than before, truly pallid, and shakier. "I know I do."

The damage Solo could have done at any other time . . .

"You should memorize their faces, and when you get out of here, you should hunt the offenders down and give them a little taste of your pain."

"There's another way, you know," X said before he could reply. Always he was there with his kindness and compassion, doing his best to build Solo up and encourage him. His color had already returned.

"Don't you dare feed him another line about forgiveness. We can't forgive this kind of behavior." Always

Dr. E was there with his flamethrower, determined to enrage Solo further.

Well, it was working.

"He can, yes," X said, "but that's not what I was going to say. This is a terrible situation, but there is a light in the darkness if you'll look for it rather than keeping your eyes closed."

"My eyes aren't closed," he growled softly. They were open, and they were peering at the human couple who'd just stopped in front of him, gaping. Why weren't they disgusted by the conditions living beings were forced to endure? Why weren't—

His gazed snagged on a cascade of blond hair, just behind the pair. He focused. Peeking out from behind the far cage, watching him, expression concerned and guilt-ridden, was Vika.

Her lip was split in the center, and there was a fresh bruise on her cheek.

"X," he snarled. X hadn't saved her. She *had* been beaten.

The human male tried to impress the female by stretching out his arm, as if he were brave enough to pet a beast like Solo.

Urges he'd battled since waking up in this cage suddenly overcame him. The urge to hurt those who wanted to hurt him. The urge to repay cruelty with cruelty. And yet, there was a new one. The urge to get to Vika. To protect.

With lightning-fast reflexes, Solo reached out, grabbed the male by the wrist, and twisted. The bones instantly broke.

A howl of pain rang out.

One of the guards surged forward, his gun already drawn.

Solo could handle being shot. Over the years he'd been shot, stabbed, beaten, and anything else the human mind could think up. Still. He shouldn't have done this, he realized. He should have remained stoic. Even without the human, he couldn't yet get to Vika.

Now he released the man and held his hands up, palms out, all innocence.

"I demand a refund!" the man shouted as fat tears ran down his cheeks. "Ow, ow, ow, and damages! And all my medical bills paid, ow, ow, ow. I was told I wouldn't be harmed, but look at this. It's crushed! Ow, ow, ow. False advertising is a crime."

Scowling, the guard replaced his gun to examine the human's injury.

"Uh-oh. You're in trouble now," Dr. E said with a laugh. Health and vitality was returning to his cheeks. He was no longer shaky.

"Focus on the light," X said. *He* was now pale. *He* was now shaky.

There was no light in a situation like this.

The guard sent the human on his way, probably to a medic, and approached the cage. "I hope you realize the money he's now owed is going to be taken out of your hide." With that, he jabbed the button Vika had once pressed—the button that brought paralysis.

Solo roared as warmth spread from his wrists to the rest of his body, exactly like the times he'd gotten angry, only this warmth was stronger and moved far more quickly. A river that had just broken free of a dam. He fought the sudden surge of weakness . . . fought the incoming vulnerability. . . .

He lost.

The last thing he saw before a heavy weight tugged at his eyelids was Vika, her hair wild, her eyes glittering with a strange sort of madness. She was rushing toward him, determined to get to him—until the second guard grabbed her by the waist and jerked her to a stop.

Solo unleashed another roar, tried to reach for her, and failed.

Eleven

〜✿〜

Do not gloat over me, my enemy!
Though I have fallen, I will rise.
—MICAH 7:8

AROUND TWO O'CLOCK IN the morning, the moon
was a mere hook of gold in the black, star-
studded sky. All of the circus patrons had gone home,
and now, all of the performers were gathering around
a great, blazing bonfire in the center of the imprisoned
otherworlders.

Vika shook with the force of her fear. Not for herself, not this time, but for the newcomer.

Blue Eyes, she'd begun to call him. The fifteen-
dollar fee her father had lost coupled with the money
for "damages" and the irritation of having to deal with
an irate human were to be taken out of Blue Eyes's flesh.

The male had not roused since the drugs had hit his
system, but only because he'd been given a fresh dose
every hour. Her father had wanted him docile until
the right time, which just happened to be when all of
his employees and Vika's charges could witness Blue
Eyes's punishment.

The performers had brought lawn chairs and now
placed them in front of the cages. There was Rasa, the

elf-size bearded lady with hissing snakes growing from her chin. There was the sword eater, the she-male with four hands, the conjoined gymnasts, and seemingly a thousand others.

Blue Eyes was on his knees, slumped over, his cuffs bound to hooks protruding from a man-made stump. The fire blazed beside him, casting rays of gold over the deeply bronzed skin of his bare back. There was no longer any hint of red. But there would be. All too soon, there would be, and it would be red of a different sort.

Jecis kicked him in the side to wake him, and cheers abounded.

As Blue Eyes lifted his head, he blinked rapidly, perhaps fighting to focus. Jecis walked around him with arms lifted high. In front of the otherworlder, he stopped, turned to face his people.

"This man—this disgusting *creature*—dared to touch a human without permission," her father called, riling the crowd. Vika continued to read his lips. "He had every intention of causing irreparable damage— *after* he had been warned to behave."

A chorus of "boo" swept through the masses, the vibrations nearly rocking her off her feet. She surveyed the people she'd grown up with, hoping, praying to find one sympathetic face, that someone, anyone, would stand up and shout, "This is wrong. I won't let you hurt that man." Someone with the strength to force her father to back down.

Instead, she discovered malicious glee and vicious enjoyment. Expressions all the more maniacal because everyone still wore their performance costumes, having come here directly after the last show. There were sequins, feathers, short fluffy skirts, lace and fishnets, oiled chests and pants practically painted on.

These people were outcasts, accepted only for how they entertained. Now, *they* wanted to be entertained. Actually, they probably felt as though they deserved a good show. Jecis had charged admission, after all.

The muscles in Blue Eyes's back knotted and his spine straightened. He scanned the area, suddenly alert. Someone threw a handful of popcorn at him, the fluffy yellow kernels raining over him.

Fury blazed in his eyes . . . a fire far hotter than the flames crackling beside him.

Please, she projected at Jecis. *Don't do this.*

"Let this be a lesson to all," her father continued, turning . . . turning . . . to face everyone in the assembly. He was saying more, but his back was currently to Vika, so she couldn't read his lips. The crowd liked it, whatever threat or insult he'd issued, because laughter erupted.

Then he was facing her again, and he was saying, "—know that to disobey is to suffer."

Cheers joined the laughter. Her stomach churned. And as much turmoil as she'd reacted to lately, she felt as if she could have made butter with it.

As her father stretched out his hand, as Matas slammed the handle of a whip against his palm, Vika shrank back into the night's gloom. Jecis wanted *her* blood, and if he caught sight of her, she would get a whipping, too.

Something strange had happened today. A few

minutes after Matas had left her trailer, the lights had flickered again. She had opened the door, expecting to have to deal with him a second time.

Instead, her father had been there. Scowling. Enraged.

"You dared disobey me? Dared place yourself in danger, when you know you're the most precious thing in the world to me?"

He shoved her backward, stormed in after her, and slapped her.

"I—I'm sorry," she'd managed.

"Why would you do this to me?" *Slap.* "Why would you force me to hurt you like this?" *Slap.*

But that time, *he* had yelped in pain. Him. Not her. As if her skin had somehow cut at him.

Then a voice had whispered inside her mind. An actual voice, the first sound she'd heard in years. Shocked to her core, she had rubbed at her ears, shaken her head, only to realize the sound hadn't sprung from outside—it had sprung from *inside* her. And yet, it hadn't belonged to her. Her shock had morphed into confusion, her confusion into dread.

Was she crazy?

You don't have to accept this, the voice had said.

Then a little louder, *You are strong.*

Then a lot louder, *You are victorious.*

Maybe she *was* crazy, but she was also empowered, as if his words imparted strength straight into her core. She'd somehow gathered the courage to scream in her father's face, "No! I won't let you do this to me!"

He'd stumbled back a few steps, as though reeling,

before stopping and popping the bones in his knuckles, gearing up for the serious stuff. But instead of hitting her with a closed fist, he had paused, a bead of fear appearing in his eyes. Fear. Directed at her!

"I'm needed in the ring," he'd muttered, baffling her further. "I'll deal with you later."

And he would, fearful or not. He never forgot a punishment due, and he never forgave, never showed mercy. Not even to her, his supposed beloved. That was why she'd decided to go back to the zoo and check on Blue Eyes. After all, a beating was already waiting for her. What better time to disobey and do what she wanted?

As she'd snuck out of the trailer, the voice had returned. *Later, you will again fight back. Later, you will again win.*

"Who are you?" she'd asked. "What are you?"

Silence. And yet, a warm blanket had seemed to wrap around her, embracing her, only to fade a second later, as if it had never been. As if she'd just been hugged and released.

But . . . that would mean she wasn't crazy. That would mean something had tried to help her. Something . . . like the absolute good in that other realm? After all, if evil could manifest, it made sense that good could, as well.

"I can't fight back later," she'd said. If she became too much of a problem, Jecis would finally make good on his threat to blind her. He might even kick her out of the circus, and she would find herself on the streets, unable to get to her money, with no skills, no protection . . . no hope.

A flash of movement caught her attention, pulling her from her thoughts. Jecis had just unwound the whip. The end was split into three parts, one with a shard of glass, one with a large nail, and one with a splintered piece of wood. A lump grew in her throat, and her chin began to tremble. Blue Eyes was going to hurt tonight.

She almost wished she were the one slumped over that stump, that she would be the one to receive the coming lashes. A stranger had tried to hurt him, and he had defended himself the way she had always wished she had the strength to do. He deserved to be commended, not disciplined!

Guilt over this would destroy her.

Blue Eyes scanned the crowd a second time, slowly, so slowly, slowing even more . . . until his gaze finally rested on her. Vika's eyes widened as astonishment and confusion flooded her. He couldn't see her. He *couldn't*. No one could. She was to the far left, wrapped in a cloak as black as the night and enveloped by shadows.

Jecis moved behind him.

Blue Eyes's gaze moved away from her, stopping on . . . the otherworlder Vika had named Kitten, who was gripping the bars of her cage, her expression laced with fury. He gave her a nod of reassurance.

He'd worked fast. At the circus only two days, and already he had romanced a female.

A spark of jealousy heated Vika's chest. Jealousy? Seriously? But why?

Blue Eyes despised her, surely, and he would continue to despise her until Vika's escape plan was enacted or until he died at this circus—whichever came first.

She looked away, her gaze catching on the Targon. "Matas!" he called.

Matas gave no reaction.

The Targon tried again. "Matas! Face me, coward. Face your doom."

Still nothing from Matas.

There were too many cheers to distinguish a single voice, she supposed. Again, she wondered why the Targon hated Matas so intently. As far as she knew, the two had never chatted.

Jecis lifted the whip high in the air. New vibration after new vibration slammed into her, and though she could hear nothing, she suspected the cheers were now obscene. A muscle jumped in Blue Eyes's jaw.

Grinning, Jecis delivered the first blow.

Specks of blood and tissue flew in every direction. Vika flinched and pressed her fist into her mouth to stop herself from gasping. But Blue Eyes never even flinched—and he was once again peering at her.

"I'm sorry," she mouthed. "So very sorry."

A second blow was delivered.

Again, Blue Eyes remained as he was and again Vika flinched. How could Jecis do this? How could anyone be this pitiless?

A third blow rained. More blood and tissue sprayed, and Vika knew the damage to Blue Eyes's poor back was deep, beyond the need for stitches. Actually, there would be nothing left to stitch.

With the fourth blow, Vika's knees gave out and

she sank to the ground. No one deserved this kind of treatment. No one but the whip wielder himself. Tears pooled in her eyes, hazing her vision. How could she let her father do this?

Shame joined the guilt and beat through her with the same force with which the whip continued to beat against Blue Eyes. She should do something. Should try and stop her father, no matter the consequences to herself.

But did she? No. She was weak. Pathetic. A coward.

You should just end it all, a voice whispered inside her head.

Another voice, she realized with astonishment. Not the same sweet voice as before, but a deeper one, suggesting she . . . kill herself?

You'll feel better. Everyone else will feel better. What's not to love about the idea?

Pinpricks of evil brushed against her skin—evil she recognized from Jecis, Matas and that other realm—and the truth hit her. She really wasn't crazy. The voices were real.

One sought to help her.

One sought to destroy her.

Well, she'd endured too much to give up now. All she had to do was stick to the plan, continuing to save and sell the presents her father gave her—and stop hemorrhaging cash to secretly buy niceties for the otherworlders. *One year,* she reminded herself.

Hope is silly. What if your treasures are stolen before you can sell them—what if your cash is stolen after you sell them? What if your father discovers your plan? Do you really want him *to have the satisfaction of killing you?*

"I'm not listening to you," she whispered. "Go away."

Surprisingly, the evil crackle in the air faded.

Another blow was delivered to Blue Eyes, stopping the most bizarre conversation she'd ever had. Another flinch on her part. Hopefully that was the end of it— but no, again and again the whip descended, until Blue Eyes had received fifteen agonizing strikes.

A panting Jecis dropped the weapon and wiped his blood-spattered hands together in a gesture of a job well done. He looked Blue Eyes over, frowned. Actually, every person in the crowd was frowning, Vika realized. They were staring at Blue Eyes as if he were a monster wearing a tiara: terrified yet awed.

Why?

"Anyone helps him, and they die," Jecis announced. "And if you think to fight your way free and run," he added, stomping over to kick Blue Eyes in the stomach, "go for it. There's a tracker in your cuffs. I'll have you back in that cage by morning, and you'll wish the whipping had killed you. Oh, and if you try to remove the cuffs, you'll activate the blade-saws and they'll remove your hands." He laughed cruelly. "A little safety precaution I had installed."

Blue Eyes didn't even glance in his direction.

Jecis whisked around. "You and you," he snarled to two of his biggest employees. "Stay here the rest of the night and watch him."

With that, he stomped away with a grinning Matas close on his heels. Most of the others followed after him. There were a few stragglers who hung back to gauge Blue Eyes's reaction to the threats. He remained just as he was, his expression blank, his gaze locked on Vika.

Thankfully, fatigue from a long, hard day's work and the knowledge that another day just like this one loomed on the horizon soon got the better of the stragglers and they tottered off, leaving only the guards. One was stationed at the east end of the captives' circle and one was stationed at the west end.

Vika gazed at the otherworlders in the cages. Most were gripping the bars, like Kitten, and some of their expressions were filled with horror while some were filled with relief. If she aided Blue Eyes and they sounded an alert, she would only bring more trouble upon his head. Or back.

But why would they sound an alert? Jecis would return, and could very well direct his anger at the prisoners. But then again, if they remained silent, he would know they'd witnessed her actions and punish them tomorrow. Or maybe he would be too angry with Vika to consider the otherworlders' part.

Either way, she wasn't going to worry about her father right now. She couldn't. Too well did she know the pain of being beaten, then left alone and hurting, desperate for someone, *anyone*, to help. Abandoning Blue Eyes wasn't an option.

Heart thundering in her chest, Vika snuck up behind the first guard. Gulping, she flipped back the hood of her cloak and tapped him on the shoulder. He spun to face her, tensed.

"Vika," he said, his expression hardening. He looked behind her, as if he expected her father to pounce. "What are you doing here?"

She forced a grin, held up her hand . . . the one with the ring she'd purchased only a few weeks ago, for just such a moment as this . . . and blew. *Has to work.* A fine, dark powder misted over the man's face, the same drug Jecis used to sedate the otherworlders. He coughed, his skin flushing with color, and she retreated into the darkness. A moment later, his knees collapsed. He hit the ground, already unconscious.

"Bernard?" the other guard said, striding forward. He reached his friend and crouched down—and Vika was there, crouching as well, blowing powder in *his* face. He too coughed and fell, landing on top of his buddy.

She waited, just to be sure. Both males remained in place.

A small measure of joy burst through her. It had worked!

In an hour, they would awaken and they would remember what she'd done, but they wouldn't tell Jecis, she didn't think. Most likely they would rather undergo chastisement for sleeping on the job than cast blame upon her and suffer an even worse fate.

Vika rushed forward, dropping to her knees the moment she reached Blue Eyes's side. His head was turned toward her, his cheek resting on the stump, his jaw clenched. His eyes were closed, the long length of his lashes fanning out. Flecks of blood had splashed onto his face. Unable to stop herself, she reached out and tenderly brushed the hair from his brow.

He met her gaze. "What are you doing, Vika?"

"Helping."

"Don't. I'm not in a nice mood."

A tide of warmth rose inside her, washing through her. He thought to protect her from himself. He was as beautiful as he was strong, she realized, and she hated seeing him brought so low by such evil.

I should have stopped this. I should have done something.

Well, she was doing something now.

"I must." As quickly as she was able, she unhooked the cuffs from the stump. Despite the fact that Blue Eyes was still awake, he slumped forward, making no effort to stop his momentum.

She caught him before he hit the ground. He was too big and too heavy for her to drag back to his cage. Plus, his back . . . oh, sweet mercy. Bile burned a path up her chest. Up close, she could see exposed hunks of muscle, decimated tissue, and blood leaking into a thousand tiny rivers.

The tears returned to her eyes. "I'm so sorry," she whispered. She eased him to the ground as best she could, felt a vibration, and suspected he'd moaned. It was his first reaction to what had happened. Either the action had hurt him worse than the whipping or he didn't mind revealing his pain to her.

She straightened, intending to rush to the edge of the clearing where she'd stored food and medicine and other supplies, knowing she would have to feed the prisoners and doctor Blue Eyes swiftly, without alerting anyone at camp. But before she could take a single step, surprisingly strong fingers wrapped around her ankle.

"I'll be back," she said, and pointed to where she needed to go.

Blue Eyes maintained his grip. Shadows and golden firelight flickered over his face, twining light with dark, and while she could see that his lips were moving, she couldn't make out the words.

"Let go," she said, and prayed she hadn't yelled. "You're too weak to do anything to me, and besides that, I have salve over there."

This time his grip tightened. "I'm not too weak. And I warned you I'm on the edge."

Her gaze darted through the area, but no one jumped out at her. A blessing, surely, and one she might not receive again. Unable to think up any other option, Vika sat down. Still Blue Eyes maintained his hold on her ankle, forcing her to curl into a ball to meet his eyes.

She placed one hand on her throat, and said, "What do you want from me?"

"I told you what I wanted."

Just now or before? Deciding to brave it out, she said, "Let me guess. Freedom. Well, too bad. You need medical attention first."

He frowned at her.

Great. Had she missed by a mile? "Let go of me, or I'll fight my way free and leave you here. And before you think that will allow you to crawl away to lady liberty, know that I'll knock you out first. My father wasn't lying. There's a tracker in the cuffs, and you'll be better off staying put."

"What about you? Will he beat you for helping me?"

"That's none of your concern."

Blue Eyes said something, but his lips were moving too quickly for her to track.

Uneasy, she gulped. "Has anyone ever told you that, uh, your accent is too thick to translate?" A question wasn't a lie, now was it?

The frown returned, darker than before. "You're staring at my mouth. Stop."

Her gaze snapped up. "I'll stop the moment you let go of me. How's that?"

The intensity of his crystal gaze held her in thrall before she realized his mouth was again moving. She looked down, and he pressed his lips together. Frustrated, she looked up—and he once again began to move his mouth. She looked down.

He paused, and just before she beat at his chest in frustration, he said, "You're deaf, aren't you?"

Her entire body stiffened. How had he guessed? No one had ever guessed. Had the other prisoners heard him?

She gritted out a sharp, "I hope you felt silly saying that." An evasion wasn't a lie, either, though it wasn't exactly the truth. But too many people tried to take advantage of her when they knew of her infirmity. "I have medicine over there. Let me go, and I'll make you feel better."

"Why?" he demanded.

Her gaze flipped up long enough to catch the slitting of his eyelids, the color darkening his cheeks. "Why what?"

"Why do you want to help me?"

Why indeed. "You're hurting."

"So?"

Before she could reply, not that she knew what to say, his gaze slid away from her, over her shoulder. Fearing one of the performers had stumbled upon them, she twisted, ready to leap up and toss out some kind of threat. But again, no one jumped out at her.

Several seconds passed before she calmed down enough to curl back up and meet Blue Eyes's gaze. "I must hurry," she said. "Or do you desire another whipping—and to watch one be delivered to me?"

A moment passed without any reaction from him, and she thought that surely no one else in the world could hide their emotions like this man. Then, to her surprise, he released her without further argument. She hopped to her feet and rushed to her supplies.

Twelve

∽

But everything exposed by the light becomes visible—
and everything that is illuminated becomes a light.
—EPHESIANS 4:13

GREAT WAVES OF PAIN raked Solo's entire body, but all he could think about was Vika's deafness. And she *was* deaf. He had no doubts. She had watched his mouth constantly, and when he'd gotten over his assumption that she was merely staring in horror at his long, sharp teeth, he'd realized she hadn't heard anything he'd said. Otherwise, she never would have approached him.

"Come any closer, and I'll chew off your face," he'd said through teeth gritted from rage and mortification, and though the words had been a falsehood, she hadn't known that.

She had come closer.

"Free my arms so I can snap your neck in two."

Another falsehood, but still she'd freed his arms.

"You're begging for it, aren't you?" he'd said. "Well, now you're mine, and I'll never let you go. You want mercy, you'll have to earn it."

She had displayed no fear.

Then he had recalled the way she had watched her

father's mouth, and the way she had watched the otherworlders' mouths. The way she had seemed to so easily tune out the rest of the world. The way her father's men were comfortable enough to discuss her while standing directly behind her.

And really, the handicap explained so much more. She had to have her hand on her throat to judge the volume of her voice, but even that wasn't 100 percent accurate. She would whisper at inappropriate times and bellow at others.

Solo wasn't sure what to make of the development . . . or of the fact that she wasn't as aloof as she wanted him to believe. She hadn't liked watching his whipping; the knowledge had struck him at the same moment the whip had, stunning him as well as strengthening him. With every blow, Vika had jolted in sympathy. Tears of genuine sorrow had filled her eyes, big and fat and rolling down her cheeks. Her knees had eventually given out.

She had become his anchor.

A laughing Dr. E had abandoned him.

A sighing X had abandoned him, though he had first promised to help the moment his strength returned. Help Solo would have refused if he'd been alone. X had already failed him. He wouldn't be foolish enough to trust the creature again.

Vika, though, she had stayed put, holding his gaze without wavering so that he was never alone and never had to concentrate on someone else, never had to consider what was happening.

What a puzzle she was. He couldn't figure her out.

And he wouldn't be given the chance tonight, he was sure. He had let her go, and she had bolted, which was probably a good thing. Right now he hung at the end of a fraying rope, ready to fall into his most dangerous at any moment. He hadn't lied about that. His mind was hazed by the ever-increasing pain he had refused to reveal to Jecis, even in the smallest degree. He would rather bathe in acid and towel himself dry with broken glass than satisfy the sick desires of such a madman. Michael had trained him better than that.

"I'm back," Vika said.

How utterly shocking. She'd kept her word without being forced.

He wanted to howl as she gently tended his wounds, but once again he remained quiet. He didn't want her to stop. He needed this. And he liked the thought of her hands on him, no matter the circumstances.

"You'll heal," she whispered. "You have to heal."

As the sound of her soft voice drifted through his mind, he was able to pretend they were at his farm, in his bedroom. On his bed. They had just made love, and he was exhausted. She had loved every moment, and now, she couldn't stop touching him, had to have more of him. But as his fellow captives marveled aloud, throwing rapid-fire questions and commands at him, he was drawn back to the present.

"Why are you just lying there?" the Mec whispered fiercely. "Kill her!"

Did he know she was deaf?

"Bob! Fred! Over here!" Criss rattled her cage door. "Fight through the pain and free us!"

"Now's your chance," the Bree Lian growled. "Do something!"

No. They didn't know. They would have told him to use the defect against her. Right now they were simply desperate for action.

"Why don't you all shut up?" the Targon snipped. "Let the girl aid the man."

Support. From the Targon. Miracle of miracles.

Vika cast a glance over her shoulder. "Hush," she said, and turned back to Solo.

Solo frowned. Maybe he was mistaken about her. Maybe—no. No mistake. She had simply followed the direction of his gaze. She had no idea the creatures had commanded him to end her life. Her expression was sad rather than angry, guilty rather than fearful.

He should listen to his companions and act. He should fight his way out. Now. He should do *whatever proved necessary.*

He wasn't against hurting a defenseless deaf girl to save himself . . . was he? Only yesterday he would have said no, no, a thousand times no. But twice now Vika had tenderly ministered to him, and only his mother had ever done such a thing for him. Vika had given him food and earned herself a beating.

His mother would expect him to aid the girl aiding him.

Yes, he was against hurting a defenseless deaf girl. *This* deaf girl.

Using every bit of his strength, Solo pulled himself into a crouch. Whatever salve she had spread over his wounds seeped deep and thankfully dulled the pain.

She slid an arm under his chest and applied pressure, helping him straighten.

"Can you lift the rest of the way?" she asked softly.

He opened his mouth to respond, realized she couldn't see his lips at this angle, and settled for nodding. He lumbered to his feet, tried not to cringe. Vika urged him toward the cage; he resisted.

"I'm not going back there," he said. New plan. He would leave with Vika and Kitten, find a hiding place, one Jecis wouldn't be able to track, even if there was a GPS chip in the cuffs, and take time to heal. He would contact Michael. Together they would come back here and destroy the circus. Some aspects of the plans would always be the same. Vika, he would . . . He wasn't sure what he'd do with her anymore.

After the circus was destroyed, he would hunt John and Blue if they were missing.

"Please," she said, giving his arm a tug. The single word was drenched with fear.

"I'm not going to hurt you, and I'm not going to allow your father to hurt you, either." He wrapped his arm around her waist and forced her into his side.

She struggled for freedom, but he merely tightened his hold. She struggled some more, but surprisingly enough, she was careful not to brush against his wounds.

"Don't do this," she pleaded.

"I must."

As the otherworlders called him over—*save me first, no me, please, me*—she finally stilled.

"Okay," she said with a dejected sigh, "that does it. I'm officially throwing in the wet blanket."

Uh, what? Maybe it was his injured state, but he so did not understand what she'd just said. "Throwing in . . . the towel?" Maybe.

She must not have caught his words, because she launched into a desperate rumble of words. "I give as much as I'm able, and I sacrifice as much as I'm able, and I sometimes endanger myself, and yet no one thinks twice about ruining my life further. So, fine, whatever. I'll go with you. I can't stop you from escaping without using your injuries against you."

"Thank you," he said, and he meant it.

"But when you're captured, and you will be," she continued, "I'll be sure to mention how you overpowered me. The last man who laid a hand on me lost it. Jecis chopped it right off. And then, to really prove his point, he chopped off the other one. And I won't even mention what will be done to me!"

"How kind of you." As she spoke, he kept a firm grip on her and ushered her to Kitten's cage. "But nothing will be done to you. I'll make sure of it."

From the otherworlders, the demands for freedom became pleas for help. As loud as they were, another guard would soon be called. He didn't want to waste precious time having Vika free them. Although . . . if Jecis and company discovered Solo's abduction of Vika, they'd have other people to chase, other tracks to follow, buying Solo more of the time he needed.

Cruel of him? Maybe. But also a mercy. They would be free. If the situation were reversed, he would want to be released for any reason, even that one.

He switched direction, approaching the cage closest to him.

"Thank you, Blue Eyes," Vika said, her tone dripping with relief. She must assume he intended to walk back into his own prison. "Thank you. You won't regret this. I have plans, and if you can just hold out for—"

"My name is Solo," he interjected, making sure she was looking up to watch his lips. She had plans? What kind of plans? And was she fond of men with blue eyes?

That last question irritated him greatly. Why should he care?

"Solo." A grin lifted the corners of her lips. "Nice to meet you."

He would have sworn the sun had just broken through a thick shield of rain clouds, lighting her entire face. He wanted her to smile every second of every day . . . but her soft amusement died a quick death the moment he stopped in front of the Mec's cage.

Dread radiated from her. "You're going to free everyone, aren't you?"

"Yes."

"Trust me. You don't want to do that. Please!"

"I must," he repeated.

Though she tugged and tugged and tugged, he forced her to place her thumb against the lock. The moment the two halves parted, the Mec burst free. As overjoyed as he was, his skin glowed a bright blue. Foolish otherworlder. He would never be able to hide that way.

"You're all dead," Vika said, emotionless. "You, me, all of them. We're all as dead as . . . things that are dead."

"I will protect you." He stumbled over his own feet and barely managed to right himself. But he meant those words with every fiber of his being. He wanted her safe. Now and al— Oh, no. He wasn't going there. He wanted her safe. *For now.*

He stopped, peered into her eyes, and again said, "I will protect you." This time he added, "I vow it."

She didn't jolt, as any other would have, and that astonished him. Maybe it was because she couldn't hear his voice, he reasoned. Maybe it was because he was drugged and in such a weakened condition. Whatever. Didn't really matter, he supposed. A vow was a vow, and he'd just tied himself to her.

A sigh slipped from her and she nodded. "Okay. I'll trust you."

Solo walked her to the next cage, and this time she offered no resistance whatsoever.

"Hey, you. Stop," a guard shouted in the distance, and Solo wasn't sure if the command was issued to him or the Mec.

Either way, there was no time to liberate the others. Kitten, yes, but not the others. He would have to come back for them. He dragged Vika to the girl's cage, and she placed her thumb against the lock's ID without any prompting from him.

Kitten raced to his side. "Let's do this thing."

"Quiet," Vika said, a desperate quality to her voice. "Please. We don't want them to catch us."

"You be quiet!" Kitten snarled, reaching for her. "Better yet, keep talking. I'll silence you myself for what you allowed to happen to me."

Solo spun Vika out of Kitten's reach. "Don't threaten her," Solo told the otherworlder. He wasn't sure what he'd do to her if she did it again. He only knew anger was already budding inside him—an uncontrollable anger. One that, when unleashed, would be unstoppable.

"Fine," Kitten muttered. "But I have a problem with her, and one day I'm going to catnip the hell out of her."

"Not without permission from me." Permission he would never give.

Jaw clenched, he lumbered forward with the women at his sides, the rest of the otherworlders hurtling curses at him . . . curses that were fading in volume, not just because he was moving farther away but because the strength of the otherworlders' emotions were engaging the cuffs and causing drugs to be pumped through their systems. They were dropping swiftly, as though Solo had targeted them for a job.

He quickened his step, trying to keep his own emotions under control.

He only made it a few more feet before a stocky man rounded a corner.

"Matas!" Solo heard the Targon shout. "I'll kill you! I'll kill you so dead!"

Not just a shout, but a spew, as if the name were a terrible curse. Bars rattled. The ground shook.

Matas. Finally they met. He'd been at the whipping.

Had been the one to hand the weapon to Jecis. The one to grin the widest as every blow was delivered.

But there was no time for a proper meet and greet. As Solo shifted directions, the male zeroed in on him. Black mist rose from the male's shoulders in thick, writhing coils. Evil, Solo knew. As many criminals as he'd targeted throughout the years, he'd seen such evil before. Slightly crooked teeth flashed in a scowl as the man withdrew a gun from the waist of his pants and squeezed the trigger.

Solo twisted so that his body completely blocked the females. Fresh pain bloomed in his shoulder, and his vision instantly hazed.

Vika released a bloodcurdling scream that joined the chant of *failed again, failed again, failed again* suddenly echoing in his head. He collapsed, no longer able to hold himself upright, and because he still had a grip on both Vika and Kitten, the two females went down with him. He managed to tuck them both underneath him, still determined to use his body as a shield in case the male decided to open fire.

He—

—knew nothing more, for darkness had eaten him alive.

Or as dead as things that were dead.

Thirteen

*Catch the little foxes for us, the little foxes that are ruining the
vineyards, while our vineyards are in blossom.*
—SONG OF SOLOMON 2:15

MATAS HAD SHOT SOLO. Matas had really and
truly shot Solo. Blood had splashed on Vika
as Solo had fallen . . . had poured over her when he'd
landed and tucked her underneath him. To protect
her. Her. His enemy. Just as he'd promised. Kitten was
struggling under his weight, trying to free herself, but
he wasn't helping her.

Was he dead?

Please don't be dead.

Hand trembling, Vika reached up and felt for Solo's
pulse. It was thready, but there. He lived. Relief bom-
barded her—just as Matas yanked her out from under
Solo's massive weight.

Glaring down at her, he snapped, "Remove the bullet from the beast. We don't want your father's precious
main attraction to die, do we?"

"N-o."

He kicked Solo in the side, rolling him to his decimated back and freeing Kitten.

The Teran jumped up, ready to bolt, but wily as he

was, Matas managed to grab her by the waist before she'd taken more than a step.

"Let me go!" Kitten snarled.

"After I've had a little fun with you."

"Careful with her," Vika commanded, her blood flashing cold. "Please. She's my charge, and I'm responsible for her."

Kitten paused, gazing at Vika with wide-eyed shock.

Icy calculation from Matas, as though Vika was giving him exactly what he'd wanted. "You'll owe me," he said, then carted the struggling Kitten to her cage.

Vika tripped her way to the medical supplies she'd brought to tend Solo after his whipping. She returned and, though her trembling had increased substantially, managed to do as Matas had commanded.

Solo's chest was more crimson than bronze, with a quarter-size hole just over his heart. Tears tracked down her cheeks, blurring his image. How much could one man endure in a single day before he died? she wondered as she wrapped his entire chest with a thick bandage.

"Good enough," Matas said. Though he was strong enough to carry Solo, he opted not to, instead dragging the otherworlder to his prison and ruining what little good Vika had done to both his back and his chest.

I'm so sorry, she thought, fighting sobs. *The night wasn't supposed to end this way.*

Dark eyes pinned her in place, mocking her for her sorrow. "Are you happy with yourself?"

"No."

"Good. Your father wants to talk to you." Matas grabbed her by the wrist and tugged her away from the clearing.

All too soon, Jecis's trailer came into view. Her father waited at the door and motioned her inside. She offered no protest, but she did stop, unable to take another step on her own. Her feet were simply too heavy.

Matas picked her up and carried her inside. To mask her growing sense of fear, she gazed around the home that no longer bore any hint of her mother's presence. Like all the other circus vehicles, the trailer boasted metal walls; multiple padlocks lined the seam of the only door. There were no windows.

However, unlike the others—excluding hers—this one boasted brand-new furniture. There was a plush reclining chair, a leather couch, a projector television, and holo-images of Audra dancing in every corner. Multihued pillows were strewn around a faux fireplace, forming a small alcove that would have been pretty if not for the bear-skin rug that was stretched out in front of it. A rug courtesy of Zoey.

Yes, Jecis had skinned Vika's precious bear. Actually, he'd put all of her beloved animals to "good use" rather than selling them. A "gift" to Vika. Sammie's ostrich feathers had been made into hats and tails for a group of performers. Dobi the tiger and Righty the ape were stuffed and on display in the main tent. Gus the zebra, Angie the horse, Gabby the camel, and Barney the llama had been dipped in some sort of alien metal and turned into a carousel. Mini the elephant had been hollowed out and dipped in the same metal, now an enzyme spout between the two public bathrooms at the circus, where people could wash their hands.

Vika could hardly bear to think about what Jecis had done to One Day.

Beyond the living area, there was a queen-size bed. Audra currently lounged in the center, the bejeweled covers puffed around her. Grinning, she sipped a glass of brandy. One of the spiders etched into her arm began to move, crawling higher and higher, until finally resting on her shoulder.

The tattoos on Audra's body had come to life a few months ago, after she'd begun her training sessions with Matas.

Audra loathed Vika, and enjoyed watching her punishments. But then, Vika kind of deserved all that loathing. Audra, Vika, and their friend Dolly had grown up together, inseparable, sisters in every way that mattered until Vika's mother died, and Jecis demanded all of Vika's spare time.

We'll be together forever, you and I. You will never abandon me. I'm the only one you can ever trust. The only one who will ever love you. Never forget.

Every chance she could, Vika had snuck away to spend time with her favorite girls. The three of them had been playing with the animals, laughing hysterically at the noises Zoey made while she napped, when Dolly had accidentally shut Vika's hand in the door of the cage.

Jecis found out and raged, saying the punishment had to fit the crime. Dolly had hurt Vika's hand, and so Jecis had removed Dolly's. When the girl's parents protested, Jecis exiled the entire family.

That's when Vika called Audra terrible names and even slapped her, hoping to send her away and save her from Jecis's wrath. Looking back, she knew she had handled things poorly.

There was no undoing the past, she knew that, but she had later sought to make restitution and apologized. Audra had refused to forgive.

Matas eased Vika into a chair in front of the trailer's kitchenette. He rubbed two of his knuckles under her chin and smiled smugly. Then he left, the door slamming shut behind him.

He shot Solo. Just shot him as easily as if the other-worlder was the main course for dinner, and now he dares to smile at me?

Would Solo live through the night?

Would she find his dead body in the morning, flies and ants covering him?

Would she even be capable of walking in the morning?

Jecis moved to the other side of the counter and took his time cutting and lighting the end of a cigar. Even with the thick slab of granite between them, dark smoke billowed around her, and she had to hold her breath to stop herself from coughing.

Jecis leaned forward and latched his hard fingers onto her jaw to keep her attention on him. His eyelids narrowed to tiny slits.

"Nothing to say to me?" he began.

"I'm . . . sorry," she said, shifting in her seat. It was

the truth. She was sorry he was the man he was, sorry Solo was here, sorry for everything that had happened that she hadn't prevented.

"I'm not talking about tonight, I'm talking about this morning," he said, surprising her with the calmness of his voice. He released her.

"I—I—" Had no reply that would encourage that sense of calm.

The only saving grace was that she hadn't challenged his authority in front of witnesses. The way the circus worked, Jecis called the shots and no one was allowed to question him. Ever. Anyone who voiced an objection would find himself—or herself—fighting Jecis in front of every member of the family, and being made a very bloody example. If that person survived, he and all of his family would be kicked out. Unless he had a pretty wife or daughter, of course. They were allowed to stay and marry other men.

"Do you like Matas, Vika?" he asked casually. Too casually.

Wait. What? "No." Violently she shook her head.

"He told me you've already given yourself to him."

Outrage stormed through her, making her stupidly blurt out, "He lies! I promise you, he lies." She had never been with a man, and, to be honest, had never had a desire to change that.

Until Solo. Until she'd kissed him.

But even then, she wouldn't. Having sex meant sharing a part of yourself with another person, binding your body to theirs . . . perhaps even your soul to theirs.

Sex was total vulnerability, just another way for a man to dominate a woman.

No, thank you.

"There's no reason to deny what happened," Jecis said.

"But—"

"I must admit, I was upset at first. However, after some thought, I find that I like the idea of grandchildren."

Oxygen congealed in her lungs. This had to be a trick. She'd yelled at her father earlier today, shoved him, and had gone to the clearing without permission. Again! Yet he talked of *grandchildren*?

A puff on the cigar, a haze of smoke, and for a moment, only a moment, she saw a mask descend over his features. One with sharp bones, red eyes, and fanged teeth.

"Matas is right," he said. "You have too much time on your hands, and that time gets you into trouble." Irritation infused his tone. "Just so you know, the Mec has already been found. Matas left us to take care of him."

A tide of remorse joined Vika's anger, but she somehow managed to keep her expression blank. *Can't give a reaction.* In circus terms, "taking care" of a person meant "torturing and killing."

Poor Rainbow. He'd reviled her more than all the others, and he'd even tormented her more than any of the others combined, but she'd admired his spirit. No matter what had been done to him, his strength had never waned.

"What will be done with the other one?" she asked, and she wasn't quite able to hide her emotions this time. There was a quiver in her voice. "The new one?"

His lips pursed with distaste, and he said, "He was shot. I think that's penalty enough, don't you?"

"Yes." *Thank you, thank you, thank you.* "That's kind of you. Daddy."

A softening around his eyes. "In the morning, I'll have Matas remove the Mec's cage until his replacement can be found." He placed the cigar in the ashtray, his gaze sharpening like a blade. "Now, then. Let's talk about what happened tonight."

Every muscle in her body tensed. He was going to ask how Solo had gotten to the Mec, and why she'd failed to scream for help, and she had no answer for him. Not one that would satisfy him.

"Do you recall what happened to you when you left the circus all those years ago?" he asked.

Another yes slipped from her.

It was a few months after her father had purchased the "perfect candidates for his zoo." By that time, she and Mara had become friends, and she'd wanted so badly for the girl to be happy. Mara, who missed her husband desperately. Mara, whose pregnant belly had grown larger every day.

Vika had bonded with her at first sight, really, the fragile-looking female reminding her so much of herself. Mara had said that, once she was free, Vika could live with her, that her husband was a mighty warrior and that he would protect her.

Vika had freed Mara and all the others—but Mara

had abandoned her, never showing up at their meeting spot. And then, Jecis had found Vika and the rest of his menagerie, all but Mara, within a week.

They were killed.

She was beaten.

But even though she'd lost her hearing that night, she'd been glad to see him. There was a dark, dangerous world out there, one she hadn't been prepared for. One that had nearly chewed her up and spit out her bones.

She'd had no protection, no money, and no one had known her father, so no one had known to fear his wrath. She'd had to walk the streets, begging people for food and money. Men had called her terrible names and had tried to drag her into abandoned alleys. She'd had to hide in trash bins. Fear of the vast unknown had tormented her mind constantly, and, well, it had been too much to bear.

All she'd known was the life inside the circus. Back then, they'd traveled from city to city in their trailers. They'd stayed in each location for two weeks, the first few days used for setup and promotion, Audra and the other attractive females going into town to spread the word and lure the males. After that, the shows began.

Always lookouts had been stationed on the roads, and if the cops were spotted, they were stopped. If the authorities couldn't be paid off, the performers packed up as much of the equipment as possible and blazed a trail into the next town.

Now, Jecis had another way to travel. One Vika despised. One she would never again have to endure once she left this place. And when she was settled into her new life and certain she couldn't be found, she would even help the police hunt her father and shut the circus down once and for all.

"And do you ever want to leave the circus again?" he asked silkily.

"I don't want to leave the circus," she said. Again, it was the truth. She wanted to stay. For now. Once she had enough money . . . once she'd found the key to the cuffs, her answer would change.

"Do you think that ugly otherworlder you fed, the one you watched while the humans were out and about, no less, will take care of you once he's free of his cage?"

He knew she had broken the rule a second time. She gulped.

Solo will *take care of you, you know. He really will protect you.*

The voice penetrated her mind, and she gasped. It was the voice from that morning. The good one. The nice one.

"What?" her father demanded.

"I . . . I . . ."

"Never mind. I asked you a question. Do you think the otherworlder will take care of you?" her father insisted.

She . . . did, she realized. He *would* take care of her. For a little while, at least. After all, he had used his body as a shield for hers. A man willing to do that wasn't a man who would throw a helpless girl into a pit of alligators. But that wasn't what Jecis wanted to hear.

"He's a prisoner, Daddy," she said. "He can't take care of anyone."

Once again, the "Daddy" worked. His expression softened, and he failed to realize she hadn't exactly answered his question. "No one will ever love you the way I do. No one will ever take care of you the way I do. Isn't that right?"

She gave a barely discernable nod. No, no one else would ever "love" her this way. She would make sure of it.

Pacified, he settled into a chair and picked up his cigar. "Good. Then you realize the otherworlder would just as soon murder you in cold blood as take you with him, so there's no reason to discuss this subject further."

Before relief had time to work through her—no more punishment for her, either!—he added, "Now, for the next order of business."

She racked her brain, trying to figure out what he was going to rant and rave about, but only drew a blank.

"Matas," he said.

And she groaned.

"He wants to marry you."

She linked her fingers, hoping to stop herself from twisting and wrinkling her shirt and revealing the depths of her sudden turmoil. "That's too bad, because I don't want to marry him."

"He'll treat you well. I'll make sure of it."

That sounded like—no, that *was* approval. "You're actually considering this?" she gasped out.

"I am. He's given me his word that he'll never harm you, and that he will forever remain here at the circus with you. With me."

Dark spots winked through her vision. A lump grew

in her throat, threatening to cut off her supply of air. All of her fine plans were beginning to crash and burn around her. Her father was changing the very fabric of her existence, trying to rewrite the future she had mapped out for herself.

Worry not, the voice said. *Evil will not win in the end.*

Worry not? How could she *stop* from worrying?

Audra abandoned the bedroom and strutted into the kitchenette. She poured herself another drink, blew a tiny stream of fire over the top, and nibbled on a cracker as the flames died down, her hips swaying to a beat Vika would never hear.

Audra grinned when she realized Vika was watching her and said, "You might as well take Matas up on the offer. No one else will have you."

Jecis sat up straighter and banged his fist into the counter, rattling the ashtray. "Anyone would be lucky to have her. She's the daughter of a champion, and she will bear strong children. The problem has been finding a man worthy of her."

A man he could control, he meant. A man who would keep her here, within reach, for the rest of her miserable life. A man who would occupy her time with one pregnancy after another, keeping her too busy to get into "trouble."

"No," she croaked. "I won't do it."

A treacherous light glittered in Jecis's eyes—one she recognized. Danger was near. "I want this, darling little girl, and so you will do this. Audra will help you plan the wedding."

"No," she repeated, her mouth so dry her tongue

felt like a strip of sandpaper. If Jecis insisted on going down this road, she would have to run away sooner rather than later, before she'd saved enough cash, before she'd found the key to the cuffs. But she would do it, no question.

Slowly her father pushed to his feet. He flattened his palms on the tabletop and leaned toward her. "You will marry him with a smile on your face, Vika, or I will give your treasures to Audra, and place the animals in someone else's care. I will be forced to express my displeasure with you . . . over and over again. Do you understand?"

Fourteen

In repentance and rest you will be saved,
in quietness and trust is your strength.
—ISAIAH 30:15

THE NEXT FEW DAYS passed in a blur for Solo. He should have recovered faster, and wasn't sure if the drugs swimming through his system were the problem, if X still wasn't able to feed him strength, or if the whip had been laced with a poison his senses were now too dulled to notice. Whatever the reason, he remained weak.

It wasn't the weakness that tormented him, though. It was the memory of his failure. He'd tried to escape, had been so close to succeeding, but "so close" wasn't good enough.

He had never before botched a job so sublimely.

At least he wasn't dead like the Mec.

The thought wasn't the comfort it should have been. Guilt filled him every time he recalled the Mec's screams for mercy that had come only with the rising of the sun. Amid the silence, Solo had watched a satisfied Matas haul the dull, lifeless body away.

Solo had fallen back asleep, only to awake to find that his cage had been removed from the clearing and placed in front of Jecis's mobile home. A monstrosity if ever he'd seen one. A skull and crossbones was painted on the side, staring at him. A giant cubby stretched over the driver and passenger seats, and the belly was almost too fat for the road.

He would have preferred something smaller, faster, sleeker, but there were no other trailers blocking the front of this one, so evacuation would be easy. He could carry Kitten and Vika away, no problem.

Yeah. He had a new plan.

Obstacle one still hadn't changed: getting out of this cage.

Most times Jecis entered or left the area, he paid Solo no attention. Every so often, he would stop and stare, saying things like, "I'm lord and master here and I'll break you yet. Just you wait."

Audra stayed in the motor home every night. The two would call each other names, fight, have sex, then fight some more. Jecis was never afraid to use physical force, but he must have avoided the girl's face, because she never emerged with visible bruises.

He wasn't sure what he would have done if he'd heard Jecis beating Vika.

Vika, the contradiction. She'd sprung from the loins of the heartless Jecis, and yet she was kind. She'd helped Solo even though he'd heard Jecis order her to stay away, placing herself in danger.

Danger. From her own father. That wasn't supposed to be the way of things. Especially with a female like her, handicapped by deafness, unable to hear her destruction coming, and as tiny as a fairy princess, unable to withstand very much abuse before breaking.

Even the thought of a single strike to any part of her body filled Solo with one of the darkest rages he'd ever experienced.

He wanted, *needed*, to talk with her. He could help her, and she could help him. She could be his biggest ally—he wanted her to be his biggest ally. But though she visited him three times a day, she never looked at him to read his lips.

Every morning she appeared mere minutes after Jecis's departure, as if she was hiding somewhere close, watching and waiting. She returned in the afternoon, though never at the same time, and then again in the evening. She would give Solo food and water, and even rags and enzyme spray to clean himself, but she wouldn't speak a word.

So many times Solo had almost grabbed her arm. If she wouldn't talk to him, he couldn't get her to help him. If he couldn't get her to help him, he would have to force her. He would have to remove her thumb with his fangs or his claws, as he'd planned the first time he'd met her. Then he could hijack the trailer and drive her to a hospital, where the thumb could be reattached. But . . . he could never get past the image of her blood running down her arm as she clutched the wound to her chest. Could never get past the horror of hearing her scream from the pain. Could never get past the idea that she would cry.

Oh, if she cried, he would be a goner.

He was disgusted with himself. Freedom should

come before *anything*, especially a woman partly responsible for his circumstances. Yet he'd come to accept two startling facts. With or without the vow, he wouldn't be able to so much as scratch her and he had to include "keeping Vika safe from everyone else" in his plans.

"Feeling better, I see," a female voice said, jerking him out of his head. "You're even sitting up like a big boy. You must be so proud."

He focused on the here and now. Audra was propped against the corner of his cage. She wore a black, bra-like top, with multicolored sequins sewn along the edges, a mix of yellow, blue, green, and red. Those same sequins were pasted to her bare shoulders and down her arms, along her—

One of the spider tattoos had moved from the inside of her elbow to her wrist.

Temporary tattoos, then. Though he'd never seen any that looked so real. He finished his study of her. Her middle was utterly bare. A pair of black panties covered her essentials, and a pair of fishnet stockings clung to her legs, though they were only visible to her knees. High-heeled boots looked painted to her lower calves and feet. A peacock tail rose from behind her, fanning up and out.

Her slick of dark, pink-striped hair was pinned into a bun, and her makeup was so thick and wild she almost appeared inhuman. Her eyes *did* appear inhuman. Contacts dusted the green with glitter. Her lashes were the color of the feathers, blue and green and black, fanning out over her brows and temples.

"Still have nothing to say to me?" she asked, and sucked a lollipop into her mouth.

One of the spiders popped its legs from her skin and walked down her arm.

No way. Just no way. Had to be the drugs, messing with his mind. He had to be hallucinating. "What would you like me to say?"

Lick. A slow, sensuous grin curled the corners of her lips, and she hummed her approval. "Why don't you start with how beautiful I am?" *Liiick.*

She *was* beautiful, there was no denying that, but Solo knew better than most how deceptive appearances could be. He'd never been one to judge by exterior.

The one and only girl he'd dated had lived on the farm next door to his. Plain but sweet Abigail, whom X had liked but hadn't wanted him to date and whom Dr. E had despised and had wanted him to bury in his backyard. Abigail was the first and only girl to ever want the man and not the monster. He'd picked her up every time she'd had too much to drink, protected her any time she traveled into the city at night, and helped her climb through her bedroom window whenever she'd snuck out. She'd kissed him a thousand times, said a thousand thank-yous, but had never given him anything more. Despite that, she had genuinely seemed to care for him—but only ever when they were alone.

One day, indignation had gotten the better of him and he'd given her a choice. Take all of him, all the time, in front of everyone, or have none of him. She had cried, she had begged him to remain in her life, but in the end she had been unwilling to change and so he had walked away.

He had never looked back.

Vika, he would think about forever, he suspected. His attraction to her scorched deeply, inexorably, and not just because she was exquisite, the loveliest female he'd ever beheld. Again, looks mattered little to him and he would have liked her if she'd been as ugly as, well, an Allorian. It was the way she'd treated him. As if he mattered.

What was he going to do with that girl?

He couldn't troubleshoot with Dr. E and X—not that he was on speaking terms with either. Both males had abandoned him during the whipping and had only returned in quick snatches, vanishing the moment he opened his mouth.

"Well?" Audra demanded.

"I will not say any such thing," he announced.

She straightened, her grin morphing into a scowl. "I have seen you transform into the ugliest beast alive, and yet you think you're better than me. Well, I'll put you in your place," she said softly, fiercely, "right underneath me."

She held out her arm, and the spider actually leapt from her skin and onto one of the bars of the cage. Okay, there was no way that was a hallucination. Eight legs crawled across the metal, tap, tap, tapping as the spider—

Hinges squeaked as the door to Jecis's trailer opened. The male stepped into the light of day. Audra inhaled sharply, and the spider jumped back onto her arm.

Some kind of dark power was at work within the girl. Now that he concentrated, Solo could feel the crackle of it in the air. It was the same crackle Jecis and Matas emitted, only at a slighter degree. He would have to remain on guard around her.

Frowning, Jecis scanned the area. He spied Audra, and his frown intensified. He stomped toward the cage.

"What you are doing?" he demanded.

As Audra pasted a seductive smile on her face and wove a lie about Solo calling her over and asking her for food, Solo performed a scan of the area himself. Tent after tent, other trailers, but no hint of Vika.

A rock slammed into his left shoulder, and he glanced down, watching as jagged silver rolled to the floor of his cage.

"Are you listening to me? I said do not dare to speak to my woman again," Jecis snarled. He curled his fingers around the bars and shook the entire wagon. "You got me? Otherwise I will kill you and send whatever's left over to your family."

Solo raised his lashes and met the man's gaze. He kept his expression blank, refusing to give any kind of reaction. *One day I will escape. One day I will end your reign of terror.* "Sorry, but I don't have a family."

After a long, flustered moment, Jecis said, "Your friends, then."

"What makes you think a man like me has friends?"

Jecis ran his tongue over his teeth. "Then we'll let the dogs have you. If they will. They like their meat tender, and you look rotten."

Solo just stared.

"Speaking of food," Jecis gritted out, "you have been eating, haven't you, Beast Man, despite asking my female for a morsel? Your color is too good for a starving man. Who's been feeding you? My sweet little Vika?"

"Probably," Audra said. She traced the lollipop over her lips. "I saw her running this way last night."

"Because her trailer is beside mine, you stupid whore."

Audra flinched. "O-of course."

Not so brave in the light of day, and he could guess why. Jecis would tolerate her temper when they were alone and there were no witnesses. But the man would not be so lenient in front of others, when every challenge to his authority would have to be defused in the most violent way possible to stop others from thinking to rise against him.

More than that, Solo knew his type. Knew Audra's type, too. Jecis was used to everyone bowing and scraping. Audra wanted to be something different, someone capable of holding such a "strong" man's attention. So she acted out. In the end, however, Jecis would tire of her and she would pay for every one of her perceived crimes. A man like Jecis never forgot a wrong.

A man like Jecis—yet Solo was the same way.

He massaged the back of his neck. He didn't like the comparison. But he wouldn't think about that right now. An important revelation had just unfolded. Vika's trailer was beside Jecis's. Solo could see no sign of it, and could only assume hers was smaller, obstructed. He could steal it instead of her father's. A kindness on his part, letting her take a little piece of her life with her—since Solo would never allow her to return.

And just how long do you intend to keep her?

"All I was saying," Audra added with a tremble, "was that she might have been feeding him to anger you and invite punishment to herself, thereby delaying her wedding."

Vika was getting married? To whom? he nearly snarled.

Jecis, who'd been watching him intently, scowled. "I finally got to you, as promised, but not for a reason I approve. You are not to lust after my daughter, slave. She is off-limits to the likes of you, and far too good. If ever again you look at her, I'll remove your eyes. If ever again you talk to her, I'll remove your tongue."

Not one to cave to intimidation, Solo said, "Try it." He would do everything in his power to ensure Jecis went down with him. "Let's find out what happens."

The man's nostrils flared with shock and anger. "Perhaps I will. Perhaps I'll even give you back to the man who sold you to me. He's not as nice as I am."

"Who sold me?" Gregory Star, he knew, but he wanted to hear the name from Jecis.

Grinning now, Jecis grabbed Audra by the forearm and said, "Let's go, woman, and leave him to wonder."

The moment they snaked the corner, X materialized on Solo's shoulder.

"Where have you been?" Solo demanded.

"Recovering."

"All this time?" He was steady on his feet, at least, his color high.

Silence.

"You were weakened yourself, but you were trying

to heal me, weren't you?" he asked, realization dawning.

X didn't confirm or deny.

But Solo knew that he had been doing just that. "Thank you," he said.

A pause. A nod.

"But I'm still angry with you," he added. "You didn't save the girl when you had the chance." He'd planned to yell, but could no longer bring himself to do so. "You told me you had succeeded."

"Such little faith," the tiny male *tsk*ed. "I did not lie. She's alive, isn't she?"

"She was hurt."

"She was, yes—*before* you bid me to aid her. I did exactly what I told you I would do. I saved her from further harm."

A good point, but one he didn't want to acknowledge. He would then have to admit the fault was his own, that he'd wasted precious minutes debating what to do.

A long-suffering sigh brushed over his ear.

That was it, just a sigh, but Solo suddenly wanted to cut out his own heart and present it to the being on a platter. Oh, how he loathed X's sighs. He could always sense the disappointment, the disapproval and the hurt, as if he were breaking a promise he'd never made. As if he were destroying something precious— something he couldn't even see!

Maybe he was. Solo's mother had raised him to be a better man than he was.

To Mary Elizabeth Judah, all life was precious and a gift from God to be treasured. Solo hadn't exactly treasured X, had he? Hadn't given back what he'd been given.

Even when Solo had been at his crankiest, Mary Elizabeth had treated him with love and kindness. She had cooked his favorite meals. She had ruffled his hair and told him how beautiful he was. She had left little notes throughout the house, positive words of encouragement. *You are strong and courageous.* And, *You are adored.* A good woman, his mother.

Maybe she had known about Solo's profession; maybe she hadn't. They'd never talked about it. Everything he'd done, he'd done for a good cause. He'd never asked questions, but then, he'd never wanted to know. He'd trusted Michael. He'd removed scum like Jecis Lukas from the streets.

But he'd grown colder over the years, hadn't he? He was not the man his mother had raised.

"Thank you," he said again, this time with more heart. "For what you did for Vika, and what you did for me."

"You're welcome," X said with a happy grin.

"Ugh. Mushy stuff," Dr. E said, never far behind. He was hunched over, as if his shoulders were too heavy to hold up. "We aren't women. Let's man this party up and kill something."

Movement at his left. Solo homed in just in time to watch Vika crawl from behind one of the trailer's huge tires. She brushed the dirt from her hands and knees as she checked the area for eavesdroppers.

"She was listening the only way she could," X said. "Through vibrations."

Her plum-colored gaze locked on Solo, and every muscle in his body tightened, clamping down on bone. The steady chatter of his companions faded as he drank her in. She wore a top and pants the same dark shade as the tire, and looked as though she'd stepped from *Biker Chick Weekly—Role Play Edition*. Her long, pale hair was sexily rumpled, her cheeks pink.

She stepped backward, away from him, finally disappearing around the corner.

He nearly shouted a denial. *Calm. Steady.* She would be back. He would tell her about her father's threat and gauge her reaction. He wouldn't ask her about the wedding. She would—

Return a few minutes later with food, causing the tension to drain from him. She had changed into white and now looked as if she'd stepped from a cloud. She'd brushed her hair, the strands glistening like molten gold. She had brushed her teeth, too. He could smell the mint of her toothpaste. She tossed a burlap sack through the bars and onto his lap, the scent of buttered toast and freshly cooked syn-sausage wafting to his nose.

She reached into a pant pocket to withdraw a rag. He waited. When she stretched out her arm to toss it through the bars, he leapt into action, scooting from the far end of the cage to the front, his own arm extending.

Contact. His fingers locked around her wrist.

She gasped. Her eyelids flipped up, and her gaze landed on him.

"Let me go," she demanded.

When the softness of her skin delighted him? When the heat she emitted blended with his own? "Or what?"

Heart-shaped lips pursed in the most adorable pout. "Or you'll lose your man parts."

Something cold pressed against his thigh, and he glanced down. She had positioned a blade at the hem of his loincloth.

X clapped at her daring.

Dr. E growled.

"Nice move," Solo said, oddly proud of her.

She sighed, a little dejected, and said, "I doubt I could actually go through with my threat. I really just carry the weapon to scare people away."

Oh, honey. That's not something you ever admit to your opponent.

As innocent as she appeared, though, her opponents could probably guess her lack of malicious intent.

He released her. "I just wanted your attention."

"Well, you've got it." She looked left, right, and sheathed the weapon. "But it's too dangerous for us to talk."

"I'll know if anyone heads this way. You'll have plenty of time to hide."

Silence as she pondered his claim.

"I promise," he said.

Another moment passed before she nodded.

"Vow it. Vow that you'll stay." He couldn't bear the thought of watching her walk away again. Not yet. "Just for a little while. As long as it's safe."

Her nose scrunched up as she said, "But I just did."

"I want the words. Please."

"Please. Wow. I don't think I've ever heard that word from another person's lips. Not without a request for freedom, that is. But okay, all right," she said. "I vow it."

He waited for any type of reaction from her, but again . . . she never gave one. Not so much as a single twitch. Were the words truly not bonding to her?

"Are you getting married?" He hadn't meant to ask—actually hated himself for asking—but there it was. He couldn't take it back. And didn't want to.

"Not if I can help it," she replied, chin lifting.

"Tell me why—"

"I'll talk about anything but that," she said.

Fury now radiated from her. Fury and more of that fear he'd noticed before, mixed with a healthy amount of desperation and resignation.

Very well. "Are you eating?" he asked. He'd felt the slenderness of her wrist, was as concerned as he was enthralled.

"Since the vow didn't include honesty, I'll say yes."

"So you aren't?"

Her shoulders sagged. "I am. A little," she admitted in that velvety voice of hers.

"Eat more." He lifted the bag she'd tossed at him. During his leap, it had fallen to the side. He dug inside and found the bread.

"I'll be okay," she said. "You need the nourishment."

He heard the hunger in her voice, and saw the way she watched the bread as though hypnotized. She'd been giving him the food from her own plate, he realized, probably not wanting to be caught grabbing extra and announce her purpose. He could barely process that information as he eased the toast to her mouth. Only his parents had ever placed his welfare above their own.

Vika shook her head, long strands of that curling gold hair dancing around her. When that failed to dissuade him, she arched backward. "You first. You're recovering from all those injuries."

"I'm more recovered than you realize."

"You're definitely stronger, and you're definitely a fast healer, but no one—"

He turned.

She gasped with amazement. "Your back."

There were a few scabs remaining, a few scars, but other than that, the skin was mended.

She reached out, traced her finger over one of the ridges. The touch electrified him, and he moaned. He . . . he . . . wanted more, wanted that finger all over him, everywhere. Just as soft, just as gentle. Just as tender.

"Well, I still want you to eat," she said somewhat shakily, as if the connection had affected her, too.

He forced himself to face her. *Control.* He wasn't sure how long they would be alone, and she needed to eat. He bit off a tiny piece from the corner of the bread, then once again placed it at her mouth—making sure her lips encountered the same spot as his own.

A cute little nibble, revealing the barest hint of teeth.

Such an innocent action, yet so lovely to watch.

Color bloomed all the brighter in her cheeks as she chewed, swallowed.

"Another," he commanded.

She obeyed.

He liked this, he realized. Liked feeding her and knowing he was helping her, even in so small a way. "Another."

"It's so good," she said, and claimed a much bigger bite.

"Isn't this nice?" Dr. E sneered.

Solo glanced over at him, intending to give him a dark enough look to send him fleeing in fear, but the sight of Dr. E stunned him. In a matter of seconds, the little man had lost weight, his cheeks becoming gaunt, and his pale skin more pallid than before.

"Do you have any idea how ridiculous you look, shoving your gigantor hand at her tiny face? Why don't you act like a man and remove her thumb, then bust free? Huh, huh? That's what you wanted in the beginning, isn't it?"

"Don't listen to him," X said, and Solo glanced over at him. "His only purpose is to ruin your life. Tell me you've realized that by now."

Where Dr. E had wilted, X had bloomed. *In a matter of seconds*, he had gained muscled weight, his cheeks filling out, his skin now glowing brightly. Was Solo's happiness strengthening X the way X had strengthened him all these years? Was that same happiness weakening Dr. E? Yes, he realized a moment later. It was. And it made sense. His worry had always caused the opposite.

How strange to think he could be happy—something he'd never really experienced before, even with his beloved parents, for he'd always felt as if something important were missing from his life—while trapped in a cage. But he was.

"This girl has only brought trouble to his door," Dr. E groused. "How is using her to escape wrong?"

"Hurting someone else, no matter who they are or what they've done, just to get what you want," X replied, "is what's wrong."

"Get off your pedestal!"

"Why? The view is better."

"Shut up," Solo snapped.

"But—" Dr. E began.

"Now!"

Fear returned to Vika's plum eyes, darkening the purple to a sickly black. "If that's the way you're going to act, I'm out of here!"

"I wasn't talking to you, you have my word," he rushed out before she could take a single step. *Must do better.* So easily frightened, this woman, though she immediately bucked up and issued some kind of verbal attack. He liked that about her. She had courage, and though she might be knocked around, she would never stay down.

"Well, then, who were you talking to?" she demanded. "I mean, *to whom* were you talking?"

Like he could really answer that. "I'm sorry for startling you," he said, and placed the toast at her mouth.

She chewed, swallowed—and asked the same question again.

Would she leave if he continued to refuse? "What if I said I was talking to an invisible man?" he asked, amazed he'd admitted that much. He was at enough of a disadvantage already, and not even Michael, John, or Blue knew about Dr. E and X.

"I might believe you," she replied, and she sounded sincere.

Shocking.

And a huge relief. He was glad he hadn't tried to lie. Eventually, even the smallest mistruth would catch up to a man, a tangled web of thorns that would leave him cut and bleeding. In fact, Solo had always told his mother the truth about everything, even her cooking. Not to be cruel, but because he had respected her too much to feed her an untruth.

A small smile lifted the corners of Vika's mouth.

Just as before, the smile lit her entire face. She looked as though she'd swallowed the sun. His heart banged against his ribs, his blood heated, and oh, he fought the urge to gather her in his arms and hold her. Just hold her.

"I think you're as weird as me," she said, then took another bite of the toast and motioned to him with a tilt of her chin. "Or is the proper phrasing as weird as I am? Anyway, your turn."

"I'm embarrassed for you," Dr. E said. "You should—"

"He told you to shut up!" X climbed up Solo's ear, stomped across his head, and jumped onto his left shoulder. He grabbed the once-beautiful blond by the ear and, as Dr. E yelped, disappeared.

I owe that man a lot more than another thank-you.

And the girl, if he was being honest. Solo took a bite of the toast. "I appreciate everything you've done for me, Vika."

Another smile, this one not quite as bright. "I wish I could do more."

"I don't want you to do more. I don't want you to risk yourself on my behalf again."

She blinked rapidly. "Are you trying to protect me? The girl who is not bound by shackles?"

"Yes. I vowed I would."

"And you always keep your promises, you said."

"Always."

The rest of the tension drained from her, and she said, "That is very sweet of you."

A female referring to him as "sweet." A novelty he quite enjoyed. But she hadn't promised not to risk herself, had she.

"So is your name really Solo?" she asked.

"It's Solomon, but my friends call me Solo." He should have given her the same Bob Fred alias he'd given Criss, but he liked the idea of his name spilling from those heart-shaped lips.

"And you're fine with me calling you that?"

"Yes." More than.

"Even though we're not friends?"

He nodded. A smoother man would have said something like "We are friends" or "I would love to be your friend," but the words would have sounded false coming from him. He didn't actually want to be her friend. He wanted to use her . . . he wanted to save her . . . and he wanted to have her.

She thought it over, nodded. "Very well. Solo."

Reality was far better than supposition. "About

Audra," he said, and she paled. "What do you know about her tattoos?"

Her head tilted to the side, her expression resigned. "She tried to use one against you, didn't she?"

"Yes."

"Matas taught her a little about black magic. Ever since, the spiders come to life and bite whomever she desires. And oh, it's painful. Makes you sick."

"You have been bitten?"

"A few times."

Strike three, Audra. "Listen, you're in trouble. Your father suspects you're the one who's been feeding me."

Her knees buckled, and she would have collapsed if he hadn't reached out and grabbed the hem of her T-shirt to steady her. How light she was. At her strongest, she would not be a match for his weakest.

"Can't I ever avoid a break?" she asked with a tremor.

Avoid a—Wait. "You mean *catch* a break."

"Why would I want to catch a break? You catch a ball. You break bones, homes, and hearts. And now, I must go."

Not yet. He wasn't ready. "Free me, Vika." The only thing he'd ever begged for was the lives of his adoptive parents, and that had gotten him nowhere. Still, he might beg for this. "Let me protect you better."

Her mouth opened, closed. Once again she shook her head. "I can't."

"You can."

"No. I'm sorry," she said, shaking her head all the

harder for emphasis. "And I know, I know. My refusal means you'll go back to being a rude little giant . . ."

Uh, that expression made absolutely no sense.

". . . and you'll start issuing death threats again, but I have to remain with the circus for a while longer. I just have to."

"Why? Jecis beats you. Why not leave him before he has a chance to hurt you again?"

"You don't understand. I can take a beating, I can, but if I leave before I've—just before," she said, stopping herself from admitting something she didn't want him to know, "Jecis will find me and kill me, *as well as* the otherworlders."

"You're his daughter." His precious. *His beloved,* Solo remembered, and had to grit his teeth to prevent himself from cursing. "He wouldn't kill you."

Another small smile, this one sad at the edges. "He wouldn't mean to. Wait. I take that back. Maybe he would. To Jecis, leaving the circus is the ultimate betrayal and deserves the ultimate punishment."

"But you want to?" He gripped the bars. "Leave, I mean?"

Hope glittered in her eyes, and she nodded. "I do."

His own sense of hope bloomed. "One day, this circus will be destroyed. Jecis has hurt too many people not to be hurt himself. That's a spiritual law, and spiritual laws are always enforced. The longer you stay, the more likely you are to be caught in the crosshairs."

"One day," she parroted hollowly.

"Yes. Free me, Vika, and that day can be today. I'll take care of him. He'll never hurt you again."

Shame obliterated what remained of the hope. "I can't let you do that."

"Why not? Do you love him?" he asked.

"When he's an evil man with no goodness left inside him?"

That wasn't exactly an answer.

"No," she finally said, "but he's also my father. I can't. I just can't. And besides that, you would have to kill Matas, too. Otherwise, he would come after us and the same fate would befall us all."

Solo would happily take care of Matas.

"And *then*, after both men are dead, and I have no means of protection," she said, "you would leave me out there in the big, bad world to fend for myself, penniless, helpless. You wouldn't mean to, I know. I can tell you're a good man. But you have a life out there, one that doesn't include the zoo owner's daughter, and you would eventually cut me loose."

"No—"

"You would also sentence the other captives to death," she interjected. "They would be slaughtered simply to punish me."

"I would come back for them."

"Yes, but would you make it in time? No, you can't guarantee that." She turned her head away, trying to end the conversation the only way she could.

Solo latched onto her wrist, giving it the barest squeeze to bring her attention back to him. "I will leave your family alone if that's what you want." He would hand them over to Michael, and the end result would be the same, but she didn't need to know that. "I'll release the otherworlders and take you with me, and you'll never have to fend for yourself. I have money. I can take care of you for the rest of your life, if you so desire."

Her gaze searched his features. "I . . . I actually think you mean that," she said.

"I do. And I'm willing to vow it."

"Don't," she said with a shake of her head. "I don't want you morally bound or anything like that, when there's a huge problem with your plan."

"And that is?" he said, urgency riding him hard. He would have a solution, whatever it was, and she would free him. She had to free him.

"The cuffs."

"They aren't actually a problem. I have a friend who can remove them." John could remove any kind of shackles. *If he's still alive.* The thought irritated him. He was. And that was final.

"You'll lose your hands."

"They'll grow back."

A moment passed. She shook her head, as if his words were too odd to keep inside her head. "The real question is, can you reach your friend before Jecis finds you? And what about the other prisoners in the meantime?"

He popped his jaw. He had no immediate solution for that, which meant he had to try another angle. "Do you like the life you lead? Hiding under mobile homes? Sneaking food to prisoners?"

Growling low in her throat, she slapped at the bars. "No, but I have a plan. A plan that will work better than yours, thank you. I just have to wait for the perfect time."

Ah. Her mysterious plan. "There will never be a more perfect time than this moment. I'm here. I'm willing." He spread his arms to draw her attention to a hard-won strength far superior to her father's. "I will do what I say I will do. I will save you, protect you. And why would you care about the others, anyway? They hate you."

Back up went her chin. "Here's a little lesson you should probably take to heart. Anyone who returns hate for hate is no better than my father, and I won't trade one monster for another."

How dare she compare him to Jecis! Even though he had done the same to himself. He wanted to yell at her.

He also wanted to hug her.

He definitely wanted to kiss her.

"If you walk away from me, Vika, you condemn me to death." A stretching of the truth, and a definite manipulation, but why not? Everything else had proved futile.

The flush drained from her cheeks, leaving her as pallid as Dr. E. "I spend every spare second searching for the key to the cuffs. I have for years, in fact. I'll find it. I *will* free you."

The announcement floored him. For years, she'd said. She'd been trying to help the captives *for years*.

Solo reached through the bars. She flinched, but didn't dart away. With anyone else, he would have taken such a reaction personally and raged. But with her, with her past, he knew better and allowed himself to trace his fingertip along the curve of her jaw. So soft, so smooth.

Her breathing quickened—but she still didn't leave.

He wasn't going to convince her to do what he wanted. He knew that now. She was too stubborn, too blinded by the merits of her plan. And there *were* merits. There just weren't enough.

He would have to join her. For now. "I've studied the cuffs. The key is probably metal, with a slender belly and two fat ends. Look for something in the shape of the letter eight."

"I will," she rasped, and licked her lips. "And thank you."

His arm fell to his side. If he continued to touch her, he would give in to his urge to cup her nape and tug her forward. To steal the air from her lungs. If that happened, he would stop listening for her father.

She backed away from him. "This is our last day in the city. After the last show, we'll pack up and leave. Jecis will keep you here, wanting you nearby during your first trip. I'll return to you when I can." A nervous laugh left her. "*If* I can."

With that cryptic statement, she spun and raced from the area, never glancing back.

"Why—" he began, only to slam his lips together. She couldn't hear him.

He punched the bars. He hated his captivity, yes, but deep down, a part of him hated watching that woman walk away more.

Fifteen

〜⚬〜

A man of understanding will acquire wise counsel.
—PROVERBS 1:5

VIKA WEIGHED HER OPTIONS. Her father suspected she had been feeding Solo. He would question her, intimidate her, and he would discern the truth. There would be no hiding it; there never was, and she'd known that before she'd acted. But still she'd been unable to stop herself from helping the injured otherworlder. Even now, it wasn't a decision she regretted. He had warned her about what awaited her, despite the fact that she could have packed a bag and left him in the dust.

I should have freed him.

But . . . she didn't want to be without him. Somehow, he had become a safe haven.

He was so beautiful, more beautiful with every day that passed. And he was so sweet to her, so wonderfully protective.

Constantly she wondered what it would feel like to kiss him while he was awake, and then, to be kissed *by* him. Because he wanted her, not because he wanted something from her. In fact, all during their conversation she'd wondered.

Now she had to know. It was a need.

He was a need.

His scent, his gaze, his touch, his heat, the calluses on his hands. His smile, his frown, his wit, his kindness. She hadn't gotten over the fact that he'd used his body as a shield to save her from a bullet already meant for him.

Everything about him appealed to her.

Yes, she should have freed him—but she was still glad she hadn't. Not just for her selfish reasons, but because he was better off here, trapped, than out there, being hunted by her father.

If she'd thought, even for a second, that he could successfully hide from Jecis with those cuffs on his wrists, she would have done it, would have risked it. But no. He couldn't. No one could.

The best course was for her to stay here, take care of the otherworlders, and take whatever discipline her father dished out. It would hurt, it would humiliate her, but if Jecis beat her, the wedding would have to be delayed to give her time to recover. Time was all she needed. But oh, knowing what she'd have to endure caused a shudder of revulsion and fear to rock her.

She just . . . she had to find that key. At least now she knew what to look for.

Vika changed into a soft, comfortable tee and flowing pants, something she could relax in while feeling as if her organs were nothing more than mush. She pulled on her most comfortable boots and reclaimed the knife she'd found in her mother's favorite trinket box a few years ago, only to stop, her attention caught on the beauty of the weapon.

The hilt was carved from mother-of-pearl and when held to the light glistened with all the colors of the rainbow. The blade was currently hidden, but when released was thin and silver and sharp.

How could something so lovely hurt so absolutely?

Her mother used to polish the metal with loving strokes, but only when Jecis was absent. Three weeks before her death, she had glanced up at Vika and smiled a little crazily. *One day he'll push me too far, and I'll kill him. We won't ever have to be afraid again, will we, princess?*

One day.

Now Vika laughed without humor. "One day" was the answer to everything, wasn't it.

"How could you leave me with him, Momma?" she whispered. He'd only grown worse over the years, more and more of his heart rotting and his soul withering. And the truly sad thing was, he had no idea he'd become a monster. He still considered himself fair and just. "How could you pick another man over me?"

With a sigh, Vika stuffed the blade inside her pocket.

Wisdom will save you from the ways of wicked men, and arming yourself for war is wise.

The voice startled her, and she spun. A swift search proved she was still alone, and her spine lost its sudden rigidity. Alarm was replaced by anticipation. Not an intruder, after all, but the return of the good . . . whatever he was.

"Who are you?" she asked. "*What* are you?"

Last time, he'd ignored her. This time, he answered. *My name is X, and I am your . . . helper.*

X. "As in, X marks the spot?"

Exactly.

"Just how are you supposed to help me, X?"

You tell me. You summoned me.

Uh, no. No, she hadn't. "I think I would remember something like that."

But you do not think I can feel your torment?

Her emotions were so strong she was projecting them into the other realm? "You mentioned war," she said. "You seem so, well, gentle. Shouldn't you have a problem with the use of force?"

Against wickedness? May it never be!

Good point. But, "I don't want war," she said. "I want peace." Finally. For once.

How do you think peace is won?

War, but . . . "How do you think people are lost?"

And you're not lost right now?

Her motions were jerky as she anchored her thick mass of hair into a ponytail. "I'm alive."

And you like your life?

Solo had asked her the very same thing. "What can I do to change it? Tell me, please, because I'm certainly doing everything I can and having no luck."

Trust.

"Who?"

Silence.

"Who?" she demanded.

Again silence.

Annoyed by such an abrupt end to their conversation, she stomped from the vehicle. Behind her, the door shut and locked automatically.

She was supposed to remain in her trailer again today, but she wanted to deal with her father rather than run, and she wanted to get it over with. Waiting would only make things worse.

The sun was bright, glaring. In an hour, the circus would open. Right now performers bustled about, setting up shop while trying to pack up everything they wouldn't need. The day would be hectic. And oh, was Solo in for a shock. When the circus left the outskirts of New Atlanta, he would meet a whole new crop of monsters—and he would grow to *love* the bars that contained him.

Don't think about that right now. She might lose her nerve.

Vika raced out of the sectioned-off area where the performers lived and through the games and rides. First she bypassed the big wheel. Soon, each basket would twirl round and round and upside down as a performer swung from the bar stretched across each cart. None of the patrons would realize those performers were anchored to the bars with flesh-colored cuffs and weren't in any danger of flying to their deaths.

Next she passed the roller coaster that would shoot through man-made tunnels decorated to resemble different planets, each one filled with bright lights, mystical holograms, and spooky mist. Only, the mist wasn't there for visual effect, as the humans always assumed. It was there for *physical* effect. In the particles was a small dose of adrenaline, making the ride seem more exciting than it actually was.

After that, the bumper cars came into view. An electric shock would be delivered to every driver who was hit. For some reason, people loved watching their fellow humans jerk against the sting, loved hearing the ensuing curses and growls, loved being chased at high speed, where revenge was eventually taken.

She turned a corner and entered the food court, the scent of fried bread and meats wafting through the air, followed by caramel and citrus. Once she cleared the canopy overhead and snaked around another corner, the games Jecis used to earn even more cash from the otherworlders who had already lost their appeal came into view. Pin the Tail on the Wedlg, Rakan Piñata, and the Delensean Rack-and-Sack were the current crowd favorites.

Tears beaded at the backs of Vika's eyes. Hardly anyone peeled back that layer of "fun" to peek at the seedy underbelly of the circus. The tricks, the lies, the cruelty. People came and they played and they laughed. They watched the performances in Big Red and marveled, captivated by feats no human—or otherworlder— should be able to do. And then they left, totally ignorant to the evil they had just supported.

Finally the main tent came into view, a big, red monstrosity her father had patterned after the circuses of old, and Vika tripped over her own feet. Jecis was inside, preparing for the first show.

Trust, X suddenly said. *Set the otherworlders free. Walk away. Today. Now. This minute. Never look back.*

How she would have loved that. "If I do, they'll only be captured again."

Trust.

"You don't understand."

Don't I?

Vika reached the entrance and swept inside. Bleachers filled every inch of space that wasn't used by the center ring, and of course, the hidden space in back where the performers changed. In the ring were spotlights, poles, wires, nets, equipment, boulders, and smoke machines.

As a little girl, she had dreamed of having an act of her own and making her father proud. Now, she was very glad he'd always denied her request, too afraid someone would see her, want her, and take her, even back then. To be stared at, judged, and critiqued by strangers? No, thank you.

A hard hand latched onto her forearm and forced her to turn. Mini-bombs of fear exploded through her when her gaze landed on Matas, who was glaring down at her, a blazing fire in his eyes.

"What are you doing here, Vika? You're supposed to be in your trailer."

I will not cower. "Have you forgotten rule number one?" she forced herself to snap.

A cruel grin lifted the corners of his mouth. "We're going to be married at the end of the month, which means your rules are out and mine are in. And do you want to know the first one? You do what I say, when I say, or I hurt you in ways you cannot even imagine. And don't forget you owe me for letting Kitten go unscathed."

There's still time to leave, X said.

I can handle this, she assured herself, even as her blood chilled in her veins. "My father will not be amused. He doesn't want you to mistreat me."

"Actually, I think he'll change his mind when he sees this." Matas held out his free hand. A small, black device rested in the center of his palm. He used his thumb to press the button in the center, and a blue screen crystallized in the air.

Colors flickered inside that screen, a picture soon forming.

Vika, inside Solo's cage. Vika, bathing him. Vika, kissing him.

Leave, Vika. Leave now, X beseeched. *Run to Solo.*

Oh, sweet mercy. She wanted to, she really did, but she had to contain this situation first. If her father ever saw this, Solo would be killed. "D-don't show him, Matas. Please."

His fingers closed over the device, and the screen vanished. "I hid a camera in the zoo a while back. I've been watching you, and I know you've been giving the animals treats they were never meant to have. Treats your father paid for. I always let that slide, but this . . . no. I can't."

Her knees shook, threatening to buckle. "I'll run away," she threatened. "If you tell him, I'll leave. I'll help the authorities find the circus and shut it down, and you'll end up without a job."

Vika, please. Listen to me. Never try to bargain with evil.

"You do *not* threaten me," Matas growled—just before he backhanded her.

Her head whipped to the side, her cheek stinging. The taste of blood coated her tongue. Another beating, and from a male who repulsed her? No. No! She wouldn't let that happen.

She grabbed her blade and struck, slamming the tip as deep into Matas's side as possible. Maybe he roared, maybe he didn't, but he did stumble away from her. And as he stood there panting and gaping at her, she looked down at the crimson-soaked blade. Horror washed through her, her blood no longer cold but frigid, little ice crystals making her feel heavy, achy.

She'd just stabbed someone. She'd just hurt someone in the worst possible way. Maybe she'd even killed him. Yes, she'd done it to protect herself, but it was still something her father would have done.

I can't be like him. I just can't.

Oh, Vika, X said sadly. *I'm sorry.*

"You're going to pay for that." Scowling, Matas thundered toward her, closing the distance before she could back away. He slammed his meaty fist into the side of her head, knocking her to the ground.

Another impact, her brain rattling against her skull.

He punched her a second time. And just like that, it was lights out for Vika.

Sixteen

When you pass through the waters, I will be with you.
And through the rivers, they will not overflow you.
—ISAIAH 43:2

SOLO HEARD THE TWO men arguing before he saw them, his ears twitching as he listened. He'd expected X, who had popped in a few minutes ago to cryptically say, "Control yourself, for she has need of your aid, not your temper," before vanishing. But no, this wasn't X.

"I'll kill you, Matas."

He recognized the harshness of the voice, knew it belonged to Jecis.

"I told you I was sorry."

"That doesn't make it better!"

"I showed you the video. You know what she did."

"And it's a problem, but it's *my* problem. You should have come to me. Should have let me handle it. Now—" A wild roar of rage Solo had heard only once before—from himself, the day he'd discovered his parents' decomposed bodies. "You were to get her pregnant, make her want to stay, give her something to do. The look in her eyes lately, just like before, when she—but you ruined everything!"

Matas was to impregnate . . . Vika? Despite the fact that she disliked the brute?

"I gave you a gift," Jecis continued shakily, "my most treasured possession, and you broke it. I should exile you from my circus."

"She stabbed me, and I reacted," Matas said, his own voice shaky. "It will never happen again. Like I said, I'm sorry."

"Not accepted! You nearly killed her with those blows."

"Let me take care of her. I'll make her better with my magic."

Her. She. They had better not be discussing Vika.

"You're not touching her again. If any other man had put me in this situation . . . if any other man had hurt my baby like this . . ."

His baby. They *were* discussing Vika. Solo didn't hear the rest of the conversation. He was on his feet and squeezing the bars a second later, dread barraging him, right along with fury and desperation . . . so much desperation . . . But he couldn't act on a single emotion, not with the cuffs shooting debilitating drugs into his system.

What had been done to her? How badly had she suffered? Would she survive?

Questions, questions, so many questions formed, but one fact crystallized: He would repay the one responsible. Not because he'd decided to use Vika to escape. Not because he'd realized she was his only hope. But because. Just because.

He was quite certain vengeance would finally feel good.

"Remain calm. Remember what I told you. She needs tenderness right now," X said, popping in and looking slightly weaker than before, his skin not quite as bright.

"Help her," he demanded.

"I tried, but I cannot help someone who doesn't want to be helped. No one can."

Finally Jecis and Matas stomped around a corner, entering his line of sight. Both men were scowling. Jecis cradled Vika in his arms. Vika, who looked like a broken doll.

Solo's knees almost gave out. Pale hair cascaded around her in tangled hunks. One arm hung limply. The other was smashed against Jecis's chest. Her face was smashed against his chest, as well, hiding any damage there.

The fury at last detonated, and he uttered a roar that rivaled Jecis's. Both men tripped over their own feet.

"Calm." X said. "You must stay calm."

The males were coming closer and closer to Solo's cage, so close their evil brushed against his skin. His heart hammered as though trying to drill a nail into one of his ribs. He'd never been one to enjoy his job, to take delight in snuffing out life, but he would have enjoyed and delighted this time.

"Calm."

It should have been easy for him. In his line of work, he'd seen the effects of domestic abuse a thousand times before, and had thought himself too hardened to ever care. He'd always told himself the people who stayed in that type of situation deserved what they got.

Now, having seen the bruises on Vika, learning she was deaf, knowing she had been raised in such an insular world, suspecting she had no idea there was something better out there . . .

But even if she had known, she would not have left the circus. He remembered what she'd said. *You would also sentence the other captives to death.*

She wanted them freed. She wanted them safe. Even at a terrible cost to herself.

Suddenly a puzzle piece slid into place, and a clear picture of her character began to form. She cared for her charges with all of her heart. Not just to assuage a guilty conscience, but because she placed others before herself. She stayed here, accepting her father's abuse, Matas's abuse, even the otherworlders' abuse, to save those under her supervision. And yes, there were probably other reasons, maybe even a thousand more, but the otherworlders were a big one, he was sure.

Even more miraculous, she understood why the otherworlders acted as they did and didn't hold a grudge. How could she, and still be willing to break the rules to distribute cookies and chocolates?

What kind of person could do that?

An answer immediately formed. The kind his mother would have loved.

A pang erupted in the center of his chest, deep and burning, probably leaving a scar. One he welcomed.

"What did you do to her?" he shouted with an emotion he'd never before used. An emotion he couldn't even name. It was too hot for mere fury and too cold for something as controlled as calculation, springing from a place deep inside him, where instinct proved to be the dominant force.

Jecis stopped a few feet away, huffing and puffing with his own rage. "You. What have you done to my daughter, beast? How have you bewitched her?"

"Give her to me," Solo demanded.

"Don't you dare." Matas, who was clutching his bleeding side, opened his mouth to say something. Shadows rose from him, high and higher, reaching toward Jecis . . . but the misty skull hiding under Jecis's skin turned—without Jecis moving an inch—and snapped its teeth. The shadows retreated and Matas closed his mouth.

"She deserves better than the likes of you two," Solo snarled.

Matas leapt forward, grabbed the bars, and shook the cage. "Keep talking, I dare you. I'll do even worse to you, you—"

Moving faster than either man could track, Solo closed the distance, wrapped his fingers around both of the man's wrists and squeezed. In seconds, the bones were crushed.

Matas howled, sending black birds scattering from their perches on top of the motor home. "Stop!"

"When I'm done," Solo growled, and he definitely wasn't done. He twisted one of Matas's arms, forcing the man to spin around or lose the limb, and slammed the lower part against the bars, breaking those bones as well.

This time, Matas screamed.

Solo still wasn't done. He jerked and slammed the

upper part of the arm against the bars, breaking the bones there, too. Matas released another scream, this one high-pitched.

The entire tussle lasted less than three seconds.

Solo could have reached out and raked his claws across the man's jugular. He definitely would have, if he hadn't feared Vika would be penalized for his actions.

Tears leaked down Matas's cheeks, and his knees buckled. But the man didn't fall—he couldn't. Solo kept hold of his arm, applying pressure to each of the new wounds.

"P-please," Matas begged.

Had he made Vika beg before he'd hit her?

Solo lifted the male's arm a few inches higher.

As if she sensed the tension, a moan rose from her. It was the first noise she'd made, and one that proved she lived, that she was still in pain.

"Give the girl to me," Solo repeated. "I would never hurt her."

"Please . . . please," Matas said.

Teeth bared with masculine aggression, Jecis said, "Oh, I'll give her to you all right. She thinks she wants you, and a little alone time with you should change her mind, teach her better, and make her appreciate what she has."

Without hesitation, Solo placed both hands in the air, palms out. Matas collapsed into a groaning heap, cradling his arms to his chest and attempting to slither away.

"Vika," Solo said. "Give her to me. Now."

"No," Matas managed to shout past his sobs. "She's mine! You said—"

"Silence!" Jecis boomed. "I have made my decision, and it will stand. Twice she has chosen the animal over you, and so I will give her what she thinks she wants. And you," he said to Solo. "I'm placing my very heart in your hands. You will guard it."

Vika was not the male's heart. A man guarded the treasures of his heart, fawned over them, placed their welfare above his own. Jecis had done none of those things.

"He's a beast," Matas cried. "He'll maul her. Look at what he did to me!"

Ignoring him, Jecis said to Solo, "If she dies, you die. If you injure her in any way, I will injure you a thousand times worse. You are only to scare her. To make her hate you."

He was done talking. He wanted the girl. "Give! Now!"

"Open the cage, Matas," Jecis demanded. "You've still got one working arm, yes? After that, change the lock. I don't want Vika able to set herself free during the solar flare."

Murmuring, still crying, Matas lumbered to his feet.

Every muscle Solo possessed tensed, his body readying to jolt into action the moment the lock disengaged. He would grab Vika, and he would run. He would get her to safety, and he would return. He would save the otherworlders, just as she wanted, and he would destroy her family, just as she didn't. Or hadn't. Maybe she'd changed her mind.

Only, the now glaring man pushed the button that caused the cuffs to pump him with sedatives, and strength abandoned him in an instant. His arms and legs became too heavy to move, and black dots winked through his eyes.

"Touch her," Matas snarled, even as he whimpered in pain, "and I'll slice you into pieces."

"Enough," Jecis said, closing the distance and peering into Solo's eyes. "When the solar flare hits, you'll discover there are monsters worse than you out there. They'll come for you, and they'll try to eat you. Keep Vika in the center of the cage, and they won't be able to reach her. You, on the other hand . . . you're so big, I bet they'll be able to get you no matter where you're lying. You'll have to fight them." He grinned, but there was no amusement to the expression. "That should be just the thing to scare her and keep her from ever wanting anything to do with you."

Solo cared nothing for the warning. He collapsed, saying, "Will . . . kill . . . you both . . ."

Eyelids splitting apart, Solo sat up with a jolt. Residual sparks of fury blazed in his chest, each one serving as a reminder. Vika. Beaten. Carried into the cage. His to save. He twisted—and found her lying on her back on the opposite side, still, too still.

Despite the aches and pains in his body—new aches and pains that proved he had not imagined Jecis setting Vika down and giving Solo a beating of his own—he scrambled over to her.

There were two cuts in her bottom lip. One was from before, and it had opened up, and the other was new. But that was it, the only damage that he could see. For her to sleep this deeply, to have moaned so thickly, there had to be more. He gently ran his fingers over her scalp, and felt two egg-size bumps. Between one heartbeat and the next, he'd partially morphed.

As gently as possible, Solo checked her vitals and the intense trembling of his hands surprised him. At least her heartbeat was strong, granting him a measure of relief. As X had said, she would survive.

He should wake her up. She needed to remain alert for the next six hours. At least. But only if Jecis hadn't given her any of the new medications available for just such a human head injury. Solo hated that he didn't know.

For once, X didn't appear with an answer or an encouragement in a time of need and Dr. E did not appear to tell him why he should be angrier. As if he needed any help with that.

How he wished he possessed the ability to heal others, as Corbin Blue did, taking her injuries into himself. Or, like John No Name, the ability to hypnotize with his voice, forcing people to do anything he wished. But no. The Allorians apparently came with many flaws, and very few benefits.

He glanced around. Night had fallen. His cage hadn't yet been moved, so Jecis's trailer was still in front of him. No one was outside. Which was strange. The circus was supposed to be packing up, moving to a new location. There should have been a ton of activity.

In the far corner of the cage, he found medicines, bandages, a blanket, bottles of water, and food. As gently as before, he doctored Vika's lip, then folded the blanket to put it under her head. Only once did she make a noise, and that noise was a low, mewling whimper.

"Vika," he said. "Wake up for me, honey." He caressed her cheek. "Come on."

Another moan, but she blinked open her eyes. They were iced over, glassy. "Solo?"

Good. This was good. She knew him; that part of her memory was intact. "I'm here."

"My head hurts."

"I know."

"And I'm tired."

"Did your father pour a sweet-tasting liquid down your throat before carting you to my cage?"

"I don't—" A pause as her features scrunched. "Wait. Yes. He did."

"Sleep, then."

"Thank you," she said with a soft sigh. Her head lolled to the side.

He traced the delicate curve of her jaw. He'd found her beautiful before, but now, knowing what he did about her, feeling the warmth of her skin surround him, inhaling the delicacy of her scent, mint and jasmine, she was exquisite. She was everything he'd ever wanted in his woman, and everything he'd never been able to have.

X claimed she belonged to him. Despite everything, Solo wanted to believe that. He no longer wanted to fight the knowledge.

And he wanted to believe she would be happy to wake up—really wake up—and find herself inside his cage, that she would not scream and cry and beg for mercy. After all, there was a big difference between seeing to an animal's care and getting close enough to be bitten.

His ears began to twitch. Finally, sound. Mumbling. Solo looked around, but saw nothing. Still the mumbling continued. And it was nearby. Frowning, he stood and approached the bars. He found Jecis on top of his trailer, meaty arms spread.

Lightning flashed in the sky.

Jecis's voice rose in volume. The wind kicked up several notches. More lightning flashed, this time arcing toward the human, as though drawn to him. Maybe he would die, Solo hoped, but the moment the bolt made contact, the man's body seemed to expand, black shadows bursting from him. A thick white fog formed at the edges of the shadows and rolled from the trailer to the cage. Solo listened, heard a whoosh of air, the patter of footsteps and slam of a door. Jecis must have gone inside.

Next he heard the crackle of flames. Even felt the heat. He heard the soft rustle of shuffling footfalls, and there were enough to form an army.

Uneasy, he stood guard. The fog began to thin . . . thin . . . and then *everything* changed—though nothing was for the better.

Seventeen

You will not be afraid of the terror by night,
or of the arrow that flies by day.
—PSALM 91:5

A WASTELAND APPEARED.

Solo looked around. He could still see Jecis's trailer, but it was now surrounded by barren hills littered with dead trees, fat insects flying from one gnarled branch to another. There were fire pits in every direction, yellow-gold flames dancing in the hot, dry wind.

The footsteps grew louder and louder in volume, until a crowd of men and women finally appeared, cresting over one of the hills. They tripped and raced in his direction.

The monsters Jecis had mentioned.

Solo had traveled the world, had seen terrible races, but never anything like *this*. The creatures were humanoid, with sagging, paper-thin skin that smelled of rot. Worms slithered along their scalps, and their eyes were dark and soulless—if they had eyes, that is. Some were blind, their sockets empty. But one thing every creature had in common, he realized as they converged on the cage: a hunger for prey. Moaning, snapping their too-sharp teeth, they reached through the bars in a desperate bid to grab him.

Moving quickly, Solo slid Vika and the supplies to the center. Then, for the first time since his capture, he put his claws and teeth to good use. He slashed, and limbs fell. Blood sprayed. He bit, and had to spit out fingers. A foul taste coated his tongue.

Adrenaline surged through him, burning, blistering, causing the drugs in the cuffs to activate. His motions slowed, but he managed to remain on his feet. Either he was developing an immunity or his determination was too great to be denied.

For hours he continued to fight, his arms bruised from banging against the bars so many times, his shins cut and bleeding, but his opponents continued to drop like stones in an ocean, so the pain was worth it. And yet, the moment he felled one of the creatures, two more stepped up to the plate. How long would he be forced to do this without any visible results?

The battle raged so long two suns began to rise in the burnt-orange, smoke-filled sky. He renewed his efforts, attacking with more fervor, desperate to protect the woman who had been placed in his care. Only, he next swiped and bit at air. The monsters were backing away from him, hissing as though their skin was too sensitive to tolerate more than the barest hint of light. They dragged their fallen with them, leaving only blood behind.

Solo stood in place for the longest while, waiting, panting, but the monsters never returned.

What *were* those things?

There was no need to rack his brain about what they'd wanted. He knew. Him and Vika, a smorgasbord of delicious.

Vika.

His muscles and bones protested as he rushed to her side. There were specks of fresh blood on her cheeks, but none belonged to her. She still slept, completely unaware of the turmoil around her, with no new injuries, and relief speared him.

He used the bottle of enzyme spray to clean her, then himself, then the cage. He didn't want her to wake up and see a single hint of devastation—or fear him any more than necessary. He wouldn't play her father's game. All the while, he kept track of the seconds ticking by, needing to know how much time would lapse between the light and the dark, the peace and the chaos, just in case the monsters returned.

He paced, swatting at the insects brave enough to try and bite him.

He watched the hills.

One hour passed, two, three . . . eight, nine. He woke Vika every sixty minutes to check her vitals, and she always told him that her head hurt and she wanted to sleep. He always let her.

At the tenth hour, the suns began to descend. Within minutes, footsteps could be heard shuffling in the distance. Moans and groans arose. The monsters once again crested the hill. Only, they were now hungrier and far more determined to dine, chomping their teeth with more force, trying to slink through the bars to reach him.

Rather than fight them, he tested the parameters of the cage by stretching out beside Vika and using his body to shield her. Jecis had hoped they would still be able to reach him, but Jecis had hoped in vain. And Solo liked this *much* better.

Perhaps this land wasn't so bad, after all.

For what seemed the most painful of eternities, Vika drifted from consciousness to unconsciousness, vaguely aware that someone was carefully tending to her needs. But that couldn't be right. No one had ever carefully tended her needs.

Oh, her father always appointed someone to bathe and bandage her after a beating, but usually that some-one was Audra, who would only sit in her trailer, paw through her treasures, or torment her with the spiders.

Was she imagining this?

No. No, she couldn't be. The sandalwood scent she'd added to Solo's enzyme spray mixed with the unique fragrance of peat smoke he emitted, penetrating the stupor around her mind. Solo must be with her. That would certainly explain why she kept imagining that she was talking to him. Well, she wasn't imagining, she realized.

They were together, and the knowledge relieved her—but it also confused her. *How* were they together? She needed to wake up, find out.

Sleep, X whispered. *I'm doing what I can to enhance the medicine your father gave you, and I'll do better work without any interference from you, thank you very much.*

She . . . remembered that he'd tried to help her inside the tent, with Matas. Yes. That's right. Matas had hit her, and—she wasn't sure what had happened after that. She only knew she had failed to listen to X and she had suffered. She wouldn't make the same mistake.

"I will. Thank you," she said, and drifted off.

An eternity later . . . or perhaps mere minutes . . . the darkness faded from Vika's mind and a fantastical dream took shape around her. She stood inside a shaded courtyard, jewel-toned flowers blooming in every direction, interspaced between towering white columns. On her right was a tall, muscled man she'd never before seen. He had dark hair and eyes the color of the purest ocean. His skin was a deep, rich shade of bronze, flecked with shimmers of gold. He wore a bright white robe and held a double-edged sword.

On her left was another robe-wearing male, and though he, too, was tall and muscled, he lacked the first male's beauty. Pale, tangled hair shagged around a face with hollowed cheekbones and chapped lips. His skin was chalk white, and his eyes so light a green they would have reminded her of diamonds set inside polished jade if they had possessed any kind of sparkle. Instead, they were dull, lifeless. He was without a weapon.

Heart slamming against her ribs, she backed away from both. "Am I dead?"

Both males faced her.

"You're here," the dark-haired one said, motioning

to the garden, "and you see me." There was a layer of surprise in his tone. "Not even my charge has come here, and no one but him has ever before seen me."

"That means you can see me, too, can't you, pretty girl?" said the blond, grinning a siren's grin despite his ragged appearance. "Let's make out to celebrate." He reached for her.

Just before contact she could not avoid, the other giant batted his hand away. "I will not allow you to harm her, fiend."

Though the blond hissed, he didn't make another move toward her.

She recognized their voices. The good. And the evil.

"Pay no attention to him. I am the one called X, by the way, and I have been helping you as much as I'm able." The dark-haired male offered her a warm smile. "You are not dead. You live. You had a lot of internal damage from all these years with your father, but you are now healing quite nicely."

X. The good. "Thanks to you," she told him.

"And Solo."

Solo. Her gaze swept the area. There was an alabaster bench a few feet away, but it was empty. "Is he here?"

"No. As I said, he has never traveled here."

Disappointment filled her. "Where's here?"

"Alloris. I am Solo's Altilium, and to protect him from rejection, I have kept him away, guarding him until he's ready."

She was more confused than ever.

"I'm called Dr. E," the blond interjected smoothly. He reminded her of her father, when Jecis spoke to the crowd inside the big red tent during a performance. A soothing tone meant to beguile, hiding a wealth of wickedness.

"He is *not* an Altilium," the other said, "but an Epoto."

"Am not." The blond offered her a smile as well, but his was far from warm. His was all teeth and no substance.

"I don't know what either of those things are." Wait. She had heard their voices. Not just inside her mind, like before, but through her ears. Ears that had not worked in years. How was . . . why had . . . this wasn't possible. Was it?

Her entire body began to shake. How long had she dreamed of such a thing? Craved it with all of her being? How many times had she cried about the fact that she would never again have it? Countless. And yet here, now . . .

Joy burst through her, as intoxicating as wine. "What do you want from me?" she asked, then blinked. Her voice! She'd just heard her own voice, as well. It was different from what she remembered, more grown-up, deeper.

I truly can hear!

"I'm not sure I'll ever have an opportunity like this again," X said determinedly, "so I'm going to throw a lot at you. Solo is a good man, and he's attracted to you. You can grow that attraction. And if you do, he will allow you to take care of him, now and always, and he will allow you to stay with him, now and always. Isn't that what you wanted?"

"No, I—"

"Need to put his needs above your own, yes."

She frowned, finishing, "Want to live on my own."

"If you do as I suggest," X continued, as if she hadn't spoken, "he will do the same for you, I promise you, and you will be happier than you've ever been. He will take such good care of you."

"Don't listen to him," Dr. E replied, waving a dismissive hand through the air. "Solo is a terrible man. Just look at him. Hideous! And you're so beautiful. You deserve better, a handsome prince to come and save the day. Besides, putting someone else's needs above your own? Stupid!"

"Solo isn't hideous," Vika snapped. He had a rough, masculine beauty that wasn't apparent at first glance, but oh, by the second, third, and fourth, all she'd wanted to do was stare at him.

X grinned at her, a proud gleam in his eyes. "Solo can help you, Vika, and you can help him. But the choice is yours."

"Choice? There is no choice. If you place yourself in Solo's care, you will be placing yourself in a worse situation," Dr. E said. "Think about it. Solo landed himself in a cage, and you earned yourself a beating. You two really only know how to get into trouble. If you get together . . ." He shuddered.

She ignored Dr. E, saying to X, "I will set Solo free." The cuffs were still a problem, but she couldn't remain at the circus any longer. She just couldn't. At long last, her new life would begin.

As Dr. E sputtered, X said, "You will free him, yes, but then you will leave him to hide from the rest of the world, despite the fact that you are meant to be joined to him, and he to you."

Joined? "As long as he's in those cuffs, he's a target for Jecis."

"Even still, you will be stronger together, two halves of a whole." He was flickering in and out of view, his voice alternating between fading and growing in volume. "Tell me you'll stay with him, no matter what."

"I can't," she whispered. She would free him and strike out on her own. She would free the other otherworlders, too, but that was all she could promise. "I'm sorry."

Dr. E laughed with glee, the hunch in his shoulders suddenly less exaggerated. "Exactly what I wanted to hear."

Sadness tinged X's frown—and she noticed *his* shoulders had begun to stoop. "A wrong turn leads to a wrong end. You'll find yourself in a place you were never supposed to visit."

"So dramatic," Dr. E *tsk*ed under his tongue. With a wink, and a chortling, "I'll be seeing you again, cutie. Real soon," he disappeared.

X sighed and peered deep into her eyes. "Sleep," he said, and sighed.

"But I'm not . . . *tired*." Her eyes closed, and darkness swamped her mind. She knew nothing more.

In the ensuing days, Solo came to understand three very important facts.

Vika was naturally seductive.

She was instinctively alluring.

She was a freaking incurable disease.

She slept off and on, sometimes mumbling to herself about wrong turns and right turns and he swore he'd go on a no-mumbles diet as soon as this was over. It was just too adorable, and he'd reached his limit. And okay. Fine. It wasn't just the mumbles that had reduced him to this state. Every time the monsters had attacked, he'd lain beside her to shield her. The warmth of her breath had caressed his skin. The sweetness of her scent had filled his nose. The beat of her heart had synced with his, making him feel as if they were one being.

Everything had worked together to propel his need for her into a new stratosphere.

Every time she stirred, he would rush to her side to give food and water. She would eat, and he would eat, and he would start praying the monsters would return so that he had an excuse to cuddle her.

He needed to get himself under control. Because, despite the raggedness of his need, he wasn't going to let himself have her. He couldn't. He'd thought about it and had come up with one hundred and two reasons why he had to avoid kissing her, tasting her, stripping her, stroking her, and having her—and the thousand other things he'd imagined doing to her.

At the moment, though, he couldn't recall a single one of his reasons.

Well, no, that wasn't exactly true. He could think of one. She might not want him the same way he wanted her. Yes, she had once kissed him, but that could have been out of curiosity. Yes, she had fed him extra food, but that could have sprung from the goodness of her heart, not romantic feelings for him.

Now she would either feel obligated to him or hope to avoid upsetting him. She might let him do anything he wanted, but not out of passion.

He wanted her passion or nothing.

So, rather than plotting ways to romance her, he would be better served spending his time coming up with a new plan of escape. Yeah. That's what he'd do. And maybe he would stop wanting, needing, craving, wishing, and hoping for what could never be.

Eighteen

～◦～

Arise, my darling, my beautiful one, and come along.
—SONG OF SOLOMON 2:10

COOL WATER DRIBBLED ON Vika's lips and slid down her throat, and food soon followed. The actions dragged her out of the darkness and into the light. She blinked open her eyes.

Though her vision was clouded, she was able to see Solo looming over her, a streak of blood under his eye.

They really were together, she marveled.

He was holding a bottle to her lips. She swallowed what he poured, never having tasted anything so magnificent, she was sure. She wanted to close her eyes and savor, but had no desire to look away from Solo.

His dark hair was in utter disarray, the locks sticking out in spikes. He had his head down, his chin pressed into his sternum. His lashes were lowered, hiding the crystal clear blue of his eyes and fanning out as prettily as any peacock's tail. She had noticed the aristocratic slope of his nose and the sharp cheekbones the day she'd bathed him, but she had missed the lush, pink lips women would have paid a fortune to acquire.

He was rugged and capable and fearsome, and for

just a second—or two—she wished she had told X she would do whatever was necessary to stay with Solo, that she would place her life in his hands and trust him to keep her safe. Now and always.

Wait. X. Alloris. The Altilium, whatever that was. The dream that hadn't really been a dream, she realized now. As much time as she'd spent in her head throughout the years, she knew the difference between fantasy and reality, and there was no confusing the two in the light of day. She really had talked to X and Dr. E, the Epoto. They really were out there, somewhere, and they knew Solo.

X, who clearly loved him.

Dr. E, who clearly hated him.

Did Solo know they were there? That X considered him "a charge"?

Solo, who was so close she had only to reach out to touch him.

So few people realized there was another world around them, just as real.

"Hey, you," she said.

Only silence greeted her.

Sharp disappointment cut through her. Her ears had stopped working, and that meant she wouldn't be able to hear Solo's voice, either. And oh, how she would have loved to hear him. He would have a low baritone, she would bet. Low and rumbling. Sexy.

Solo glanced up, blinked in surprise. "You're awake."

Again, silence.

The disappointment intensified, but she easily beat it back. She was alive, and she was with the best man she'd ever met. What did she have to complain about?

"I am." She stretched her arms over her head, arched her back. The bones popped.

Heat exploded in Solo's eyes, the blue suddenly reminding her of living flames. The callused hand at her nape eased her to the ground. He moved away from her, taking his delicious body heat with him.

"How do you feel?" he asked.

Not as good as I did a few seconds ago. "Wonderful, thank you." Better than she had in years. "But how . . ." She scanned her surroundings. She was inside his cage, the bars all around her. Beyond them stretched the vast expanse of the Nolands. Random fires blazed, ribbons of thick smoke wafted, and green and black insects buzzed in every direction, even swarming a tree that had dared to survive, its limbs budding with life—but quickly withering.

Her father . . . he'd . . . he'd . . . *caged* her. The man responsible for her well-being, the man who professed to love her above all things, had placed her with one of his "animals" during a solar flare, leaving her vulnerable to the attack of the Nolanders.

She should not have been surprised, but she was. He'd done many, many terrible things to her, but this . . . Grief pierced her, wounding her far more than Matas's fist. Matas, who must have shown Jecis the video.

She'd known her father was cruel, had known he enjoyed lording his power over her and everyone else. Had known he thrilled in punishing anyone who defied him, but . . . but, she was his little girl. His princess. His beloved.

Well, this would make leaving the circus that much easier. *If* she was ever allowed outside the cage, she thought, fighting a wave of panic. Was she to be one of the sideshows now? Was this to be a life sentence?

Was she to be treated as a lowly animal?

Oh, sweet mercy. All these years, she'd done nothing to stop her father from locking up innocent people. People who had experienced these very emotions, but without any hope.

She couldn't free them while they still wore those cuffs, as she'd finally decided to do. She couldn't allow Jecis to find them and bring them back. She had to stay, no matter the pain inflicted upon her, and she had to continue her search for the key.

First, though, she would have to get out of the cage.

Sorry, X, but I can't pack up Solo and let him go just yet.

Solo tapped her gently on the shoulder to gain her attention. "Is there anything I can do for you?"

For her. Her. One of his tormentors. After everything, he still desired to help her. "I . . . I . . ." Wanted to cry. Wanted to sob and beg for his forgiveness. "I'm so sorry. I know there's nothing I can say—"

"Vika," he said.

"—to make things better, but I'll try. I will. You have my word. I won't let him keep you—"

"Vika."

"—locked up anymore than necessary. The moment I'm free, I'll look for the key more intently."

He leaned down, getting in her face. "Vika!"

She blinked up at him. "Yes?"

"I'm not going to hurt you," he said, settling back on his haunches.

Confusion returned. He thought, what? That she was apologizing simply to keep him calm? Well, if that was the case, he wouldn't believe a single word she uttered on the subject of freedom, would he?

"Your father left a blanket for you. I let you use it as a pillow for a while, but when you began to heal, I took it and rigged it in the corner as a curtain. For privacy . . . when you need to use the chamber pot he also left. I think that's what it's called."

Heat flooded her cheeks. "O-okay. Thanks." She shouldn't be embarrassed. She actually deserved this. He and the others had had to endure that kind of violation since their capture.

"Just so you know, I bathed you," he said, "but I never removed your clothing and I never looked where I shouldn't."

As she had done to him. The heat intensified.

She looked herself over and saw that she was wearing the same clothes she'd worn to confront her father, the plain tee, and the flowing pants. At least she was comfortable.

"Thank you, Solo. Really. For everything."

A stiff nod. "You're welcome."

Her gaze swept over him. He still wore the loincloth, his big, beautiful body on display. His skin was a luminous bronze, each of his muscles so well defined they looked painted on.

Breath caught in her throat. "So, uh, how long have we been here?"

"Three days."

Three whole days. Fifty hours rather than seventy-two, for time was not the same here. During those fifty hours, Solo could have bound her. He hadn't. He could have threatened to withhold medicine and food until she swore to aid him. He hadn't. He could have fed her to the Nolanders to save himself. He hadn't.

I'm the monster in this relationship. "Are you all right?" she asked hesitantly.

He blinked, frowned. "Why?"

"You have blood on your face."

He reacted as if she'd slapped him, spinning to hide the fact that he was scrubbing his skin with a vigor that astonished her.

"Let me," she said, but he acted as if she hadn't spoken. She sighed. "Did the monsters hurt you?"

"You know about them?"

"Yes. To keep them out of the trailers, Jecis had the windows removed, the walls reinforced with steel, and the doors padlocked."

"He should have put us inside your trailer, then," he said, still wiping at his face.

"And allow you to find and hide weapons to use on him later?"

He popped his jaw. "Do you know of a safe place to hide outside the cage?"

Hoping to bust out of here, was he, while there were no armed guards? "I don't recommend fighting the Nolanders on their home baseball court. Now, will you stop doing that and let me help you?"

He stilled. His hand fell to his side. Slowly he turned

and met her gaze, his eyes so frosted over she shivered.

Still, she held out her hand. "Rag." He'd helped her. Now she would help him, even in so small a way. Despite the fact that he had scrubbed so hard he'd left a red welt on one side of his face, the blood remained.

Reluctantly, he gave her what she wanted.

"Lean down here."

Inch by inch he obeyed, a mask falling over his features.

She gently wiped at the crimson streak. Her arm trembled, the action almost too much for an arm that hadn't been used in three days, but still she persisted.

"People play baseball on a field," he rasped.

"That's what I said. Isn't it?"

"You said court." Solo's gaze never left her. He watched her every reaction, as if . . . what? As if he wanted to know her every emotion? Well, he would discover that she liked tending him and looking at him. Especially at his lips. Those beautiful, lush lips.

Right now they were pink. When his appearance changed, they would turn as red as his skin. Would they still be as soft as she remembered? she wondered. As sweet?

"You're staring," he pointed out, his voice tight.

"Does that bother you?"

His tongue flicked out, swiped. "No."

To have that tongue in her mouth . . . to know what it was like to press her own against it . . . She shivered forcefully. "It did before. You threatened to kill me."

"That was before."

Before . . . what?

"And I will never hurt you, Vika." He reached out, his thumb tracing the seam of her mouth.

At the moment of contact, her lips began to tingle. They parted of their own accord, and a heated, needy exhalation escaped her. "I know you won't. Just like I will never hurt you." She forced herself to finish cleaning him—before she did something they might both regret. "See? I'm harmless."

He didn't pull back. *He* stared at *her,* the fire in his eyes intensifying. Finally, he leaned toward her. "I'm sorry," he croaked, "but I have to do this."

"What—"

He kissed her, silencing her. His lips pressed against hers, lingering for one second, two, as though testing her reaction. Yes! This was what she'd wanted. And no wonder. It was magnificent, his lips softer than before. When she offered no protest, he lifted his head and studied her face. Whatever he saw, he must have liked, because he lowered a second time. His tongue flicked out, and she eagerly opened for him.

Their tongues thrust together, and, oh, this kiss was so much better than the one before, when she had taken what she shouldn't have. He went slowly at first, coaxing her, but she didn't need coaxing. She needed more.

Somehow, he understood what she couldn't vocalize. He increased the pressure, the speed, and forced her head to tilt, giving himself deeper access, dominating her mouth, branding her soul-deep, consuming her. She loved every second of it, was engaged body and mind, swept up, lost. Happy to be lost.

He was so hot, a fire against her skin. He was so necessary. Suddenly she couldn't imagine trying to take a breath without him. He was here, and he was hers, and this was beautiful. A beautiful kiss from a beautiful man.

His hand slid underneath her shoulders, angled up and cupped her nape. The rough texture of his skin delighted her, tickling her. He massaged the muscles there, drawing a groan of pleasure from her. Then his hand began to lower . . . stopping midway down her arm, kneading . . . angling again, this time toward her breast . . .

Her aching breast. A place that had never been touched by another. She'd caught enough illicit acts in the shadows of the circus to know that once a man got his hands on a woman's breasts, he couldn't stop himself from taking more, all.

Vika tensed, not sure she was ready for what "all" entailed.

He must have been attuned to her every nuance, because he jerked backward, severing contact.

As she fought for breath, her fingers sought her tingling lips. "Solo," she said, wanting to call him back. She might not be ready for all, but that didn't mean the kiss had to end.

His hands fisted at his sides.

Had she angered him? "I—I—" Had no idea what to say. How did you tell a man you wanted to kiss him, but you didn't want to do anything else with him? Not yet, at least.

"When are the monsters due to return?" she asked, changing the subject.

He looked away from her. "A few hours. But don't worry. You'll stay right where you are, and I'll lie beside you."

He'd done that every time before, hadn't he? The idea of his weight pressing against her . . . didn't frighten her, she realized. It delighted her, her blood bubbling and fizzing with warmth.

Perhaps she was closer to wanting "all" than she'd realized.

"They'll be unable to reach us," he added, "and I won't have to touch you."

"I don't mind—"

"What is this place?" he interjected.

Message received. Subject closed. Maybe that was for the best. "A world between worlds."

He frowned. "Explain . . . please."

Another rusty "please." How could she resist? "Through his dark arts, my father learned how to move the circus from one city to another without ever having to take down or set up the tents and equipment or move the vehicles, and without ever having to take a step. Somehow he creates solar flares that open a portal from one location to another, but he has more trouble closing the flares, especially if we're going a great distance, and sometimes we become trapped here."

His frown deepened. "I know inter-world travel is possible, and that's how the otherworlders came to earth, but I didn't know average citizens could open portals on their own."

"I doubt that they can. But then, my father isn't exactly average, is he?"

"Well, I need to know what he knows."

"Trust me, you don't want to mess with the dark arts."

Well, well. Good thing you listened to me, Dr. E said, his voice seeming to come out of nowhere. She couldn't see him, but she could *feeeeel* him. There was a strange sort of crackle in the air, sparking against her skin. *He's about to try and talk you into spying for him.*

Had Solo heard the male?

His expression remained the same: pensive. "If I asked you to find out what kind of spell he casts," he said, watching her intently, "would you?"

See? Told you!

"No," she answered honestly, ignoring Dr. E. She couldn't blame Solo for wanting more information. "He invited evil into his life, and I'm not going to do the same to mine. Why do you want to know about the flares, anyway? To stop him?"

Solo pondered for a moment, then once again waved a hand through the air. "What's the longest you've ever been trapped in the Nolands?"

So. He wanted her to endanger herself, but he didn't want to tell her why. That, she *could* blame him for. "Six days," she said a little snippily. "But guess what? We're not done with the other topic. I could say yes, I'd try to find out how he does it, because I owe you and I always sometimes try to pay my debts."

"Always sometimes?" he interrupted.

"Exactly. So, here's a question for you. Would you prefer to have the info about the solar flares or the key to the cuffs?"

Without any hesitation, he replied, "The key to the cuffs."

I could have guessed that one, Dr. E muttered.

"Are you willing to give it to me when you find it?" Solo asked with the patient stillness of a predator. "Not just use it on me but give it to me."

"Of course," she replied, and he blinked in bafflement. "*If* my father lets me out of the cage, I've already decided to increase my efforts and do whatever's necessary to unearth its whereabouts."

"Vow it," he rushed out. "Vow to free me, to remove the cuffs when you find the key, and place that key into my sole custody."

Him and his vows. She fought the urge to roll her eyes. But she noticed he'd said "when" and not "if." Either he had more confidence in her than she did, or he simply refused to admit defeat in anything.

Don't do it, Dr. E pleaded.

"So vowed," she said, wanting to smirk. She kind of liked disobeying Dr. E.

He cursed at her.

Solo watched her intently, relief and suspicion in his eyes.

"What?" she asked.

"Did anything strange happen to you?"

"No. Why?"

"Never mind." He rubbed the back of his neck. "Tell me something. Was your newest beating because of me?"

"No," she said, and that was the truth. Matas had hit

her because she'd embarrassed him with her continued refusal of his romantic pursuit, choosing an "animal" over him.

You should have blamed Solo. There was now a pout in Dr. E's voice. *He would have felt guilty and would have done anything you asked.*

"Will you just shut up already," she snapped. "I'm sick of you." She didn't want anyone feeling guilty on her behalf. Guilt was a terrible thing, a consuming thing, and Solo had enough to worry about.

The crackle in the air instantly vanished.

Solo scooted away from her. "I will do what you wish."

"Not you," she said, sitting up to reach for him. She managed to wrap her fingers around his wrist. A wrist so big her fingers weren't even close to touching. He was strong, amazingly so, and that should have scared her, *would* have scared her, until she'd woken up and discovered everything he'd done for her. "You are—" Dizziness had her swaying, moaning.

Solo returned in an instant, pulling from her grip to cradle the back of her head. He eased her down, and she battled an urge to snuggle into the warmth of his body, to know she was safe and protected for once in her life and maybe even . . . cherished.

He didn't cherish her, though, did he. He liked kissing her, she was sure, and had wanted more, but sex had never been and would never be proof of someone's affection.

"You sat up too quickly, after lying down too long."

"I wasn't talking to you," she assured him. "Before, I mean."

"Then to whom were you talking?" He paused to shake his head, perhaps recalling the other time they'd had this conversation, when the question had been directed at him. "And why were you beaten? You never told me."

She licked her lips. "You once told me you talked to invisible men."

He sucked in a breath and moved away from her. "No, I didn't say I did. Only that I might be."

Fine. "Do you believe there's another world at work around us?"

"Very much so."

Her eyes widened. He'd admitted that so easily, as if he had no fear of her reaction. "Really?"

"Yes."

"Me too."

"And?"

"And, I . . . was talking to someone in that realm," she said, and waited for him to admit to knowing Dr. E and X.

A minute passed.

Another.

"So, why were you beaten?" he finally prompted, no hint of his emotions revealed.

Maybe he *didn't* know the pair kept tabs on him. If not, she didn't want to be the one to tell him. "Matas is twisted, warped, and on a power trip. That's why."

Solo reached out to smooth the hair from her brow. He caught himself just before contact and dropped his arm to his side. "I know you aren't a fan of violence, but when you were delivered to me I broke his arm in a way that it can never be put back together. He won't be hitting you again."

Another deed to protect her. "Thank you," she said, fighting a sickening deluge of dread. Clearly he was done touching her, even in the smallest way, and he might even regret kissing her. Why else would he want to maintain such a great distance between them?

But . . . but . . . she wasn't done with him, and didn't want him to be done with her.

He looked at her, thought for a moment. His shoulders bunched with tension. "How long has the circus been in operation?"

I can do this. I can chat as if nothing's wrong. "Jecis's great-great-grandfather opened it, and the oldest son has always taken over."

"How has he not been shut down?"

"He not only uses lookouts to prevent cops from making it into the circus, but when he can, he pays the higher-ups to ignore him."

"You've seen these higher-ups?"

"Oh, yes." Jecis loved to entertain, and though Audra was the candy on his arm, the one he kept at his side during any such events, Vika had watched from the shadows whenever possible.

"And you could point them out if I showed you photographs?"

Hold everything. "Are *you* a cop?" she asked, the idea not surprising her. It did concern her, however. After she freed him, he might try and arrest her.

A pause. A flicker of guilt in his eyes. Then, "Let's

just say I have a vested interest in closing the circus once and for all."

Relieved that she wouldn't have to worry about being tossed into another prison cell, she said, "Yeah, me too."

He arched a brow. "Where do you plan to live when you escape?"

She pictured the beautiful cabins in New Colorado, the ones she wasn't yet able to afford—the homes that could be sold at any time while she scrimped and saved. "I'll find a place."

He rubbed two fingers over his jaw. "Wherever it is, modifications will need to be made."

For her deafness, he meant. "Are you going to come over and fix it?" she asked, and promptly wished she could snatch back the words. How wonderful it would be to have him inside her sanctuary, just because he wanted to be there. But with the way he was currently acting, there was no way he would—

"I would be willing to do so, yes."

Pleasure was a soft, sweet rain against her skin. "Really?"

"Really."

"Would you demand payment?"

His eyes narrowed to tiny slits. Scowling, he pushed to his feet and stomped to the far corner. Only then did she realize her mistake.

"Solo," she said, but he ignored her. "Solo. I'm sorry. I didn't mean to question your honor or anything like that."

Silence.

But of course, she lived in a world of silence. "I really am sorry."

Again, silence.

"I was afraid you were angry with me, because I had stiffened during our kiss, but I only stiffened because I was nervous about what we were doing. I've never done anything like it before. And then, when you said you wanted to come over to my new house and help me, I asked if you would demand payment because I wanted you to say yes. I was going to tell you that I would pay you in kisses. I just . . . I wanted you to know that I liked what we did, but I didn't know how else to tell you."

She had zero experience with men who were not the spawn of the devil or related by blood. Or both. Townies had never been an option, and none of the boys at the circus had wanted to risk her father's wrath. And after her time in the big city, alone, frightened, and witnessing the cruelest of deeds, she'd wanted nothing to do with *any* male . . . and maybe even ladies with mustaches.

A few days ago, she would have balked at the mere idea of being handled by hands as big and rough as Solo's—and probably had! Now, with his sweetness so fresh in her mind, she just wanted another kiss.

She inched into a sitting position, but even still, the dizziness returned full force and she had to close her eyes. This time, Solo didn't rush to her side.

Could nothing go right for her? Ever?

"Fine. Be that way," she said, riding the tide of resentment. "Act like a baby princess." If Solo wanted to pout because she'd inadvertently insulted him, whatever. That was his prerogative. "Normally I wouldn't say something like this, but I'm going to make an exception for you. I hope you enjoy your solitude. And by that I mean I hope you choke on it!"

Nineteen

Hope deferred makes the heart sick,
but a longing fulfilled is a tree of life.
—PROVERBS 13:12

H ER FINAL WORDS WERE certainly fitting. Solo *was* choking on his solitude. His mind refused to settle, was stuck on one thought. She had liked his kiss, had wanted more. Not because she'd felt obligated to him or because she had wished to soften him. Just because.

He almost wished she hadn't told him. Now his body hungered for her on a level he'd never before experienced, a level that mocked everything else he'd felt, as if he'd never really known what it was to crave something. Now he knew.

He wanted her desperately.

He needed her frantically.

He had to have her. Couldn't hold out much longer.

But he had to hold out. Not for any of the reasons he'd previously entertained but for a new one. Reason one hundred and three. Already he reacted terribly when she was hurt. If he claimed her, he would grow more attached to her, and if he grew any more attached to her, he wasn't sure how he would react when Jecis came to take her away. And Jecis *would* come to take her away.

Solo needed to think about the best course of action, the best way to handle this.

Vika had moved to the far corner of the cage, where the strongest beams of light hit but fewer bugs approached her. He claimed the center and lay flat on his stomach. He balanced his weight on his hands and his toes and pushed up, lowered, pushed up, working out the tension in his arms.

By the two hundredth descent, a slow burn had worked its way into his biceps. He did two hundred more before rolling to his back and performing just as many sit-ups. Sweat trickled down his chest and back in little rivulets. His mind whirled.

If Vika ever found out about his past . . . about his side job . . . she would no longer trust him on any level, and would not want him out of the cage. She would dump him into the same category of evil as her father and Matas.

She wouldn't understand the difference between a necessary kill and a cold-blooded one. But then, she wouldn't need to, he realized a second later. His kills hadn't always been necessary. Sometimes he'd had to take out innocents to get to his targets—and those operations *had* been performed in cold blood.

Those were the jobs that had left a dark film of acid over his skin.

Those were also the jobs that had caused him to

question his line of work, to debate leaving the agency. And really, he would have left a long time ago, if not for John and Blue. They'd needed him.

"What are you doing?" Vika asked, ending the cold-shoulder treatment.

"Exercising. Getting oxygen to my brain." And maybe it was working.

His thoughts suddenly jumped from a curved road to a straight one. So what if he reacted terribly whenever she was hurt? So what if he grew any more attached to her? So what if she wouldn't be happy with his job situation? No other man had ever kissed her. No other man had ever held her. Solo had been the first. A sense of possessiveness rose up inside him, consuming him.

Solo would be the only.

He would have her, he decided, and his motions slowed. He would enjoy her for whatever time they had left in these lands. He would be her man, and she would be his woman.

His woman. Oh, how he liked the sound of that. He would work to make it so. *Whatever proved necessary.*

With the decision, relief filled him, and inside, where instinct swirled, a sudden knowing bloomed. This was right. This was supposed to happen.

The revelation left him reeling. Used to be, he'd had a knowing each and every day, an internal knowledge that had nothing to do with an external voice. Truth had risen up inside him, urging him to do exactly what he needed to do to survive—and not just to survive, but to thrive. Go here. Don't go here. Do this. Don't do this.

But after too many promptings to do things he hadn't really wanted to do—turn down a job, stay away from John or Blue for a certain length of time—he'd begun to rationalize. Maybe he had misunderstood, he'd told himself. Maybe he was missing it.

After he'd ignored one too many knowings, they'd just stopped rising, and he'd had only X to guide him. He'd convinced himself he was happier that way. But he hadn't been happier. He'd ignored his companion, too, and had made stupid decisions, as evidenced by the explosion in Michael's office. Well, no more. He wasn't going to ignore another knowing. Not this time. This *was* right, and he would win Vika's trust.

Before, he had scared her, had pushed for too much too fast. Solo would rather rot in this cage forever than frighten Vika in any way. He never wanted her to look at him as she looked at her father and Matas. He would go slowly this time, would ease her into every new experience.

And there was no better time to start. He straightened, his gaze locking on his beautiful Vika. Target acquired. Poor darling.

"What?" she asked, shifting uncomfortably. "Not that I'm speaking to you."

Hadn't ended the cold-shoulder treatment, after all. "I'm thinking."

"About?"

"About our arrangement." He looked her over, this fairy princess come to save the beast. Blond hair was tangled around a dirt-smudged face. Her hands nervously twisted the fabric of her shirt. He definitely had some preliminary work to do. But . . . he didn't mind. Was actually thrilled by it.

He wanted more than sex, he realized.

He wanted to soothe and comfort her, to talk to and laugh with her. He wanted . . . *everything*. Her mind, her emotions, her thoughts, hopes and dreams. He wanted to learn about her, every little detail, and tell her about himself. He'd never before had that with a woman.

He wanted to know about the invisible man she'd mentioned. He'd wanted to question her right away but hadn't let himself. That line of conversation would invite her to ask about X and Dr. E, and he wasn't ready to confess. Did she have a protector, like him? Did she have a tormentor?

"Well," she huffed, "there's nothing you can ever say to make me speak to you again."

His lips twitched with an amusement that was just as potent as his desire, astonishing him. "I'll come up with something."

"Want to bet?"

Oh, Vika. You are too adorable for words.

Now that he'd decided to have her, adorable was no longer such a terrible thing.

Solo considered his options. Exactly how was a man like him supposed to entice a female? What could he give her that she didn't already have?

Well, he could think of one thing she'd probably never received. An apology. Determined, he closed the distance and sat directly in front of her. She refused to meet his gaze. He cupped her cheeks, paused to savor the softness of her skin, then forced her attention on him.

"I'm sorry about earlier," he said gruffly. "I *would* have wanted kisses from you. I still do. You're a beautiful woman, and I have wanted you since the first moment I saw you, even though you were appointed my keeper."

Her eyes grew larger with every word he uttered. "You wanted me, even though I'm—"

"As small as a twelve-year-old boy? Smart-mouthed? Yes, even though."

Expression beseeching, she curled her fingers around his wrist. "Be serious. Even though I'm Jecis's daughter?"

Right now, she wasn't the zoo owner's daughter. She was Solo's woman, and nothing else. But just like the physical aspect of their relationship, she wasn't ready for that kind of boldness or that intense of a possession. So he did the only thing he could. He ignored the question and changed the subject.

"Just so you know, I've won our bet. You're definitely speaking to me."

A moment passed. A soft smile brightened her face. "And *you're* forgiven for earlier."

"That easily?" Surely not. If she were anything like him, she would keep a checklist of his transgressions, whether he apologized or not. After three, she would wash her hands of him. But then, no one could maintain a relationship when they kept a checklist, could they? The record keeper was always too conscious of the bad to concentrate on the good.

"You look astounded and suspicious," she said, that smile widening. She could not be a mere mortal; she just couldn't be. "I'm not sure why. You used the most pleading tone when you apologized, practically dripping with sincerity. I'm just sure of it."

He laughed with hearty amusement, carefree in a way he'd never been, even outside the cage. But the sound cut off abruptly the moment he realized what he was doing, and only the crackling of the fire and the buzzing of the insects could be heard. He'd set out to charm her, but she was the one charming him.

"I want to play a game," Solo said a little while later. He'd taken a bit of time to try to fortify himself against Vika's allure, because he'd known he couldn't dazzle her if he was always being dazzled. He'd thought he was ready.

"And you always get what you want?" she replied, her nose going in the air.

He'd thought wrong. "Is this a fit?" he asked, fighting a grin. "This seems like a little-girl-princess fit."

She gasped with mock outrage. "How dare you! I do not have little-girl-princess fits!"

Will not laugh again. He sat across from her, a position he enjoyed. She was close enough to scent, close enough to touch, but just far enough away that he wasn't tempted to dive on her—more than a few times. "Tell me. What do you do in your spare time?"

Her brow furrowed, her mock pique fading. "I don't understand. What does that matter? What about the game?"

"We're playing it right now."

"Oh. And it is . . ."

"The question game."

"Oh," she repeated, still dazed and somewhat confused. "Well, what are the rules?"

"There's only one. If I ask a question, you have to answer it."

Understanding took hold, and her eyes twinkled mischievously. "Well, good luck. I'm playing to win."

"Me too." And he planned to win more than the game. "Toss out question number one, and listen to me dominate."

He enjoyed seeing her like this. Excited. Perhaps even happy. "I already did."

"What did—oh, yeah." Toying with the ends of her hair, she said, "On the days I'm forced to remain in my trailer I count my money and plan my future. What about you?"

He had to force himself to stare at anything but her hands. Her beautiful hands. So gentle. So feminine. Capable of delivering the most undeniable pleasure, he was sure. "I farm."

Her mouth formed a large O as her gaze swept over him. "You don't look like a farmer."

Perhaps he shouldn't stare at her mouth, either. "And you've met so many of us?"

"Well, no." She lifted to her knees, practically bubbling over with enthusiasm. "Did you notice how quickly I answered that? I'm winning, aren't I?"

The muscles in his stomach clenched as he said, "You're definitely losing, and I'm definitely winning."

She frowned, and he had to fight another laugh. "How?" she demanded.

"The more questions you can get a person to answer, the more points you earn. I've asked more questions."

Her eyes narrowed, two lasers locked on him. "Perhaps I misunderstood the rules."

"That's understandable. You're foreign."

"But perhaps I didn't," she added. "You can't just change them whenever you want."

"I can, too. I'm the game's inventor."

"And what's the score, Mr. Inventor?"

"Fifteen to one," he said, choosing a number that wasn't so high she couldn't catch up, but wasn't so low she could best him. "But because I'm such a nice guy, I'll let you ask me the next question. Okay?"

"Okay."

He *tsk*ed with false pity. "Another two points for me. One because you answered an unnecessary question and another because you fell for my trick. Better luck next time."

"You dirty little swindler," she said with a choked gurgle of delight that caused the muscles in his stomach to once again clench up. She tapped a finger against her chin, brightened. "Oh, I know! Will you tell me about your farm?"

"Of course."

"Got you," she said in a singsong voice. "Another point for me."

Really will not laugh. "It's situated miles from any other residence, and surrounded by rare clusters of trees." Most forests had been burned to the ground during the human-otherworlder war. "There's a natural spring that's filled with fish, and birds constantly fly overhead. There are multiple flower and vegetable gardens, and there's a pesky rabbit that likes to ruin both. I've named him Dead Man Hopping."

Expression glazed with awe, she said, "I've never heard of such a promised land and cannot even picture its like."

Maybe one day he would take her there.

The idea registered, and he froze. He'd once thought about locking her there, but now . . . he knew he would do no such thing. He wanted to have her there, yes, but he wanted her there of her own free will, happy and smiling. And naked.

"Do you have any secret talents?" she asked, unaware of his inner turmoil.

He had *many* secret talents, but there was only one he could share without scaring ten years off her life. "I can wrangle a bull with my bare hands."

"Really?"

"Really."

"Got you! That's four points for me, for using your own trick against you twice, and practically in a row," she said with a smirk. "And before you can ask, I'll just tell. My secret talent is a backbend kick-over."

He . . . had no idea what that was. "One day, I'll want to see that."

In a snap, all of her enjoyment drained. Her sparkle died.

"What?" he demanded, unsure what he'd done wrong.

"Those words . . ." she muttered. " 'One day.' I hate them."

"Why?" They were so innocent.

She waved the question away. "What's, uh, your favorite memory?"

He wanted her back the way she was, and decided not to push for the truth. Not yet. Instead, he leaned forward, placing his lips at the hollow of her neck. "I'll tell you, but I have to whisper because it's personal."

She shivered, the motion brushing her skin against his mouth.

He moaned. So soft, so warm.

She gasped. "Tell me."

"What if I said it was when I kissed you?" he rasped through a throat gone tight.

Her pulse quickened, and he leaned back to study her expression. Spots of color had darkened her cheeks. Color that spoke of arousal, not panic. Exactly what he'd hoped to see.

"Was it?" she asked, hand fluttering over her heart.

"Yes." And that was the truth.

"I would say . . ." She nibbled on her bottom lip, and his blood hummed with exhilaration.

Steady.

Another slow, luscious smile bloomed, lighting up her entire face. "I would say you owe me another point."

A moment passed before her meaning sank in, and he nearly swallowed his own tongue. What a sneaky little vixen she was—a fact he liked. "What about you? What's your favorite memory? And keep in mind, you'll lose eight points if you refuse to answer."

The nibbling started up again. "Do I get an extra point if my answer is the same as yours?"

Gonna kill me. "You get thirty extra points," he croaked.

"Well, good." She was the one to lean forward this time, warm breath stroking over his neck. "Because it is."

The arousal heated, becoming white-hot, consuming. "Vika—"

In the distance, he heard footsteps. Moans, groans.

He checked the sky, saw that the sun was in the process of setting. Cursing under his breath, he dragged Vika to the center of the cage.

Her arms flailed as she struggled to remain upright. "What are you—"

"Lie down." The moment he had her on her back, he stretched out beside her.

"The monsters," she gasped.

"Concentrate on me."

She paled, but she obeyed.

"What's your greatest wish?" he asked to distract her.

The cage shook. Arms reached through the bars.

Vika looked, cringed.

Solo flattened his palm against her cheek, forcing her attention back to him. He marveled anew at the perfect texture of her skin, the purity of her features. "Do you want me to win?"

She shook her head, swallowed. "Well . . . for a long time, I wanted a baby brother. Then, after my father changed, I was happy I was an only child. I never wanted another child to suffer through the Wrath of Jecis."

"He wasn't always like this?" Solo asked, his thumb stroking her delicate bones. For once, he was beside her, her softness pressed against his hardness, and she was awake—yet still he couldn't have her.

"No. He changed when he took over the circus. He actually wasn't supposed to be the one to run it, because he had an older brother. But my grandfather and uncle died fighting each other during the passing of the scepter. Jecis was then thrust into the spotlight, and I guess he grabbed the reins of control with both hands."

The change had to have startled a little girl unprepared for what loomed ahead. "I'm sorry."

Her smile was soft, sad, and sweet all at once. "Thank you."

One of the monsters stuck a leg through the bars in an attempt to kick them both to the other side, where other monsters waited, hoping to grab them. That was a new move. One he didn't appreciate, especially when he was making such sweet progress with Vika.

Anger created little bonfires in already hot blood, the flames crackling and spreading.

He grabbed the monster by the ankle and jerked with all of his might. The leg detached from the body, and he tossed the appendage through the bars.

He regretted the action immediately. Blood had dripped across the cage floor. Worse, Solo had partially morphed. His skin was now red, and his fangs and claws peeked out. Vika had to be scared out of her—

"Do you have a best friend?" she asked him, as if nothing had happened.

For a moment, he could only lie there, staring at her. "You don't want to discuss what just happened?"

"Why would I?"

"I just ripped—I mean, I just helped that creature shed twenty pounds in less than a second."

"I know. You saved me. Again. So, a best friend," she prompted.

Perhaps she would always amaze him. "John and Blue. They're like brothers to me."

"What about the names etched into your arm?"

"Mary Elizabeth and Jacob. My parents. They died in a car crash." An ache in his chest.

Sympathy in her eyes. "I'm so sorry."

"I would have given anything to have them back forever, and still would. Or at the very least, to have them back for five minutes, just to tell them just how much I loved them and how sorry I was for my behavior."

"I'm sure they knew how much you loved them."

He hoped so. "I moved out at the age of seventeen, when I found out how much they were being paid to keep me. I thought they'd been nice for the money rather than because of any affection they had for me." A supposition Dr. E had encouraged. "But my mother called me at least once a day. At first I ignored her, but she never gave up. We started talking again, and she told me they'd placed every cent in an account for me. I felt so bad, so foolish."

"But I bet she forgave you right away."

"She did." And Solo had fallen that much more

in love with Mary Elizabeth Judah. "But one day she failed to call me, and I was out on a . . . I was unable to call her. Six days passed before I could get to a phone. She didn't answer. I returned to the farm—and found her and my father inside their truck, deep in the heart of their land, smashed into a tree, their bodies slumped over in the seats." He still wasn't sure what had caused the accident. Not a faulty break line. Not gunshots.

They'd been there seven days.

After an autopsy, it was revealed that his father had had a heart attack and wrecked, and Mary Elizabeth had died on impact, her side of the vehicle taking the bulk of the damage.

"Oh, Solo. I'm so sorry," Vika said again. She cupped his cheeks as he'd often done to her. "Such loss . . . it's a terrible thing, something that hurts you on an indescribable level."

Yes. "Do *you* have a best friend?" he asked, changing the subject before he broke down. He didn't want her to see him that way.

"I . . . well . . . hmm."

Surely she did. She was so lovely, so kind and perfect. People had to flock to her.

Although, she had grown up in an abusive home and such an upbringing could warp a person's mind. It had John No Name's. Solo had watched, helpless, as the happy, loving boy he'd met for the first time in Michael's office all those years ago had quickly become quiet and withdrawn. And then the outbursts had begun. Anytime anyone had touched him, John had reacted with a cutting rage even Solo had not displayed.

Solo had no idea what had been done to the boy John had been, but, as many criminals as Solo had studied over the years, he could guess. And even after Michael had pulled John from the home and placed him somewhere safe, the boy hadn't relaxed his guard. In fact, he'd become *more* determined to remain aloof.

John trusted no one, believed in no one, and believed the worst of everyone he encountered. That was no way to live.

Yet it was exactly how *he* had been living, Solo realized.

Solo wasn't sure what was worse. His and John's determination to remain alone, or Blue's determination to have a partner, any partner. Over the years the male had plowed through women as if they were disposable tissues. He had lived with a woman for a year and was now engaged to another, but he had not been faithful to either one, choosing the job over romance, always doing what Michael told him to do.

They all had.

"You want the truth?" Vika asked, hesitant.

He pulled himself from his mind. "Always."

Softly she admitted, "You're the only friend I've got."

The knowledge floored him. Humbled him. "I consider that a privilege, Vika."

She patted around until she found his hand, and then she twined their fingers, shocking him, delighting him. He'd never held a woman's hand, not even Abigail's.

He brought her knuckles to his lips, kissed each one. "You would like John and Blue, I think. We've known each other since the age of five, and we've always looked out for each other. They're big, like me, and they're fierce, but they would protect you with their lives." Just because he asked.

Her features softened, becoming wistful. "Once, I had friends like that. They were the animals I used to tend. The lions and apes and bears."

This little fluff of nothing had handled dangerous predators? "Did they ever hurt you?"

"At first, they were quite leery of me. We soon got to know each other, however, and everything changed." The wistfulness vanished, replaced by a dreamy haze that even saturated her voice, and he would not have been surprised to learn she had actually stepped from a storybook and the animals had followed, licking at her feet.

"You loved them?"

But even the dreamy haze vanished. "Yes," she said flatly.

"What happened to them?"

"They died. The end." The words, so sharply uttered, told him far more than she'd probably intended.

"Vika," he said. For this, he *would* push. He had to know. "I'm willing to forgive you as easily as you forgave me, and you won't even have to apologize."

Her brows furrowed. "For what?"

"For . . ." *Making my body ache and my mind crave an impossible future—*

". . . interesting me in your past, and then holding the stories hostage."

Her lips curled in a sensual grin. "You want a story?"

"I do."

"Give me one first. How were you captured?"

How much to tell her? "An explosion injured me. A man decided to sell me to Jecis, while I was too weak to fight back. Now, how did your animals die?"

A shiver moved through her, and she nervously licked her lips. "My father."

Thought so. "He killed them." A statement, not a question.

"He did . . . right in front of me. He even made me shoot my lion, One Day."

One Day. Why were those words so—ah. He got it. The words made her think of her pet, of what she'd lost, of what she'd had to do.

Solo could feel the bones in his fingers curling, knew it was only a matter of time before the nails in his left hand dug into her pretty cheek and the nails in his right dug into the top of her hand. He withdrew both, flattening his palms beside her temples.

The action shouldn't have been arousing, but it was. He surrounded her, was all that she could see.

"I've known people like your father," he said. "If you stay at the circus, Jecis will eventually kill you."

Twin spots of pink painted her cheekbones, and whether they were born of shame or anger, he wasn't sure. "He wasn't the one who beat me this time."

"I know. Matas was, but your father *has* beaten you. Yes?"

She meshed her lips together, refusing to answer.

"Yes," he answered for her. "You don't deserve what they do to you, Vika. You need to leave them."

"I will," she said with the determination he'd come to expect from her. "And I told you, I plan to. I've been selling everything of value that I can, saving and hiding the cash as quickly as possible to buy a new identity and to be able to support myself. *I have to* be able to support myself. I don't have any skills, and I cannot place myself under another man's control."

She wanted out, which he'd known, but she was wisely trying to achieve her goals, which he hadn't known. Good girl. He was proud of her, and utterly relieved. "You nearly sliced off my balls when I grabbed you," he reminded her. "I'd say you can protect yourself."

"I also stabbed Matas," she whispered, with just a hint of shame.

"I'm glad," he replied, clearly startling her.

The suns began to rise, and the monsters began to back away. Perfect timing.

"You lack confidence, however, and I can remedy that." He stood, held out his hand, and waved his fingers in her direction. *This is dangerous. If you handle her, you won't be able to mute your body's reaction. Hunger will consume you. You'll push her to do something she's still not ready for.* "I will teach you everything you need to know."

Twenty

The night is almost gone, and the day is near. Therefore let us lay aside the deeds of darkness and put on the armor of light.

—ROMANS 13:12

SOLO WAITED.

Vika resisted, clearly unsure.

"You have a kind heart, and you deserve to be cherished," he said. "Until that happens . . ."

She frowned, eyeing him warily. "Violence isn't always the answer. I'm too weak to defend myself against the muscle and brawn of a man. I tried, and this was the result."

She'd gathered her courage once. She'd risked everything. She could do it again.

"You're right. Violence isn't always the answer. But sometimes violence *is* the answer. Don't ever go looking for a fight, Vika, but when it comes to something like survival, don't back down when one comes looking for *you*. Your opponent will simply keep coming back for more and things will get worse. I know you understand and accept that on some level, or you would have reacted to what I did to the monster."

A moment passed. She nodded, whispered, "But if I try, I'll keep losing."

"Of course you will. Right now you're fighting from a place of defeat. You have experienced the same results for so long, you no longer expect anything different." He'd done the same thing. He'd taken one look at her and decided she could never want him. He'd acted that way, too. Had spoken that way.

The moment he'd decided to fight to have her, things had begun to change between them. They had talked, and they had laughed. They had grown closer. Soon, he would have his hands all over her.

"You have to force yourself to stand up again." He kept his arm extended as he told her one of the stories his mother used to read to him. It was one of his favorites, about a sword-wielding giant who had caused an entire army to tremble with fear. Along had come a young boy who'd had no formal training, but who had managed to kill the giant with only a slingshot and a stone, saving the entire army.

As Solo spoke, interest sparked in Vika's eyes. "And you think someone like me can save an army?"

"I will give you something better than a yes or a no. I will give you something to think about. We have both admitted that we believe there is another world in operation around ours. I've seen it."

"I have, too!" she said.

Her enthusiasm made him smile. "Humans, otherworlders, it doesn't matter. At our core, we are spirit beings. We have souls and bodies."

"That's what I thought!"

"You are a spirit, eternal; you have a soul, your mind, will, and emotions, and you live in an aging body. Your spirit is attuned to the unseen world. Why else do you think you can see into it?"

"How do you know this?" she asked.

"My mother taught me." And so had X and Dr. E. "I wasn't sure I believed her at first, but intense study proved her right." He'd wanted to know more about the creatures following him. He'd wanted to know whether or not he was crazy.

"Go on," she said, interest clearly intensifying.

"As spirits, we have more direction than we realize. Listen deep inside yourself. There's a knowing that supersedes emotions and mental capabilities. That knowing will lead you to victory every time, if you'll pay attention to it."

She closed her eyes, concentrated. One second passed, two. Her eyelids flipped open, and she frowned with disappointment. "I listened, but I didn't sense anything."

"Sometimes it takes time and practice, shutting out the rest of the world, the noise."

Her lips pursed with a hint of irritation. "There's a problem with your theory: I don't hear any noise."

"Actually, you do in your head," he said, and she couldn't refute it. "Everyone battles their thoughts at some time or another. Negative thoughts, wrongful thoughts, wicked thoughts. You have to cast them down and refuse to dwell on them."

"Why?"

"If you entertain one, it will welcome another, and the more you entertain those, the stronger they become, developing roots and sprouting thick sprigs of leaves, until you can no longer see through the dark forest in your mind." He knew that firsthand.

She deliberated for a moment, nodded. "You're right."

"Always."

She snorted. "So what happened to the boy after the fight?"

"He became a symbol of victory to his people and was later crowned king. Now, allow me to help you, Vika. There's a very good chance I was placed in your life for this reason. And besides, if you want a different life, you have to do something different." The words gave him pause. He was beginning to sound like X.

Well, that wasn't such a bad thing.

Solo waved his fingers. He would be careful of her injuries, but he would teach her the way Michael had taught him: hand-to-hand combat, inflicting whatever was necessary to force the knowledge into the well of instinct.

"Truly?" she asked.

"Truly. You must always be ready to defend yourself against whatever comes against you, and learning the rules of battle is a good start."

She deliberated for a moment more, sighed. "Oh, all right, but only because I've always wanted to be a queen." Her hand at last fluttered to his, and he gently tugged her to her feet. She inhaled sharply and swayed, and he wrapped an arm around her waist to hold her upright.

In the place where his own instinct swirled, he wanted to shout with satisfaction. A beautiful female—

this beautiful female—leaned against him, resting her head in the hollow of his neck, trusting him.

"Just need a moment to steady," she murmured.

He caressed the line of her spine, the exquisite curve of her waist, and had to grind his molars to stop himself from groaning. Slow and easy, he reminded himself. He'd known this would be difficult.

"You're so hot," she said.

"Sorry," he said, but he knew she couldn't hear him.

"It's nice."

Really gonna kill me.

"This won't make me like my father, will it?" she asked.

And there was the crux of the problem, he realized. He moved his hand up, up, and tilted her chin. "He fights to inflict pain. You fight to save. You're nothing like him, and you never will be."

Tears of gratitude welled in her eyes, and his heart suddenly felt as if it was being squeezed by an iron fist.

"Ready?" he asked. Any more waiting, and they wouldn't get to the fighting.

"Ready."

For the next several hours, he taught her how to (properly) make a fist, exactly where a lightweight like her could punch a man to inflict the most damage, to disable, and how to use even the most innocent of items to slow an attacker.

She was timid at first, and even frightened to the point of trembling, but she soon found a core of strength and met his attacks with vigor. She absorbed everything he said and concentrated with every ounce of her being to do the best she could.

"You keep tucking your thumb under your fingers," he said. "Don't do that. You'll break it."

"See! I once told you that breaks were bad, but you pretended not to believe me." Once again she made a proper fist. "Like this?"

"Yes. Now swing."

She did, going out and around. An ineffectual action that would have irritated her attacker rather than hurt him.

"No. Forward. A jab, jab." He demonstrated what he meant, then tapped the ridges of his stomach. "Hit me."

Her eyes went wide, shimmering amethysts backed by black velvet. "No."

"Yes." The only way to get her comfortable with fighting back was to get her used to hitting actual flesh. "Don't be a princess babycakes. Hit me as if it's the only way to free the otherworlders."

He expected her to yell at him. She punched him instead. Just straight-up nailed him in the gut, not once, not twice, but three times. If he'd been any less of a man, he would have doubled over.

"Good," he managed. "That's good."

She punched him again.

He caught her wrist, studied her, worried she would revert to her earlier fear of becoming like her father. But her cheeks were flushed and her lips parted, on the verge of grinning. She wasn't about to break down. She was about to celebrate.

"I'm impressed with your . . . technique," he said.

"Did I hurt you?" she asked, reaching out to stroke her fingers over his stomach.

He sucked in a breath.

"I'm surprised these kitties didn't break my hand," she said, gaze locked on the ridges of muscle. "They're so hard."

Darling, you have no idea. "These puppies," he corrected.

"Puppies . . . kitties . . . both are baby animals and therefore appropriate." *Still* stroking.

He took her hand before the training session switched gears. "Now it's time to learn what to do when someone tries to hit *you*. I'm going to swing at you slowly." Very, very slowly, every inch measured. That way, if she failed to heed him, he could stop himself before contact. "I want you to duck before I reach you, then come up swinging yourself, okay?"

A nod of determination.

They performed the action over and over, until she could defend and attack in quick succession, without pausing to consider her next move. And oh, was she gorgeous as she worked. All that golden hair danced around her shoulders, down her back. Her chest rose and fell; her tee soon became streaked with sweat— hers and his—causing the material to cling to her breasts. Her more-than-a-handful breasts.

Breasts he *would* hold in his hands. One day. Soon.

Her legs kicked out, and she knocked his ankles together. He stumbled to one side, but caught himself on the bars.

Clapping, she jumped up and down. "I did it! I really did it!"

"You sure did."

"Wow! I'm amazing! And I have to say, this is much easier than I anticipated."

A growl lodged in his throat. It should have been more difficult! *Get control of yourself, Judah.* He was a trained assassin. He could do better than this.

"Let's take this up a notch," he said.

"I'm ready."

He varied his pretend hits, forcing her to think while staying in motion. She began to anticipate his moves before he knew in what direction he was going. A survival technique she must have developed growing up as Jecis's daughter.

He was saddened and angered by that, but proud of what she'd accomplished, too, and all the more determined to teach her more than survival. He would teach her how to win.

"You're very good at this," she said.

"I have to be."

"Why?"

Uh-oh. Dangerous territory. "When I was little, I had several run-ins with humans who hadn't yet accepted the otherworlders living on this planet. I had to learn how to control my strength, as well as inflict enough damage to save myself."

Her hand fluttered over her heart, and she looked ready to burst into tears. "That's so sad."

So sensitive to other's pain. "It's more common than you realize. But Vika?"

"Yes?"

"You shouldn't have let me distract you." Solo sprang into action, knocking her to the floor, catching her before she hit to prevent her from banging her head, and pinning her in place. No matter how forcefully she squirmed, she couldn't manage to free herself. The sadness had left her, at least.

But desire had taken its place.

She smelled of the jasmine and the mint, and he needed more of both, but one second passed, two, and he stopped breathing. This was too important to mess up. So far he'd kept his touches mostly business, never slipping his fingers past clothing and onto bare skin. Now, the restraint caught up to him, his own desire rampaging through him. He could feel her, every inch of her. Could feel every curve he'd previously denied himself.

"I want to kiss you," he said.

"Yes. Please."

"I won't do anything else."

"Okay."

"Afraid?" he asked.

"No," she whispered.

He looked at her lips. So pink and pretty, with only the barest hint of a wound.

Was she ready?

He prayed she was ready.

He couldn't stop himself.

He leaned down, pressed the softest of kisses onto her mouth. Her nails dug into his chest, and he wasn't sure whether she meant to push him away or drag him closer.

Well, well. He *could* stop himself. He lifted his head to peer into her eyes. Wonder stared up at him, more intent than ever before and as thrilling as it was tantalizing. She definitely hadn't meant to push him away. So he did it again. He kissed her, lingering this time, and a needy little moan left her.

"Open," he commanded.

The moment she obeyed, he slid his tongue into her mouth. And oh, her taste was *exquisite*, just as he remembered, like summer berries dipped in fresh cream. Last time, he'd become instantly addicted. This time, he was forever changed. He could not exist without this—without her. She was the only light in a vast expanse of darkness.

Her body heat enveloped him. Her fingers tangled in his hair, and she tilted his head to the side, forcing deeper contact. As if she needed to force him. He took and he gave. He drank her in, greedy, ravenous, using what remained of his willpower to keep his hands on the ground beside her shoulders.

She began to meet his tongue thrust for thrust, asserting more pressure. Her panting breaths mingled with his, and he liked that almost as much as the kiss. He was taking of her, and she was taking of him, and they were becoming one, even in so small a way.

He wanted to touch her.

He *had* to touch her, all of her, soon, soon, *soon*, and he would. There would be no part of her he ignored.

But even that wouldn't be enough. That would never be enough—nothing would. If he touched her, he would take her. And he couldn't allow himself to take her on a bloodstained floor. Not today, and not tomorrow. Not for their first time. Not with Jecis's trailer beside his cage. Not until she was ready, until regret would no longer be an issue.

And if he didn't stop now, he never would.

Solo rolled back, sitting several inches out of reach. Surely the most difficult thing he'd ever done. Vika sat up, her fingers going straight to her mouth. Did her lips throb as deliciously as his?

"No more for today," he said, more gruffly than he'd intended.

Her fingers lowered, and the pink tip of her tongue emerged, as if she wanted to capture more of his taste. "I like doing that with you."

Killing him. He stood, strode to the supplies. "Drink this," he said, and tossed her a bottle of water. "You need to stay hydrated."

She missed by miles, and had to lean over to fetch the bottle from where it had rolled.

"How did you know what I was planning to do during training?" he asked to distract himself.

She struggled with the lid as she said, "You ignored me, but I'm supposed to answer you?"

"Yes."

She laughed, and it was a beautiful though rusty sound, and when she blinked in amazement he knew she had not had cause to laugh in a very long time. "Very well, then. I will reward your honesty." She drank half the bottle, and motioned for him to take the rest.

"The knowing you told me about. When I got quiet inside my head, I could sense the changes in your body just before you leapt into action."

"Good." She needed every advantage she could get. "Use that knowledge, no matter how big your opponent is."

A reluctant nod greeted his words. "Who taught you those skills?"

"A friend."

"John or Blue?"

"Neither. Michael. John and Blue trained with me."

"Are they like you?"

He knew what she meant. "They are otherworlders, but not the same species." This topic usually propelled him into a rage. No one knew about the Allorians, and because they didn't know, and he refused to say, they invented names for his race. But Vika meant no insult, and he knew that, too. "I'm Allorian."

A curious glitter in those velvety plum eyes. "Have you ever been there?"

"Not that I remember."

"Well, you're definitely one of a kind. And I mean that in the best possible way, of course."

"I know you do." He shifted from one foot to the other, suddenly uncomfortable. All his life, he'd wanted someone other than his parents to like him for who he was. To admire him. And now, his pretty little human was doing just that, and he was unsure what to say or how to react. "Will you use what you learned today?"

"I hope I won't have to, but yes. If anyone comes at

me, I'll leap on them like a wounded wolverine with a blood-cream fetish."

He tried to hold back his chuckle, but failed.

Vika's expression softened. "I love seeing you like this. So . . . relaxed. And I want to know more about you," she said. "I want to know everything."

And he wanted to give her whatever she desired. As he scanned the crackling fires, the hills with their dead and gnarled trees, he said, "I told you I own a farm. I actually grew up there. My parents were human and adopted me."

"Ah. So that's why you thought they were being paid to take care of you. I assumed it was an alien custom."

He knew very little about the Allorians. Only what X had told him. They were a peaceful race, very loving. Very joyous. Everyone had a helpmate, like X, until they were strong enough to take care of themselves.

Perhaps that was why Michael had paired him with the Judahs. They fit so well with his ancestors.

The couple had more than adored Solo. They had more than adored each other, too, and deep down he'd always wanted what they'd had—what he'd believed he could never hope to have.

"I still can't imagine you tending the land," Vika said.

"I did more than tend the land. I raised the animals. Not the clones all the farmers raise today, but the real thing. Pigs, sheep, goats, chickens, cows. We refused to sell them," something that would have made his parents millionaires, "because we hoped to help with repopulation."

He still refused to sell. Thankfully, he didn't have to

worry about them while he was gone. Always before a meeting with Michael, he hired a team to see to their every need.

"You were blessed."

Very much so. And he yearned for her to experience the same. "I want another vow from you, Vika." *You shouldn't do this. You know better. She could accidentally give the information to her father.* Still, he said, "If ever we're separated, I want you to go to the farm." He gave her the address. "Memorize it."

A huge smile bloomed, only to fall into a frown of devastation. "Why would you welcome me there?"

Why the change in her? "Maybe I could use a house-keeper." He would rather pamper her than watch her do chores, but those kinds of details could be worked out later. First, he had to get her there—an idea he liked more with every second that passed.

"I—" Paling, she rubbed at her throat. "How long would you want me there?"

"I don't know." Right now, he couldn't imagine *not* wanting her there. In his bed, morning and night, her pale hair spread over his pillow, her slight body snuggled under his covers. Her mint and jasmine scent would permeate the air. He would be able to protect her at all hours of the day and night, to empower her so that she would bloom as she had during their training session, watching the sparkle light up her eyes and the flush darken her cheeks.

"What would happen when you tired of me? Where would I go?" She shook her head, adamant. "No. I'm sorry. I can't rely on your offer. I'm sorry," she repeated.

"If necessary, I'll get a job somewhere else. I'm highly skilled."

Uh, a while ago she'd said she had no skills.

"At *something*, I mean," she added hastily. "I'm skilled at something. Surely. I just, I have to do this on my own. Out there, in the real world, I'm the only one I can trust. And besides, I told you. I'm saving."

"You're scared of men. I get it. But you don't have to—"

"I'm not scared of men! I'll have you know—"

"—worry on my farm," he interjected, forcing her to be quiet or miss what he was saying. "You'd cook, clean, and feed the animals. You're used to that, right?"

Her mouth floundered open and closed. "That was a low blow."

"How so?" he asked, confused and irritated that she wasn't more willing. That she didn't seem to want him as much as he wanted her.

Golden brown lashes fused together. "You think that's all I'm good for."

"I do not."

A thick white fog suddenly rolled through the bars, black burning at the edges and claiming his attention. What the—

"We have arrived," Vika said, her voice now devoid of emotion. "The fog should clear within the next half hour, and we will be in our new location."

Twenty-one

~~✦~~

Hold on to instruction, do not let it go;
guard it well, for it is your life.
—PROVERBS 4:13

NEVER WOULD VIKA HAVE guessed she would mourn the loss of the Nolands. But she did, and she would have given half of her treasure to return for a few weeks. She might have given *all* of her treasure to stay forever. In a matter of days, Solo had become one of her favorite things in the whole world. He was even better than chocolate!

She no longer feared his temper. After all, she'd angered him several times, but not once had he struck her. She'd even hit him, but instead of raging, he'd showed her how to hit him harder.

He was pragmatic and morose, but he was also kind and caring. And he had an unexpected sense of humor, one she didn't think he'd known about. One *she'd* managed to bring to the surface, surprising them both. He'd even offered her a home and a job, and maybe he'd done it out of pity, maybe he'd done it to keep her from changing her mind about freeing him, but still he'd done it. He was such a good man.

She shouldn't have rejected him so forcefully,

shouldn't have hurt his feelings, but when the sudden burst of joy his offer had brought had faded, new fears had surfaced. What if she moved in, he got tired of her, and kicked her out? Or what if he got tired of her, let her stay, and brought a girlfriend home?

Vika's hands curled into tight little fists at just the idea of Solo pressing those soft lips onto another woman's mouth.

Why did she feel this way? No matter how much she wanted him, no matter how possessive she realized she was, she couldn't allow herself to fall into a relationship already doomed to fail. Yes, they seemed to have gotten past the circumstances that had brought them together. Yes, she loved spending time with him. But what about the future? How was she supposed to make him happy outside the circus?

It would be better for her to stick with her current plan. She would buy a new ID for herself, find the cuff key, free the otherworlders once and for all, and cut her ties with the circus. And if not the ID, then the home in New Colorado. No one would ever be able to kick her off her own land, or escort the woman who'd won Solo's heart to her door.

A hand on her shoulder, tugging her from her mind.

"Are you okay?" Solo asked, crouching beside her, his features tight with concern.

Oddly enough, she could truthfully say, "Yes. Why?"

"Look at yourself."

She did. Her clothes were a little dirty, a little wet. Nothing was out of place, though she was trembling from the chill.

The chill. Sweet mercy, but the temperature had taken a nosedive. She realized she'd wrapped her arms around her middle, trying to huddle into herself for warmth. "C-cold," she said, teeth chattering now that reality had made itself known.

Solo, who wore nothing more than the loincloth, wound their only blanket around her shoulders and tugged her against his chest.

His heart drummed against her shoulder, soothing her. She could have stayed in his arms forever—which was exactly why she had to pull away from him. And she would . . . after just a minute more . . . no, two minutes more . . . three . . . he was hot, a living furnace, and . . . and . . . and he had kissed her just a little while ago, and she still craved another, *loooonger, deeeeper* one.

He was the first man to ever be willing to risk her father's wrath, just to be with her. Matas had often claimed to want her, yes, and had even told her father they had been together, but Matas had never tried anything. Solo, though . . . he must really want her, because even though Jecis controlled his fate, he had pressed his lips against hers with such gentleness, as if she were precious, perhaps breakable, only to lift and study her expression before going back for another taste. A far more intense taste.

The memory alone caused her skin to prickle with longing, her insides to ache with need. Oh, how she ached.

Can't think about Solo's kisses right now. Any moment she would have to face her father. The fog would vanish and Jecis would look at the monitor inside his trailer and realize he was no longer inside the world between worlds, and he would emerge. She couldn't be found enjoying her punishment or she *and* Solo would be given another.

"They can't see us together like this," she said, lifting her head and scooting away from him.

He dropped his arm, nodded. She frowned at him. His face was an emotionless mask, giving none of his thoughts away. And yet, he suddenly radiated a frigidness that far surpassed what wafted from the mountains.

A sigh left her as understanding crested. He'd taken her words and action as a rejection.

"Solo," she said.

He pushed to his feet, miles of bronzed skin coming into view. If *she* was cold, he had to be closing in on frostbite. Standing, she unwound the blanket and thrust the material in his direction.

"Here," she said.

"No." He shook his head, adamant. "You keep it."

She couldn't hear his tone, but the vibration of his words packed a powerful punch. He must have been throwing each one like a baseball.

"Listen, you. I moved away from you because my father will erupt if he sees your hands on me, and I won't allow another whipping." After everything Solo had done for her, she wouldn't be able to bear the guilt.

That failed to relax him. "Just so you know, I'm not afraid of him. But don't worry. I understand. You and I can be friends in private, when you need my help, but we have to stay mere acquaintances in public. Right?"

Oh, that burned! "You need to get over yourself and stop the tantrum right now."

His gaze narrowed on her.

"Let's gather all the poker chips, all right?"

He blinked, a different reaction than she'd expected. "Poker chips? Do you mean we should put our cards on the table?"

"No, I don't mean we should put our cards on the table! A new game cannot start until all the chips are *off* the table." Why did he always question her about this stuff? "I'm trying to end your bad mood and start a good one, so help me out and listen."

"Very well." He pressed his lips together, as if to stop himself from . . . scowling? Laughing?

Whatever! "Here goes. I don't know you outside of this messed-up situation, and I certainly don't know how to handle whatever's happening between us. After we've ditched the circus, and if *you* haven't ditched *me*, and if you still want me, and if you don't want someone else, ask me to work for you and my answer might be different." Might be, but probably wouldn't be. Not that she'd tell him that. "And I'm not embarrassed to be with you. Though I should be! You're so foolish! I told you already, but I'll tell you again. I won't have you tortured simply because I like you. Why can't you get that through your head?"

The blinking started up again, though his eyes were brightening. "You like me and hope to protect me."

Finally! He understood. "Yes. I know staying away isn't much, but it's all I can do for you right now. Foolish man," she muttered.

He looked so surprised, she knew not many people had dared to call him such an irreverent name, and that she had just proved how comfortable she'd become with him. Otherwise she wouldn't have risked his increased ire when he clearly had no fear of her father.

Solo pondered her words for a moment, the light in those ocean blues still brightening, brightening. "If you aren't careful, Miss Vika," he said, "I won't ever be able to let you go."

She . . . had no idea how to respond. Keep her forever? Her silly mind was shouting, *Yes, please.*

Despite everything.

I have returned.

The familiar voice whispered through her mind, and she whipped to the right to confront the speaker. Her initial torrent of alarm subsided when she saw a tiny version of the dark-haired X perched on her shoulder. He appeared younger than before, stronger.

But never before had she seen *this* clearly into that other realm—while she was in *another* realm—and she wasn't sure what to think.

When your father comes, and he will, do whatever is necessary to escape the cage with Solo. His mouth wasn't moving, and yet his words reverberated inside her head. *You need to leave. Now.*

Liar! said Dr. E, causing her to swing to the left. He, too, was now a tiny version of himself. He appeared older than before, weaker. *You know Solo will be captured. And if you're with him, you'll be captured, too.*

A tap on her shoulder had her spinning back to

Solo—who was right in front of her, concern once again radiating from him. "Are you okay?"

"D—did you see them?" she asked, rubbing her hands up and down her arms.

"See who?"

"*Them*." She looked left—Dr. E was gone. She looked right—X was gone. "But . . . but . . ." Her shoulders drooped. "Never mind."

"What did you see?" he insisted.

Twice they'd discussed that other realm, yet he'd never mentioned X or Dr. E, even though he had to know them. And he was Allorian, and somehow, during her dream that wasn't a dream, she had appeared on Alloris. But she wasn't going to be the one to mention their names. Solo would demand to know what they had said to her. He would agree with X, she knew he would, and then she would have to turn him down yet again. Despite the fact that she knew X was right. He was always right. But she couldn't see a way to obey him.

"Vika."

Forget her father. Forget the future. She threw herself into his arms. They probably wouldn't be together much longer, and she needed to savor every moment.

He didn't grab hold of her. She felt a vibration, knew he was speaking. "I don't know what you're saying. And honestly? I don't care. If you want me to move away, sorry, because I'm staying right here. Just hold me tight and warn me if you hear anyone coming."

Several moments ticked by before he obeyed.

A sigh of relief left her at the feel of his strength

and heat enveloping her. "I vowed to do my best to find that key, and I meant it. I will. But where should I start? What if I fail?"

At the right, she heard a moan.

At the left, she heard a cackle of laughter.

Her nails sank into Solo's chest, as if he was her only anchor in a turbulent storm. Actually, he was. Dr. E and X were still here, listening.

Warm hands cupped her cheeks, a beautiful caress she would remember all the days of her life. He lifted her chin, hope and flickers of what looked to be apprehension peering down at her. "He would keep the key close by, and it might even be something he wears every day. And you won't fail."

"But I've looked through his jewelry."

"Look for secret compartments in his trailer. And if you get into trouble, run. Run, and never look back."

Oh, yes. Apprehension. She could barely process the knowledge. He was putting her needs above his own. Not just for the aid she could render, but for *her*.

"I can't do that, Solo." No matter what. "I just can't."

His gaze searched her, drilling all the way to her soul. "Then run to me."

She rubbed against his palm, practically purring with the warmth and pleasure of the sensation. "What would you be able to do?" she whispered. She didn't ask to be cruel, but to point out how futile such a thing would be.

Anger suddenly overshadowed the apprehension, but his grip remained gentle. "I'll think of something."

That anger wasn't directed at her, she knew, but at

the circumstances. "I don't want to get you into more trouble."

"I can handle trouble."

"And I can't?"

His thumbs stroked, making her shiver. "You've handled too much already. And one day, you're going to tell me everything that's been done to you. One day you'll have the life you deserve."

One day.

Panic bubbled to the surface because she knew, *knew*, something bad would soon happen. Something bad always happened when those words were voiced. Still, all she said was, "F-fine. I'll come to you. And before you say anything, I vow it."

A speck of color flashed toward the left. The fog was thinning now, she realized. Different parts of the circus were appearing, everything in its place, nothing so much as an inch off. The cage that had become Vika's safe harbor was exactly where it had been left—right in front of Jecis's trailer.

Only the landscape had changed. A single sun shone brightly in a baby blue sky. Rather than hills of soot and ash, with gnarled trees stretching grotesque limbs in every direction, snowcapped mountains painted the area.

"One day, you will—" Solo's ears twitched. The corners of his lips turned down as he jerked his head toward her father's trailer. "He comes."

Swallowing a yelp, Vika jumped away from him.

A second later the door swung open, and Jecis pounded outside. Audra trailed behind him, wearing a lovely golden hat, coat, and boots—all made from One

Day's pelt. The bald patches from age and the holes from Jecis's gun had been filled in with another animal's fur, creating the illusion of a healthy lion in the prime of his life.

Anytime Vika saw the outfit, she struggled with the urge to rip Audra's face off.

I will not react.

Solo shifted, as if he meant to leap in front of her. Somehow, he stopped himself.

"Vika," Jecis said, looking her over with . . . a confusing mix of disappointment and relief in his eyes. "You have recovered."

"I have."

"You even appear content." His gaze moved to Solo, and the tension returned. "And you look as if you want to cut my heart out with a rusty spoon and feast."

Solo remained quiet.

"You were gentle with my daughter, weren't you, beast? I bet you even controlled your darker urges, just to impress her."

Again, there was only quiet from Solo.

"You taught her nothing," Jecis shouted, his face turning red. "Nothing! I expected the animal to act like an animal. I expected to find her on her knees, begging me to free her."

Audra backed up a few steps, turned, and raced to the trailer, as if she feared he would focus all of that rage on her. Tremors began to slide down Vika's spine.

"An animal would make her feel the need to beg, yes," Solo finally replied, leaving no doubt he considered Jecis the actual animal.

Jecis popped his jaw.

"Do you want me to beg?" she asked her father, bringing his attention back to her. "I will." For Solo, she might do just about anything.

"Beg? Now?" He spit on the ground. "When it will mean nothing?"

Still. She had to try. With dread churning in her stomach, she said, "Daddy, please release me. Please." She hated the idea of leaving Solo trapped, all alone, to suffer humiliation when the circus kicked off and new humans came to view him. As poorly as he reacted to rejection, it had to be a special kind of torture for him. But she had to. "Please."

Solo placed a hand on her shoulder and squeezed, a bid for silence.

Her father's eyes nearly bugged from his face, and the red tint returned to his skin, darker now. "How dare you touch her, beast!"

Vika tried to step away, but Solo applied just enough pressure to keep her in place.

"Daddy," she said, desperate. "I . . . we can have dinner tonight. And we can talk. Just like before, when I was little. Remember? And afterward, I'll return to my former duties, if you'll let me."

Jecis inhaled sharply, released the air slowly. Finally he nodded, as if he'd just made a decision. "I will release you, Vika."

"Thank you. Thank you so—"

"On the condition that you perform in the ring tonight," he added.

"What?" she squeaked, even as Solo's grip tightened enough to cause her to wince.

Immediately the pressure let up. But . . . she no longer wanted to move away.

Jecis ignored her question. "And you, beast, are going to suffer. You think it was bad before? You'll soon be *praying* for those days. Not only will you be returned to the menagerie, but you'll become the main attraction at the new petting zoo."

Solo roared with rage he'd probably suppressed far too long. "I will kill you first."

"Threaten me again after your nap, and see what it gets you." Grinning now, her father reached up and pressed the button on the cage.

Thump.

Vika watched, helpless, as the man who had spent the last six days protecting her dropped to the floor, motionless. Vulnerable.

Jecis opened the cage door and stomped inside. She dropped the blanket, determined to leave it behind for Solo to stay warm. Her father grabbed her by the arm and jerked her outside, slamming the door shut behind him.

"I've been too lenient with you," he said, tugging her forward. "I realize that now. I've let you waste your time with the animals when I would have been better served using you in the ring. Perhaps then you would have appreciated all the work I've done for you. For you and you alone. I even considered killing Matas after what he did to you, and how do you thank me?"

"Daddy—"

"Silence! I'm taking you to the seamstress. The two of you will have to work all night, but whatever it takes, you will ensure you have the best costume or you will know my displeasure."

"Y-yes. Of course," she said, wanting to look back at Solo but not allowing herself the luxury.

I have to find that key. It's our only hope.

Twenty-two

The faithless will be fully repaid for their ways,
and the good rewarded for theirs.

—PROVERBS 14:14

JECIS HADN'T LIED ABOUT the petting zoo.

Vika gazed at it with growing horror.

Early this morning, Matas—whose arm had mysteriously healed from Solo's abuse, though the skin was now veined with a sickly black—had drugged each of the captives, rendering them unconscious. He then dragged them into the tent Jecis had had his employees set up. There, the two men had stripped the captives to the skin and bound them to giant spinning wheels with thick iron bands.

Solo never had a chance to fight, his muscles paralyzed by the sedatives. And now, he *wouldn't* have a chance. He couldn't even use his teeth. A muzzle covered the lower half of his face.

The circus had kicked off a short while ago, and humans had begun to parade in and out, allowed to touch whichever otherworlder they desired, in whatever manner they desired.

It didn't help that they peered at the captives with wonder in their eyes.

It didn't matter that they didn't try to hurt a single one.

The otherworlders were humiliated. Defenseless. Helpless.

The tent was warm, encouraging the sale of ice cream in the corner, despite the frost outside. Strawberry, vanilla, and chocolate melted as the humans studied and petted the otherworlders one by one, discussing their "magnificence."

Jecis had escorted Vika here a few minutes ago, and they now stood at the edge of the tent. She wanted to run from him. She wanted to attack him. How dare he allow this?

"There isn't a key to the cuffs, you know," he said. "Years ago, I destroyed the only one that was ever made."

The words penetrated the dark shroud around her mind and nearly sent her to her knees. He wasn't lying. He couldn't be. There was too much glee in his eyes.

No key, she lamented, her insides hollowing out. There was no key. All this time, her search had been for nothing. Forget the money she wanted to save. If she'd found the key, she would have freed everyone ahead of schedule. If she'd known it couldn't be found, she would have still freed everyone ahead of schedule. Yet staying to aid the otherworlders had been for nothing.

They were doomed. They had always been doomed.

"Your beast will wear the cuffs to his grave," Jecis said with an evil grin.

He meant to remind her of Solo's fate. He rallied her determination instead.

He was a nasty, hateful man and he would never change. He would only ever cause more hurt. And Matas, too. He had been demoted to hired hand while off duty for his actions against her, but one day, he would snap. He and her father would fight for rights to the circus. Once, she had thought her father would always win against him. Now, after Matas had "healed" his arm? She wasn't so sure. But she did know only one of them would walk away—and she didn't want to be around to find out who it was.

She was leaving tonight, Vika decided. After the performance, when everyone was too drunk or too tired to notice her actions. There would be no more waiting. She would gather up as many of her jewels as she could carry, free Solo and all of the others, and she would run. Run and never look back, just as Solo had said.

Finally.

If Jecis found her, well, she would rather die than come back. And there were ways to ensure that happened.

"Welcome to the amazing, spectacular Cirque de Monstres!" Jecis's voice echoed through the darkened tent. Vika stood on the sidelines. She couldn't hear him, couldn't read his lips, but she knew the routine by heart and recognized the distinct vibrations.

Red, blue, and green spotlights suddenly switched on and swept over the crowd filling the bleachers that surrounded the center ring. As expected, twitters of excitement erupted, brushing against her skin. The lights switched off, once again leaving the tent in total darkness.

Then, multicolored sparks sprayed in the air above, fireworks that weren't really fireworks cascading over the humans. Judging by the buoyant expressions, she knew everyone was squealing with delight.

When the sparks died, the spotlights were once again turned on—but this time they were focused on the happenings in the ring. Smoke billowed from strategically placed boulders, and as cymbals clanged to set the beat, out leapt one of Jecis's more beautiful female performers, followed by another and another.

Each woman wore a sequined bra top and tiny underwear bottoms. After they climbed on top of each other to form a pyramid, they raised and spread their arms, awaiting cheers.

At least the majority of Vika's skin was covered. She wore an evening gown the same ruby red as her lipstick. It conformed to her curves, dipped low in the back, and flared at the bottom. Her hair was down, brushed to a golden shine and falling to her waist in perfect waves.

A clown was the next to jump from the smoke, surprising the viewers, but rather than helping the ladies with the pyramid, he dove on top and tried to kiss the star. She resisted. The pyramid teetered. He maneuvered to the lower level and tried to kiss another. She too resisted, and down the pyramid fell. Laughter abounded as the females stood, and, lifting up their hands, seemed to tug the clown into the air with an invisible rope. He dangled there, suspended and strug-gling, and the crowd ate it up.

Two other clowns bounded from the smoke, and they desperately tried to help their friend, but they were soon caught up in the same bubble of air, and the females began to juggle them without ever touching them.

Ten more minutes, and it would be Vika's turn. Even the notion caused her heart to pound erratically. Where was X? She wanted to talk to him, wanted to ask him for advice. He would tell her the truth, noth-ing held back, and this time she would listen, whether she knew how to proceed or not.

Audra was stationed beside her, to ensure she didn't miss her act. Vika was to be part of Matas's magic act. Just another punishment, she knew.

"Why did you sell your soul for *this*?" Vika asked her. She wanted a distraction, but she also wanted the answer.

Up went the girl's chin, though she didn't bother glancing in Vika's direction. "What else was I going to do? Where else was I going to go?"

"Anywhere."

"I believe you discovered the joy of trying *that*," Audra replied with a roll of her eyes. "Our kind isn't accepted out there."

Our kind. "I'm not anything like you."

A greater vibration stroked over her, and she knew the crowd was cheering madly. The clowns were van-ishing one by one, and when there were no more, the females looked at each other, looked behind the boulders, as though they had no idea what had happened.

"Don't kid yourself," Audra said. "You're exactly like me."

"How so?"

"We're tainted. And without this circus, we're nothing."

No. She wouldn't believe that.

"I loved you once, you know," Audra said.

"And I loved you." Part of her still did, despite everything. She remembered the little girl she'd played with, laughed with.

"You destroyed me when you rejected me."

"No. I saved you."

"No! Destroyed! My family was so proud that I was friends with Jecis's daughter, and when you cut me from your life, they cut me from theirs. At twelve, I had to find a man to take me in. He was awful, always using me, and the sad thing is, I'd still be with him if Jecis hadn't decided he wanted me."

"I'm sorry, I am." She'd known Audra had begun living with one of Jecis's men, but hadn't known . . . hadn't thought . . . "You saw what Jecis did to Dolly. I couldn't let that happen to you."

Audra laughed without humor. "Dolly. I always hated how much you cared for her."

What! "She was your friend too."

"No, she was a nuisance. Who do you think told your father that she slammed your hand in the cage?"

"No," Vika said, shaking her head, refusing to believe what her former friend was implying.

"Oh, yes. I wanted you all to myself."

But how could she live in ignorance, when that former friend so boldly proclaimed her crime? Anger rose. "You ruined an innocent girl for your own selfish gain. Tell me, Audra. Are you happy with what your actions have wrought?"

Applause rang out, signaling the end of the act and saving Audra from having to form a reply.

Vika focused on the ring. Her palms began to sweat.

Matas stepped front and center. He operated with his usual charm and flair as he waved his hand over a big black top hat—and out flew twenty birds, each painted with all the colors of a rainbow. They soared through the tent, circling the crowd before disappearing in a haze of smoke, just as the clowns had done.

He tossed the hat aside, shadows rising from his shoulders, forming . . . lion heads. That was new. The lions turned toward Matas, opened their mouths, and ate him in one bite. He vanished. Then, even the lions vanished. Everyone looked around. A few people even stood. One second passed, two, then three. The lions reappeared at the other side of the ring, opened their mouths, and out spewed an uninjured Matas, earning more cheers.

He spread his arms and grinned . . . but the expression lacked any kind of sincerity. "And now, I summon my lovely assistant," he called.

Audra gave her a little push, and Vika stumbled into the ring. There was a burning around her ankles, and she looked down to see the girl had blown a flame onto the hem of her gown. She stopped to pat it away, causing the crowd to laugh and her skin to heat. Smoke curled around her.

The shadows Matas always carried shot out and wrapped around her, tugging her forward. Dread threatened to consume her, but still she offered no resistance when he shackled her to a spinning wheel—the same kind of wheel Solo had been tied to in the petting zoo—with her arms above her head and her legs apart. A flick of his wrist and round and round she spun. Her surroundings blurred, and her stomach clenched.

This had not been part of his act for years, and never with Vika.

But her father wanted her scared, didn't he? He wanted to prove his utter control over her. He wanted to break her down and remake her into something dark, like him. He wanted her reliant on his mercy. Mercy he did not possess.

Her mind blanked as, in quick succession, blades sank into the wheel beside her left and right temple. Beside her left and right hip. Her left thigh. Right thigh. Both of her ankles. Finally the spinning stopped, and Vika was surprised to find Matas hadn't purposely nicked her.

He closed the distance between them and removed the shackles. Forcing herself to grin, Vika straightened and nodded to the crowd. For the next ten minutes, Matas had her fetch his props, "relax" on a table while he sawed her in half, his shadows hiding the fact that she was still in one piece, and he bent her over and kissed her for dramatic effect. She barely stopped herself from biting his tongue and spitting out his vile taste.

The crowd cheered. There. She had done her part. She was done.

Head held high, she strolled back to the sidelines. Several other performers patted her on the back for a job well done. For once, they weren't treating her as if she were a leper, and she didn't have to wonder why. They now considered her one of them, no longer set apart. And . . . a part of her liked knowing she was no longer despised, there was no denying that.

Perhaps Audra was right. Audra, who was now stepping into the ring to swing on the trapeze.

Perhaps Vika was tainted.

A vibration behind her. A big hand on her shoulder.

Jecis stepped up beside her, and her nervousness returned.

"Well done," he said. He wore a formfitting red jacket, skintight black pants, and knee-high boots. He wore more makeup than she did, probably to prevent his aging skin from appearing washed out in the light.

"Thank you," she replied, happy he wasn't here to yell at her.

"Did you have fun?"

Even now, she wouldn't lie. "No." She might have liked the admiration she'd received there at the end, but the feeling had been fleeting—just like the admiration. These people would turn on her in a heartbeat.

Jecis swept out his arm. "Look. Look out there, at their faces. Feel the adoration of the crowd. You can have that every week."

"I don't want it. You had to sell your soul to get it." Just like Audra. "I won't do the same."

"Sold my soul? Darling, when I took over this circus, I finally *found* my soul."

How could he not see what he'd become? "Daddy, you found something dark and twisted. I liked you the way you were."

A flare of frustration and impatience in his eyes. And . . . was that a skull hiding under his skin, peering out at her, its teeth chomping at her? "When I was weak?"

"When you were sweet."

"And you don't like me now?" he asked, his mouth moving contrary to the skull's.

She pressed her lips together, refusing to answer.

He didn't hit her, and he didn't push her. He didn't even speak another word to her. He simply stalked away.

Vika remained in the same spot for the rest of the performance. And, she had to admit, even she was captivated by the colorful lights, the exuberant beat of the music, and the antics of the twirlers, spinning, spinning, round and round from cords hooked to wooden beams in the ceiling, their bodies contorted in what should have been impossible positions. Some even dove through fiery hoops, lightning flashing from their hands as they met in the center.

A giant glass cannon was wheeled to the far right. A man made a big production of slipping inside the barrel. Audra swung from one of the ropes, nearing the cannon, and shot a spray of fire from her mouth, lighting the fuse. As she swung in the opposite direction, the male blasted from the center, and the fish inside the glass burst free. Only, they weren't injured. The glass turned to glittering snowflakes, and the fish to stuffed animals several lucky people in the crowd could catch.

Finally, though, the show was over and everyone in the stands rose to their feet. They ambled out, talking and laughing, marveling over what they had seen, speculating about how certain things were done.

When the last body cleared the door, the performers offered up their own cheer, breaking out the hard liquor they'd made in their own trailers rather than any kind of champagne. Jecis was in the center of them, drinking in their praise.

Now was her chance.

Vika snuck out the back of the tent and raced to her trailer. Once there, she locked herself inside. Jecis had a key, but even if he decided to use it, the lights would flicker on and off, alerting her to his presence.

She exchanged her high heels for boots, but didn't bother taking the time to change out of her dress. Not yet. If her father spotted her, she wanted him to think she was just out and about, intending to enjoy herself with the other performers. That way, he would be less inclined to stop her or even talk to her.

Well, it's about time, a voice said.

X!

"I know," she said. "Better late than never."

Hands trembling, she stuffed as many necklaces, bracelets, and trinkets as possible into the largest bag she could carry. She ignored the chocolates, but also grabbed the cameras her mother had loved—besides the blade, they were all she had left of the woman who'd given birth to her, and she couldn't force herself to leave them behind. There was barely any room for a sweatshirt and winter pants, but they were necessary, so she crammed them in.

"Did you know there wasn't a key to the cuffs?" she asked, recalling the times he'd told her to grab Solo and go now rather than later.

No. I simply had a knowing that you needed to leave without worrying about the cuffs.

Before donning her coat, she put on several pieces of jewelry that hadn't made the cut for the bag. Six necklaces, seventeen bracelets. Rings on every finger. What a sight she must be.

"Well, I wish you would have told me," she said.

I did. Several times.

"Why not several more?"

Why not listen the first time?

A point she could not refute. "All right, I'm ready to go." The bag was almost too heavy to lug, but lug it outside she did. Cold air instantly enveloped her, the heat of her breath causing a fine mist to form in front of her face.

"Do you know where Solo is?" she whispered.

I do. He's in the same tent as before. The one for the petting zoo.

Suppressing a groan, she flattened herself against the side of the trailer, hiding in the darkness, waiting and listening the only way she could. Thankfully, there was no vibration at her feet.

Before you save the day, X said, *you'll need to steal Solo some clothing. He's currently naked.*

"All right."

You'll need a few other things, too.

As if she would argue with him about anything ever again. "Just tell me what to get, and I'll make it happen."

He rattled off a list of what seemed to be ridiculous items, and she swallowed another groan.

"All right," she repeated. Heart hammering, she raced forward.

Twenty-three

For you have girded me with strength for battle. You have subdued under me those who rose up against me.
—PSALM 18:39

SOLO HAD LOST TRACK of time. He wasn't sure how long he'd been bound to this wheel. He only knew his arms and legs were numb, tied as they were to the board, and that people had eventually stopped coming into the tent. Staring at him. Stroking his flesh as if he were a tame little house cat. Rousing the beast inside him to a fever pitch.

The otherworlders around him were quiet. Not because they were muzzled—they weren't—but because they were in shock, still utterly humiliated, still reeling about all that had happened, about how vulnerable they'd been.

He couldn't do this again. He would rather die.

Even now, his fingers were curled into fists, his claws slicing into his palms. His blood was hot, so hot, tongues of fire licking through his veins. Something even hotter had been pooling in both of his bound wrists, but now, in the face of his burgeoning resentment, that heat spread. The cuffs had just sped into another level.

No matter what you have to do, stay in control. He would tolerate nothing less. He just had to . . . what? Since the death of his parents, he'd had no luck with his temper. Not until Vika, who would have teased him and—

Vika. Where was she?

He pictured her, his sweet, kind Vika, and his fingers actually uncurled. He pictured her peering up at him, her lips swollen and glistening from his kisses, her eyes wide with bafflement and need, and his muscles relaxed.

To be with her, he *could* do this again. He could do anything.

I will have that woman. One day. Soon. Often.

And when that "one day" came, he would make her forget her aversion to the words.

"You deserve this, you know," said Dr. E.

Right on time to try and revive Solo's anger.

"No, you deserve what's *about* to happen. Rescue."

And there was X, here to build him up.

"Where were you guys while I was in the Nolands?" he demanded quietly, the words muffled by the muzzle across his mouth. "Wait. Rescue?"

A moment later, Vika raced into the tent. She was dressed in a glorious red dress, and he forgot his questions. Her arms were covered by a thick black coat, but the material was split in the middle and he could see that the top of her gown scooped low enough to reveal a hint of cleavage. The bottom was so long it swept across the floor, curling around her feet as if it were enchanted mist. The material clung to her every curve, and her body . . . it was a work of art. Small and lush, with hips that flared into a heart.

Her. *She's mine,* he thought. He didn't need X's help anymore, not for this. He'd already realized that, yeah, but now the knowledge swirled where instinct beat with a heart of its own. Never again would he allow her to walk away from him.

She reached him, dropped the bag she was holding. Expression pale and pinched despite the bright makeup she wore, she immediately tried to undo the metal bars draped over his cuffs, pulling and tugging.

"We're leaving tonight," she said. "Now. No matter what we have to do." But no matter how valiantly she struggled, she couldn't remove the obstacles. "Argh! What should I do?"

He opened his mouth to answer, not sure she would be able to understand him, but she stiffened.

"Shh!" She raced behind the wheel, out of sight.

It was then that he heard the oncoming footsteps. "Your bag," he whispered fiercely. She'd left the thing at his feet. But she couldn't hear him, he reminded himself, and she had no idea she'd left evidence behind.

Three of Jecis's guards suddenly entered the tent, each drinking from a half-empty bottle of booze. The trio stumbled toward Criss's wheel, two of them arguing over who would get to have her first, and the third vowing to tame Kitten after he watched the other girl's violation.

Solo scanned the rest of the otherworlders. Except for the Targon, all eyes were closed, as if the prisoners couldn't bear to watch what they couldn't stop. Not the Targon, though. His eyes were open. His body was tense, each of his muscles knotted, as if he prepared to fight.

"Kaamil-Alize," Solo growled.

The Targon's attention swung his way, and they shared a moment of understanding. They had to do something. Anything.

Bottom line: He couldn't allow this. For the women, and for Vika. She would try to stop the men. They would turn on her, Jecis's daughter or not. They were drunk. They wouldn't care.

The thought of Vika attacked . . . hurt by these disgusting humans . . . perhaps thrown down and stripped, perhaps even touched in ways she would forever despise. No! A new spurt of the drugs flowed through Solo's veins, but not even that could dampen the chill of his determination.

Gritting his teeth, growling, he put all of his strength into his right arm, lifting . . . lifting . . . Muscles pulled and tendons tore, but still he lifted—until the metal from the wheel could no longer handle the strain and snapped away. Warm blood trickled down his arm.

The humans had reached Criss. They were too busy fondling her to notice Solo.

"What are you doing?" Dr. E demanded. "Stop! You're hurting yourself."

Funny thing. The being sounded incensed rather than concerned.

Solo ripped off the muzzle, and his arm dropped

limply to his side. The cuff was still there, still active, but at the moment he only cared about range of motion. Immediately he began to work on the other arm, lifting despite the pain, until those shackles fell away.

One of the guards heard him and glanced back. He noticed Solo's half-free state and paled, slapping at his friends to get their attention. They spotted him and finally stopped laughing.

"What're you doing?"

"Enough of that."

They surged forward, and out raced Vika, whipping in front of Solo and spreading her arms.

"Leave him alone!" she shouted.

They paused, Solo momentarily forgotten.

"And what do we have here?" one said.

"A naughty little girl, that's what."

"I've always wanted me a piece of you, Vika Lukas, and here you are, throwing yourself at me. Jecis will surely understand if I take you up on your offer. Especially since he's made it more than clear he's done protecting you."

The three moved toward her, only to freeze in place halfway. Each had a foot lifted in mid-stride. Each leered at Vika, expression unchanging.

"I'll hold them as long as I can," the Targon said through gritted teeth.

Solo had known Targon warriors possessed the ability to manipulate energy molecules and control the human body, but he'd assumed this particular warrior was too drugged to ever do so.

Vika swung to face Solo, her eyes wide. "I don't understand what's happening."

Solo didn't waste any time. Only his legs remained bound. As he tugged and jerked, one of his kneecaps popped out of place, but that didn't stop him either. Nothing could, and finally he was free, falling from the wheel . . . crashing into the ground.

Through sheer grit and willpower he lumbered to his feet. Black dots wove through his vision as Vika rushed to his side, her soft hands flattening on his chest.

"Oh, Solo," she breathed. "You're hurt."

He picked her up by the waist and set her behind him.

"Do what needs doing," X said, his voice strained.

Even as he spoke, Solo felt another flood of warmth through his veins. Only this warmth didn't spring from the drugs. It came from X. Bones began to snap back into place. Muscles began to weave back together.

The moment he was completely healed, X vanished. And Solo. Utterly. Un. Leashed.

He surged forward, arms pumping at his sides, legs increasing in speed, until he left a trail of fire in his wake. He plowed into the guards and they jetted to the ground, hit hard. He ripped out the trachea of one—with his teeth—while clawing through the throat of another. Both acts happened in two seconds flat.

The third, finally able to move, tried to scramble away from him, but Solo picked him up. He stood, blood dribbling down his chin, and slammed the male into the ground from left to right, left to right, over and over again, until he was panting, until his arms burned, until there was nothing left and he was holding only a blood-soaked coat.

Dr. E said something. The otherworlders called out to him. Solo was too lost to his rage to understand the actual words. He had to destroy this place. Had to ensure Vika never again suffered at the hands of these monsters. Had to save the others like him.

He plowed into the little ice cream shop, tilting the tin building to its side. The equipment scattered to the floor. Bottles of flavoring spilled, scenting the air with strawberries and vanilla. The fragrance only incensed him further, reminding him of the humans. Of being touched when he hadn't wanted to be touched. He shredded the building, leaving only confetti, uncaring when jagged shards of tin cut him.

A group of males rushed into the tent to find out what was causing such a commotion. Eight, Solo counted as he straightened, ready for more. *Wanting* more. They spotted him and ground to a halt. Solo knew his skin had turned red. Knew his bones had enlarged, his ears had extended into sharp little points, his fangs had sprouted, and his claws had lengthened. He was the monster their mothers had probably always warned them about. The one under their bed, or in their closets. The one who would steal their souls.

He leapt into motion and slammed into them, a bowling ball to the pins. They fought against him, but they could not contain him. They tried, oh, they tried, but Solo ripped arms from sockets, ripped spines from beneath their fleshly coverings, bit and clawed and tossed his opponents in every direction—in little bitty pieces.

"Solo," he heard.

Soft, whispery. Frightened.

He whipped around, panting, nostrils flaring, his big body tense, his claws raised and ready to slash whatever had dared to frighten Vika. Wide plum-colored eyes peered over at him—and he was the target of her fear.

"Vika," he said, his voice nothing more than a broken scrape.

She was still standing in front of his wheel, her little body quavering, her arms wrapped around her middle. "The others," she said, and motioned to the otherworlders. "Let's free them and go."

She still wished to leave with him.

He would do whatever she asked.

He rushed to Kitten's wheel. She had been struggling against her bonds, and blood was dripping down her arms. He reached out, yanked, and ripped one of the bars from the wheel, taking a huge hunk of wood with it.

"Watching you work was a real pleasure," she said. "But you aren't part of AIR, are you? I'm guessing you're black ops all the way, baby."

Silent, he reached for the second bar.

Footsteps sounded behind him, and Kitten paled.

"Go," she said. "Come back for me later. With guns. And Dallas."

He turned. Four other males and two females had just run into the tent. They stopped to catalogue the carnage, as if they couldn't quite believe what they were seeing. One of the females unleashed a blood-curdling scream.

His gaze swung to Vika. She was at Criss's wheel, tugging ineffectually at one of the bars. Tears streamed down her cheeks as the rest of the otherworlders begged and pleaded with her to hurry.

He had a choice to make. Vika, or all the others. Right now, he couldn't have both. The knowledge frustrated him, enraged him further, and guilt immediately began to chew on his bones. Because honestly? He didn't need a moment to think. He already knew what he was going to do: grab Vika and run.

He *would* come back, though. There was no question about that. He wouldn't leave these people defenseless for any longer than necessary.

Decided, he rushed to Vika's side and scooped her up.

"If you want to save anything here," the Targon called, "I'd return in nine days."

Why nine days?

"My bag," Vika gasped out. "Please! I need it."

The males had finally looked past the pile of dead bodies and the pools of blood and noticed him. Shouts erupted. Solo backtracked, grabbed the bag's strap, and fit it over his shoulder. The moment the weight settled against him, surprise filled him. Little Vika had carried this thing? On her own? It had to weigh a hundred pounds, at the very least.

Another group of men entered the tent, claiming his attention—and Jecis occupied the center. His stormy gaze locked on Solo, and the skull he always carried with him, the one that moved of its own accord, separate from his own bones, that dark presence, tilted back, stretched open its jaw, and shrieked.

One day, we'll have our showdown, Solo vowed, and ran in the opposite direction. *One day very soon.*

Twenty-four

∽◈∾

Hurry, my beloved, and be like a gazelle or a young stag
on the mountains of spices.
—SONG OF SOLOMON 8:14

SOLO CARRIED VIKA AND her bag through the night, into the mountains. He had to be freezing. She was. And he was naked, and frost practically coated the air.

"I brought you clothes and shoes," she said through chattering teeth. "They're in the bag."

Maybe he replied, maybe he didn't. Either way, he kept going.

What had happened inside the tent . . . Total devastation was the only way to describe it. He had morphed into the raging red beast the others had called him. He had hurt people. He had killed.

He had protected.

She hadn't been afraid of him, and the knowledge had stunned her. He would never hurt her, and deep down, where the knowing he'd taught her about swirled, she'd understood that. She'd been afraid *for* him.

Any moment, someone could have walked into the tent with a gun and shot him. If that had happened, her father would have killed him, not just to punish him for what he'd done but because Jecis would have feared him, even behind the cage.

"I can walk," she said, not wanting him to have to carry the entire burden of their escape.

He set her down without ever breaking stride, clasped her hand, and dragged her behind him. They maneuvered around trees—so many trees!—and over thick stumps. An eternity later, he glanced back at her.

"Questions? Concerns? Comments?"

"Where are we?" she asked. Jecis hadn't said. All she knew was that she'd never been here.

"The New Kolyma region of the Russian Far East."

"Siberia?"

"Yes. Don't worry. I've got this."

Up, up, faster and faster, he led her through the snow. Snow on the ground, snow on the beautiful trees. A true winter wonderland, stunning in its beauty. Harsh in its treachery. How quickly could a person freeze to death out here?

Sadly, that wasn't the least of her troubles. Jecis would follow. Maybe not tonight. Maybe not tomorrow. He would feel no rush. After all, he could locate Solo at any time. But he *would* gather the troops and come after them.

Vika would be wise to ditch Solo now and strike out on her own. It was what she'd planned to do while they were trapped in the Nolands. Now . . .

She just couldn't bring herself to leave him.

He looked back at her, saying, "Shout if you need me to stop."

"I will." And she almost shouted a thousand times in the next five minutes, but somehow, she held the sound inside. She wanted as much distance between them and the circus as possible, even if she had to suffer to get it.

The higher up the mountain they went, the thicker the trees became and the rockier the terrain. Eventually, Vika lost track of time. All she knew was that she was shivering uncontrollably and her muscles were as heavy as boulders. Her lungs burned.

Solo glanced back at her a second time, slowed his pace, then stopped. "We'll stop for the night," he said. He wasn't winded and didn't seem cold.

"Because you found a safe place?" she asked hopefully.

"Because you're tired."

As she'd suspected. "I don't care. Keep going until you find a safe place." They needed every advantage they could get.

He studied her intently, pride glowing in those baby blues. "Very well."

Was that pride directed at *her*?

She expected to leap back into motion. Instead, he dropped the bag and unzipped the top. The clothes she'd stolen from her father rested on top. Although not a single garment belonged to Jecis. Rather, Jecis had stolen them from the Targon and were the perfect size for Solo.

Size—the reason no one human had bought them. The material was as black as night, and possessed a soft, luxuriant quality.

He slipped into the shirt and the pants, then withdrew the clothes she'd brought for herself and tossed them at her.

"How about we leave the bag behind?" he asked as he tugged on the socks and boots.

What? "No!" Removing her coat was actually painful, the cold air biting at every section of exposed skin, but somehow she found the strength to do it. Next she shucked the dress.

Solo averted his eyes, saying, "It's excess baggage, and I mean that literally."

"It's my life." The sweatshirt and pants bagged on her, but oh, they were toasty warm, having been snuggled up to Solo's body during the entire trek.

"I heard jewelry banging around in there."

"Exactly."

An eager gleam that rivaled the beauty of the moonlight entered his eyes. "I'll buy you new ones."

When she'd gone to hell and back for these? "Give the bag to me, and I'll carry it."

Frowning, he once again fit the strap over his shoulder.

"Solo," she said.

"Vika." Without another word, he linked their fingers and urged her forward.

Solo reveled in his freedom. He still wore the cuffs, yes, but he was no longer behind bars. He was no longer strapped to a wheel, a scratch pad for anyone with an itch. He had his woman at his side, and the only danger currently stalking them was the weather.

He'd listened, he'd watched, and he knew Jecis had

stayed behind. Still, Solo wanted as much distance between them as possible tonight. Tomorrow, he would
drag Vika what would probably seem to be a thousand
miles, and the more they ran tonight, the less they'd
have to trek while she was sore and hungry, her adrenaline depleted.

No, he thought next, he wouldn't allow her to become hungry. The moment he had her tucked into a
warm little crevice, she would fall asleep and he would
hunt. But wow, already she was holding up better than
he'd hoped. His tiny little fluff of nothing had a stubborn streak that wouldn't allow her to quit—or even
slow. She might appear to be asleep on her feet, but she
matched him step for step.

"What are we going to do?" she huffed.

"Avoid the towns, for one." Many Americans had
moved to Siberia immediately following the human-
alien war, since Siberia was supposedly the only land free
of the otherworlders' "taint." Actually, otherworlders
were usually shot on sight here. "My boss, Michael, has a
cabin on the border." Michael had homes in every state,
every country. Maybe even every city. That was how he
kept his agents hidden, no matter where they were or
what they had to do. "We'll make our way there."

They reached a little clearing, where a tree had
fallen, the center hollowed out by weather and age. No
one would be able to hide nearby. He would see and
hear anyone who approached. And he could share his
body heat with Vika inside the stump. This was as good
as it was going to get.

He dropped the bag beside the tree, urged Vika to settle inside the center, and worked on gathering nearby stones. He'd wanted ten but could only find eight. Oh, well. That would have to do. He cleared the snow from a small section of land and used the rocks to form a circle. Next he gathered twigs and piled them inside the rocks.

He sat beside Vika, claimed two of the stones, and struck them together.

"As much as I'd love to watch you create a fire that way, because it's very manly and impressive and everything," she said, "I'd feel guilty if I didn't tell you there's a lighter in the bag."

He paused, looked at her, and arched a brow. "You came prepared."

"I had help," she admitted after a brief hesitation.

"Who?"

"Well . . ." She nibbled on her lower lip as she dug into the bag. Several minutes passed, and she began to mumble under her breath. "Found it!" Grinning, she pulled out a lighter and slapped it into his hand.

"You never answered my question, Vika."

"Oh, yeah. Well, do you remember those invisible men we've talked about?"

"Yes." He lit the end of one of the twigs, flames quickly catching and crackling and spreading to the others. Heat wafted toward them, and smoke curled through the air.

"I wasn't ever going to tell you, unless you spilled first, but waiting kind of seems silly now, after everything. So, here goes. One of them helped me. His name is X and he—"

"X? My X?"

"Your X? You *do* see him, then."

"I do. I've seen him most of my life."

"Well, I started seeing him a few days after you were captured."

He had no idea what to think about this development. X had never revealed himself to another person, never expressed a desire to do so, never *mentioned* doing so, and Solo had assumed it was an impossible feat.

"What has he said to you?" he demanded.

Vika groaned. "That question is the very reason I never mentioned his name."

Same for Solo. But just like she'd inferred, they were past the point of holding back. "You're going to spill whether you want to or not."

"Fine." Her cheeks bloomed a lovely pink. "X says he's an Altilium and Dr. E is an Epoto, but I have no idea what either of those words mean."

"They are Latin for 'a charger' and 'a drain,' and they certainly fit." And they'd certainly told her more than that.

Mist billowed in front of her, creating a dreamlike haze. "So how is Dr. E a doctor?"

"Well, for starters he earned a doctorate in annoying me."

She giggled as she said, "Make that two doctorates. I really like X, but I want to find a way to get rid of Dr. E."

Solo was the reason the being had been bothering her, but she threw no blame his way. He did not deserve this woman, but he wanted to. He wanted to do whatever was necessary to become the man she needed. "Are they with you now?"

"No. You?"

"No." So where were they? "What else did they tell you? And you had better fess up. Otherwise I'll be forced to utilize my world-famous interrogation technique."

Another giggle. She assumed he was kidding. But at least she'd stopped blushing. Solo didn't want her embarrassed with him. He wanted her comfortable enough to confess anything.

"Well, X said I'm supposed to stay with you."

And that's why I like him best. He waited. She remained silent.

"That's all?" he insisted.

"That's the gist of it, yes, and all I'm willing to admit at the moment. Interrogation or not."

That wasn't so bad.

Then, she added, "Dr. E suggested I leave you behind to rot."

His hands fisted, and he could feel the drugs begin to drip into his bloodstream.

He wanted to talk to both creatures right there, right then. He wanted to ask how and why, what else had been said, and command they leave his woman alone. She wasn't to be bothered with their antics.

"Let's change the subject," he said. Before the sedatives got the better of him.

He stretched out beside her and she immediately snuggled against him, angling her head to watch his lips and sighing with what seemed to be satisfaction. He toyed with the ends of her hair, content.

"You aren't afraid of me, are you?" he asked.

"No. Why?" Golden light danced over her, making her look as if she'd just stepped from some ancient painting of a magical land with fairies and pixies and a happily-ever-after.

"I . . . hurt people today."

"In an effort to help others. Trust me," she said with a yawn. "I'm beginning to understand the difference."

Thank the Lord. "Good." He kissed her forehead. "Close your eyes now, sweetheart. You need to sleep."

"But I'm not tired."

She was, but she was fighting it. Too much adrenaline, perhaps. Too much concern for what the future held. "Want to play the question game again?"

Her features brightened. "Yes, please."

"Good, because I'm wondering . . . what's your favorite color?"

"Blue," she'd said, and then admitted softly, "the exact shade of your eyes. I've never seen anything so lovely."

He stilled, not even daring to breathe.

"What's *your* favorite color?" she asked.

"Vika."

"Yes?"

"No," he said, fighting a grin, "that's my favorite color."

Her brow furrowed with confusion, the same way it had done in the cage when he'd said something she couldn't quite figure out. "But I'm not a color."

"Are you sure?"

A pause. A second later, a laugh bubbled from her. A laugh that heated him far more thoroughly than the fire.

"You know, that's the most wonderful thing I've ever not heard," she said, petting her fingers through his hair. "You're the first man to ever truly compliment me, and I think I'm already addicted to it."

"I'm truly the first?"

A beat of silence. "You will be," she whispered, and they both knew she wasn't just talking about the compliment.

Instantly the tide of need he'd experienced for her all these many days flooded him, his body reacting to her on a primal level. He'd known she was a virgin, but here, now, the knowledge caused a sense of possessiveness to rise up—one stronger than before.

This woman was to be his, and only his.

"Forget the game. I want to kiss you," he croaked. They were alone. No one was watching them, no one was listening. There was no better time.

Her lips fell, the humor draining from her.

"But I won't," he forced himself to add. Clearly, she wasn't ready.

Well, he would have to get her ready again.

"Why not?" she said. Then, "Oh. That's right. It's my turn to kiss you." She leaned over and licked her way into his mouth.

Surprise hit him first, followed closely by intensified desire. Their tongues met, rolled together, and the sweetness of her taste arrested him. Heat blasted through his entire body, his cells coming alive, his nerve endings shooting out electric sparks, and he groaned as the absolute, utter devastation of his need consumed him. This woman . . . he had to have her, all of her, and soon.

"Vika," he said.

"Solo."

He gave her sweet and he gave her tender . . . at first. The more they nipped at each other, the more concentrated his motions became. He played with the edges of her shirt, running his fingers along the hem, teasing the bare skin of her belly, trying to prepare her for a more intimate invasion.

Soon she was moaning, following his every movement for more prolonged contact.

"I want to touch you, sweetheart."

"You are," she whispered.

Such an innocent comment, reminding him to go slowly, to be careful—no matter how great his need. Her peace of mind was more important than any fleeting pleasure. "I know, but I want to go higher, to touch your breasts."

Out came the pretty pink tip of her tongue, swiping over her lips, leaving a delicate sheen of moisture.

"I won't touch anything else," he told her. Not until she was ready.

A moment passed. She gulped, nodded.

Slowly he slid his hand under her top and cupped her, flesh to flesh, palm to female. Her skin was cool, but he quickly warmed her up. He grazed his thumb across the center peak, drawing a moan from her, this one straight from the deepest depths of her. All the while he watched her expression. Fear never registered. Only pleasure.

And when she arched into his clasp, a silent request for stronger pressure, he fought the urge to bellow with sublime satisfaction.

He would get her there.

"Do you like this?" he asked, already knowing the answer.

"Oh, yes."

"I want to replace my hands with my mouth, all right, and—" Solo's ears twitched, and he stiffened.

"What—"

He withdrew his hand and placed his finger against her lips, silencing her. With his other hand, he doused the flames. Darkness descended.

His eyes adjusted in seconds, and he watched as a fox pranced into and out of the clearing. No threat, then. Still. The intrusion served as a necessary reminder. He was Vika's sole means of protection, and that had to come before anything else.

Solo met her gaze. "I have to put a stop to our extracurricular activities. We can't risk any kind of distraction, and besides that, we've got a big day ahead. Sleep."

"No."

"Yes." He relaxed into the stump and pressed her head into the hollow of his neck.

"Fine. Night, Solo," she said with a bead of frustration, warm breath caressing his neck.

"Night," he replied, even knowing she couldn't hear him.

Only a few minutes later, she melted against him, signaling that she'd fallen asleep, as ordered. But just as he was about to rise to hunt the morning's game, she began to toss and turn, before jolting upright, gasping for breath.

"I'm here," he assured her. "Solo's here."

"Solo," she said, sighing and settling back against him. Once again she drifted off. This time, she remained motionless, quiet.

She felt safe with him, trusted him, and he was glad—even though holding her was the sweetest and the worst sort of torture, her decadent scent in his nose, her soft curves pushed against the hardness of his body.

But this was what he'd always wanted, wasn't it? A woman in his arms, happy to be with him. And that the woman happened to be Vika . . .

Despite everything else, Solo grinned.

Twenty-five

∽◦∾

Awake, sleeper, and arise from the dead.
—EPHESIANS 5:14

LIGHT PIERCED THE DARKNESS in Vika's mind, and she stretched, roused from the most peaceful sleep of her life. The smell of roasting meat filled her nose, and her mouth watered.

She eased up, rubbed at her eyes. Right away, she noticed a few startling facts. She was warm, draped by a thick, furry blanket she hadn't had last night, and except for the diamond choker locked around her neck, her jewelry had been removed.

Solo crouched in front of a small fire, turning a skewer of meat he'd rigged across two sticks he'd planted in the ground. On her own, she probably would have starved. But Solo was beyond capable, beyond resourceful . . . and far more beautiful than her necklace as golden rays shone and danced over him, highlighting his strength, his utter masculinity.

"Good morning," she said.

He turned toward her, looked her up and down, a heat every bit as fiery as the one in front of him blazing in those baby blues. "Morning."

Her heartbeat quickened as she recalled the sheer mastery of his kiss. And when he'd cupped her breast, oh, sweet mercy, the reaction he'd sparked had been unexpected, the sweetest sort of pleasure, the most agonizing sort of pain.

She'd needed more. Wanted more, yes, that, too, but *needed* was the better word. When he'd stopped, she'd expected to die. She would have traded her next breath for one touch.

And all right, okay, she'd understood his reasons, she had, but she'd still wanted to growl with dissatisfaction. She'd never experienced so much pleasure, and he'd just taken it away.

You're pouting, she thought, and sighed. Solo deserved better than a whiny female more concerned with lovemaking than safety—especially since that very same female had stopped *him* from continuing a time before.

"Solo," she said.

"Yes. That's me. What's with the snotty tone?"

Snotty tone! "I don't have a—Fine, I do. I'm sorry."

"Still frustrated?" he asked her.

"Maybe." She glanced down at her hands; her fingers were wringing together. "I want you to know . . . feel like I should explain . . . why I wouldn't let you do more than kiss me that time in the cage."

"You told me. You weren't ready."

"And that was true. It's just, when I was younger, just a girl, the things I witnessed in the shadows . . ." she said, and a shudder raked her. "Then I ran away and I was captured by a group of drunk boys and barely managed to wiggle my way free to hide. The things they did before I got away . . . they squeezed and it hurt, and I was so afraid, so happy when my father showed up and rescued me, and I'm rambling, I know, but that's one of the reasons I stayed with him so long. He saved me from a terrible fate. At the circus, his name offered me some sort of protection."

Solo moved to crouch in front of her. "Vika—"

"No, don't say anything. It happened. I learned, and I grew. I'm okay. I just wanted you to know."

"You were a child," he said. "A child who grew into a guarded woman, desperate for a way out, yet still taking care of those less fortunate than herself. I understand that now." He sighed. "I threatened you during our first meeting, and I'm not proud of myself for that. I wish I could go back and do a thousand things differently."

She ran her fingers through the chilled locks of his hair, entranced by the softness. "Typical Solo, trying to make me feel better."

"Always." He kissed the tip of her nose. "Listen. I revved you up last night and failed to finish you because watching you climax would have pushed me over the edge. I know you don't blame me for deciding to wait, but your body doesn't get it, and that's understandable. When we're finally together, it will be in a bed and you'll be safe. We can do whatever we want to each other."

"Yes, well . . ." Even talking about what they could and would do was revving her up again. She hurried to change the subject. "What's that we'll be dining on?"

"Don't ask, and I won't tell."

"Well, how did you manage to kill this mystery meat?"

"I stumbled upon a group of hunters, waiting in a blind, and confiscated their weapons."

She wouldn't ask what he'd done with the hunters themselves.

"Speaking of weapons . . ." He straightened and walked to the other side of their tree trunk bed, where he lifted two rifles. "Have you ever used one of these?"

"A gun? Yes. Something that big? No."

"I'll give you a mini lesson before we head out. And you don't have to worry about using it and drawing Jecis to our location with the noise. See the ends? I created a special paste to muffle the boom."

"Oh, well, that's great, but I already have a gun," she said, and dug inside the bag until she found it. "It's even loaded and everything."

He looked at the weapon, shook his head, then looked again, a strange light entering his eyes. "The safety is off," he said through gritted teeth.

"What safety?" She turned the barrel toward her face and—

The weapon was swiped from her grip. Solo fiddled with it, and she heard a click. He checked . . . whatever it was called, the little round center that spun, before saying, "I've been carrying this thing around, Vika."

Now probably wasn't time to say "duh." "I know."

"I could have shot myself. Or you! And I thought you said you'd used a gun."

"I had. My father put one in my hand and forced me

to squeeze the trigger. And guess what? I've got some good news for you. You didn't shoot yourself, or me."

He ran his tongue over his teeth. "Let me guess. This is X's doing?"

"It was a suggestion of his, yes," she said, not wanting to get the little guy into trouble when he'd only wished to help.

"What else did he tell you to bring?"

"I'll show you." She withdrew a fork, toothpaste, lipstick, a condom, and scented body spray. "He told me that each one of these things was a necessity."

"O-kay. So why the fork?" he asked.

That was the first question he had? Really? "X says we aren't savages, and we aren't to act as if we are."

"And the lipstick?"

"That, he didn't say."

"No bottles of water? No food?"

"No. But I'm guessing that's because we can melt and drink the snow, and X knew you could catch"—she waved her hand toward the fire—"things."

"And the condom? The *single* condom?"

Annnd there was the question she'd assumed he would ask at the start. "It's not my fault," she said, fighting a blush. "I'm embarrassed, too, but he said to grab it, so I grabbed it."

"Yeah, but we probably aren't embarrassed for the same reasons," he muttered.

Why was he embarrassed, then?

He took the fork and stomped back to the make-shift kitchen, where he placed juicy chunks of meat on a large, flat stone. "There's a river a few yards north, and I've already cleaned the stone," he said, handing it to her. "We aren't savages, right, and I won't have you eating off a dirty plate."

A beat of surprise as she absorbed his words. What a sweet, sweet man, considering her in all things, even the little things. "Thank you," she said with a bright smile.

"Welcome. Now, here's the fork." He held out his hand.

She shook her head. "No, thank you. That's for you."

"I'm not going to use a fork while you're stuck using your fingers. Take it."

"No."

He frowned but stuffed the utensil back into the bag. "Fine. We'll both be savages."

"Fine." After she'd taken a few bites of the most delicious meal of her life, she moaned and said, "Is there anything you *can't* do?" And maybe she *was* a savage, because she wanted to continue stuffing her face while she was talking—and she wanted to chew what remained of the meat off the bone. "You have no need for a chef at your farm."

"And yet I still want one," he muttered.

Did that mean what she thought it meant? That he still wanted Vika there? "Sweet" barely scratched the surface, she realized. "I want you to know, while we're on our journey, I'm not going to let you down or hold you back. I'll keep up, I promise."

"Don't push yourself too hard."

"I won't," she said, which was the truth. She planned to push herself *way* too hard. He'd only helped her. She wouldn't hinder him.

Solo finished eating and stuffed all the "necessities" back into the bag, as well as the blanket he'd stolen, and hefted the stupid thing over his shoulder, then one rifle, then the other. He would have given Vika one of the weapons, but no, that was never going to happen now. Not even if his life depended on it.

"I rigged a place for you to take care of any pressing needs you might have," he said, and watched as color once again brightened her cheeks.

"Thank you," she replied, comprehending. "But, uh . . . where is it?"

He pointed, enchanted by her unease for some reason. They'd spent six days together, trapped in a ten-by-ten cage. They'd gone over this type of thing. But his little Vika was prim and proper, he supposed—until he kissed her.

Any time he remembered their kiss, a fire ignited in his blood, and a deep awareness bloomed where primal instinct seethed. It was wonderful. . . . It was terrible. . . . He wanted her, but he couldn't have her. Not out here, in the open, where anyone else could stumble upon them.

At least he understood a little more about her now—and how much he'd misunderstood her in the beginning and even moments before. No wonder she'd always wanted to live on her own. No wonder she had wanted to spend the rest of her life alone. It was a miracle she'd ever allowed Solo to come near her.

Vika stood, stumbled through the snow, and soon disappeared behind a wall of winter leaves. The area was close enough that he could hear if anyone approached her, but far enough away that she would feel comfortable enough to do whatever she needed to do. Plus, a good number of trees would form a circle around her, shielding her from any prying eyes.

He dismantled the spit, put out the fire and scattered the rocks. He hid the evidence of their stay as best he could, and by the time he finished, Vika had returned.

"Are you sore?" he asked.

"Surprisingly, not too badly."

Good. "We're going to keep a brutal pace today. I checked our coordinates, and if we hurry, we can make it to the cabin a little after nightfall."

"I'm ready," she said, and she sounded as if she truly was.

He linked their fingers—something he was fond of doing. He liked knowing she was nearby. Liked knowing she trusted him enough to remain by his side.

They trudged forward, silent for the first hour.

"I have something to tell you," she said, "but you're not going to like it."

"You can tell me anything."

"Well . . . you see, there isn't a key to the cuffs. Jecis destroyed the only one, which kind of explains why I was never able to find it."

Kind of explained?

"I'm sorry!" she added.

No key, he thought, dazed by the realization, even though he should have guessed a long time ago. Jecis was just cruel enough, just smug enough, to do such a thing, uncaring about the lives he was ruining. Actually, *happy* about the lives he was ruining.

And Vika was waiting for a response from him. She expected him to rant and rave, most likely.

"Don't worry about it," he finally replied, and turned left, maneuvering around a small pond of ice. After a while, the drugs in the cuffs would run out. They would no longer be able to affect him. But . . . he still wanted them off. Never wanted anyone to have this kind of power over him again. Never wanted to be located by a few clicks of a computer.

He'd hoped to search for the key when he went back to rescue the otherworlders, but now, that would be unnecessary—one less thing to do. And really, this was probably for the best. Now he could remove the bands the moment he had Vika tucked safely away and knew Michael was on his way.

Michael, who should have found him by now.

But Solo still refused to believe his friends were dead. In their line of work, you had to see the body to believe. And even then it was iffy.

John was wily. Blue was a charmer. They were both survivors. No one could keep them down for long. And Solo, well, he was the fixer. He'd always been the problem solver and he would solve this.

Together, they had saved this world from many,

many terrible people. Drug suppliers, human slavers, murderers, and those thinking to put together an army and rise up to power. The boys were due for a rescue of their own. And they would reap it, he assured himself. He would make sure of it.

For the next six hours, he was careful to avoid the areas with heavy wolf and bear tracks. And he did well, until a pack of wolves stepped to the edge of the cliff above him. He wanted to curse, but really, there was nothing he could have done. There'd been no tracks to avoid—because the animals had clearly been hunting him.

Bright yellow gazes scanned the daylight, diligently searching for the tasty treat that had been scented. Solo stopped and tossed a narrow glance at Vika, a demand for silence. She nodded to show she understood. He lifted her off her feet and carried her to the nearest boulder. He might outweigh her by more than a hundred and fifty pounds, but still his steps were lighter.

He set the bag at her feet and placed a swift kiss on her lips. Her eyes were wide, glazed with fear and fatigue, but she remained upright as he moved away from her. He was prouder of her with every second that passed.

A low, menacing growl split the air, followed by another.

The wolves had spotted him. Now they jumped, landing behind him in quick succession. He heard the thump of their paws, and could calculate the location of each.

Solo spun around, palming the rifle and squeezing off a shot. There was no loud bang, only a mild pop, the makeshift silencer doing its job. One creature stilled, his leg now sporting an open wound, while the others leapt at him. Rage engulfed him. Rage that these animals had placed his woman in danger, that they could have harmed her.

Just before contact, he morphed into his other form, making it impossible to use the rifle. He dropped the gun and grabbed two of the wolves by the scruffs of their necks, slamming them together, blocking one of their friends from his jugular. The other bounced to the ground, and he tossed the ones he held on top.

The remaining three had latched onto his legs and were chewing on his calves. Red dripped and splattered across the snow, scenting the air with a copper tang. He tossed one to the left, one to the right, and grabbed hold of the last. Lifting the creature high, he threw back his head and roared.

The others began to back away from him. He launched the one squirming in his grip, and the wolf slammed into its friends. No longer content to inch away, the entire pack turned tail and ran.

A strange sound behind him had him looking back, concerned. Vika stood in the very place he'd left her, but she was holding the gun X had told her to steal. And she was shaking, pale.

"I . . . I couldn't fire. I'm sorry. I tried. I wanted to help you, but I couldn't. I just couldn't, because all I could think about was One Day, and the way he looked at me when Jecis made me shoot him, and the others as they died, and I . . . I'm so, so sorry!"

An apology. After everything she'd just witnessed. Once again, she wasn't disgusted by his fighting ability and the knowledge floored him.

He held his hands up, palms out and moved toward her. His nails retracted. "Sweetheart, it's okay. It's actually better that you didn't. You haven't practiced with a gun, and you could have shot me. Do you want to shoot me?"

"No!"

Gently he pried the gun from her kung fu grip and stuffed the barrel into the waist of his pants. He tugged her into his arms and held her, just held her as she cried, very glad he had allowed the wolves to live.

"I'm sorry. Now isn't the time for emotion." She lifted her head, revealing watery eyes that hurt his very soul. "I need to tend to your injuries."

"And you can, the moment we get to the cabin." He cupped her cheeks, his thumbs dusting away the tears that would always be his undoing. "*I'm* sorry for everything you've had to endure over the years, sweetheart."

She sniffled out a trembling, "Thank you. But Solo? If you were smart, you'd leave me behind. I know I've been trying my best to keep up, just as I promised, but I'm still dragging you down, aren't I?"

If you were smart, she'd said, obviously clueless about just how badly she'd insulted him.

Why did he want to smile?

"You would be miles and miles from here if you didn't

have to worry about me," she continued. "Wouldn't you?"

Probably. "Body heat is important in weather like this." Not for him, though. Solo didn't experience cold the same way the humans did. Still he said, "Maybe you're saving me from frostbite. Maybe you're saving me from dying of boredom. You're quite entertaining."

That mollified her somewhat, and she fiddled with the collar of his shirt. "You're right. I'm sure I am saving you. And by the way, you're welcome."

"Well, it's about time you two started trusting each other," a familiar voice said. "It was the lipstick, wasn't it? I knew you wouldn't be able to resist her."

Solo didn't have to look to know that X had just landed on his shoulder. "Where have you been?"

Vika frowned up at him. "Right here."

"X," he said with a shake of his head.

"Really?" She looked right. She looked left. "Where is he?"

"You can't see or hear him?"

"No."

"Why can't she see or hear you right now?" he asked X.

"I am only able to manifest to one person at a time. And to answer your earlier question, I have been recharging. I've had to do that a lot lately."

"It's taking you longer than usual."

"I'm using more energy than usual."

"Where did you go, anyway?"

X looked down, kicked out a sandaled foot. "You know I will not tell you where."

No, he never did. Still, "thank you" hardly seemed adequate. "I owe you."

"And I'll collect, I'm sure," the little man said with a grin.

But he wouldn't. He never did.

Why did Solo suddenly feel like ruffling the male's hair? "Where's Dr. E?" And how odd to have this conversation in front of someone. He'd never done that before.

"He's somewhere nearby, that's all I know. I plan to hunt him down. But first . . ." He walked down Solo's arm and stopped at the metal bands around his wrists. He peered inside the keyhole, mumbled to himself and nodded. "If I could heal the wounds the wolves left behind or open the cuffs, which would you prefer?"

"I think that's the stupidest thing you've ever said."

X laughed. "Noted. This might take me a while, since I have to disable the motor in the needles to prevent you from losing your hands." Then he placed his own hands inside the keyhole and a bright light erupted from him, almost blinding Solo with its intensity.

One minute passed. Two. Three. Finally, the cuffs disengaged. The bands remained attached to his wrists, the needles still embedded in his bone, but all he had to do was rip out each of the needles, causing sharp pains to lance through his arm, and he was free. Sweetly, blessedly free, able to keep both of his hands.

Vika gasped with delight.

"If you had the power to do this," Solo said to X, "why didn't you do it before?"

"It was the circus. The black magic. My power was limited."

That, he understood.

Again, "thank you" hardly seemed adequate. "X . . . I don't have the words."

"I don't want words. I have only ever wanted to see you happy and settled, Solo. I hope you know that."

X loved him, Solo realized. Really loved him. He'd thought Mary Elizabeth and Jacob Judah were the only ones, but no. He'd always had X, he just hadn't known it. And he totally should have known, should have looked deeper than the surface. But he'd been so blinded by his problems and his distorted expectations.

"I do," he finally said. "I really do."

"Then do whatever proves necessary to stay that way, eh?" X said, and vanished to recharge.

Next time I see him, I'm going to kiss him on the mouth.

"Oh, Solo," Vika said, jumping up and down and clapping. "How wonderful! Jecis will never be able to find you now."

But Solo would find him, he vowed to himself, and that was a vow he would not break. "Come on, sweetheart. Only eight more hours of travel to go."

A little whimper escaped her, but all she said was, "Tomorrow, while we're in the cabin, I get to plan the day's activities."

"As long as those activities include a bed."

Maybe she knew what he meant. Maybe she didn't.

"Deal," she said, and grinned as sweetly as sugar—as playfully as a kitten. Sealing her fate.

Twenty-six

*O my dove, in the clefts of the rock, in the secret place of the
steep pathway, let me see your form, let me hear your voice.
For your voice is sweet, and your form is lovely.*
—SONG OF SOLOMON 2:14

*F*INALLY!

The cabin came into view, small and partially
hidden by trees and snow.

Solo knew there would be a security box somewhere
on the property and searched every inch in a thirty-
foot perimeter, until he found it inside the trunk of a
tree. He had to scrape off the ice with his claws, prov-
ing no one had been here in a while, and punched in
his personal code.

Blue and yellow lights flashed, signaling that the
traps set along the borders had been disabled.

Next, he typed in the code for information. It had
been six months since an agent had entered the prem-
ises, and four weeks since one of the trip wires had
been activated, sending bolts of electricity through the
offender's entire body. Either a human had gotten a
little too close or an animal had stalked his dinner a
little too long.

"Sleep now?" Vika asked.

Her words were slurred, the poor darling. He had

showed no mercy, had stopped only twice to make sure she ate the extra meat he'd packed, and drank the water he melted for her.

"Sleep now," he replied, and swooped her up in his arms.

Her head rested on his shoulder, her body instantly going limp.

He got her inside, in the warmth. The furnishings were quaint and homey, here for comfort rather than war. A long cloth couch. A love seat. A recliner. A coffee table with old magazines spread over the surface. He was glad. He wanted Vika calm and at ease here.

He entered the master bedroom but bypassed the queen-size bed. In the bathroom suite, he stepped into the shower stall. At the circus, she had used a cheap, wet enzyme spray to clean the captives. That's why she'd had to move their clothing aside and use rags. Here, with the more expensive dry enzyme, the removal of clothing was unnecessary.

His weight on the tiles triggered the automatic switch, and the spray began to mist over them, cleaning them inside and out, as well as their clothing. His skin tingled, and a minty taste even coated his tongue.

That done, he entered the bedroom and settled Vika atop the soft mattress. A mass of pale hair spilled over the pillow, and a soft sigh parted her lips. She curled to her side. He couldn't help himself. He reached out, traced his fingers along the curve of her ear. She was such a stubborn woman. Such a beautiful woman.

His woman.

He removed her coat and tucked the covers around

her. His fingers ghosted over the diamond choker he'd left on her. The stones were cold but pretty, and he wished *he* had bought the jewelry for her. Still, something about seeing so delicate a woman wearing it tempted the animal inside him. The animal he would have denied with his dying breath only a few days ago. The animal he'd once hated.

Somehow, his biggest fault had become his greatest asset. He hadn't used his strength to intentionally harm but to protect someone precious. And she was precious, wasn't she? Precious to him in so many ways.

The need he had for her spun into the most sublime sense of satisfaction as he realized he would finally be able to have her. In every way. No interruptions. No distractions. No danger. And she was ready for him. He knew she was. Last time . . . the way she'd moved . . .

And then, this morning . . .

"Still frustrated?" he'd asked her.

"Maybe," she'd snipped.

He'd worked her up but hadn't given her any kind of release.

"Soon," he promised her now, even though she couldn't hear him. He placed a kiss on her forehead and stalked quietly through the house. It was two stories, though the second story was underground and only a trained eye would be able to find the doorway to below.

The heat was already on, the air warm, but he started a fire in the hearth in the living room anyway. The kitchen was small, with granite counters; cherrywood cabinets held enough boxed and canned food to see a family of four through a few months of seclusion. There was only the one bedroom. The other had been turned into an office.

An office Solo took over. He claimed the only chair in front of the wall of computers, and started typing on the center keyboard, reengaging the traps outside. He sent a message to Michael, John, and Blue, waited five minutes, ten, but no response was forthcoming from any of the three. He would check again after he ate, he decided.

The pantry was stocked with even more canned food, and he devoured an entire gallon of chicken noodle soup. And . . . still no response from the boys.

That didn't mean anything, he assured himself.

He padded to the bedroom, eased onto the mattress, and tugged Vika into his side. She didn't wake, but she did mold herself against him. He anchored a hand in her hair and a hand on her bottom, loving how perfectly they fit together.

But . . . half an hour passed. Two hours passed. He lay there, simply peering up at the ceiling. He was too primed to sleep, his mind too active. What a journey he'd undertaken. Forced to become a sideshow freak. Surrounded by evil, but tended to by a saint. A race through a frozen tundra, with a beautiful little blonde at his side. An attack by wolves. And now, this. Satisfaction.

And, honestly, if everything he'd endured had been necessary to bring him to this moment, knowing Vika was safe, that *he* had saved her from a life of torture and torment, he wouldn't have changed a single thing.

Sunlight poured through the bedroom window. Solo hadn't slept at all, but he still lay in the bed, Vika still curled up beside him. She had remained in the same position all night, not a sound to be heard from her.

He wanted her. He needed her.

When would she wake up?

He counted the beams in the ceiling. Twenty-three. He counted again, just to be sure. Twenty-three.

He counted dust motes. Two thousand and sixteen. Two thousand and seventeen. Eighteen. Nineteen.

Finally, she sighed and shifted to her back. Arched and stretched.

The ferocity of his need strained and bucked against the tight leash he held. Had she been any other woman, he would have pounced then and there. But she wasn't. She was Vika. *His* Vika. He would rather die than frighten her or press her for something she wasn't ready to give. Right?

But he had nothing to worry about. She *was* ready; he'd already come to that conclusion. And he was never wrong. Right?

"Solo?" she said, her voice scratchy from sleep.

Right. "Vika." He rolled on top of her, clasped her by the nape, lifted her head, and fit their mouths together. Her taste, her heat, her softness, her gentleness, every curve of her luscious body fanned the flames of his desire.

He kissed her thoroughly, deeply, branding her, being branded by her, kindling a fire that would always burn between them. After a moment's hesitation, she welcomed him with the sweetest of moans, wrapping her arms around him and arching into him. He nearly roared at the intensity of the pleasure.

She was ready.

"Are you going to stop this time?" she asked.

"Only if you want me to."

"I won't."

"Then I'm *never* going to stop."

On and on the kiss continued, until she was panting, struggling to breathe.

"We've done this before," she said. "Now I want to know what comes next."

"We've done the next part, too, but we're going to do it again. And probably a third and fourth time." Until she was ready with more than her body. Forcing himself to move slowly, he slid his hands underneath her shirt, until he encountered warm, bare skin. "Tell me if I scare you."

If she caught his words, she made no reply. However, she leaned into his touch, telling him all he needed to know. He cupped the heavy weight of her breasts, just as before, and groaned. Another perfect fit. She mewled her excitement, encouraging him to knead . . . until his hands were trembling, until she was arching continually, trying to press more fully against him.

"Gonna go lower now," he said.

Maybe she read his lips. Maybe she didn't. He moved his attention to the plane of her stomach, dabbled at her navel. When she offered no protest, he traced his fingers along the waistband of her pants.

A gasp slipped from her. Her gaze locked with his, and she trembled.

"Change your mind? Want me to stop?" he asked, swallowing a denial.

"No. Keep going, please." A needy entreaty.

He continued, moving lower still. He kept his caresses light and easy, and she responded to every movement, every brush of his thumb, again mewling . . . soon begging.

"More. *Please.*"

"Yes. I'll give you more. But I want to see you first, sweetheart."

"I . . . I have a few scars," she replied tremulously.

A burst of fury, quickly subdued. "You're beautiful. All of you. Every inch."

She licked her lips. "Really?"

"Really."

"Prove it."

With pleasure. He whisked the shirt over her head and tossed it aside, then removed her bra, baring her to his view, and oh, was she gorgeous, perfect in every way, just as he'd known she would be. She . . . the first woman to ever tempt him to the brink of losing control.

He saw a pale, thin scar on her right shoulder and kissed it. There was a puckered pink scar on the left side of her rib cage, and he kissed that one, too. Goose bumps broke out over her skin.

"You are the most exquisite creature ever created," he said, rising from the bed.

If she had other scars, they would be lower, on her legs, and when he got down there, he wouldn't want to pause to take a moment to shuck his clothing. Best to do that now.

"Where are you going?" she demanded.

Such a fierce tone from such a tiny creature. He almost grinned.

Silent, he stripped, then leaned over and stripped her the rest of the way. His breath caught in his throat. He'd described her as perfect before, but this . . . *this* was perfection. Every inch of her was encased by luscious rose-tinted skin, her supple curves creating a canvas of the sweetest femininity.

As he'd suspected, she had other scars. Just a few, but they formed puckered circles where her bones had broken through skin; they somehow only added to her beauty. She had survived a kind of hell that would have destroyed countless others. Every mark of abuse was a badge of her incredible strength.

"So powerful," she said, looking him over. "Come here."

"Want to kiss your other scars."

"Soon."

"Soon," he parroted. He would take such good care of her, he vowed as he stretched out beside her. He would treat her as the treasure she was, make her feel so special she would never doubt his determination to protect her.

Heat radiated from her, enveloping him, but still she shivered.

"Scared?" he asked.

"Blissful."

"I want to make you feel even better." Wanting to urge her back into that state of total arousal, he gave her another kiss, seeking, tasting, taking, giving. Finally, she needed more—she needed everything. Yet still he only caressed her face, toyed with the ends of her hair. He traced the line of her shoulders. Every touch was innocent, yet strategic.

"Solo," she finally said, a command.

"Yes," he replied, a promise.

"More."

Exactly what he'd been waiting for. He explored her the way he'd longed to do from the start, leaving no part of her untouched. He learned her. He enjoyed her, this sweet, vulnerable girl with a heart more exquisite than diamonds. He licked and laved at the scars on her legs.

"So beautiful," he told her. "So perfect."

"Me? You're the beautiful and perfect one."

When she looked at him with pleasure and passion and need in her eyes, he felt like the handsome prince he'd wanted to be as a little boy. "You would not change anything about me." A statement, not a question.

"Only if you wanted to leave this bed before we actually got to the good stuff!"

He chuckled. Humor. In sex. He had never known it was possible. But then, he'd never been with a woman like her, a woman of love and light. "I'll show you the good stuff," he growled with mock ferocity.

He set out to do just that. His own need should have overpowered him, should have driven him to hurry, but this was too important to rush, he craved her satisfaction too desperately, was so determined to make this a memory she would cherish for the rest of her life, that he was careful to study her reactions.

When she gasped, he knew she liked what he was doing.

When she moaned, he knew she really liked what he was doing.

But when she writhed, he knew he *owned* her.

All the while, she kneaded and scratched at his back. She couldn't seem to get enough of him, seemed to *need* him, some part of him, and grabbed his hand and sucked his fingers into her mouth.

He nearly burst out of his skin. "Are you ready for me, sweetheart?"

"*Pleeease.*"

She'd stolen the word right out of his head. "I need to grab the condom. I'm safe, I'm clean, but we don't want to risk a baby."

"No. I want to feel you. Only you. Just this first time."

Oh, yes. She was surely plucking the words out of his mind. He knew the risk, just as he'd told her, but he couldn't seem to make himself care just then.

He shifted into position, getting ready, but not taking her. Not yet. She wrapped her legs around him, and their lips met in another fevered kiss. Finally he moved forward. He meant to be gentle, but as small as she was he had to exert more pressure than he'd intended. She gasped when he at last slid home, her body jolting from the shock of his invasion.

"Okay?" he gritted.

"Yesssss," she said on a moan.

Then he'd done his job, had prepared her properly. As he moved against her, she offered another moan and gave him more than he'd ever imagined possible, nothing withheld. She surrounded him, clasped at him, breathed in his ear, shouted his name, arched into him, moved with him, cried out, pulled his hair, scratched at his back some more, kissed and kissed and kissed him. And when he knew she verged on losing her breath, he lifted his head and peered in her eyes. Deep, so deep.

"Vika," he intoned. "I'm going to give you everything I have to give, this I vow to you, and you're going to like it. Vow it to me."

"Solo, darling, Solo." Her trembling increased. "I vow it. And I'll give you everything. Everything I have."

"Make you so happy you said that." As he kissed her and claimed her, he went a step beyond what he'd promised, giving her all that he would ever be. She was everything he'd ever wanted, everything he'd thought he would never have, and she began to gasp his name, over and over, calling to him, drawing him ever deeper.

As her back bowed off the bed, she shouted with the force of her release. He felt her relief, and lost the rest of his control.

And when he collapsed on top of her a few minutes later, he quickly rolled to his side, not wanting to hurt her. His eyelids were unbelievably heavy—and he could only smile wryly about it. He'd trekked through the ice-caked mountains carrying a hundred-pound bag of jewelry without ever tiring, yet this one little female had exhausted him.

He was keeping her, he decided as he drifted off, and woe to anyone who ever tried to take her away from him.

Twenty-seven

❦

Sustain me with raisin cakes, refresh me with apples,
because I am lovesick.
—SONG OF SOLOMON 2:5

WHILE HER SWEET, EXHAUSTED Solo took a nap, Vika dressed and enjoyed a wonderful dry enzyme shower. She heated a bowl of tomato soup and ate it while studying the cabin. It was bigger than she'd expected and quite homey, with log walls and comfortable, well-worn furniture. A soft brown rug covered the living room floor, and pictures of roses and lilies covered the walls. An even softer rug covered the kitchen floor, and pots and pans hung from a metal rack just above the granite island counter.

An eclectic mix of old and new, as though a man and a woman had shared the decorating responsibility. The man had decided what belonged on the floors, and the woman had decided what belonged on the walls.

Was Solo's boss married? she wondered. If so, what would the female think of Vika? She had never socialized with people outside the circus, and wasn't sure she knew how to make a good impression.

For that matter, what would Solo's friends think of her? Would they slap Solo on the back for a job well done, as males sometimes liked to do, or would they pull him aside and warn him to stay away from her?

How would Solo react if they did?

He'd once told her they would protect her, but that didn't mean they would like her or approve of her. A burning heat inched up the center of her chest, one that had nothing to do with pleasure.

"Worry only buys you wrinkles," her mother used to say. "Well, those and rotten bones."

Vika forced the depressing thoughts out of her mind and peered out the ice-fogged window. Now that she was toasty warm, she could enjoy the sheer winter majesty around her. And maybe . . . maybe her love also stemmed from the fact that, for the first time in her life, she didn't have to fear doing or saying the wrong thing and "earning" a beating. She was safe. Solo would never physically hurt her, something he'd proven again and again as he'd fought to save her.

She was . . . cherished. Yes. She was. No matter what his friends might say about her!

The man had kissed and touched her, and he'd done it with unabashed relish, intense need, and a hint of joy. She had loved every second and had only craved more. Nothing he'd done had scared her. Everything had excited her, softened her.

I'm so glad I waited for him.

Was that the way making love was for everyone?

No. No way. The things she'd witnessed throughout the years had confirmed the opposite. Sex could be violent, explosive, angry, or laughing, fun, and seemingly carefree. But tender? No, she'd never witnessed that. What she and Solo had done was special, and she would hold the memory in her heart for all of eternity.

A movement outside claimed her focus.

Heart picking up speed, she abandoned her soup to race around the kitchen counter and press her nose against the window glass. Roughly forty yards away, a gorgeous white tiger prowled from one patch of trees to another, leaving a ruby line in his wake.

Ruby . . . blood? Was he injured?

Had to be. Only desperation for help would have brought him so close to human life.

But . . . she shouldn't help him. She wasn't foolish. Well, not all the time. She knew he was a wild animal, unlike her tame, fun-loving Dobi with the marking problem. She suspected he would bite her head off if given half a chance. Or even one-third of a chance. Fine, even if she failed to offer him any kind of chance. But . . . she couldn't leave him out there, injured, without at least trying to aid him.

I know what you're thinking, X suddenly said, appearing on her shoulder. *And it would be my pleasure to help you. I can prevent the beast from attacking you.*

"Really?"

Yes, really. But first, I want to show you something. It's the reason I came, and I might be too weak after we help your little friend out there to show you later. He flattened his tiny hand on her nape, and pictures of Solo's life began to flash through her mind.

Solo—a little boy only his parents had loved.

Solo—a kid no one had wanted to hang around.

Solo—a teenager the girls had laughed at. He'd never even been on a genuine date. The only girl he'd liked had used him for her own selfish needs.

Solo—a man only the most depraved of women had desired.

"You're ugly," a thousand people had said to him.

"You're disgusting," a thousand more had said.

Solo—a warrior who had decided to spend the rest of his life alone. That way, no one else could hurt him.

Oh, the pain this man had endured . . . so like her own. How dare anyone treat him so poorly? While she had deserved the hatred thrust at her, he had not. And how, how, *how* had he survived the circus? How could she have left him in that cage, time and time again?

Tears trickled down her cheeks.

I didn't show his past so that you would pity him or even feel guilty, X said, *but so that you would understand him a little better.*

"He really is wonderful, isn't he?"

He is. Now tend to the tiger before Solo wakes up and decides to stop you.

"You're helping me. He won't mind at all."

And you are too innocent for words. Go!

As quietly as possible Vika tiptoed into the bathroom. It was the largest one she'd ever been in, triple the size of the one in her trailer and almost as large as the bedroom itself, with calming blue walls and a sink in the shape of a seashell. She stuffed the supplies she would need inside a basket she'd found in the living room—and there was plenty to choose from! She'd never seen so many bandages and medications.

Clearly, Michael was a man who liked to be prepared for anything.

As she tiptoed out, she kept her gaze on Solo. He was utterly still, his chest barely even rising as he breathed. His thick lashes were spiked, curling up at the edges, and his lips were parted, relaxed. He looked so wonderfully boyish.

A warm sense of contentment filled her, practically busting her skin at the seams. *I don't want to be without him,* she realized. Ever. She wanted to hold on to him and never let go.

How did he feel about her? Truly feel? He desired her, yes. And he'd asked her to live on his farm. But how did he actually feel? How would he feel when all of the danger had passed?

Worry and wrinkle and rot, she reminded herself, swallowing back a sigh.

Hinges squeaked as she opened the door to the backyard, and she cringed. But Solo didn't shout or come running so she continued on. The tiger was still there, still prowling—still bleeding.

"How are you going to calm him?" she asked X.

I have my ways.

They were several yards apart, but she could see that the blood flowed from the tiger's front left leg. He'd stepped into some sort of trap, she would bet, for the skin and muscle had been punctured in three separate places.

Slowly she approached, X directing her steps. Cold

air slapped at her, stinging. The tiger caught sight of her, blue eyes locking on her, and he stopped. One step, two, she continued her journey. His lips pulled back and he bared his saber teeth—long, sharp, deadly.

"Uh, X?" She considered dropping her basket and running.

I've got this.

The tiger crouched, as though ready to leap at her and feast on her bones. Her steps faltered.

He's not going to leap. Now, move three inches to the left. Good. Now hop and angle toward the right.

Again she obeyed. "Why am I walking like this, anyway?"

To avoid security. Now, take a giant step forward, as if you're stepping over a fallen tree. Good, now stop. Give me just a moment. With that, the being vanished.

He never appeared on or even near the tiger (to her knowledge), but suddenly the creature dropped to the snow-laden ground. He pushed out a heavy breath.

He's all yours, X said, once again on her shoulder.

Vika closed the rest of the distance with much surer steps. She knelt beside the magnificent beast and scratched him behind the ears. "I'll make you feel better," she said. And, now used to Solo, added, "I vow it."

Pain-filled blue eyes watched her warily. She would not fail this creature.

Working swiftly yet gently, she cleaned each of the punctures.

Not many people would have come out here, X said.

"I couldn't leave him."

I like that about you.

"Thank you."

You're exactly what Solo has always needed.

A small thrill lit her up inside. "What was he like as a child? Other than what you showed me, I mean."

A fond chuckle. *He was the sweetest little boy ever created, following his mother around, always making her gifts.*

Only yesterday, he'd offered to buy Vika new jewelry. She'd convinced herself the offer stemmed from irritation over the heaviness of her bag, and maybe it had, but what if it had also stemmed from a desire to please her?

Hands trembling, she smoothed numbing cream over the feline's injuries and wrapped his leg with a thick white bandage, applying pressure to stop any more bleeding. A final scratch behind the creature's ear and she stood to walk back into the cabin. Once again X ordered her steps, making her zig and zag and leap.

Inside the cabin, warm air instantly enveloped her. She shucked her coat and carried the basket of supplies to the bedroom, desperate to see Solo again. He had begun to stir. He'd kicked the covers from the bed, leaving his body bare. He was on his stomach, his back to her. His luscious, luscious back. He was all bronzed skin and chiseled muscle, his bottom tight, his legs . . . injured, just like the tiger's.

Concerned, Vika rushed to his side.

All right, then. This is where I say good-bye, X said, and vanished.

The wolves had bitten Solo, she recalled, and the

teeth marks were still there, still leaking. She set the basket down and withdrew the only remaining clean rag.

The moment the fabric brushed against his skin, he jerked around, arm swiping out, his claws elongating—but he caught sight of her and stopped the momentum just in time.

The claws retracted, and Solo moaned, as though in pain. "I'm so sorry, sweetheart."

"My fault," she said, and there wasn't a single beat of fear inside her. *That's* how much she trusted him. "My babies used to react the same way when anyone roused them from sleep. I knew better." Smiling softly, she gave his warm chest a little push. "Lie back. You promised I would get to tend you when we reached the cabin. Well, happy news. We've reached the cabin."

As strong as he was, the action forced him to do nothing. Still, he fell backward, the pillows plumping around him. He watched her as she doctored him, silent. When she finished, she traced her fingertip along one of his toenails.

"So pretty," she said. "Like diamonds."

"I want you again, Vika."

He was totally and completely naked. "I realize that, Solo," she said with a grin.

Their gazes met, and she suspected the same fire that crackled in his also crackled in her own.

"Do you want me?" he asked.

"More than anything."

"Then have me."

She did. Oh, she did.

Vika propped herself up on one elbow and peered down at Solo. He met her gaze through heavy-lidded eyes. His hair was in complete disarray, the dark strands sticking out in spikes. The strong bones of his face were overlaid with skin flushed from the intense pleasure they had shared. His lips were soft and red from her kisses, a little swollen.

He was breathtaking.

"I think I liked that time better than the first," she announced.

"You'll like the third time even better," he promised.

She laughed with delight. "So, when we get to your farm, are you going to let me feed the animals? Can that be one of my chores?"

A pause. A hesitant "You've decided to stay with me?"

"For now," she said, thinking, *forever*. But she wouldn't tell him that part. Not yet. Not until she was certain he wanted her in his life that long.

"That's good." He scrubbed a hand down his face. "But I have to tell you something, Vika. You might change your mind."

Her stomach bottomed out. In a single blink of time, he had gone from playful and aroused to serious and grim. "What is it?"

He looked away from her. "I don't want to lie to you, want to give you full disclosure even though I told myself I'd keep this a secret, and I know I should have told you before you ran off with me. But I'm a smart man—really smart—and now it's too late for you to ditch me, so this was the wisest path and I'm not sorry."

O-kay, she'd never seen him this uncomfortable. And she'd seen him stripped and fondled by strangers! "Just tell me."

His fingers tangled in his hair. "You're not going to like it."

"Well, you're just gonna have to use your man parts and do it!"

He stilled, his lips twitching. "My man parts? Do you mean my balls?"

Heat blasted from her cheeks. "Maybe."

"Say it," he said with a grin. "Say the word. I want to hear it on those candy-apple lips."

"No! Now stop stalling and—your eyes," she said with a frown. There was a slight ringing in her ears, annoying and yet wonderful. "Your eyes used to be a light blue, but now they're a dark purple, like my father's used to be. Like mine are." And she could see far more clearly than she'd ever seen before, she realized as she looked around the room.

Before, she'd thought everything was clear. Now she realized how wrong she'd been. *This* was clear. Dust motes swirled in the air, floating . . . floating . . . and the overhead light provided an undeniable radiance that caused her to tear.

Confused, she eased all the way up. "What's going on?"

"Your eyes are now a light blue," he said. "I noticed it a few minutes ago, but I figured it was a trick of the light."

"My eyes aren't dark purple?"

"No. They're blue, like mine used to be."

So . . . they had changed, both of them. "I don't understand this."

"Could we have . . . switched?"

Maybe. "But I've never heard of anything like that happening. Not with humans, or even humans dating otherworlders." The ringing stopped abruptly, and in its place, she heard her own voice. "I can hear," she said with a gasp. "I can hear!" And oh, her voice was gorgeous! She knew it was wrong to brag, but she couldn't help herself. Her voice was the most beautiful thing she'd ever heard!

"What?" he said, rubbing at his ears. "Say that again."

Scratch that. *His* voice was the most beautiful thing she'd ever heard. Rough and raspy, dark and masculine, full of power and undeniable vigor, causing her to shiver. "It's a miracle! My ears are working. Do you have any idea how long I've—"

"I can't hear you," he interrupted. "I can't hear anything."

"What?" she screeched. She could hear, but he couldn't? No. No, no, no. That would mean they'd done more than switch eyes. They'd switched ears. His perfection for all of her flaws.

"The vow." He gave her a dazed look. "I vowed to give you all that I was."

So had she. The moisture dried in her mouth. "Oh, Solo, I'm so sorry." She flattened her palms on his chest, felt the hard thump of his heartbeat. "I never would have agreed to such a switch—"

"Hush," he said. "In my line of work I had to learn to read lips, too, so we won't have any problem communicating."

Yes, but he'd helped her and she'd hurt him. "I'll never be able to forgive myself. After everything you've done for me, I go and do something like this to you, adding to your misery. It's not fair to you. It's criminal, actually. I should be punished!"

"You stop that right now. This hearing thing? It doesn't matter." He tugged her down so that she sprawled across his chest. "Now listen to what I have to say." He traced his fingertips along the ridges of her spine. "I will tell you about my past, and you will vow to stay with me anyway."

An order. One she would heed. There was nothing he could say to change her mind about him.

"I was a contract killer for the government." He paused, as if expecting her to leap up and run.

She didn't—she was too stunned.

He continued. "I killed humans, otherworlders, males, females, it didn't matter. If I was told to kill someone, I killed that someone, no questions asked. I've killed a lot of people, Vika."

She wouldn't lie. The words were hard to hear, and she flinched. Her man, a killer. But he wasn't anything like her father, she reminded herself, and she would never think of him that way. Jecis had enjoyed the pain he inflicted. Solo never had, something she would stake her life on.

"I cried after my first kill, and I'm not embarrassed to admit it. I stared at the body for a long, long time, shaking, sick to my stomach. But I still took the next job, and the next, and eventually what I was doing no longer bothered me. I was cold inside, and glad of it."

But not now. There was too much regret in his tone.

"Most of what I did was for a good cause, and I know men like me are needed to keep our world safe. But the things I had to do to complete certain jobs . . . I think I've always been more like you, because, no matter my reasons, what I was doing was also killing the man I was meant to be. I wish I could undo my past. I wish I could go back and live a different life, but I can't. I have to live with what I've done. And now, I'm asking you to live with it, too."

She heard the regret, now mixed with insecurity, doubt, guilt, and sorrow. A desire to clean the slate and start fresh. A desire she knew very well. She was surprised she could judge the emotions so precisely, and doubted she could have done so with anyone else, but this was Solo, her Solo, and she knew him in a way she'd never known anyone else.

Vika sat up, her hair tumbling around her shoulders. He waited, tense.

"Everyone regrets things in their past," she said, and he tensed a little more. "Even me."

As he watched her lips, he relaxed, but only slightly. "You have done nothing wrong."

Oh, no. He wasn't going to absolve her. "Rather than finding a way to free the otherworlders right from the start, I enabled my father to use them. And don't you dare say I did what I could. I could have done more.

My actions were selfish. I wanted out of there permanently and I let them rot while I saved my money."

"You searched for the key."

"I could have searched harder. I could have asked Jecis about it."

"And placed yourself at greater risk."

"All I'm saying is, we *both* could have acted differently."

"Vika—"

"I still want to stay at your farm," she interjected. "You're not the man you used to be, and you aren't a monster." And she didn't like that she'd ever implied he could be. No one could see into the heart of a man and know what he felt or why he did what he did. You had to wait and watch for the fruit. An orange tree would always bear oranges. A lemon tree would always bear lemons. "I'm not the girl I used to be, either, and I'm so very—"

"Don't you dare apologize," he said sternly. "With your past, the fact that you helped me at all is amazing enough."

"Sorry," she finished anyway.

His frown was chiding.

"We have to forgive ourselves," she said with a nod. "We can't live with self-hatred. It's a terrible emotion, and it will open the door for us to hate others. Hating others will make us like Jecis, and I don't want to be like Jecis."

"We can only go on from here," Solo agreed. "Doing better."

"We start fresh." From this moment on, she was no longer the coward who slunk around in the shadows, the timid mouse that cowered in corners, or the victim of constant cruelty. She was filled with hope. She was empowered.

She was with the most magnificent of men.

"As long as you never forget what we've done here at this cabin," Solo said, his voice tender.

Shivering, she replied, "Believe me, I'll be dreaming about this cabin every time I close my eyes."

"I have a feeling I will as well." He reached up, brushed a fingertip over her cheeks. "We've talked about the past. Now let's talk about the future. After I free the otherworlders from the circus, I have to find my friends, John and Blue. They were injured, like me, and from what little I know about the man responsible, terrible things were done to them."

"I understand." And she wouldn't have it any other way. "I'll do anything I can to help."

A fierce light in eyes she was used to seeing stare back at her from a mirror—a light she'd never before seen in them. "No matter what happens, I'll take care of you."

"And I'll take care of you," she promised. "And when we succeed—and we will, because we're unstoppable—we're going on a date. *Many* dates. You're going to wine and dine me, and I'm going to dress up and seduce you. We'll dance and eat and talk and laugh, and have the best time."

"I'll agree to those terms on one condition," he said, and reached down to cup her bottom.

A thrum of need, a breathy moan. "What?"

He licked and sucked at her collarbone. "Solo no good with words. He have to show."

Silly caveman. "Again? Oh, dear. However will I survive?"

He kissed her, relearning her, tasting her, but the kiss soon spun out of control. Just as before, Vika was confounded by the absolute and utter delight she found in the act of making love with him. Solo was gentle, and he was rough, he was careful and he was undisciplined, he was . . . everything to her, and more than she could have ever dreamed.

There was no part of her he left unpraised. Nothing was taboo. He delighted in all that she was, and erupted into a frenzy of growls and commands when she took over, showing him just how much she loved him.

Love?

She did, she realized. She loved him with all of her heart. The emotion burst through her, warming her, delighting her, thrilling her—frightening her, but she wasn't going to dwell on that, and she wasn't going to think about wanting more from him than he might want from her. His feelings wouldn't change her own. And she wasn't a mouse, she reminded herself. She was brave. She was strong. She would go after what she wanted with everything she had.

Twenty-eight

*The flowers have already appeared in the land,
the time has arrived for pruning the vines, and the
voice of the turtledove has been heard in our land.*

—SONG OF SOLOMON 2:12

S OLO STARED AT THE computer screen and scowled.
Finally, he'd gotten an e-mail. Three, in fact. One
from Michael, one from John, and one from Blue. But
all three were bounce-back messages.

Their e-mail addresses had been changed. And so
had their phone numbers. That was standard operating procedure when an identity or a location had been
compromised—or an agent had died.

Solo's own code to this cabin should have been disabled, but it hadn't been. He wasn't sure why. What he
did know? He needed a new plan. If Michael was alive,
he knew Solo was here, despite their little communication problem. He would have known the moment Solo
punched the code into the alarm. He would have called.

To Solo, that still didn't prove the man was dead.
But. Yeah, but. There was always a but when doubt and
uncertainty were involved. Solo might have to proceed
as if Michael was out of the picture and unable to help
him.

Now that the cuffs were out there in the wild, Jecis

wouldn't be able to get a lock on Solo. He would be watching the nearest cities, maybe even the airport and bus station. But that wasn't really a problem. In the garage underneath the cabin, there was a truck and an ATV. But . . . There was that word again. He didn't like the thought of taking Vika out in the elements. She'd held up well the first time, but he'd since made the mistake of allowing desire to overshadow duty, and hadn't used the condom the first time they made love. He'd used it the second, and should have stopped since they'd had no more. But then he'd rationalized that the damage was already done. So he'd made love to her a third time—and he would make love to her again.

She could now be pregnant. And if she wasn't, she could be by day's end.

The possibility should have disturbed him. The possibility should have frightened him. He wasn't ready to be a father. But he couldn't deny he liked the thought of Vika round with his child, tied to him on so visceral a level.

A loud ringing erupted in his ears, and he frowned, ignored it. He didn't like that Jecis knew Vika's general vicinity. He didn't like father and daughter even being in the same country. But though Solo now had the resources, he didn't have time to take her somewhere else.

He would stay here one more night, he decided, and wait for Michael. Then, if his boss failed to contact him or arrive, he would lock Vika inside the cabin and return to the circus—with guns, as Kitten had requested. After all, more than vehicles filled the garage.

He didn't want to run the risk of Jecis moving the

circus again. Right now, Solo doubted the man would do such a thing. He would want to stay here and search for Vika.

"You're happy," a familiar voice said.

Solo blinked, momentarily confused. He could hear. Did that mean Vika, who was currently napping, exhausted from his insatiable lovemaking, was once again deaf? If so, he wasn't sure he liked that trade.

"I am," he replied. "No thanks to you."

Dr. E appeared on the desk, glaring up at him. His hair was tangled, hanging limply around a gaunt face. His eyes were sunken, his cheeks hollow. "Why not? I helped you."

"You only ever got me into trouble."

The being hissed at him, and if there had been tiny pebbles on the desk, Solo felt certain they would have been hurtled at his head. "You won't ever listen to me again, will you?"

"No." He liked to think he learned from his mistakes.

Dr. E popped his jaw. "X was given to you the day of your conception, a gift from your parents to minister to your needs, to protect and teach you, but he was never to override your free will, even when it got you into trouble."

"I know that," Solo said, sitting up straighter.

"I used to be like him. Did you know *that*? Long, long ago, I was an Altilium. But I chose a different life, chose to take rather than ask and wait for an answer, and the source of my power drained. I had to find another. So I joined you and X without permission. Had you ignored me, I would have been forced to leave, but you did not. You listened to me, welcomed me, and I was able to attach myself to you and feed off you."

"Like a parasite," Solo gritted.

A dismissive wave of Dr. E's tiny hand. "I prefer the term 'energy receptor.'"

"Whatever. Go on. You have a point, I'm sure."

Before the little guy could open his mouth, Vika poked her head into the room, and said, "Solo?" Her mass of pale hair was brushed and gleaming. Her eyes were once again the color of plums, and though they were sparkling, she was frowning.

Solo jumped to his feet. "Everything all right?"

"Everything's fine. But I'm deaf again, and I just wanted to make sure you could hear."

"I can," he said.

Relief painted the edges of her sudden smile, dazzling him. "I'm glad." She came the rest of the way inside and leaned against a wall. She must have dug through the dresser drawers, because she now wore an oversize sweatshirt that had to be rolled at the wrists and pants that had to be rolled at the ankles.

Never had she looked younger, fresher, and his heart actually swelled in his chest. But he wanted to see her in clothing he had bought for her. Or clothing he had first worn. Wanted her surrounded by his things—their things. Wanted to give her . . . everything.

"I wonder why the switching of our senses keeps happening," she said. "I know you said you think it's because we vowed to share all that we are, but do you think there's more to it than that, since nothing's sticking?"

"Like what?"

"I don't know." A shrug. "I was hoping you'd be able to tell me."

Like the fact that he wanted to give her *everything*? Like the fact that he loved sharing this with her? "I'm glad it's happening, and I hope you are too. No one else has ever had the chance to see the world through another person's eyes, but we have. No one else has ever had the chance to hear through another person's ears, but we have."

"We're special?" she said, a question when she'd probably meant to make a statement.

"We are. And maybe the abilities aren't sticking because that's what sharing is all about. Give and take. Ebb and flow."

She nodded, satisfied with that. "Well, Mr. Special, I'm going to raid the pantry and cook up a feast," she said. "Are you hungry?"

"Always."

"Give me an hour. Meanwhile, prepare to be amazed." She blew him a kiss, turned, and padded down the hallway.

"You'll never give her up, will you?" Dr. E demanded from behind him.

Solo pivoted on his heel and faced the being who had so often given him terrible advice, laughed during his torture at the circus, and abandoned him time and time again, when Solo most needed help. "No."

Dr. E popped his jaw. "Not even to save my life?"

"Not even."

A pause. Heavy, oppressive.

"Very well," the being said. "You have brought this on yourself." With that, he vanished.

Vika found green beans, peas, carrots, and potatoes, and mixed them all together. She also found several packages of syn-chicken and was able to heat the pieces over the stove and drizzle them with a tasty butter glaze.

There were so many spices to pick from, she was a little overwhelmed. There were things she'd never even heard of. She used only the ones she knew about, not wanting to ruin the first real meal she would prepare for Solo.

At the farm, he would have chores for her. He'd already said so. She wanted to prove she could do anything he asked, that she could take care of him properly. And she prayed that she could!

She had no formal education. Her mother had taught her to read and write, and her knowledge had been limited, too. *I have a quick mind,* she assured herself, *and I can learn anything.* And . . . and . . . she knew how to sew. Yes! That was a perfectly acceptable skill. She would mend Solo's clothing, and he would be the best-dressed farmer in the entire world.

And she could sell her jewelry and use the proceeds to buy him something special. Something he'd always wanted. She just had to find out what it was that he'd always wanted.

When the chicken was warmed all the way through and the vegetables were boiling, she turned off the stove and prepared two plates. Steam rose, and the scents caused her mouth to water.

Gold star for me, she thought, proud of herself. She'd sometimes watched the cook at the circus, knowing she would one day have to care for her own meals.

She picked up the plates to carry them to the table, but caught sight of her tiger outside the window. He had returned. He was no longer prowling, but lying between the trees, his tail waving slowly. He yawned.

A warm, strong body pressed against her back, and she shivered. Soft lips slid along the side of her neck, and the shivers intensified, wringing a moan from her. She set the plates down. Solo clasped her by the waist and turned her.

He kissed one eyelid, then the other. "I'm ready to share again."

"Sharing *is* kind of fun, I guess."

"You guess? No, you know." He kissed the tip of her nose, one cheek, then the other. Then he hovered over her lips, his warm breath caressing her. "So what were you doing, staring out the window? Dreaming of me already?"

She walked her fingers up the ridges of his stomach, to his shoulders, and around, to his nape, intending to pull him down the rest of the way. "No, Mr. Ego, I was watching my tiger."

His muscles bunched underneath her hand. "Tiger?"

"Mmm-hmm." She pulled, but Solo resisted. "He was injured, but he's doing better."

Frowning, he lifted her off her feet and set her aside to press closer to the glass. He watched for a moment before jerking his head in her direction, his eyes wide.

"He's wearing a bandage," he said.

"I know." Her ears began to ring.

"Who put that bandage on him, Vika?"

She heard him that time, and he had not sounded pleased. "Well . . ."

"Vika."

"I did."

"What?" he shouted. "You went outside? Approached a dangerous predator? When? While I was sleeping?" he added, answering his own question.

Exasperated now, she threw up her arms. "Yes, but X helped me. I was never in any danger."

"There are traps out there, Vika."

"Which is why X made me walk in strange places."

A red tint darkened his skin. "That's the second time you've mentioned him. X knew about it and didn't wake me?"

"Why would he? You were sleeping so peacefully. And again, I was never in any danger."

He worked his jaw, obviously trying to get himself under control. "X could have weakened, and the tiger could have maimed you."

"But neither of them did."

"How could you . . . why would you . . ." Shouting a curse, Solo pounded his fist into the kitchen counter, rattling the dishes.

Vika jumped, startled by the volume.

"Do you want to put me in an early grave?" he snarled. "Is that what this is about?" Another shout, another pound of his fist.

This time, the dishes bounced off the counter and fell to the floor. Nothing broke, but the delicious, amazing food she'd spent forever preparing was ruined. Vika peered down at the mix of yellow, green, and orange and despaired. Not only would Solo not discover what an excellent cook she probably was, he now needed a lesson about his temper.

"That kind of outburst won't be tolerated," she said sternly. "I dealt with that kind of thing all of my life, and I know you would never hurt me, but I won't let you talk to me that way. I won't have that kind of relationship with you."

He placed his hands on her shoulders, but she tore out of his grip. Head held high, she turned and marched away.

Twenty-nine

*You are altogether beautiful, my darling,
and there is no blemish in you.*
—SONG OF SOLOMON 4:7

SOLO CLEANED UP THE kitchen, a bit sick to his stomach. He'd allowed anger to get the better of him, and he'd hurt his woman's feelings, perhaps even frightened her. With her past, he'd known better. Had known to be careful.

He was ashamed. He'd just . . . he'd been so scared for her. She'd entered the harsh cold and, unaware that one wrong step could shock her or kill her, she'd done it to approach a wild, injured beast. Did she have no sense? Could she not understand that Solo didn't want to live without her?

He stilled.

He didn't want to live without her.

He played the words through his mind again and again, and realized they were true. He wanted her with him now, always, and forever. He didn't just want to keep her, either. He wanted to *be* with her. Every minute of every day, he wanted to talk to her, laugh with her, make love to her. He wanted to learn more about her, think about her, and know *he* belonged to *her*. He wanted her to crave the same things from him.

And he didn't want to change her. Taking care of others was in her nature. She couldn't look at the sick and hurting and not desire to help, and that was a beautiful quality to have, one that had drawn him to her, one that had captivated him, enchanted him.

He never should have yelled at her, reminding her of her father, and he definitely owed her an apology.

He searched the house and found her in the bedroom. She was removing the jewelry from her bag, placing what seemed to be thousands of necklaces, bracelets, and rings on the bed. The only other thing she'd brought, besides the items X had requested, were disposable cameras.

"I'm sorry."

Vika stilled, her wide purple gaze swinging to him.

Without a word, he swiped up a camera and then Vika herself. She offered no protest. He settled in the chair across from the bed, and directed her body like a master with his puppet, forcing her to sit on his lap.

Even though she was angry with him, utter contentment flooded Solo. Who would have ever believed someone trapped by such hideous circumstances could find such bliss? A woman as lovely as this one. Pleasure beyond imagining. Laughter. Sharing. Acceptance.

The loss of his hearing, in short bursts or forever, truly was a pleasure for him to bear. Vika was taken care of. She was with him, his to protect and cherish. He would have to quit his job, of course, but then, he'd planned to do so anyway. He had warred all his life.

Now it was time to rest. To enjoy the life he'd been given.

"Sweetheart," he said, "I'm sorry I yelled at you. I won't do it again, you have my word. My only excuse is that I was scared, thinking of you out there, hurt and bleeding, and I was completely unaware, unable to help if you needed me."

A moment passed. She ducked her head.

He felt the vibration of her words and had to interject, "I need to see you to understand you, sweetheart," stopping her.

Her hair swished around her shoulders as she straightened. "I'm sorry," she said. "I was telling you that I just couldn't leave the tiger to his suffering."

It was odd, knowing she was speaking, watching her mouth move, yet hearing nothing. It was odder still, knowing *he* was speaking and hearing nothing. But that had always been the norm for her. "I know. Do you forgive me?"

Her eyelids flipped up, revealing those plum eyes he found so irresistible. Interesting. This time, they'd only switched ears, not eyes. "Of course."

Again, she offered her forgiveness so easily. Another quality he had never been able to resist.

She reached out and twisted the collar of his T-shirt. "So what do you want with the camera? Why'd you grab it?"

"Maybe I wished to take naughty photos of you."

"In that case . . ." Grinning, she grabbed the camera from his hand and held it in the air. "What are you willing to do for it?"

"Anything," he said, utterly serious.

"Anything?" A carefree laugh. "You vow it?"

"I do." An open bargain. Something he'd never before made. Something he would never make with anyone else.

She planted a loud, smacking kiss on his lips before she relinquished control of the camera.

"And what is it you're going to want?" he asked, not the least bit concerned.

"We'll start with three more wishes."

Won't grin. "Hate to break it to you, sweetheart, but I'm not a genie in a bottle."

She ignored him, saying, "I'll make a list and let you know everything you'll be doing for me."

Really won't grin. "I'll look forward to reading it."

"Expect to be riveted."

Okay. He grinned.

"Let's take a look at these photos before I toss you on that bed." He pressed the buttons on the disposable and discovered pictures of little Vika, no more than five years old. In each of the photos she was grinning so widely she was all teeth. Her hair was brushed to a glossy shine and hanging in pigtails at her ears. In one, she was in the middle of a twirl. In another, she was holding a large sequined bra up to her tiny chest. In yet another, she was pressed up against an older version of herself, and the two were blowing kisses to the camera with chocolate smeared all over their faces.

"You have an addiction to chocolate, I think," he said, a pang in his chest.

"Only a small one. I can go through an entire five-minute span without thinking about or craving a piece."

He would buy her a chocolate factory, then. She could swim in the stuff, if she so desired.

"And who is the other woman?" he asked, already suspecting the answer.

"My mother," she said wistfully. "She was flighty and emotional, but I loved her."

"I'm sorry you lost her."

"Me too."

The loss of someone you loved could leave a big gaping hole in your chest. One you feared would never be filled. That was how he'd felt about his parents, and yet this woman had filled him in such a way that he doubted he could ever be hollowed again. He would carry the memory of her forever.

He couldn't let her be hurt.

He set the camera aside. "How about we do a little practice fighting?" If he left her here—and with every second that passed he was more and more certain he would have to—he wanted her as prepared as possible.

"All right," she said, and if she was confused by the change of subject, she didn't show it.

"Give me a few minutes to get everything ready." He stood with Vika in his arms, placed her in the chair, and stalked to the living room to move the couch and coffee table.

When he finished, he returned to the bedroom. She was in the same place he'd left her.

"Ready?" she asked.

He frowned. He'd heard her voice, soft and sensual, but his ears hadn't rung. Not this time.

She frowned too. "Solo," she said, standing.

He'd heard her that time, too. "Can you hear me?"

A shake of her head, as she said, "No. Can you?"

"Yes." So they'd switched back again.

And they would probably switch yet again.

She displayed the same relief as before. "I like sharing with you, I do, but I'm glad you can hear. The guilt was going to fry me like battered chicken."

He . . . had no idea which adage she'd butchered that time. "I told you not to feel guilty."

"You did. And do you not recall me telling you to bite someone?"

So gorgeous when she's feisty. "No. But just for the record, you're supposed to tell me to bite *you.*"

"Why would I want you to bite me?"

"Because I'll make sure you like it. Now, come into the living room and *force* me to bite someone."

"I will, and you'll be sorry." Radiating eagerness, she followed after him.

They stopped on the rug he'd cleared and faced each other.

"What's first on the agenda?" she asked, fisting her hands at her sides and bracing her legs apart.

"You're going to practice what I've already taught you and learn a few more tricks."

"What if I want to teach you something?" Without any more warning than that, she kicked out and knocked his ankles together, sending him to his knees. She was on him a second later, pushing him back and straddling his waist, a blade poised at his neck. "Like that."

So gorgeous when she's fierce. "Where'd you get the knife?"

"Snagged it from the counter when I left the kitchen. I was going to carry it in the bag since you were so against me carrying the gun."

And he'd missed the action. Either he'd lost his edge or he had no defenses against this woman. "Good girl." Swiftly he rolled her over, pinning her to the ground with his weight. "But whatever will you do now?"

She laughed.

So gorgeous when she's amused.

"I'll take pity on you and keep my knees to myself."

"Not sure that's wise. I have no plans to take pity on you."

Thirty

〜✤〜

Do not let kindness and truth leave you. Bind them around
your neck, write them on the tablet of your heart.
—PROVERBS 3:3

NIGHT FELL, BUT SOLO wasn't tired. And neither
was Vika, judging from her flurry of activity.
She had raided the dresser drawers and the closet and
had withdrawn everything in need of repair. Now, she
sat in front of the living room fire, sewing, a soft orange
glow enveloping her, the pile of clothing beside her.

Six times she'd shown him the work she'd done,
watching his features intently. He wasn't exactly sure
what was going on, but he made sure to lavishly praise
her efforts. And she was good. He just wished he knew
what thoughts rolled through her mind.

A light pressure on his right cheek had him turning.
X stood on his shoulder, frowning at him.

Can't you hear me? His voice filled Solo's head.

"No. My ability to hear has been given to Vika again."

Vika looked over at him.

How—Never mind. I have to tell you something. And
I'm so sorry. I didn't know until too late. I tried to stop
them, but I failed. I'm so sorry.

"What are you talking about?"

Dr. E. He's here.

"I know. I spoke with him."

No. He's here. With Jecis. Dr. E told him where you were and led him to the cabin.

Solo jolted to his feet. Vika followed suit.

"What's wrong?" she demanded.

Silent, he stalked to the living room window and, kneeling, peeked through the crack in the curtains. All appeared to be well. There were no moving shadows. The trees weren't swaying. And there was no way Jecis could have bypassed the security as Vika and X had. He was too big, too heavy.

Still, Solo sealed the crack and stood, grabbing Vika's hand and leading her toward the secret passage to the garage. It was in the bedroom, underneath the bed. He crawled under, shoved the rug out of the way, and pushed open the door. A yawning pit of darkness greeted him. He'd already been down there and checked everything out. Had already loaded the truck with everything they might need, just in case.

Dust coated the inside of his nose as he maneuvered onto the first step, helped Vika do the same, then shut the door and quickly descended. He reached the floor and flipped the light switch.

Nothing.

He flipped it again.

A vibration against his chest, and he knew Vika was speaking.

"I need to—" he said, and stopped. Something about the air . . . wrong, familiar . . . terrible . . . thick and cloying, filled with evil.

Jecis and Dr. E were here, in the garage, he realized.

Laughter suddenly reverberated inside his head. Again, familiar. Dr. E's. A moment later, a fiery skull with red, glowing eyes appeared at the other side of the room, its mouth open, its sharp teeth revealed.

That skull sped into motion, a mere inch away from Solo in a single blink. He jerked Vika behind him, hoping to shield her from whatever was about to happen, just as those flame-drenched bones reached him—and swallowed him whole.

Vika heard a thump.

A second later, light flooded the cold, underground room Solo had led her to, and she saw that he was on the ground, motionless, his eyes closed. Concern overwhelmed her, and she began to bend down to help him—when she caught sight of Jecis, Matas, and Audra, standing at the far wall, and froze.

They'd found her.

Horror and dread mixed, forming a toxic sludge in her veins. Jecis was scowling, Matas was grinning, and for once Audra was gazing at her with sympathy. She was pallid, and she was shaking, no longer a pretty woman. Her face was swollen, discolored and scabbed from Jecis's rings.

Scabs Vika herself had borne many, many times throughout the years.

Despite his amusement, Matas, too, looked as if he had come into contact with her father's fists. One of his eyes was swollen shut, and there was a knot on his jaw.

They each wore summer clothes: tanks, lightweight pants. Yet still their corruption managed to cloak them. The misshapen skull she'd glimpsed inside Big Red stared at her through her father's eyes. Dark shadows hovered over Matas's shoulders, thicker than before.

"No," she said with a shake of her head. "No."

"Thought you would have a better life without me, did you?" Jecis said, a hint of madness in his tone. Madness, fury, and evil. Pure evil. "Thought some disgusting otherworlder would care for you in ways I could not?"

He had no idea she could hear him, she realized. A fact she could use to her advantage. She just had to figure out how.

"Well?" he demanded.

"Yes," she said, happy to discover there wasn't a tremble in her voice. "I did. I do."

Surprise widened his eyes, and he stomped toward her. *I will not cower.* When he reached her, he grabbed her arms in a painful vise grip and shook her. "I loved you." Spittle rained over her face. "How could you betray me like this?"

"You never loved me."

"I gave you everything."

"You gave me nothing but pain and sorrow."

He raised his hand to hit her, but rather than back down, rather than plead for mercy he would never show, she lifted her chin. The surprise returned, now magnified, and he slowly lowered his arm.

"You've changed," he said, and he didn't sound happy about it.

"I have." And she would never go back to the way she'd been. She had traveled too far down this current road, had gone from cowardly to courageous. Even looking back, she couldn't see where she'd started. "How did you get here?"

"A little man, Dr. E, came to me. He told me where to find you and vowed to empower me in ways I could only dream of . . . if only I vowed to kill you."

Kill you. The words echoed in her mind, leaving an empty ache in her chest. "And did you agree?"

He flashed his teeth in a parody of a smile. "I did. And you deserve to die, after what you did to me. But first," he said, "I'm going to teach you the same lesson I taught your mother: Leave me and suffer."

He motioned Matas forward.

Her former guard walked over, bent down, and, straining under the muscled weight, hefted Solo over his shoulder. So badly Vika wanted to lash out, to do something, anything, to save him. But she didn't. Not yet. Right now it was three against one, and she had no way to transport Solo. Solo, who had not moved or made a sound since falling. What had her father done to him?

"With the power Dr. E has given me," Jecis said, "I can create stronger solar flares. I can choose where I end up, *when* I end up—up to a certain point. I can only go short distances, but the more I do this, the better I become." He raised his arm, mumbled a string of words she didn't understand—words that lifted the fine hairs on her body and left a sour taste in her mouth.

Suddenly white lightning speared the air just in front of her, creating a split in the ether. The edges were drenched in fog, but through the center she could see . . . outside the cabin. Cold, wintry air even blustered inside the garage.

Jecis jerked her through, and a second later, she was standing outside, in the exact spot she'd seen. Matas and Audra followed, and the pocket of air closed behind them.

"One more, and you'll be home," Jecis said. Once again he raised his arm, mumbling, and once again lightning lanced down, creating a crack in the air. A curtain that had just been opened, revealing another location on the other side.

Revealing the nightmare she'd left behind. The circus. Only, now it was surrounded by sunshine and light.

Just before Jecis could tug her through, a ferocious roar resounded through the night.

"What was that?" Audra whispered.

"Come," Jecis commanded, his gaze roving the distance.

The injured white tiger leapt from the darkness and slammed into him before he could take a single step, propelling him off his feet and onto the snowy ground. He maintained his hold on Vika and took her with him. On impact, oxygen burst from her lungs.

Her father howled with pain as the tiger bit into his arm, dragging him several feet, shaking him. Finally Jecis released Vika, but only to throw a bolt of lightning at the tiger, causing the animal to fly backward.

"No!" she screamed, attempting to jump up but slipping on the ice.

A bleeding Jecis stood, grabbed her, and jerked her through the new opening. This time, Matas and Audra didn't walk through but ran, practically pushing her out of the way.

Another roar, and she could hear the frantic clomp of the tiger's paws against the ice. He was running, determined to make another play for her father. But Jecis reached back and waved his hand, and the air sealed shut, blocking the creature from view and preventing him from entering the circus.

He'll be fine, she told herself. *He's better off.* She didn't want him near Jecis ever again. Her father would have used the tiger's wounds against him.

Just like he would use Solo against Vika.

"Home," Jecis said, and spread his arms.

Vika breathed in . . . out . . . as she looked around, the sights that greeted her caused her stomach to churn with sickness. White tents, Big Red, trailers, games and rides, and performers walking in every direction, setting up for tomorrow's show. The cold had been replaced by sultry heat, and the mountains with flatlands.

"After you left," Jecis said, "we changed locations, thinking you meant to bring the authorities to my door. Thankfully, we were only gone for a few days since the little man had approached me and showed me a better way."

An avalanche of sounds suddenly assaulted her ears, and she barely stopped herself from cringing. Voices, so many voices. Chatter, laughing, arguing. The grind of metal against metal. The squeal of tires. The crunch of stones beneath shoes.

Jecis pushed Vika at Audra. "Lock her in her trailer. I'll deal with her once my wounds have been bandaged. And if she escapes, I'll blame you, my darling Audra." With barely a pause, he looked to Matas and said, "And you. Put the beast back in his cage."

Thirty-one

∽∾

Be dressed in readiness, and keep your lamps lit.
—LUKE 12:35

SOLO AWOKE WITH A jolt, panic instantly infusing him. He remembered the cabin, and the fiery skull propelling toward him. But after that? Nothing.

"Vika!" he shouted, bounding to his feet. Where was she? Had the skull gotten her, too? "Vika!"

"Calm down, warrior."

The Targon's voice penetrated his mind, and he spun. The sun shone brightly in the sky, and he had to blink rapidly to focus. Through familiar metal bars he could see the otherworlder, his caged neighbor.

Bars. Cage.

Dread beating at him, he looked around. He was back in the cage, he realized. Back at the circus, back in the menagerie. He'd . . . he'd been captured. The rest of the otherworlders were watching him. Some with anger. Some with pity. Kitten, with hope.

"Don't despair," she said. "You did it once, something no one else has ever done, and you can do it again."

They were dirtier than when he'd left them, as though no one had bothered to clean them even once.

They were thinner, too, as if no one had bothered to feed them. But at least they were alive.

And he could hear them. Once again, his ears were working. That meant Vika, wherever she was, was once again deaf.

"Where's Vika?" he demanded of the Targon. "How long was I out?" The landscape had changed. Mountains had been replaced by planes, snowy tundra by red dirt, and trees by rolling wheat.

"She's been locked in her trailer, and you were out only for the night."

His relief was so potent, it buckled his knees. He tumbled down, shaking the entire cage.

"She's your woman," the Targon said. "You've claimed her."

"She is. I have." And he would not lose her. Not this way. Not in *any* way. "Where's Jecis? Matas?"

A flash of fury in the Targon's eyes. "They're setting up for tomorrow's show."

It was time for information, Solo decided, time to learn the Targon's motives. "You hate him. Matas. You hate him more than Jecis, the man responsible for your predicament. Why?"

"Hey, Jolly Red," Criss called. "You don't call, you don't write. You have some nerve showing your face here again. My brothers are coming for me, you know, and they'll have something to say to you. You just left me behind!"

The Targon held out his arms, and the world just . . . stopped . . . moving, even going silent. Solo frowned—

or tried to. Like the world around him, he was motionless. His body felt as though it had been covered by cement, even his arms too heavy to lift. The only part of himself that he had any control over was his eyes, and he kept those trained on the otherworlder.

Only the Targon could move. He stalked to the side of his cage, his lips curling into a smile that wasn't a smile. "Don't worry. Unlike you, their minds are on lockdown. They have no idea what's going on. And did you notice I'm stronger than before? I've been practicing."

Stronger, despite the cuffs.

The cuffs!

"Yes, you are bound, too," the Targon said, and suddenly Solo's head could move.

He looked down. Sure enough, the metal of the cuffs circled his wrists. Jecis . . . oh, Jecis would pay. "There's no key, you know."

The otherworlder absorbed the news and shrugged, as if he simply didn't care.

"How are you able to wield so much control with the drugs pumping through your system?" Solo asked.

"The drugs are inhibitors."

"I know. So?"

"So. There is a fatal flaw to such drugs. A flaw spelled out in the name. They inhibit, they do not wipe away."

"Why have you remained, then?"

A return of the rage, now laced with sadness. "Your woman once took care of mine. Mara was her name, and she and her friends heard about a magical circus called Cirque de Monstres and came for a visit. Matas saw her, wanted her, raped her, and vanished with her before I could get to her. He had no idea that we were linked, and that I knew everything he was doing to her, as he was doing it." More and more rage seeped from his tone. "I could have killed him from the start, and maybe I should have, but I wanted to experience everything my Mara experienced. I wanted to see my tormentor every day—until I destroyed him."

He wanted to punish himself for not saving his woman, and he understood. He did. He wasn't sure how he would react if he discovered Vika had been harmed in any way.

Vika . . . the girl he loved.

Yeah. He loved her. With all of his heart, with all of his soul, he loved her. She was the one. The other piece of him. Somehow, she had entangled herself in his life, as if he were a tree and she the ivy, and he could no longer distinguish his foliage from hers. They were two halves of a whole, better together, dependent on each other.

"Nothing to say?" the Targon quipped.

"Nine days," Solo replied through a throat now raw, recalling what the Targon had said the night of his escape. "You plan to destroy the circus."

"Yes. But now, there are only four days left."

"Do not wait. Act now."

The Targon pretended he had not spoken. "I saw the way your Vika took care of my Mara. I heard the conversations they had—until Mara severed our connection. I was glad when you came along and began to watch out for little Vika." Tension branched from the corners of his eyes. "I didn't see into Mara's mind again until the night of her death, when Vika's father found her, gave her to Matas, and the male . . . the male . . . *destroyed* her."

"I'm sorry, Kaamil-Alize. I know you have a plan, and you want to stick to it, but my woman still lives and she needs me. Help me now. Today. Together, we can end this."

A shake of that dark head. "I told you. I must first experience everything Mara did."

"Were you raped?" A harsh question, but one that needed to be asked.

A tic of the muscle beneath the otherworlder's golden eyes. "No."

"Then you have not experienced everything she did, and you never will. There's no reason not to act. You can have Matas, I can have Jecis, and we ensure no one else ever suffers this way."

Silence.

"We can save Vika, the girl who helped your Mara."

Again, silence.

"If you do nothing, you're as bad as the male you despise."

The Targon popped his jaw. "We all watched Jecis increase your dosage of the inhibitor. If you become emotional, or if anyone presses that magic little button on your cage, you'll be too weak to fight."

"Never." Not when it came to Vika's safety.

"And we all heard them discuss your new and improved cuffs," the otherworlder continued, as if he hadn't spoken. "If the bones in your wrists expand, and

I'm guessing they do when you transform into your prettier half, you'll activate the saws in the needles and you'll lose your hands."

No need to think about his response. "That's a risk I'm willing to take."

The Targon studied him for a long while. "I think I like you more with every second that passes. And I think I'm even willing to help you . . . for a price."

"Name it."

A fleeting smile, without a hint of amusement. "Reading minds is a little hobby of mine. I know about your farm, and I want it."

Again, no thought was necessary. "Done. Help me today, help Vika afterward, if anything happens to me, and it's yours. I vow it."

Vika paced from one corner of her trailer to the other, reminding herself of the tiger in the forest. Only, her wounds weren't visible. Her heart was breaking inside her chest, a sense of helplessness razing her.

She'd lost the ability to hear, and all of her furniture and the trinkets she'd left behind had been removed, leaving the space barren, devoid of a single weapon. In fact, there was only one weapon nearby and it was clutched in Audra's hand.

Audra, who stood by the only exit, guarding it with her life.

Vika stopped, just stopped, and faced her child-hood friend, her tormentor. Actually, that gun wasn't the only weapon, she realized. *She* was a weapon. Solo had made sure of it—and she wouldn't make light of his lessons.

"Let me out, Audra," she said. "Otherwise, you won't like what happens to you."

"I won't like what happens to me if I do. Your father will kill me."

"If you stay with him, he'll kill you anyway."

"No." Green eyes glittered. "He's not going to hit me anymore. He promised."

"He lied."

"No, he loves me."

"He knows nothing of love! And neither do you, I think. Love protects. Love cherishes. Love lifts you up rather than tears you down. Love makes you fly, and *I love Solo*."

A flicker of sorrow, quickly gone. "Your beast is going to be the first to die, Vika. You can't save him. No one can."

No! She refused to accept such a thing. She *could* save him. She would.

"One last chance," she said, making a proper fist.

"Shut up, and—"

Vika slammed that proper fist into Audra's nose.

The girl yelped as blood spurted from her, and she dropped the gun to clutch at the injured cartilage. Vika dove for the weapon, and when she straightened, she aimed the barrel at Audra's chest.

Wide-eyed, Audra flattened herself against the door.

"I'm sorry I hurt you," Vika said, "but I'll do worse if necessary. Worse that will happen in three seconds, if you fail to move out of the way."

"I don't care," Audra replied with a defiant shake of her head.

"One."

"*Jecis* will do far worse."

"Two."

The defiance drained, and tears welled in her eyes. Audra stepped out of the way.

Vika brushed past her and stepped into the sunlight. But before she'd taken three steps, X appeared on her shoulder, wringing his hands together.

Duck under the trailer, he commanded. *Now!*

Heart suddenly slamming against her ribs, she dove for cover. She knew better than to pause and question him. Good thing, too. The moment the ground was pressed against her back, she felt the vibration of footsteps. A few seconds later, she saw her father and Matas's boots.

The pair disappeared inside the trailer. Several seconds passed.

Solo's in trouble, X said. *He and the Targon have worked up a plan. They began shouting for your father and Matas a few minutes ago. But rather than confront them head-on, your father wants to use Solo's feelings for you against him.*

So low. So like Jecis.

"What should I do?" she whispered.

You know what you need to do, Vika.

She did, didn't she? And it was brutal. It went against everything she'd ever believed. Or rather, everything she'd ever thought she had believed. Afterward, she would probably cry.

Probably? No. She would. But this was war. This wasn't business as usual. Action had to be taken. Things had to be done. The strong could not trample on the weak and continue to reign.

The trailer shook and she barely silenced her gasp. Jecis had either punched the wall . . . or Audra. Two sets of boots again appeared, this time stomping away. She waited one minute, two, then rolled into the light.

Can you do what needs doing? X asked.

"Yes," she said, and stalked forward.

Thirty-two

YOU! WHAT HAVE YOU done with my daughter?" Jecis pounded to Solo's cage and, with a spat of curses, jabbed at the button to pour sedatives through his system. Dr. E sat on the male's shoulder, laughing. "I planned to wait, to kill you slowly, but I want her to hear your screams and come running. I want her to see what I do to you—and I want you to see what I do to her."

Solo remained silent as he dropped to the ground.

"Matas," the Targon snarled.

"Shut up," the guard snarled in return.

"I'll shut up the day I carve out your black heart and dance in your blood."

Matas snorted, not the least bit intimidated. "Yeah, good luck with that."

Jecis was too lost to his rage to notice the two men were arguing. And he was too lost to his rage to notice Solo wasn't actually asleep. Because of that, he made the mistake of opening the door to the cage.

"Now," Solo shouted, his jaw heavy but still workable.

In the process of stepping deeper into the enclosure, Jecis froze, the Targon taking control of his body. Every ounce of Solo's strength was needed to pull himself into a sitting position, but he did it. His gaze met his enemy's, and he smiled slowly, with relish.

Dr. E stopped laughing. "What's going on? How are you doing this?"

Ignoring him, Solo said to Jecis, "Just so you know, the only one who will suffer today is you."

Fear joined the rage in Jecis's eyes. Solo could see the skull writhing beneath his skin, attempting to jerk out of the Targon's control. Gritting his teeth, Solo kicked out his leg, nailing Jecis in the stomach and sending him propelling to the ground.

Dr. E vanished.

Solo was quick to follow his opponent, jumping out of the cage. Every action loosened his muscles and lifted some of the weight of the drugs. Now it was time for a little dirty pool. He threw his leg into another kick—nailing Jecis between the legs.

Air burst from the man's mouth, but that was it, his only reaction.

"You're free!" Kitten said, fist pumping the air. "I told you this would happen. Didn't I tell you?"

"Let me out!" Criss shouted.

"Me too! Come on, man. Over here!"

The Bree Lian jumped up and down. "Beast Man! Over here!"

"Can't . . . hold them much longer," the Targon called. "Their magic . . . fighting me."

Solo bent down and grabbed Jecis by the wrist. He dragged the man past an equally frozen Matas, and to the Targon's cage, where he pressed Jecis's thumb into the lock. A flash of white light, and the tumbler gave way.

The Targon burst from the cage and launched himself at Matas. That's when he lost his hold on the bodies, both Matas and Jecis erupting into action.

Jecis jerked from Solo's hold and rolled to his feet. There was no exchange of words. They simply dove toward each other, fists flying. Solo landed several punches, but he took one, too. The ensuing sting enraged him. What had Vika endured at this man's hands over the years?

Rage . . . cold, harsh.

Drugs . . . drip, drip, dripping, trying to weaken.

Calm, he told himself. *Remain calm.* He couldn't allow himself to morph, not in any way. And for once, it wasn't an impossible task. Vika had taught him a better way to live.

He blocked a punch, ducked, and threw one, smashing into Jecis's kidney. He heard a hiss, though he knew the man wasn't out for the count. Far from it. The violence must have engaged his dark side, because the skull shot out, little gold flames appearing in the darkness as it tried to chomp on Solo. Just before contact, a giant version of X swooped in, catching the skull like a basketball and falling to the ground with it clutched to his chest.

Jecis unleashed a pained wail, as if the evil were attached to him, and he could feel its defeat. Solo struck, nailing him in the temple once, twice, three times. The man's head rattled from side to side, but on Solo's fourth swing, he managed to get his hands up and block.

Solo aimed lower. Contact. Again, air burst from Jecis's mouth.

From the corner of his eye, he saw that the Targon had Matas pinned to the ground. The shadows that had always hovered over Matas's shoulder had stretched out and were biting and biting at the otherworlder, but the male paid them no heed. He continued to rain fists of fury into his opponent's face. Again and again. Until it wasn't just blood flinging in every direction. Until the shadows slowed . . . stilled . . . flopped to the ground and vanished.

Jecis used his distraction against him and landed another punch to his jaw. His head whipped to the side, and he went with the motion, dropping to his side and kicking up his legs. His boots knocked Jecis's teeth together, sending him stumbling backward.

Solo straightened and followed him, grabbing him by the collar. Swollen, bloodshot eyes peered up at him.

"Kill me, and she'll never forgive you," Jecis spat.

No. He wouldn't believe that.

Boom!

Jecis's body jerked, his eyes going wide. He fell to the side, but Solo maintained his grip, keeping him upright. He recognized gunfire when he heard it and held on to the man to use him as a shield if necessary. He tracked the noise with his gaze. Vika stood a few yards away, holding a smoking gun, tears streaming down her cheeks.

Solo loosened his fingers, intending to drop the man to the ground and race to her side, to gather her in his arms, to offer comfort, or whatever else she might need. What she'd done . . . all to protect him . . .

"My own daughter," Jecis gasped out. "How could you?"

Boom! Boom! Boom!

The shots came from a different direction, from behind Jecis, but still the man jumped each time. And as three sharp stings registered in Solo's chest—all straight in the heart—he looked to find *Audra* with a smoking gun. Dr. E sat on her shoulder, and he was laughing all over again.

"If I can't have you," the little man called, "no one can."

The girl had shot Jecis, but the bullets had gone straight through him and into Solo. He finally dropped the man, but not to get to Vika. He no longer had the strength. The man responsible for his torment all these weeks flopped lifelessly to the ground, and Solo fell to his knees beside him.

"Solo!" Vika cried out, rushing to his side. Her hands patted at him, trying to stop the flow of blood. "You'll heal, yes? You did before. Many times. I've watched you. You have to heal from this, too. Right?"

He heard a cry, watched as X collided with Dr. E, knocking Audra to the ground. As X and Dr. E fell, Dr. E's body elongated, growing to the same size as X's. Maybe he was seeing things.

Dizziness consumed him. Black dots wove through his vision. With every pump of his damaged heart, his life slipped away a little more. "Vika," he managed to choke out as blood bubbled up in his throat.

"Tell me what to do, and I'll do it," she rushed out. "Just tell me!"

"Nothing to be . . . done." His injuries were too severe. He'd caused this kind of damage in others. He'd seen the results too many times. He knew.

"There is!"

"Can't lie . . . Vika . . . This is . . . it." He struggled to keep his gaze on her as his fingers and toes grew cold.

X moved in, kneeling at his side. Still giant, as big as Solo. "Tell him good-bye, Vika."

"What? No! Never."

Solo pitched forward, no longer able to hold his own weight. Somehow, Vika managed to catch him, balancing him against the softness of her trembling body.

"Tell her good-bye, Solo," X commanded.

"No!" Vika shouted again. "Not good-bye. Just good night. You'll go to sleep, Solo, and we'll patch you up. You'll revive in the morning. You will. You'll see. You vowed to give me anything I wanted and this is what I want."

"Love . . ." He had to tell her how much he loved her. He had to explain everything she'd come to mean to him. Until her, he'd never really lived. But the black dots still winking through his vision expanded, thickened, and the blood bubbling in his throat cut off his airway. Suddenly he couldn't breathe.

"He will die at home," X said. "And don't you dare protest, Vika. It must be this way."

"No! He's not leaving me. He promised to take me to his farm, too, and he always keeps his promises." To Solo, she said, "You're going to get better, I know it. I feel it. I have a knowing. Just . . . get better. Please, Solo. Please. *Please.*"

Strong arms banded around his waist, pulling him backward, tugging him away from Vika.

"No," she said, and now she was sobbing. "X, don't—"

They were the last words Solo heard.

Thirty-three

∽◈∾

For where your treasure is, there your heart will be also.
—LUKE 12:34

VIKA WASN'T SURE HOW long she knelt in place, staring at the pool of crimson Solo had left behind. X had put his arms around him, and the pair had vanished. All she knew was that, when she finally looked up, the circus was engulfed in flames.

She laughed without humor. Her father's pride and joy was being destroyed bit by bit, all of his work soon to be ruined. Justice had at last arrived. But then, it always did, didn't it? Somehow. Someway.

The otherworlders were still in their cages, screaming to be released. Performers were shouting and running in every direction. Her father's body was motionless beside her. Matas was splayed a few feet away from her. Or rather, what was left of him. The crimson-soaked Targon stood over his body, arms lifted as he danced in the man's blood. Audra stood in the same spot she'd occupied before, still holding the gun. She was pale and shaking—and she was no longer tattooed. The spiders were gone.

Audra noticed her gaze and shuddered. "I didn't mean to kill your beast," she said. "I just wanted to hurt Jecis the way he'd hurt me."

"Solo wasn't a beast! He was the best man I knew." Horrified by her words, Vika hurried to correct herself. "He *is* the best man I know." He was still alive. She wouldn't believe otherwise. He was too strong, too vital, and he'd promised. He never broke his promises.

Audra nodded, as though ashamed, and dropped the gun on the ground. Sirens blared in the background. Sirens Vika heard. Not as clearly as before, in the cabin, but enough. Still, she couldn't bring herself to care.

"What should I do?" Audra asked.

She could hear the girl's voice, as well. "Start a new life," Vika told her.

Where was Solo? Where had X taken him? Home, the creature had said. Did that mean the farm? Or perhaps X's home, in that other realm?

A tap on her shoulder caused her to look up.

The Targon peered down at her, and he was smiling. Splattered as he was with blood, it was a chilling smile. "You might want to close your eyes for this next part," he said.

He didn't wait for her response, but turned to her father and unsheathed a blade. Vika watched. With one sharp motion, he cut off Jecis's thumb. The brutality of the action barely registered. She knew what he planned to do with the appendage, knew it was necessary.

He picked up the detached piece and rolled it along his palm. "Mara was my wife. Matas killed her."

Mara. Vika's Mara. "Killed her? No. I freed her."

"You did. Your father found her and gave her to Matas. I was bonded to her, and I witnessed the entire thing through her eyes."

Mara was dead. Mara hadn't abandoned her. Hadn't forgotten her. She'd been caught, killed. "I'm so sorry. I—There are no words. I loved her."

"I know you did. That's why you're still alive." He moved to the cage nearest him and began freeing the otherworlders.

Most sprang from behind the bars and ran, never looking back. Tawny fur grew from Kitten's pores, covering her entire body as she disappeared around the corner, but she quickly returned with an unconscious, bleeding circus performer. She dumped the body on top of Jecis, kicked it—the performer was still alive, judging from that gust of pained breath Vika heard— and disappeared again . . . only to return with another body. This time, she was a little bloody herself and missing several patches of fur.

The Bree Lian raced toward Vika, his claws bared.

The Targon grabbed him by the back of the hair and jerked him to the ground. He loomed over the otherworlder and scowled.

"You don't touch the girl. Ever. She took care of you and was your only means of protection."

A trembling "All right."

The Targon freed him, and he lumbered to his feet.

He didn't bother glancing or glaring in Vika's direction, but sprinted away.

Criss strolled out, stopped and checked her cuticles.

"Run," the Targon said. He'd finished releasing the otherworlders and dropped her father's thumb on the ground. "I don't owe you any protection, Cortaz, and I won't offer it. You've got an attitude that needs adjusting."

"I think I'll stay," the girl said with a confident smile. "When Jecis died, my brothers were finally able to get a lock on me. They showed up a few seconds later."

The Targon spread his arms. "And where are they? Because they can feel free to bring it."

A brighter smile. "You see the fires?" Looking beyond the otherworlder, she called, "The circus is charbroiled now, guys, so stop showing off. I'm ready to go home."

A second later, five glittering lights surrounded her, blocking her from sight. Those lights were shaped like men, and when they faded, Criss was gone, her footprints nothing more than charred grass.

Kitten dropped another body in the ever-growing pile and turned to grab another victim. But cops suddenly swarmed the area, their guns raised, stilling her. She held her hands up and said, "Don't shoot. I'm with AIR, and the Targon and the blonde are with me."

"Kitten?" a male voice growled.

"Dallas?"

A handsome dark-haired man with otherworldly blue eyes that reminded Vika of Solo—a sharp pang in her chest—shoved his way forward. Kitten caught sight of him, squealed, and threw herself in his arms.

He hugged her, but he never lowered the barrel of his pyre-gun.

Pyre. Something only AIR agents carried. And Kitten had said she was an agent, hadn't she. And yet, Jecis had enslaved her. Well, he had signed his death certificate the moment he'd done so. If Audra hadn't shot him, AIR would have eventually found him. Everyone knew they never gave up.

"What are you doing here?" Kitten demanded. "This isn't New Chicago . . . I don't think. Unless we're in a contaminated section I've never visited."

"No. Not New Chicago," the blue-eyed agent said. "Word got out that a certain circus had a Teran in a cage. We hoped it was you, but didn't really think it was. Still, we kept out feelers, and the moment we heard the circus had landed in the flatlands last night, I hopped a plane."

Oh yes. Jecis's downfall would have happened one way or another.

"A family reunion. How sweet." The Targon chuckled, and in the next moment, the entire world stilled. The flames stopped crackling, the smoke stopped wafting. "Come on, little Vika. I told your man I would take care of you. Vowed it, in fact."

How like Solo. "What did you demand from him in return?" She doubted the creature had been willing to help out of the goodness of his heart. Daddy Spanky wasn't the type.

He tugged her to her feet. "Doesn't matter. I didn't really want what he was offering, just wanted to see how much he was willing to give up. By the way, he was willing to give up *everything* for you."

Just like that, tears burned the backs of her eyes. She blinked them away—they were silly. X would bring him back, Solo would insist on it, if Solo wasn't at the farm already, and she would have the opportunity to say thank you, to tell him of her love.

"Now, come on. I'm weak, and I know that's not saying much. My weakness is actually the strength of ten men, but I'm not sure how much longer I can hold such a big group of people with the magnificent power of my mind. If we stay, they'll question us. If they question us, they might decide to keep you. I don't relish the thought of springing you from prison."

"Yes. Let's leave."

They wound around the now-blackened tents, darted around the frozen bodies, the flickering fires, the wafts of smoke. "In case you're wondering, I'm going to do you another solid," the Targon said. "I'm going to take you anywhere you want to go. Anywhere in the world. I can't open solar flares like your father, but I can drive and I can keep the cops off your tail. I doubt you'll receive a better offer."

"The farm," she rushed out. "I want to go to Solo's farm." She rattled off the address Solo had forced her to memorize.

"That's a few states away. If I buy a car, give you time to clean up and rest, I can have you there in three days.

If I steal a police cruiser, I can have you there in two. If you ask me to drive all night, I can have you there in one."

"Steal and drive all night," she said. "You can mail the local PD a check."

"Thought you'd say that," he grumbled.

"There it is," he said. The Targon stopped the car, put it in park, and emerged.

Vika opened the passenger door, warm air bathing her, amazingly fresh and clean, layered with scents she remembered from long ago. Animals. Fur, hay, pine.

The sun beat down on a white, two-story house, a picket fence around it. Beyond that, mountains formed the perfect backdrop. Trees stretched in every direction.

Her knees nearly buckled, but she managed to race forward, calling, "Solo! Solo!"

An older man with silver hair stepped out from behind the house. He wore dirt-stained gloves. "Can I help you, ma'am?" he asked.

"I'm looking for Solo." She pounded up the porch steps, heart galloping in her chest. The front door was unlocked and she soared inside, leaving the Targon to handle the human. A lovely little living room greeted her.

A soft leather couch. A well-worn love seat. An oblong coffee table, with books scattered across. An unlit fireplace, a plain but soft-looking rug. The kitchen reminded her of the one in the log cabin, with an island counter and pots and pans hanging from the ceiling, only these were a lot higher up. She would never be able to reach them without a ladder—or Solo.

Two bedrooms were upstairs, and she had no trouble picking out Solo's. It smelled like him, with a subtle hint of peat smoke. The bed was huge, the biggest she'd ever seen, and there were no covers, only a sheet. A sheet without a single wrinkle. The closet was filled with shirts, pants, and shoes, all black. But there was no sign of Solo.

And the other bedroom was empty.

He wasn't here, she realized.

Shoulders slumped, she made her way down the stairs. The Targon leaned against the doorpost, his arms crossed over his middle.

"Didn't find what you were looking for, I take it," he said.

This was Solo's farm. His home. But he wasn't here. She burst into tears.

Thirty-four

∽∾

*The path of life leads upward for the prudent to keep
them from going down to the realm of the dead.*
—PROVERBS 15:24

DR. E IS DECEASED. I killed him." X leaned against
a column, his arms crossed over his chest. He
was still tall, still muscled.

Solo could hear him, but his voice—and all sounds,
really—had been turned to a lower volume. "I wish you
had done it sooner."

"Had you told me to do so sooner, I would have.
You had accepted him into your life, and I was never
to interfere with your free will. But the moment you
rejected him, I was able to act."

All these years . . . all the torment . . . and the fault
was all his own.

He was outside, lying atop an alabaster dais. A sheet
was draped over his lower body, but the rest of him was
bare, allowing rays from the three suns glowing in the
white sky to stroke over him. Rays that were actually
healing him. The cuffs were gone, thank the Lord.

He wanted to rise, but he didn't yet have the energy.
The three gaping holes in his chest were still in the
process of closing.

"How are you so big?" he asked.

"In this realm, I am big. In your realm, I am small."

"You were big in my realm, too. For a little while."

"No. You saw into my realm."

"Why haven't I changed, then, now that I'm in yours?"

"You are not like me. And besides, this might be my realm, but it is not my world. It is yours. Alloris."

He looked around with new eyes. Fresh green grass surrounded him. Flowers of every color bloomed in lush gardens, sweetly scenting the air. Men and women just like him strolled down a cobbled road. Each wore white. Each was smiling.

And behind every person was an even taller being with translucent skin.

No one seemed to care that Solo was out in the open, half-covered.

X grinned. "You will love it here, I promise you."

"Not without Vika." His sweet, darling Vika. With every second that passed, he was more determined to return to her.

Where was she? Not on the farm; he'd given that to the Targon. Or maybe she *was* there. The Targon had vowed to protect her, and the male would not renege. Not just because doing so would cause him pain but because he had the heart of a guardian underneath that irreverent exterior.

Did she think Solo was dead?

Had she cried?

He hated the thought of her tears. He wanted her happy. Only ever happy.

"Why did you never tell me you could bring me here?" Solo asked.

"Because you would have wanted to return," X said, "and you would not have been welcome."

"Why?"

"Your temper. Your job. Dr. E. Many other reasons."

"Am I the reason my parents left and went to earth?"

"No. That was your father's doing. He took your mother from another man and hid with her so that she could not be taken away."

"So the husband traveled to earth and shot them?"

"No! Of course not." X spun around and faced him. He closed the distance and eased down at the edge of the dais. "Your father got into trouble while on earth. He . . . Are you sure you want these details?"

"Yes."

"He again stole another man's wife, a man of the worst sort. Your mother didn't know he was planning to leave her."

And me, Solo realized. He thought back, and realized he mostly only remembered his mother standing over his crib, singing to him. He didn't have many mental pictures of his father. "You were there the night they were shot. Why didn't you save them?" There wasn't an ounce of accusation in his tone. He was simply curious.

"Everything happened so quickly. The next thing I knew, you were terribly injured, and I had to use my energy to save you."

"Is that why I didn't see you until years later? You were healing?"

"That, and you somehow blocked me. But I was

always there, always doing my best to protect, whispering suggestions for better choices into your ear, suggestions you always assumed stemmed from your own mind. But then you fought that child at school and you were so upset. The intensity of your emotions must have broken through whatever barriers you had built."

"I'm glad I was able to see you."

"Me too."

"But . . ."

"But you want to go back."

"Yes."

There was sadness in X's eyes as he said, "I do not travel by solar flare. I was merely tugged between this world—and you. I could bring you here, because I'm still bound here, but I can't take you back to Earth."

"No," Solo said, shaking his head.

"You were the only thing that bound me, and you are no longer there. I . . . hoped you would be pleased, despite losing Vika. It was the only way to save you."

Losing Vika. Losing. Vika. No. Never. He needed her. Had to have her. "I have nothing without her. I'm bound to her, to Earth. I should be able to travel to her."

X's shoulders drooped. "You can't. I'm sorry, Solo. I really am."

Thirty-five

*I have fought the good fight, I have finished the course,
I have kept the faith.*
—2 TIMOTHY 4:7

THE TARGON REMAINED AT the farm for several days. He helped Vika pay and dismiss the ranch hands Solo had hired, and finally left her with a promise to return in a few weeks to check on her. She liked him, appreciated his help, but she was glad for the solitude.

She didn't want an audience when Solo returned. She wanted to run into his arms, kiss him, hug him, strip him, and tumble to the floor and make love to him. And she would. One day.

Yes, one day.

But a few more days passed, and Solo never appeared. Her hope began to wane.

A few more weeks passed, and Solo never appeared. Her hope crashed and burned.

He was never coming back, was he? Her one day wasn't ever going to come.

The horror of it hit her while she was inside the kitchen, peering out the window and remembering their time in Siberia, and she collapsed, sobbing uncontrollably, sobbing until her tear ducts swelled shut, sobbed until she was choking, barely able to breathe. What was she supposed to do without him?

What are you doing, feeling sorry for yourself? He's not dead.

But if he were alive, he would be here.

What of the knowing?

That's right. Before, while she'd held his bleeding body in her arms, she'd had a knowing that he would survive. She couldn't allow noise to fill up her head and distract her from the truth.

She closed her eyes and focused on Solo's image. So tall and strong and beautiful. So perfect. Deep inside her, where instinct swirled, was a bouquet of hope that had managed to withstand the flames, the petals blooming . . . opening . . . and knowledge rising.

Oh, yes. She still had the knowing. He was alive.

Relief rolled through her, and she laughed. Laughed! He was alive, and he would come back. Whenever he was able, he would come back. For her, or for the farm, or both, she didn't care. All that mattered was that he *would* come back.

In the meantime, he would want her to stay and tend to the animals and the gardens. He would want her to take care of his things. That was what he'd tried to hire her to do, after all. Now she would do it. Free of charge.

Vika stood to shaky legs and made her way to his bathroom to use the enzyme shower. She dressed in one of his T-shirts and a pair of his sweatpants. She had already burned her clothing from the circus, so she had nothing of her own. And besides, she liked knowing she was wearing something that had been in contact with Solo's strong, beautiful body.

She marched outside. The sun shone brightly, warming her skin. She spent so much time outdoors, she had developed a tan. The cows, chickens, pigs, sheep, donkeys, and goats still wanted nothing to do with her, always shying away from her as she approached.

"You'll come to love me," she told them. "I'll make sure of it. And if not, I'll go get my tiger from Siberia and he'll teach you a few lessons."

One of the cows mooed. A few pigs snorted.

"Fine. I want to go get him, but I would never use him against you."

No response.

"I have experience with your kind, you know."

A donkey kicked at her, and she had to jump out of the way to avoid being pummeled.

Wagging her finger at him, she said, "Do that again, and I'll name you Princess Fluffy Cakes."

He put his nose in the air and pranced away.

Midday, she began to pull weeds from the garden, pluck the vegetables that were mature enough, and pick fruit from the trees. There were acres and acres of land Solo hadn't yet put to use, and there were countless women out there. Abused women. Women who thought they had nowhere to go. Women who assumed they were trapped by situation and circumstance just as she had. They didn't yet know there was something better out there.

But they would. Solo had taught Vika, and she would teach others.

Yes. She would build cabins and create a place for women and their children to run and hide. A place of protection and safety. Perhaps her purpose would come out of her pain. The women could help her with the land and the animals and finally come to understand how valuable they really were.

Solo would definitely approve.

As the sun set on the horizon, casting a haze of purples and pinks through the sky, she carried a basket of edibles into the kitchen. The screen door squeaked as it shut behind her. She—

Saw a strange man reclining behind the table, a gun resting just in front of him. Even as relaxed as he appeared, she had no doubt he could reach the trigger in plenty of time to put a hole in her chest if she made a single move in his direction. He had the same *I'm prepared to do anything* glaze in his eyes that Solo had had.

"Who are you, and what do you want?" she asked with a weary sigh.

"I'll be asking the questions, girl. Who are *you*, and what are you doing here?" he demanded. "And don't you dare lie to me. I'll know it, and I'll get angry."

"Sir, there's nothing you can do to me that hasn't already been done," she said. More than that, the worst thing that could ever happen to her had already happened. "And to be honest, I'm too exhausted right now to care what you do."

He frowned. "Who are you and what are you doing here?"

"Who are *you*?" she repeated.

"Someone who was invited."

"Well, so was I. I'm Vika Lukas." If he tried to take the farm away from her, she would fight him. With everything she had, she would fight. "And I'm here waiting for someone."

A pause as he studied her. "My name is Michael, and I want to know where Solo Judah is."

"Michael. You're Solo's boss, aren't you?" she asked, as a little bead of excitement formed.

His eyes widened. "You've heard of me?"

"Yes. Solo mentioned you. Have you seen him? Heard from him?" Maybe Solo had contacted him. Maybe "home" was someplace Vika didn't know about.

"I haven't, no."

Disappointment was a crushing weight on her shoulders, obliterating the excitement.

"He would never mention me to a woman," Michael said.

"Because you forced him to kill people?"

His jaw dropped. "I never forced him."

"Well, he's not working for you anymore. He's done with that way of life. He told me so, and as you know, he never breaks his word."

Dark eyes narrowed on her. "How long since you've seen or heard from him?"

"Thirty-two days." She set the basket on the table and flopped into the seat across from him, wiping sweat from her brow. "You need to eat." His skin was pale and his cheeks hollowed out. He had scabs on his face and hands, and those scabs stretched all the way to the edges of his clothing; she would bet they even stretched underneath.

Another pause. Another frown.

"I want to know everything," he said coldly.

She sighed. "The last time I saw him, he was . . . he was . . ." Stupid chin, wobbling. "We were at the circus. He kissed me good night, and he . . . and he . . ."

"Tell me." A ragged command.

"Vanished," she whispered. "But he's not dead, I assure you."

He demanded the details she had omitted, and she gave every single one, leaving nothing out. She told him how Solo was captured, how he was kept, what her father had done, what she had done, how they had escaped, the fight at the end, his final words to her.

Michael did not react the way she'd expected. He rubbed two fingers over his chin. "Until I see a body, I won't believe that he's dead."

"That's good, because like I said, he's still alive," she replied.

"And you know this how?"

"I just know."

A small smile greeted her words. "Years ago, Solo used to say the same thing to me. He stopped." The smile faded and he scowled, tugged at his earlobe. "Had my assistant not betrayed me, there wouldn't have been an explosion. And had there not been an explosion, my boys would be on a case right now." His hands curled into fists. "Did Solo mention anything about Corbin Blue or John No Name?"

"Yes. They're his friends, and he loves them. He plans to look for them."

"I could really use him. I've had men on the hunt

since I woke up in the hospital, and we've even found a few leads but with zero success. They're still out there somewhere. *I* know it. As for Solo, I had nothing on him until he invaded my home in Siberia, but I had no idea how deep my assistant's betrayal went or if someone else was working with her and didn't want to reply to his attempts at contact. I waited, hoping a traitor would reveal him- or herself." He pushed to his feet, the chair skidding out behind him. "One did, and the moment I had him, I rushed to the cabin, but by the time I got there, Solo was already gone."

And they really could have used the help. "Do you think everything happens for a reason?"

"No. Of course not. I think bad things happen, but those bad things can be worked to our good. *If* we'll let them. I have a feeling you're the good that sprang out of Solo's situation." He peered down at her for a long while before nodding. "That's why I've decided to let you stay here."

He sounded so sure of himself. "That's very kind of you, but honestly? Had your decision swung in the other direction, you would have been unable to force me out. Solo taught me a few tricks."

He gave a sharp little bark of laughter. "If there's ever anything I can do for you, let me know."

"All I want is for you to contact me if you hear from him."

"I will, and I'll expect the same from you. Here's my number." He tossed an identification card, an IDC, on the table, a small round device she had only to touch to activate. The patrons of the circus had used them.

A screen would appear in the air just above the base, and on that screen would be his number and any other information he'd added. "See you around, Vika."

He padded from the house, his footfalls quiet. If he had a car hidden somewhere, she hadn't seen it. If not, he'd be doing a lot of walking. The house was miles away from any other home, and even farther away from the only grocery. Solo had a car parked in the barn, but she hadn't found the key.

Sighing, Vika dumped the fruit and veggies into the sink and began to wash them.

A flash of bright light erupted behind her, and she grabbed an apple and turned, ready to launch it. The last bright light she'd seen had ripped her out of the only real home she'd ever known and taken her back to the circus . . . to Solo's destruction and disappearance.

A tall, muscled man stepped from the center, and she launched the fruit. It slammed against his chest, bounced to the floor and rolled.

"Some greeting," a familiar voice said.

Breath caught in her throat. "Solo?"

The light faded, and she was able to make out his features. He'd lost a little weight, and there were bruises under his eyes, but he was the most beautiful sight she'd ever beheld.

"You were expecting someone else, sweetheart?"

"Solo!" She threw herself into his arms, and he wrapped her in his embrace. He pressed his nose into her neck and breathed deeply. "I knew you were alive! I knew it, I knew it, I knew it! And I knew you'd come back!"

"Of course I came back. *You're* here."

Wait. Her face was buried in his neck, and yet he'd heard her. "We can both hear," she said, gazing up at him.

"My ears are operating at low volume."

"Mine too."

"We're sharing the ability, then. And before you start to feel guilty, you should know that I'm happy to share. I . . . love you, Vika Lukas."

Her bones nearly liquefied. "You love me?"

"With all that I am."

"Oh, Solo, I love you, too. So very much."

He cupped her cheeks, kissed her. "Where's the Targon?"

"He left."

"Really?" Confused, he peered down at her. "But I gave him the farm."

Her heart nearly burst. "You traded the farm for me?" The otherworlder had mentioned Solo had been willing to give up a lot for her, but she'd never suspected his farm. His paradise.

"I would trade my *life* for yours."

"Oh, Solo," she sighed.

"Vika, my Vika." His thumbs stroked her. "You're going to marry me, and I won't tolerate an argument."

"I'll argue only if you want a long engagement."

"That's good, because I plan to marry you today."

"That's too long," she said, and laughed with abandon. "Oh, we're going to have the most amazing life."

"Yes, we are." He picked her off her feet and spun her around. His heart beat against hers, the two forming the perfect rhythm. She let her head fall back, watched as the ceiling spun round and round. Then he carried her to the bed and tossed her atop the mattress.

He was on her before she finished bouncing, his weight pinning her.

He kissed her, then lifted his head and peered into her eyes. "Are you ready to exchange vows?"

"It's that simple? Really? Just like that, you'll be mine?"

"Forever."

"Do it, then. Vow."

He grinned at her exuberance. "I am yours, your husband now and forever. What's mine is yours, and what's yours is mine. I vow it. You will now say the words to me," he instructed.

With pleasure. "I am yours, your wife now and forever. What's mine is yours, and what's yours is mine. I . . . vow it."

She didn't expect anything to happen; she'd made vows to him before, and nothing ever had. But oh, was she wrong. Her back bowed, and a cry split her lips. *His* back bowed in the opposite direction, and a cry split *his* lips. Suddenly she felt torn apart, limb by limb, piece by piece, and even down the middle.

Slowly, so slowly, though, the pieces began to return, as though she were Humpty Dumpty, being put back together again. Only when the transformation was complete was she able to relax into the mattress.

Solo sagged against her. He was panting, sweat-damp.

"What *was* that?" she asked.

"I'm not sure."

"Well, don't ever do it again."

"Me?" He somehow regained his strength and placed a thousand kisses along the curve of her jaw. "Maybe it was you."

"No, you. So are we married now, or what?"

"We are, and don't you forget it." He lifted and meshed his lips to hers.

Thirty-six

~

I am my beloved's and my beloved is mine.
—SONG OF SOLOMON 6:3

SOLO'S HANDS SHOOK AS he stripped his wife. His beautiful wife. Pale hair was spread out over his—their—pillow. And now . . . now, her rose-tinted curves were atop their bed, just the way he'd once imagined.

He could have her here every night. Every morning.

They could talk and laugh, and hold each other. They would grow old together. Have children.

"I once thought the three most important words in creation were 'whatever proved necessary,'" he said.

"And now?" she gasped against his mouth.

"Now I know I was wrong. The three most important words in creation are 'I love you.'"

Her expression, already soft, utterly melted. She held out her arms, tracing her fingers through his hair. "My one day has finally arrived, and it's more wondrous than I ever supposed possible."

"For me too. I missed you more than I can ever say. I missed trading senses with you. I missed your scent and your voice and your laugh and your touch."

While on Alloris, he'd briefly considered hunting

down someone who knew how to use black magic to open a solar flare. But then he'd recalled the price Jecis had paid for such an ability, and the way the man had changed over the years, and he had known not to dabble in such things, even to obtain what he wanted most.

Thankfully, there had been another way. The way his mother and father had used.

Natural solar flares.

All he'd had to do was wait in a quarantined area all of Alloris avoided. Only a rare few had ever left Alloris or had ever wanted to leave. It was a land of beauty, of peace, of joy. A few, like his father, had turned their backs on the utopia, choosing to break the rules, which was why the area had not been destroyed.

Solo hadn't turned his back. He just hadn't wanted to stay there alone. One day, he would take Vika there. One day, he would see X again.

"I missed you, too," she said. "So much."

He pressed his lips into Vika's, tasting her, enjoying her, relearning her. He caressed her, and when she could take no more, when she was fighting for breath, trembling uncontrollably, he forced himself to slow.

He was so on edge, so ready, so close, and he needed her, needed her so desperately, had been lost without her, wanting so badly to have her back in his arms, to claim her once and for all, permanently.

She nipped at his jawline. "I missed this."

"Sweetheart, you have no idea."

"Don't ever leave me again."

"Never."

She released a moan as he claimed her the way he'd dreamed, branding her, branding himself.

Her head fell back, and the ends of her hair tickled his thighs. Even that served as a stimulant. But then, everything about her delighted him. And that's the way it should be. A man and wife should see the best in each other, should work together, should enjoy each other.

Solo would never take this woman for granted. He would never forget the beauty of her heart. And he would always strive to be the man she needed. They wouldn't just have a life together. They would have a future and a hope.

"Oh, Solo," she cried. "Yes!"

In an instant, pleasure slammed into him, undeniable, uncontrollable, and he shouted her name.

She collapsed on his chest, panting.

His wife, he thought, content. Their sweat-drenched skin rubbed together, and utter contentment overflowed inside him. She had given him everything she had to give, and he would cherish her always.

There was only one thing left unfinished.

"I hate to bring this up now," he said after he'd caught his breath. He traced his fingers along her spine. "But I have to work one more case before I can become a full-time farmer."

"Smart man, waiting until I was too weak to move." There was no condemnation in her tone. Only amusement.

"Exactly."

"You plan to search for your friends," she said.

"Yes."

"I understand, and, like I told you before, I can even help. I met some pretty shady characters at the circus, and even tried to buy a new identity from one. Of course, he raised the price the more time that passed, causing me to have to raise more and more funds, but that's okay. The wait brought you to my door."

"Something I will be forever thankful for." He kissed her temple. One day, he would replace all her bad memories with good. She would look back and smile, only smile.

"We'll find them," she said. "Don't worry."

"I know we will. Together, we can do anything."

Fantasy.
Temptation.
Adventure.

Visit PocketAfterDark.com, an all-new website just for Urban Fantasy and Romance Readers!

- Exclusive access to the hottest urban fantasy and romance titles!

- Read and share reviews on the latest books!

- Live chats with your favorite romance authors!

- Vote in online polls!

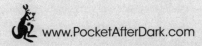